# *Inferno*

She's a trucker
tried and true
driving the line
seeing what life can be

a kind and gentle woman
who loves to sail
She's far more than
what she seems

with the wind in her hair
billowing out her soul
for all to see
riding the roads free

T. Shields
122603

# *Inferno*

## Trish Shields

Baycrest Books
**One-In-Ten Imprint**
Monroe, Michigan

Cover art by Shannon Lynch.
Edited by Nadine Meeker and Susan Carr.

Visit us on the World Wide Web at baycrestbooks.com

# Dedication

This book is dedicated to the many firefighters and EMTs I've contacted, both in Canada and the United States, over the course of the past four years as I researched the subject for this book. They come from every walk of life, different religions and lifestyles, but with one purpose in mind – to serve and protect.

What I found during my quest for information was a vast network, a brotherhood of men and women who put their lives on the line every day as they perform their duties as protectors in cities both large and small. These men and women rush into burning buildings where other mortals fear to tread as they battle the beast that is fire.

I also want to thank my family who has put up with my endless bouts of research long into the night, the numerous re-writes and long distance phone calls with friends and other professionals during the writing of this book. To my family and my children, I thank you for always supporting me from near and far. Sue, you are an amazing woman and I thank God that you are in my life.

# Acknowledgements

There are many people that have helped me over the years with my research. Lieutenant Pat Price, from Station 16, Seminole County Fire and Rescue, spent many hours getting information, pictures and web links so that I could look into burn trauma, treatment and its aftermath.

I'd also like to thank Miryam Ramos, Fire Apparatus Engineer, from the California Department of Forestry and Fire Protection, who helped with my investigations into exactly how a fire moves.

The following companies provided instruction through pamphlets and web sites on everything from burns, smoke inhalation and chemical fires, to skin grafts, the nature of scarring and firefighter equipment: Armstrong Forensic Laboratory, National Institute on Disability and Rehabilitation Research, The Phoenix Society for Burn Survivors, Inc., National Institute of General Medical Sciences, National Institutes of Health, Bethesda, Maryland and Rocky Mountain Model System for Burn Injury Rehabilitation, University of Colorado Health Sciences Center, Department of Rehabilitation Medicine.

I also want to thank Mike Ertel and Gregory C. Berk for writing an invaluable volume of basic information entitled, Firefighting - Basic Skills and Techniques.

# Chapter 1

The crowd watched in horror as flames shot out of the top floor of the old five-story brownstone. As the fire spread from the front of the building to the back quarter, a siren screamed as yet another fire hall in the area responded to the call. Nearby homeowners watched nervously, wondering whether the blaze would spread destroying their homes as well. It was an older part of Chicago, and there had already been a dry hot spring; each of the dilapidated apartment buildings turning into tinderboxes as summer got under way.

People in various stages of undress wandered about, uncertain as to what to do or where to go, their lives as they knew them going up in a black puff of smoke. Tear stained faces greeted loved ones who had been lost in the rush to flee the burning building and still the firefighters went back to seek more.

A scream filled the air as a figure eased out of one of the top windows, flames appearing alive and attempting to snatch at the hair and clothing of the victim. Standing hesitantly and silhouetted by the inferno behind, the person searched hopelessly for another means of escape. Finding none they jumped into the darkness of the night. A cry arose from the crowd as a few more people trapped in the building followed suit. Curses rose and ebbed as the firefighters scurried from area to area, attempting to dissuade further jumpers as they readied equipment to catch those in immediate danger.

A ladder truck was eased closer to a back window on the fifth story. Inside a mother handed her small child over to a firefighter high above the ground in the basket. Flames shot out and the tendrils of the sudden burst of flame seemed to tangle in her wild hair. The situation went from bad to worse when she panicked.

In her haste to escape, the mother jumped before the firefighter could get a firm hold her and she dangled precariously on the edge of the basket. Below people watched with hand over mouth as the rescuer tried to reposition, hanging almost completely out of the bucket, his legs wrapped securely around the water gun. The firefighter's comrades saw the situation immediately and began to lower the basket as close to the ground as possible, unsure how long their associate could hold on. The building seemed to groan in despair as the ladder was cranked away from the grip of the beast-like fire. Other firefighters rushed about frantically trying to cover the area beneath the trio any way they could.

The ladder slowly finished its descent and a cheer rose from the crowd for a job well done. Emergency medical technicians checked them for injuries and whisked mother and child away. A few firefighters shook hands with the hero, but soon the throng of survivors and rubberneckers lost sight of him as the team went back inside the building.

The apartment building continued burning well past midnight. Some of the exhausted firefighters sat on the curb, their faces blackened by soot, weariness mixed with the sweat that seeped from every pore.

Ambulances came and went and a truck was set up to dispense ice water to those who could rouse themselves from the destruction around them. Only two of the four water guns were still on duty, the others were in various stages of being disassembled and packed away. A woman in the crowd raised her face skyward and watched the fine mist create halos around the streetlights.

She wasn't sure what had drawn her to the fire but Abby Dean felt an uncontrollable need to be there, waiting for something she knew would happen. She was twenty-six years old and hadn't held many jobs for longer than a year, two at the most. She'd worked mostly in customer service jobs at restaurants and diners all across the U.S – a dishwasher, a cook and even as a swimming instructor but none seemed to hold her interest for long. Right now she worked for a greasy spoon diner, hopping tables and avoiding the pinching hands of drunks that came in after happy hour.

She lived a solitary life for the most part, having few friends and even fewer lovers. And although she lived on the streets after leaving home at age 16, she was still rather young looking given her hard past. Abby liked her life but still...something always seemed missing but she just didn't know what it was. So she went from place to place, job to job, just wandering through the streets of life. At the moment those streets were in Chicago where she'd spent the last few months. In that time, there were many fires in the area but tonight felt different. It was as if this fire was calling her, demanding her presence. Her intense focus kept returning to the one firefighter from the basket escapade. She had an almost uncontrollable urge to approach him but hesitated, uncertain of her own motives. She felt as if she knew this person but then again Abby did see many people around the area because of her work. Still she couldn't shake the feeling she knew this brave individual.

As she watched the firefighter from the road, Abby wondered what kind of person took up that line of work. As the reflection of the flames danced across his helmet, casting his face in shadows, she noticed the slump of his shoulders, the weariness in his body language. There was a sense the man believed he'd fallen short somehow; that he couldn't contain the blaze or halt the destruction.

Abby was hit by an overwhelming feeling that she was intruding. She looked away, trying to avoid his gaze, knowing the pain she'd see there on his features. The firefighter removed the helmet, tousling the short hair as the beads of sweat rolled down tanned cheeks. The shock on Abby's face must have been visible as her eyes fell into a sea of blue of the beautiful woman standing a few feet away from her. She had strong arms and shoulders, a sleek neck and a well-formed chin. And then there was the expressive mouth, full lips, incredible bone structure and those brilliant eyes Abby could see despite the lack of light and the distance between them. Abby watched the woman as she wiped a dirt-smudged hand across her brow. After removing her coat, she let it drop by the rest of her equipment.

As Abby took in the sight before her, she felt her heart stop. The woman stood like a goddess of fire, her tanned skin seemed to glow in the reflection from the blaze. Abby swallowed deeply and found it hard to concentrate on anything except the woman's profile, her shoulders and the strong line of her jaw.

She watched as the firefighter turned to a person in a pair of pajamas walking around as if in a daze.

"You live here?" Abby heard the firefighter ask the unknown victim in a rich and sultry voice. Abby felt her mouth go dry. Something about the voice made her feel both safe and frightened. It was comforting but authoritative. For a moment Abby could imagine getting lost in the arms of this woman.

The firefighter appeared to wave Abby over but turning around Abby noticed it wasn't her that she was motioning for at all but a medical team behind her.

As the team ran over to check on the victim that's when the firefighter looked past them and noticed Abby standing there. She gave Abby a slight grin before turning back toward the conversation with the patient and the medical team.

Abby just had to know more. She had to speak to this woman.

She began to make her way over to do just that but stopped when she looked near the entrance. Abby watched as firefighters began to bring out one body bag after another. She cringed, thinking of what lay within. Guilt for her attraction to someone during such a dire time also began to take hold of her. Still, she did want to know more about this woman. Being certain they had prior contact, Abby decided that the firefighter's unit was from the local fire hall and she'd seen this woman in street clothes at the diner. *That must be it,* Abby decided silently.

The firefighter seemed to have a similar knowing expression on her face and even began to take a few steps toward Abby. The smaller woman watched the soot covered fighter start toward her with confident steps but suddenly a man's voice called out and she stopped.

"Yo, Dray! Think we got a coupla kids missing in one of the back apartments. Ted and I are going in. We need you as point."

Without delay she bent and retrieved her coat and helmet, struggling to get back into her gear as quick as she could. Abby walked a little closer and watched as the three of them checked the other out, making sure the gear was in place and functional. At last, the firefighter gave Abby a friendly smile and propped her mask securely on top of her head. She turned and looked at Ted and their associate, waiting until each man had given her the thumbs up before turning and jogging towards the burned out apartment building.

Abby crept closer to the entrance where the firefighter had disappeared when a tug on her shoulder startled her.

A tall, bulky woman stood beside her and chuckled. "What's got you so jumpy?"

"Just snuck up on me is all," Abby replied.

"Well we have to get back. Break's over and you know how Frank gets."

Abby nodded. She knew her boss could be a real pain when he wanted to be. So she started on her way but not before looking over her shoulder at the building, hoping for one more glimpse of the mysterious woman.

Dray flexed her fingers around the cannon of the flashlight, gaining a sort of comfort from its reliable weight. She fought the urge to toy with the toggle switch, instead she focused on the task at hand. Pete, with axe in hand, followed deeper inside, past the smoldering timbers. Ted brought up the rear dragging a hose, its nozzle oozing a bit of water with every step he took.

Removing her heavy gloves, Dray placed a tentative hand on the inner metal door and nodded. It was hot but not instantly scorching to the touch. Pete gave her a nod, which she understood without comment. They both put their shoulders to the door and pushed. It gave in with an anguished scream as the metal bent and warped. Their vision was immediately filled with an eerie luminescence and visibility was cut down to about fifteen feet. The dense fog had descended making the ceiling all but lost to the billowing smoke.

"Ted!" she shouted, grabbing the tall man by his sleeve. The easygoing southerner brought his face close to hers, their masks touching and eyes locked. "Lay a light spray near the ceiling. This shit's gonna really play havoc with our vision." Ted confirmed with a nod and went to work. Dray caught Pete's eye and then jerked her jaw forward.

The two of them began making their way down the darkening corridor, their bodies always in contact. All three firefighters instinctively ducked as they heard a loud groan from the ceiling above, threatening to give way and crash on top of them.

*It ain't gonna take much*, Dray mused and then adjusted her helmet and mask, the dripping sweat making the seal incomplete. She fought the urge to scratch and knew she'd be wearing 'mask face' for hours afterwards. A smirk played on her lips briefly as she thought of the guys on her squad who slicked facial hair with Vaseline every time they needed to wear their headgear. It really put a crimp in any thoughts of having a fashionable beard. Lucky for her, it was one of the benefits of being a woman in the department.

They knew from the information provided by a neighbor, the missing kids would be somewhere in the back apartment on the first floor. Because kids were young there was always a chance they might not stay in one place. It meant that every alcove on the floor had to be checked.

The pace was quick yet methodical and thorough, the difficulty of their job compounded by the decreasing visibility. If the kids were inside then time was of the essence. Sadly, Dray understood first hand and found herself quickening her pace. She knew they had to get to the kids as soon as possible; any chance of their survival dwindled as the minutes dragged by. Fire had a life all its own and had a nasty disposition at the best of times. It was strange, but whenever kids were involved, Dray could swear the fire's greed for consumption increased.

Finally making their way to the apartment in question, Pete felt a tap on his shoulder and let Dray take his position. She kicked in the door, keeping to the side in case of back draft. The woman dragged her sleeve across her faceplate and looked up. Ted had been slowly making his way behind them, providing a steady mist. It helped and Dray gave Ted a thumbs up sign for a job well done. She clipped the flashlight onto her belt and pushed a dark lock of hair off her forehead. She removed her glove and quickly glanced at the time. Ten minutes already. This had to be it. An image of a small boy trying to hide behind furniture, thinking the fire couldn't find him filled her thoughts. Dray swallowed convulsively, the bile having risen in her throat. She pushed the image away and concentrated.

She motioned silently to Pete and pointed down a hallway and began to move in the opposite direction.

Cranking her arm Dray motioned for the two men to put their shoulders to the locked door. Ted threw the hose down and began rocking steadily against the door, trying to break it down. The nozzle fell open and began dousing the trio. Pete groaned in relief as some of the cool water trickled down his neck. Then he smiled, hearing the hinges begin to go.

Dray however, was finding it very hard to see, the cascading water obscuring her vision and tweaking her already high frustration level. "That's it, I'm goin' in. Get outta the way!" Both men stood back as Dray stepped away and then, with a roar and a sturdy kick of her boot sent the door off its hinges. The new supply of oxygen seemed to awaken the fiery beast within and both she and Pete darted back as flames shot forward. Ted aimed the flow of water full force onto the blackening ceiling until the flames retreated. Dray pointed to the ceiling tiles and drew a finger across her throat. Both men nodded, knowing they were probably asbestos-lined and would have been deadly had there not been enough ventilation.

Pete made a quick check of the room and then pointed to the far window.

"Look! C'mon!"

Dray dodged around the blackened furniture, staying close on Pete's heels. Over by the screened window, crouched a lone figure of a young girl. A deep barking cough rattled her small frame and her eyes had a vacant look as Dray came to kneel before her. Pete was now scanning the rest of the room in search of the other child. At least the billowing smoke was at a higher level, the damage being minimal where the girl crouched.

"Hey."

Dray got no response whatsoever. She quickly took off her mask and gloves and brought her face close to that of the child, who looked to be about eight or nine. She tipped the child's face up trying to establish eye contact but she could see there just wasn't any acknowledgement. The girl had gone into shock and Dray knew her time was even more limited now.

She pressed the mask to the little face but still she got no reaction. Sighing, she placed the mask back over her own face and then, knowing it might scare the child even more propped it up on her forehead. She stood up and tried to get the girl to just settle into her arms but she wouldn't budge. Another cough shook the child's slender frame and the brunette hugged her close, starting to cough herself. The oily scent of the air seemed to make every breath labored. They had to get her out...now. Dray noticed that the child's hand was firmly wrapped around the arm of what appeared to be a well-loved doll.

As Dray pulled on the doll that was under a half charred sofa, she felt her heart slow down and a strangled cry escape her lips. Pete heard the noise and came over to check. He saw the look on his partner's face and bent down to help. There, under the chair, was the body of a little boy of about three. His hair had been burned almost clean off, as had most of his clothing. The child's clear blue eyes stared vacantly up at her and Dray was filled with the urgent need to just...run away.

Pete saw the play of emotions on his partner's face and gently pushed her out of the way, picking up the body of the small boy.

"Dray! Mask! Now!"

The death of Dray's own son, consumed by fire, came to the forefront of her mind. The child's eyes were blue. So blue like hers...like her son's eyes.

"Dray!" Pete yelled again, giving her a small shake. "Focus! Get this girl out of here!"

Dray started and then nodded, sliding her protection back down. Pete was right. She couldn't save the boy, just as she couldn't save her own, but there was still a young girl that needed her help.

With a mixture of sweat, tears and acrid smoke covering her face, Dray blinked the mess out of her eyes and pulled the girl to her in a fierce hug, gently prying open the fingers that would not let go of the boy. All she could do was hold the child tightly as the girl began to scream and struggle as if startled from her catatonic state. She felt her neck and shoulders being hit and just closed her eyes tightly, riding out the emotions until they slowly petered away.

Meanwhile, Ted was finding no matter how much he pulled on the hose, there just wasn't any further slack. He opened the nozzle wide and sprayed the room liberally. Hearing a terrible noise, Ted turned and watched in horror as parts of the second floor came crashing down just feet from where he stood. The hose was totally useless and seeing both his lieutenant and Dray carrying the kids, he tossed it and began looking for another exit.

"Y'all stand back," he shouted in the accent he never managed to lose although he'd spent years on the Chicago department. Taking his axe out, he began breaking the glass in the windows, knocking all the shards out so they could make their escape safely. Workers from outside heard the commotion and ran to the window, helping clear the path from the other side. She handed the girl through the opening to one of her comrades who immediately sprinted her to the waiting medical unit.

Dray climbed out into the night air. The child now gone, her arms felt vacant. And she felt numb. Suddenly though, the loss of her son five years ago came back full force.

As she watched her fellow rescuer disappear around the corner, she remembered the girl's face. Her son would have been around her age had he survived. But he was gone and she spent many nights wondering if she herself would survive. Yet survive she did, finally being able to sleep without the nightmares of his burned and twisted body filling every corner of her mind and soul. Now it was all back again, leaving her more than a little shaky. How was she to get through the next dozen shifts if she couldn't sleep?

She barely registered the EMTs taking the dead boy away from Pete or Ted leading her over to the pumper truck to sit on the tailgate. A cup of hot coffee was pressed into her hands and she sipped absently at it, lost once more in the hell that brought her into the world of the firefighter. The southerner patted her shoulder and then took pencil and paper and went over to the truck to fill out his report. He looked upon Dray as a younger sibling and knew a bit of her past. Heck, the whole crew did. They knew emotions could affect judgment but still...*There just ain't nobody I want actin' point but Dray*, Ted said to himself, looking at the woman and wishing there was something he could say.

Lieutenant Pete Melrose sat nearby, filling out his own paperwork, spared a glance to his partner. Didn't matter how long they'd worked together, Andrea Khalkousa, Dray as she preferred, just wouldn't refer to him by his rank. It didn't really bother him, though; it was just her way.

He glanced at his watch and sighed. Three more hours and then he could sleep in his own bed – the word 'sleep' being somewhat figurative. He knew the vision of that poor kid would haunt his dreams for quite a few weeks as well as the look on the father's face when he saw them coming out of the building.

*Yeah, that woulda killed me*, he muttered to himself. Pete later found out the whole story, which he now documented.

The children's grandmother had been watching them while the father was at work. She had been unconscious from smoke inhalation and unable to tell the rescuers about the children. Scared and frightened the children hid from workers on the first walk through. If not for a neighbor asking about them, they wouldn't have learned about the children's presence until much later, perhaps too late. Yes it was true they lost one child tonight, tragedy that it was. But Pete tried to focus on the positive – they saved one and that shouldn't be forgotten.

Pete looked up from his report again and he saw a tear slowly work its way down Dray's sinewy jaw. As Pete looked at his partner he remembered meeting the brunette for the first time. She'd come to the station four years ago, had taken the extensive training and gotten over being a probie just fine. There had been a few glitches in the finely oiled machinery that Dray was but they'd been sorted out, one way or another. Although there had been talk of just cutting the woman loose, Pete hadn't been about to let that happen; he knew she had the right stuff.

Dray had kept to herself mostly at first but it became apparent that she was a natural in the business, the practical side of her training coming almost too easily. Pete had found himself drawn to the dark beauty, seeing past the brooding exterior regardless of just how hard she tried to hide the caring side of her nature. Theirs had been a tentative friendship but one that had blossomed over time. Dray confessed what had happened to her family shortly after and Pete went in search of more information on his own, not wanting to press for details.

Someone fell asleep with a cigarette in his hand or mouth and that's all it took. The building had caught quickly and there had been twelve deaths in all when the blaze had finally been put under control. And most of them had been children, Dray's 3-year-old boy being one of them. The babysitter had panicked while looking for a way out, and Dray's son used her inattention to hide behind the couch where he'd gotten stuck. Not being home at the time, much like the father tonight, Dray felt responsible for his death.

Shortly after Dray survived the probation period Pete admitted his growing feelings for her. Working with her, seeing her strengths, her indomitable will and giving personality had allowed for an easy progression from friendship to a deeper kind of love. *Too bad I had the wrong chromosomes*, he smirked ruefully as he watched her now.

He never begrudged Dray her choices, though. After all, it was the person she was inside that he was in love with, as well as her outside shell. And he accepted that although he couldn't have the place he wanted in her heart it was still a special place nonetheless. He could accept that because her friendship was important.

Putting the clipboard down Pete walked over to his partner. It was only when he was standing next to her that Dray noticed his presence.

"This seat taken?" he asked.

"Go right ahead," she said trying to muster a grin for him.

He knew it was for show and he grabbed her cup, taking a sip before handing it back, wincing.

"Damn! Each night it's getting worse. Whadya think? 10W30 oil or mud?"

Pete watched a genuine grin come to Dray's face. "I think it might be both," Dray quipped, twirling what was left in the cup.

A small silence passed between them until Pete spoke up.

"Dray I know there's nothing I can say that's gonna-."

"Then don't," Dray told him, trying to hold back her tears. "Just sit here a while okay?"

Pete nodded. He understood on a certain level what the loss tonight felt like even if not to the extent that she felt it. So in keeping with her wishes he did the best to make his partner feel better. He put his arm around her shoulder and did just as she asked. They just sat locked in unspoken closeness.

# Chapter 2

Abby sighed and placed a hand at the base of her spine. The resulting crack made her wince and groan with relief and not pain. Tucking a rag into the apron tie at her waist, she slowly made her way out of the sweltering kitchen and into the back of the restaurant. A couple of other waitresses exchanged nods but most of the other staff didn't give the short blonde a second glance. They knew she was temporary.

The current rumor was that she was from up town. Perhaps she'd fallen out of favor with her rich father and had to spend some time rubbing elbows with the great unwashed. It was obvious to many of them, regardless of what talk was being passed around, that the small blonde didn't fraternize with the rest of the crew and she came off as being snooty. Despite the absence of a decent wardrobe, her flawless looks, good skin and polite ways certainly backed that particular notion up. It was equally obvious to them that Abby had heard some, if not all of the gossip during her stay. She never rose to the bait. In fact, although she was certainly civil, Abby didn't offer any personal information whatsoever which might dispel the nasty thoughts. She was an enigma and most of them held it against her.

A large woman pushed through the doors into the locker room, stripped off her soiled apron and tossed it into the laundry bin.

"Well, that's another shift over with."

She glanced at Abby briefly, and then engaged two other women in conversation.

"You guys wanna hit the bars with me this weekend? I for one could use a nice tall one."

The brunette just pulling on her shirt guffawed. "Hell, I could use a nice tall one, too, but all I'm gonna get is some slobbering idiot who'll probably pass out before he can do a thing for me."

The large woman grunted in disgust, and began to strip off her cook's uniform.

"Yeah, I hear ya. That's why I'm gonna settle for a drink, or nine, and leave it at that. At least I'll be able to look myself in the mirror the next morning and not wonder what the hell I was thinking. Can't tell you how many assholes I wake up with that looked like a real catch the night before."

The room erupted with ribald laughter, and some equally amusing snippets were bandied about the locker room. Abby reached in and snagged her torn jeans from the back of her locker. She fingered the holes that were almost connecting. It was almost time to buy a new pair. Mentally adding the funds she had saved, she bit her lip. *Rent's due, gotta eat, jeans can wait.* With a small shrug, she stepped into her pants and continued to dress.

She could feel their animosity toward her although she'd done nothing to deserve it. And a part of her really wanted to turn around and join in the conversation. But that would mean sarcastic comebacks and mocking glances to show she wasn't part of the 'gang.' Abby tried to avoid confrontation at all costs so she found it better to keep to herself. Instead of attempting to banter with them, she closed her locker, took a seat on the bench and began lacing her sneakers.

The conversation continued around her, and Abby felt a small ache in her chest. Sure, she had her friend Arleen who came over to the fire to warn her about punching in the other night but it wasn't the same. It had been a long time since she'd been in the company of a group of women. Abby's lips tightened as she thought of her time with a community action coalition in Florida. It was a great experience trying to change the world but they soon found out money seemed to be a big key to everything in life. They were forced to close their doors and once more Abby was left to find a new direction in her life. The friends she thought she'd gained slowly became shadows and she found herself moving on again. That had been the first and the last time she'd actually let her walls down around people.

The thought of Arleen brought to mind the interesting firefighter she'd seen almost a week ago. She remembered her name – Dray. She loved the way it sounded. But more so, there was something about the tall brunette that made her want to dismantle those walls she had built. Maybe it was just that friendly smile or the self-assured walk that captured her.

Regardless, she'd spent each day inspecting each patron that walked in, hoping she'd recognize her but no such luck.

The idea of getting close to some one again was exciting and terrifying all at once. If only she'd been able to speak with the firefighter, for even a brief moment, perhaps she'd be meeting her after work instead of grabbing a bus and heading back to the lonely shoebox hotel room she'd managed to get a few days ago. It wasn't much, but it certainly beat life in the shelter she'd been living at when she first came to town.

The idea she was always one paycheck away from homelessness again caused a brief shudder and her shoulders to twitch. Pushing the thought away, she finished buttoning her jeans and quickly tucked her t-shirt into her pants. As she turned, Abby could see the mistrust in the other women's eyes. It was natural not to trust someone who kept you at a distance. She understood that, but opening up wasn't something that came easily to her. Every time she did she seemed to get burned. For Abby, it was easier to be solitary than be hurt again.

Abby sighed as the women left the room, chatting away. *Yeah,* she decided. *Alone was better.*

Grabbing her kit and slinging it over one shoulder, Dray waved at a group of her crew as their truck eased back into traffic. It had been a long and uneventful shift. Stifling a yawn, she contemplated the small café across the street. She waited a few seconds to see if her stomach would rise to the bait but it remained silent. Giving a shrug, she resettled her kit and walked towards her apartment building.

A city bus slowed down half a block in front of her, and Dray began checking out the occupants. For some reason she felt something pulling at her. It came as no surprise when a familiar blonde woman stepped off the bus and walked towards her. Dray checked the figure from head to foot, and was certain that it was the same young woman she saw standing with a group on onlookers at the apartment fire. She was even wearing the same beat up backpack, Dray was certain it was her.

As the woman walked abreast of her, Dray cleared her throat and issued a greeting.

"Hi there," Dray said hoping to catch the young woman's attention

Abby continued for three or four steps before the words registered in her brain.

"Huh?"

She turned, a frown creasing her brow, and checked out the people around her. It was only 6 a.m. but the hustle and bustle of people going on early shift was already picking up. Her eyes moved from person to person before settling on a tall figure carrying a duffle bag. The moment of recognition hit her seconds later, making her feel elated and yet somehow pensive.

"Oh! Hello," she answered with a grin. Putting her arm through the loose strap of her backpack, Abby wiped her hand on her jeans. "I remember you. The firefighter. I've been look-." Quickly, Abby stopped. She didn't want the woman thinking she was a stalker. *That's great Abby. Scare the woman away why don't ya?* "I've been thinking about you since that night – that woman in the basket? That was pretty hair raising but a job well done." Abby commended, extending her arm. *Good save.*

Dray accepted the proffered hand and wondered at the calluses she could feel before the smaller hand was withdrawn.

Abby felt uneasy as the tall woman eyed her hands. Sticking them quickly into her pockets, she smiled and waited for the other woman to say something.

Dray's throat seemed to close up, leaving her feeling awkward. Placing her kit between her boots, she coughed and tried to get her mouth to work.

"Well most calls are pretty routine but anything can happen as that night proved. It's hard to see things going well when people die and we did lose some in that fire." Dray answered.

Glancing up every so often as Dray spoke, Abby was struck again at the intense hue of the firefighter's eyes. They were soothing mountain streams occasionally fed by a glacier. She wanted to look into the woman's eyes openly, without reservation, but was unsure of the woman's reaction. Thinking back to the night of the fire, Abby was partially convinced there had been an attraction going on between them, but feelings of doubt plagued her. She could be reading too many things into the brief encounter.

"Yeah I read about it the next day. Five total but you know…"
"What?"

Abby grinned in nervousness. "I don't want to offend you but five could have been ten. One victim would have been that woman hanging on the basket so I think you did a good job. That's all I wanted to say."

The butterflies in Dray's stomach turned into bleating sheep as they stomped around, urging her to shut up and run away. Clenching her jaw, she forced both hands into her pockets, cleared her throat, and tried to ignore people as they pushed by them.

"Maybe you're right," Dray said, trying to avoid too deep a discussion. "I should look at the positive and just promise to do my best again next time." Abby didn't know how to respond to the comment and she was grateful when Dray continued without prompting. "So, how ya been? I was gonna come over and talk to you that night but duty called."

The blonde smiled and Dray felt a bit of unease dissipate. It was the kind of smile that made her forget she'd just done a long and boring shift.

"Oh, really?"

"Yeah," Dray admitted.

Dray reached into her back pocket, retrieved her wallet, and pulled out a couple of ragged business cards.

"Say," she began again. "If you need to see someone, I've got a couple of contacts here. Losing a home can be pretty traumatic. And we've got information too on hospitable services. You know, places that can give you shelter, clothes, toiletries – stuff like that."

Abby wanted to tell the firefighter that she hadn't been in the building at all, but the faint reddening of the woman's cheeks enticed her curiosity. Perhaps the woman was interested in more than her state of health? Abby looked fully into the woman's face. Even without flames to highlight the woman's natural beauty, she really was quite the picture of perfection.

"You're something. Ya know that?" Abby told her, remarking on her striking appearance and demeanor.

Dray's eyebrows shot up high on her forehead and she quickly stuffed the cards away. *Very smooth with offending the woman Dray. She must think I see her as a basket case.*

"Sorry. I didn't mean you can't handle things on your own. I just thought-."

The firefighter's apologetic reaction pulled the blonde from her flight of fancy.

"Oh no! I'm impressed actually. You're worrying about someone you saw briefly a week ago. It's very...endearing."

"Endearing, huh?" Dray asked.

"Very," Abby nodded with a smirk.

*Okay. It's official. She's flirting.* Dray began to chuckle when she realized she felt a bit smitten and had no idea with whom.

"If you don't mind me asking...what's your name?"

"Abby. My name is Abby Dean. And you're Dray."

"You know my name?"

Abby's face turned crimson and she began to fidget with the straps of her backpack.

"I heard them say it before you went into the building that night."

"And you remembered?"

Dray couldn't contain her grin at the knowledge that Abby recalled who she was. Many people she helped over the years recognized her but all she and Abby had exchanged was a brief smile. Yet still Abby remembered her and it warmed Dray in a way she hadn't felt in a long time.

Abby debated her response for all of three seconds.

"You're hard to forget," she countered honestly.

*Don't say something stupid Dray. Keep it simple. Play it cool.* "So, you wanna grab some food? I'm just coming off shift, and I could eat. How 'bout you?"

Abby's lips curled at the brunette's words. "I don't think I'm on the menu. Well, not yet."

Abby's smirk and sexy comeback caught Dray off guard but the firefighter enjoyed it immensely.

The response also stunned Abby on a certain level. She didn't know this woman or even if she was interested in her romantically and here she was throwing Mae West type zingers at her. Abby figured she must be more desperate for attention than she realized by the impetuous reply but instead of getting embarrassed she decided to hold her ground and wait for Dray's retort. One way or another she'd find out if Dray might consider her for more than friendly chitchat.

"I really need to say something here, don't I?" Dray finally mumbled with a slight chuckle. She cursed her blank mind for not having something to send Abby's way.

Not sure if Dray was flattered or unnerved by the comment, Abby decided to give Dray an escape.

"Look," Abby told her. "I like you and I think you're sexy. Correction: you are sexy. *But* if I misread your interest in...well, me," Abby added with a playful grinned, "I apologize. I will bow out gracefully of the food offer and wish you a long and happy life with my presence far, far away from you." After she finished, Abby began to chant in her head. *Please say no. Please say no. Please say no.*

"No!" Dray answered immediately. "There's certainly attraction. Believe you me. There's attraction all right."

*Yes!* Abby's mind hissed while her exterior remained calm.

She listened as Dray continued. "I just didn't want to be presumptuous. So...thanks for being the one to presume," she added with a chuckle.

Abby bit her lip. "It's settled then? A little food and a lot more flirting if you'll indulge me?"

Dray grinned ear to ear. "I can indulge. No problem with the indulging."

At that point Abby's stomach rumbled loud enough for both of them to hear it and Abby blushed again. "I think it's time to feed this beast."

Dray was about to make a comment on the anticipated size of the monster that belonged with the growl when her own belly began to howl in harmony, making them both chuckle.

Linking her arm in the brunette's, Abby tugged her along and they both made their way across the street.

Dray peered in the window and checked her watch. "I see 'em working inside, so they should be open in another half hour. Can you wait, or do you wanna check out the local fast food joint?"

Abby grimaced. "God, I need real food. I'm just coming off shift, too, and I really need to get some digestible stuff into me before I crash. Here is good."

Dray nodded, pushed her duffle bag against the door of the café and bowed deeply. "Well then, ma'am, may I suggest we relax and take in the fine Chicago air until the owner of the premises deems the establishment is available to patrons?"

Abby covered her mouth in an attempt to hold in a belly laugh, but it was no use. Dray stood with one hand on her hip and watched the blonde in her merriment. It was like music to her ears, and yet she couldn't really say why.

But soon she realized the reason. It had been years since she could make someone roll with laughter. In fact, the last person had been her son. She thought about him everyday since his death but the past week had been even harder in light of the apartment inferno.

A feeling of melancholy washed over her for a brief moment but she pushed it aside. She was determined to have fun with this vibrant stranger. 'We gotta keep moving forward,' Pete once told her. Dray knew it was true and decided to live up to the words by enjoying her time with Abby.

After a few moments, Abby perched herself on the firefighter's kit bag and offered the other half.

"I'm sorry I laughed. You just sounded so stuffy and pompous."

Dray wiped her thumb against her lower lip. "Funny, I used to think the same thing when my mother used that same tone of voice."

Abby was soon peeking from behind both of her hands. "Oh my God, I'm sorry. I didn't mean to...I mean, I'm sorry for saying..." And then she shut up as Dray sat beside her and patted her arm.

"It's okay, really. Marion means well, but she can certainly be a pain."

"You call your mother by her first name? I'd have been clocked a good one if I'd called my parents anything but Mother and Father."

"Really?" Dray asked.

Abby wasn't willing to share everything just yet so she only nodded. Dray's face screwed up with disdain for Abby's upbringing but she didn't press. She just continued.

"Well, I never called her that to her face," Dray explained, "but I called her that behind her back. That and other things." She sighed. "But let's not go there. Right now, I want to enjoy the company of a pretty woman and simply relax."

"Pretty? Me?" Abby snorted. "Well, I could say the same thing, you know."

"And you have," Dray answered. "Just thought it fair to return the compliment."

They sat in companionable silence for a few minutes, each wrapped in their own thoughts, remembering their histories and wondering a bit about each other's but not saying anything. Abby cleared her throat, and started to talk.

"I think I've always called my folks that – Mother and Father, I mean." She shrugged. "Beats Gladys and Martin, I think. Happy Homemaker meets the Sleazy Used Car Salesman. Sounds like a soap opera, huh?" Dray just grinned and waited for Abby to continue. "And I just can't imagine Mother being shortened to Mom." She shook her head quickly. "No way. That would indicate some sort of bond, relationship other than warden and prisoner. Can't have that."

Dray bit at the cuticle on her thumb. She was reluctant to go into bits of her past, but found herself unwilling to deny the blonde's path of candor. She waited a few minutes, but when Abby didn't continue, she crossed her arms and settled back against the doorframe. "I was never a prisoner, I don't think. A trophy, an object certainly, but I was never restricted as to whether I could come and go." Then she thought about the early curfew, and whom she could fraternize with when she was growing up. And then of course there was life with Brian.

"Okay, amendment – I lived in a gilded cage." Sticking her legs out and crossing them at the ankles, Dray hooked her thumbs in the front pockets of her jeans and gazed over at her newfound friend. "Ever wonder how we survived them?" the firefighter asked.

All Abby had to do was nod.

"I mean, I don't know much about your background," Dray continued. "But you don't sound like you had the greatest upbringing either." She put a hand up as the blonde began to speak. "I'm sorry if I'm speaking out of line here, okay? But as for me, well let's just say I came from parents that had enough education between them to know better and they still screwed me up. I guess you deal with what you have and make the best of it." She shrugged again. "Hey, we survived." Dray's belly growled again, and she groaned. "God, they better open up soon or I might just fade away."

Abby elbowed the woman. "Yeah, just skin and bones, that's all you are." She reached over and pinched a bit of flesh at Dray's side, making the brunette squirm. "Hey, quit that, you!" The impromptu tickling fest came to an abrupt halt as the door was yanked open and a very large man stood behind them, tapping his foot. "You two comin' in or should I just close the door and give ya's privacy?"

Dray jumped to her feet, her face crimson. "Uh, we were just waiting for you to open."

Abby nodded and straightened her clothes. "Yeah, breakfast, we need breakfast."

They were led inside and seated at a nearby booth. Another couple entered shortly after and the owner told them to sit where they like before turning back to Dray and Abby.

"Wanna look at the menus or do you know what you want?"

Dray's belly rumbled again, and she pushed the menu away. "Got a bacon and eggs special?"

The man nodded. "How you like 'em?" asked the owner.

"Over medium and a side of white toast," Dray answered.

"Coffee?"

"Yes please."

The owner then turned to Abby, "And you?"

Abby hesitated, trying to quickly calculate the money she had with the menu and trying not to be too obvious.

"Get what you want," Dray told her. "It's on me."

"Dray," Abby grinned. "I appreciate it but really-."

"Eggs? French toast? Tell him quick because I'm gonna order for you if you don't," Dray teased.

Blushing Abby looked up and told him. "I'll have the same."

The man grunted and walked back towards the kitchen for their drinks.

"So," they both said in unison, and promptly laughed.

"You go first," Abby offered.

Dray's stomach made a few peculiar noises and she rubbed it.

"Maybe I should have ordered something more off the menu? I don't think my monster will be appeased with just bacon and eggs."

"Just bacon and eggs? That's more than I usually have for breakfast. Toast and coffee, and that's good for me."

She casually stuck her hand in her right pants pocket and released a slow inaudible breath as her fingers closed around a few bills. Sure Dray offered to pay but still. She had her dignity. She'd made her own way in life so far and she would continue to do so.

She had about twenty dollars left of her last paycheck. The bulk of her funds had gone towards getting the apartment, leaving her with very little on which to live. Her stomach growled again. It didn't seem to matter how many days, weeks or years she went through having little more than one or two meals per day, the monster inside never seemed to take the hint and adjust. At least working at the diner helped. She got a free lunch and dinner from the owner if he was in a good mood. It was rare but still those times of generosity did happen. A gentle sigh escaped her lips and she tore her gaze away from the kitchen area. The smells were wonderful.

"When the guy comes back, I think I'll ask for some pancakes or waffles, too," Dray told Abby.

As if on cue, the owner came toward the table, two mugs in hand. "There ya go. Anything else?"

"Yeah can you put in an order for a short stack and an extra plate if you would?"

"Sure thing," he nodded as he left.

Dray's mouth was watering at the thought of the pancakes and she chuckled at the mirrored look on Abby's face.

"You like pancakes too huh?" Dray asked knowingly.

"Very yummy," Abby nodded.

"Not as yummy as you I bet." Dray suddenly became embarrassed by the brash remark. "Oh geez, I'm sorry. I don't know where that came from," she apologized.

"From your heart," Abby told her. "Orrr, some place lower," she added with a wink to let Dray know she wasn't offended.

Dray was about to speak again when the owner's voice boomed.

"Wendy, front and center with that damned coffee, wouldja?"

A petite, redhead pushed through the doors at the back, a stricken look on her face. "Yeah, I was just coming, Buddy."

The owner, Buddy, waved a hand in the other couple's direction. "No excuses, just do it. How many times I gotta tell ya, when we got customers you grab the coffee pot?"

Wendy opened her mouth but closed it quickly as her boss glared at her.

"Yes sir."

Quickly pouring the coffee, she grabbed a dish full of creamers and plunked it down between the other patrons and dashed back towards the kitchen.

"Good help is real hard to find, so don't mind her." They overheard him tell the other customers. "She's on her way out, anyhow."

Without another comment, he went about setting the stacked chairs in the corner around the tables. Soon Wendy and the other waitress were busily setting the tables with utensils and napkins.

Dray's tongue contemplated her front teeth as she watched how nervous the waitresses seemed around their boss. Having been browbeaten for years by her own father, she couldn't abide seeing others under the same kind of wrath.

"What a jerk," she told Abby. She narrowed her eyes as the man continued to harangue the waitress. "That guy's a real pig, you know?" She shook her head and then went into preparing her coffee. Three creams and 6 sugars.

Abby chuckled softly. "How bout a little coffee with your sugar and milk?" she teased.

Dray grinned. "You sound like Pete, my best friend. He's my boss too so that makes him double the pain in my ass but I love him anyway. Truth is, I hate coffee. This helps kill the taste," Dray told her.

"Then why not order juice?"

"I hate juice even more."

"Do you like anything?" Abby chuckled.

"I like you," she replied with a smirk.

The owner began to grumble again and Abby snuck a look while he pulled the blinds up, frustrated that his ranting was ruining the mood. For a restaurant owner he wasn't too bad, and she'd certainly seen worse but still he was ruining their attempts at flirtation.

"I don't think it's poor service that keeps the customers away," Dray offered, nodding toward Buddy.

"Well, I don't think he should be name-calling his staff, that's for sure. But hey, if they don't like working for him, they can leave. It's a free country, right?"

Dray nodded and paused before taking another sip. She was surprised that Abby sounded so complacent. There was no way that she'd have taken such behavior from any employer, whether it was at the fire hall or anywhere else.

"Sometimes you gotta draw the line, you know, show folks you deserve respect. Unless you do that, you gotta take what others dish out. It's just too bad Wendy hasn't gotten to that point yet. But I sure hope she does."

Abby was relieved when Wendy arrived bearing their order. They ate in relative silence aside from an occasional comment about how good everything tasted. The owner might be a pig but Dray had to admit he had a good cook.

Abby continued to soak up the remaining egg yolk on her plate with the last of her toast. Burping gently, she reached for her cup and finished her coffee.

"Well, that sure hit the spot."

Dray wasn't even half way through her meal, and had barely put a dent in her coffee. Her mouth hung open as Abby pushed her empty plate away.

"Sheesh, you win. Your monster is way bigger and certainly hungrier than mine." Dray glanced under the table, and then picked up Abby's thin wrist. "Where the heck do you put all that?"

Abby blushed and let the touch linger, offering nothing but a shrug.

The brunette frowned as her beeper began squawking. She glanced at the number and turned to Abby.

"Excuse me a moment. The station's calling."

"No problem." Abby told her. She watched as Dray looked around and moved to the pay phone.

Not more than two minutes later, Dray was back and grabbing her wallet.

"Hey Buddy," she yelled to the owner. He walked over and she handed him a twenty-dollar bill. "This is for the food. Keep the change and buy yourself a better disposition."

Abby snickered in response to the comment. Unable to issue a retort Buddy scurried away as Dray turned back to Abby. "Listen, they need me at the station. Can I call you sometime?"

22

Abby opened her mouth but no words came out. She didn't have a private phone, but had no intentions of telling the firefighter that. "Um," she mumbled as she tried to think of what to say.

*Maybe I shouldn't have told off the owner,* Dray considered when Abby didn't want to seem to give her number away. Unfortunately, Dray didn't have time to question her.

"Look," she said quickly, pulling out a ten-dollar bill and a pen from her pocket. "Here's my number," she told her as she wrote it on the bill. "I really would like to see you again. So if I'm not home be sure to leave me a message, okay?"

Dray was moving so quick it was hard for Abby's mind to keep up and she mutely nodded. But before she knew it, she was sitting alone at the table, feeling as if she'd just witnessed a tornado. Making sure that no one was looking, she exchanged her empty plate for Dray's half full one and finished what was left. After all, there was no sense in letting it go to waste.

# Chapter 3

Abby's mind played out a scene in what appeared to be a hospital or a medical facility of some type. Difference being, this didn't feel like a place of care or well-being. She couldn't quite define it but the overwhelming feelings of fear and being trapped consumed her. It was as if she didn't want to be there; she had to escape. But nothing seemed to be holding her there as she casually walked along, taking in the sights around her.

Perhaps it really was a hospital but something was amiss – this place seemed dark and soggy. The stench of burning flesh and hair hung in the air and although she knew she was sleeping, try as she might she couldn't wake herself up.

A vision of injured people floated by but soon her eyes settled on a dull surgical instrument being slowly passed through a flame. Images became clearer and she felt as if she belonged here – these people were her people; people she knew although she was sure she'd never met them in the waking world. She could try to escape but by doing so she would be leaving a part of herself behind. So Abby stayed and continued to walk.

As the scene played out, Abby found she couldn't take her eyes away from the far end of the room and she crept closer. She watched a victim being held down, her flesh being carved open by a dull scalpel. This wasn't a standard operation – Abby could tell. The woman on the gurney wasn't unconscious and she certainly didn't look willing to be under the knife judging by the tears on her face and the straps around her body.

Neither woman couldn't run or scream or even attempt to save themselves from their fate. The woman would continue to be cut and Abby was helpless to watch. Immediately, the sound of a woman's scream pierced Abby's ears.

Abby took a shuddering breath and tried to will the image away from her mind – trying her best to wake up. Instead she found herself walking closer still, totally unnoticed by the doctors moving around her. Her vision centered on the bloody instrument as it moved across exposed flesh. The strong hand, muscular arm, broad shoulders of the surgeon was all so familiar.

Suddenly she felt her hand being held and she looked up to see Dray standing beside her. Abby blinked slowly, bringing her eyes away from the woman on the table before looking down at their locked hands. She frowned, trying to figure out how both of them had gotten there and how they could both escape.

"We have to leave," she warned Dray. "It's not safe here."

"It's never safe around me," the firefighter answered.

Dray wore her uniform and her face was covered with soot as if she'd just returned from battling a blaze.

"Was it a bad one this time?" Abby asked, taking in Dray's appearance.

She watched as Dray nodded toward the doctor and the patient in front of them.

"It was the worst," she answered.

"The worst fire ever?" Abby asked. "Did you lose Pete or someone you love?"

Dray nodded slowly, still looking at the table in front of her, as if time was beginning to freeze. "Yeah."

"How did it happen?"

Dray turned her attention back to Abby. "Because it was the one fire I should have prevented. But I let it happen."

"What? Dray, that doesn't make any sense?"

Abby was certain she was still dreaming but instinctively she knew Dray was telling her something. It had depth and meaning she was sure. But she couldn't pinpoint it. She felt like she was trying to put together a jigsaw puzzle without using her eyes, just her fingers. But at the moment the pieces just weren't coming together.

"Sometimes in this world things just don't make sense," Dray told her. "But they happen anyway, don't they?"

Consciousness ripped Abby from the dreamscape and she darted upright in bed, half expecting to be on one of the gurneys she had seen moments before in her mind.

But she found no gurneys – just a lumpy mattress at the 18-dollar a night hotel she'd recently moved into. And the only screams she heard were coming from the room next to hers.

Probably an adulterous couple who paid for an hour's time to shack up. Abby lay back down and heard the woman give a final scream. Convinced it was just her overactive imagination that incorporated her neighbor's sounds of passion Abby tried to get some rest.

Dray's words however stayed with her. 'Because it was the one fire I should have prevented. But I let it happen.' She glanced at the ten-dollar bill on her nightstand. Although she'd been saying it for three days now, Abby thought about it again: *Maybe tomorrow I'll get the nerve up to call.*

In another part of town, Dray found herself tangled in her sheets, tossing and turning, reliving the night of the worst fire she'd seen in quite some time.

The night she first saw Abby to be precise.

In Dray's dream they were sitting on the back of the pumper truck, much like she and Pete had done. It was an odd sensation. Dray knew the events that had happened that evening were similar but still the dream felt fake, as surreal as the dreamscape itself.

"So?" she asked the petite woman. "You live around here? You work out this way?"

Dray felt rather uncomfortable asking such personal questions but she owed it to her own peace of mind to know that Abby was going have a place to stay after they left. There was just something about the woman that seemed so familiar. A sudden feeling of nausea overwhelmed Dray and she gripped the bumper. Time and space seemed to just wink out at that moment and she found herself standing in a bleak landscape, a few gray buildings just to the right. Dray blinked a couple of times and then cleared her throat.

Suddenly they were both sitting at a table in a café instead of on the back of the truck. Dray's mind raced to catch up to the change of scenery.

She could tell that Abby, who sat across from her, was saying something but there was a buzz in her ear and she couldn't make sense of what was being said. She watched in curiosity as two men materialized out of nowhere and the scene behind the blonde changed yet again. The walls of the café slipped away and Dray was looking at an open courtyard. What was even more confusing is the fact they still sat at the café table facing each other.

Dray's mouth dropped open as a small woman in rags appeared out of the haze in front of her. A large tower and some high barbed wire fences sat even further back. Dray struggled between trying to understand Abby's words who stood in front of her and the commotion going on over the woman's shoulder that she seemed oblivious too.

Then Dray's attention shifted yet again. One man rolled up the sleeves of his uniform, eyed the woman coldly and then began to yell in another language she didn't understand. Dray dragged her eyes away momentarily to look at her companion, the only woman she did recognize in all of this.

"Look," Dray pointed behind Abby. "Can you see that?"

Casually Abby turned back, "Oh that? Yeah I do. You can't change it so it doesn't matter. Anyway as I was saying..."

Abby prattled on about something but Dray was too focused on their surroundings. When she looked down Dray saw Abby's eyes narrow, filled with cold anger and strength of purpose.

The gaze washed over Dray, scalding her and she blinked a few times trying to get a handle on why she'd received it. Nothing in this dream made any sense whatsoever and her heart began to pound, and she felt dizzy.

Dray pushed Abby aside, reaching to her belt as a figure approached them. Dray glared at the men, her fist tight around the handle of the...gun? *What Goddamned gun?*

Dray pulled up the item her fingers were wrapped around to reveal a flashlight. Abby suddenly cried out and fell to the ground.

"Ksenka," whispered Abby.

"Huh?" replied the dazed and confused firefighter.

A gunshot ran out and immediately Dray sprung out of bed, literally coming to her feet in the middle of her bedroom with a host of sheets wrapped around her sweating legs.

Her breathing was quick and shallow as her mind tried to compute all the information it had thrown at her. She knew the nights after the fire that claimed the boy's life would be fretful but this was something she didn't expect at all. This was bizarre. *Jeez, beyond bizarre* she decided as she collected her sheets and crawled back into bed.

It had been three days since she had taken Abby out to breakfast and not a word from her. Dray felt a sense of frustration. *Not only does this woman want nothing to do with me, she also invades my dreams. You sure know how to pick 'em.*

Dray lay back down and closed her eyes but she knew it was pointless. She wouldn't be getting much rest anytime soon.

That night, after sleeping most of the day, Abby reassessed her job situation. *Why work for someone you don't want to? I should take my own advice and get a new job.* Perhaps something that paid a bit more.

A couple of blocks away from her previous employer Abby did find such a place. The staff was small and the establishment no better or worse than the one she'd left. She felt no remorse about leaving her former employer without giving the usual two weeks notice. They paid her minimum wage and although it was barely enough to live on it did give her certain privileges. Leaving like she did the day before was just one of them.

The owner Jake handed her an apron and went through what he expected of her.

"You come on time lookin' respectable. You're late, you get docked. You break anything, you bought it and it'll be deducted from your wages. You keep your nose clean and we got no problems." He looked Abby up and down. "You from around here?"

"I've lived in Chicago for nearly three months now," she replied.

The man grunted. "Yeah, whatever. Go get to work."

Then he was gone, leaving Abby with a pile of crusty dishes still stacked from breakfast.

Folding a rag quickly into a headband, Abby sighed heavily and began to work her way through the mountain of dirty dishes. Two hours later, the stack was at a manageable level and she decided to take a break. She frowned a little as loud voices could be heard from the other room.

Poking her head through the doors, Abby's shock to what she was seeing was complete. Jake stood in the center of the room, his hand raised over his waitress, who was crouching on the floor. She had just met the woman today and her mind raced to remember her name. Rachel? Rebecca? Robin!

"Whoa! Wait a minute here!" Abby moved quickly between her new boss and the waitress and that's when she saw her split lip. Abby glared at the large man. "What the heck is going on?" she demanded.

Jake lowered his hand but didn't make a move away from the brunette. "You wanna go back to washin' dishes, little girl. This ain't no business of yours." His meaty hand reached past Abby and closed around Robin's upper arm. With one quick movement, he yanked the waitress to her feet. She stood awkwardly, her knees quivering as she tried to remain upright.

Two groups of patrons sat at their table as if they were watching a floorshow. No one tried to intervene or put a stop to the abuse that was taking place. This, more than anything, made Abby's blood boil.

"What're you gawking at?" she asked one couple and took some satisfaction as the woman looked away. Turning her gaze back onto her employer, Abby's temper shifted into full gear.

"Nothing gives you the right to manhandle her," Abby challenged.

Jake's eyes became slits of anger as the young blonde stood defiantly before him.

"In the first place," he said poking his index finger into Abby's shoulder while still gripping the woman's arm, "it ain't no business of yours. And in the second place," he poked her again, this time with more force, "this is my business and I'll run it any way I wanna."

Abby was forced back with each push of the larger man's finger. She locked eyes with the waitress, who simply shook her head sadly, silently pleading her to just let it go. It was obvious to Abby that the woman had been abused before.

"Listen scum. You don't have the right to treat anyone like this and if you touch me one more time-."

Jake raised his hand to strike her and Abby took a cautious step back.

"I dare you to hit me," Abby growled.

No sooner had the words left her mouth then she felt his backhand swipe across the face, the blow sending her to the floor. She lay there dazed and confused while he dragged Robin into the back of the café. Even though Abby's ears were buzzing from the force of impact and her vision blurry, she could still hear the waitress's screams as he hit her again.

Struggling to her feet, Abby ripped the apron from her body and staggered from table to table. She made her way back to the double doors leading into the kitchen. Jake stood with his back to her, his hand coming down on Robin's face and shoulders. Soon her cries diminished completely and Abby threw herself at the man, grabbing his right arm with both hands with her entire body weight. Jake stopped his downward momentum only long enough to shake the blonde off before administering another blow to the hapless brunette. Then he turned on Abby who was sprawled on the floor.

"Stupid broad don't know when to shut up. Well, I'll do the shuttin' up for ya."

Picking Abby up by her hair, Jake slapped her hard. He reared back to strike her again but the impact didn't come.

"You better let go of her or else." Abby heard a familiar voice issue the warning.

Next she blurrily watched as Jake was shoved half way across the kitchen and three rather burly looking men proceeded to block his impending departure.

The room swayed precariously and Abby felt her knees buckle. But the expected impact with the floor never came. Instead she was cradled to the ground with a soothing voice in her ear. She tried to focus.

"It's okay now, Abby. C'mon, let's get you cleaned up. The cops are on the way."

Abby's right eye was starting to puff closed, and she was suddenly conscious of a bitter coppery taste. Although she had a difficult time focusing she knew it was Dray. For a moment she thought maybe she was dead or it was just a hallucination. How and why she was there Abby didn't know but without a doubt it was Dray's voice she heard.

"Son of a bitch split my lip and made me dizzy," Abby muttered.

"Well, I'm gonna close this fucker down, even if it means siccing sanitation on him. The cops might not keep him in jail long enough to force him out of business but I can make his life Hell."

Some of the perks of being a firefighter were that you came in contact with people in high places. She knew a certain inspector at the Health Department who respected her and Pete. She made a mental note to call him in the morning. One way or another this man would suffer for the pain he caused the people around him.

Dray nodded, putting her arm around the blonde's waist to steady her as they moved to the sink. Taking a damp rag, she proceeded to hold it gently against the dazed woman's eye. Dray winced as the blonde groaned with pain. "Aw, Abby. What happened? What are you doing here?"

Abby tried to focus in front of her but she just couldn't.

Dray recognized Abby's trouble and pushed a bit of wayward lock of hair behind her ear that fell from Abby's ponytail. "You tell me later Honey, deal?"

Abby could only give a slight nod. A dull ache was forming behind her eyes and she felt slightly nauseous. She groaned again, and Dray took the wet cloth away. Quickly inspecting the blonde's wounds, she decided there weren't any broken bones but the dizziness was a real concern.

Dray looked around at the people in the kitchen and began barking orders. She pointed at a scared looking waitress with short, brown hair.

"Tell everyone out there that you're shutting down for the evening. They can take their food with them if they like in a box but they have to go." She waited until the woman scurried from the room and then called over to the dazed woman sitting on the floor. "What's your name?" she asked.

"Robin," she answered.

"We've got medical units in route so just sit tight Hon."

The brunette shook her head, pulled the hem of her uniform up and began to clean her face. "No thanks, I'm fine. I think I'll just clean up and go home. Just about time to quit anyways." Dray frowned at the woman's detached comments.

"We can't make you stay. But I'm asking that you let the team look at you first. You might have a concussion so let's find out to be sure, okay?"

Robin slowly got to her feet, shaking her head the whole time, and started picking up the mess around her.

"You should've stayed out of it," she told Abby and Dray who stood next to each other. Abby realized the chances of Robin pressing charges or even leaving her job most likely were slim to none.

The other waitress pushed through the doors a few moments later and stood silently, wringing her hands. Dray looked at her expectantly, but the woman just stared in her direction. The firefighter tried to keep her temper in check, but it was hard.

"Yes?" she asked impatiently.

"I did like you said, they're all gone. Can we finish up and go home now?"

The speech pattern of the woman struck Dray and it suddenly occurred her that the two women were probably mentally handicapped. She hadn't noticed it at first but it was starting to make sense.

They were cheap labor who Jake felt he could order, or in this case batter, around. And judging by their meek behavior, this was most likely the usual fare for both of them. The firefighter's lips twisted into a sneer as she looked at Jake who simply groaned piteously from the floor.

"Not yet, Sweetie. Why don't you and Robin just go have a seat at the counter?" Dray told her, turning back with a gentle demeanor. "We've got some police officers coming by and we need you to tell them what happened. You can even tell them about other things that might have happened before tonight."

"You're not a policeman?" she asked. "You have a badge," she noted.

Dray spared a glance to her shirt looking at the emblem. "Yeah, I've got a badge but I'm a firefighter like these guys," she said pointing to Pete, Ted and John behind her. "We stopped in for dinner when we heard the trouble."

"I thought you fight fires."

Dray grinned. "Yeah usually, but sometimes we have to do more...Actually I got an idea. Why don't you two have a seat at the counter and Pete will wait on you for a change and get you something to drink? Will you do that for me?"

Both women nodded and Pete followed them to make sure they were okay and settled in before taking their orders. Before he could return, two officers walked into the kitchen and looked at the mess around them.

"You causing trouble, Khalkousa?" One of them asked with a teasing grin.

Dray looked up. It was Eddie Marshall. He was a bear of a man or as Eddie described himself – big, black and beautiful. He and Dray often crossed paths over the years. She had to agree there was some justification to his arrogance. Over six feet tall, more than 200 pounds and a head as bare as the day he was born, Eddie looked like someone you did not want to defy or get angry.

"Hey Eddie! Not me this time," she grinned. "That loser over there," she added as she pointed.

"Hey!" Jake shouted indignantly from behind Ted and John who still stood guard.

Eddie bore his eyes into Jake. "Mind your manners and don't interrupt a lady when she's talking," his deep voice boomed before he calmly turned back to Dray. "Please continue," he told her.

"From what I can figure he's got a few members on the staff who might be a bit slow, mentally. I think he's been abusing them for awhile and today things got extra ugly."

"Okay, thanks Dray. We've called in another unit to keep an eye on him so you guys can get out of here." Eddie saw Abby's injuries and nodded. "What about you?" he asked.

"This is my friend Abby," Dray answered for her. "She was here when we came in but I don't know her whole story yet. I was hoping to talk to her 'cause she got banged up pretty good too."

"No worries," he told her. "We'll start out there."

Eddie and his partner walked out the double doors but he quickly peeked his head back inside. "Medics are out front," he told Dray.

"Thanks Eddie," Dray nodded.

With that bit of police business done for the moment, Dray turned her full attention back on her charge. "Hey, Abby? Honey? How you doing now? Wanna tell me what happened?"

Abby blinked and without warning pulled Dray into a tight hug. Dray stood rigidly for a few seconds before she returned the embrace. Finally pulling away, Abby placed both hands on the side of Dray's face, and smiled through the tears running down her cheeks. Abby was convinced now that Dray was the most beautiful sight she had ever seen.

"How did you know? I mean I didn't even know I'd be here until yesterday."

"I don't know why myself, Abby. We were off duty, just sitting around the firehouse when we decided to grab a bite to eat. The guys wanted to go one of the regular haunts but I wanted to try something new. This place just caught my attention for some reason." She shook her head slowly, trying to get a handle on her emotions. "Thank God it did," she added softly. "I just wish I got here sooner."

Abby placed her hand against the taller woman's lips. "You did come, and you did save me. And I thank you for that." Leaning her head carefully against the firefighter's shoulder, Abby released a shaky breath. Dray was glad to comfort Abby but she wanted answers.

"Is this guy your boss?" she asked. "And why didn't you leave if things were this bad? And-."

"Remember what I said about freedom of choice that morning at the restaurant." Dray simply nodded. "Well I decided to look for greener pastures. I wasn't happy at the place I was at so I came here. Needless to say things went from bad to worse. I mean my old boss was temperamental and paid me next to nothing but...he never did anything like this today. No boss ever did anything like this."

"Well that's because this guy is obviously a psycho," Dray told her. Her hands bunched into fists and it was obvious to the blonde that Jake was a lucky man to have the cops as protection.

Suddenly Abby remembered that she hadn't spoke to her since the morning at the restaurant. "I meant to call you. Honest I did but I've been busy trying to find a bigger asshole to work for," she explained, mustering a grin. Immediately a pain shot through her cut lip and she held the wet washcloth to it.

"Don't worry about that," Dray told her. "I'm glad to hear it but let's focus on getting you bandaged up first."

The paramedics came in and taking one look at Abby made their way over. Dray stood back and let them do a series of tests on the young woman. They asked her various questions and the firefighter bit the inside of her cheek nervously as Abby got all of them right except one. When Abby failed to tell them which president was on the one-dollar bill a warning flag went up.

"We need to take you in. Just to be sure you're okay," the medic told her.

Abby shook her head. "Sorry. Can't afford it. No insurance. Just get me some aspirin and I'll be fine."

"You really should be held for observation if you start to get worse," he told her.

"But I'm already getting better," she argued. "The room is no longer spinning and I don't see twins of everyone anymore," she quipped. "I'll be fine."

"Okay," the medic conceded. "As long as you've got someone to look after you and get you medical attention if you need it then you can go home. How's that?"

*Guess I really need to rethink this solitary life.* "Fine," she told him. "Are we done now?"

"Yeah," he told her. "If your dizziness or nausea returns make sure to see someone okay? Even if it's not the emergency room then at least go to a clinic, alright?" the technician asked.

Abby didn't want to be difficult. He seemed like a sweet guy who was genuinely concerned about her well-being. "Okay," Abby acknowledged with a nod.

"I'll make sure she's taken care of," Dray added to the medic.

Satisfied, he nodded and finished packing his supplies away before leaving the room.

After he was gone, Dray turned to Abby. "Do you want me to call someone for you?"

Abby was undecided. Should she lie or be honest? She had no one to call. Arlene maybe but she really didn't know her well enough. Besides, was Arlene had been a bit more than miffed when Abby turned in her nametag to Frank.

Abby did want to get to know Dray better and she didn't want a relationship built on lies.

"Yeah about that," she told Dray. "I moved here just recently and I...well..."

"You've got nobody here."

Abby could hear the disapproval in her voice.

"Kinda. Sorta."

"You're staying with me."

Dray's voice didn't leave it open to debate but that didn't stop Abby from offering a protest.

"You've done so much already and I couldn't ask you."

"Do you think I'm some kind of nut case and I'll harm you? Honestly?"

The peculiar dream came back to the forefront of Abby's mind – 'It's never safe around me.' Abby certainly didn't feel that way in Dray's company despite what Dray told her in her dream.

"No, it's not that. I'm just not gonna burden," Abby said with a small grin, being careful not to smile too full again thereby hurting her lip. "And for the record I trust you. You've more than proven that in my eyes here today."

"You've proven something tonight, too," Dray told her. "He's a big guy to take on to protect someone you just met. So why don't the two heroes here look after each other?"

"I think you're doing just fine on your own," Abby countered.

"I could use the company," she said honestly. "And you could use someone to look after you for the next day or so. You might not think you have a friend in Chicago but you really do Abby...So what do you say?"

Abby gave a sigh and considered it. She'd always been self-reliant, ever since she left home 10 years ago. She grew up fast and maybe being a real grown up was asking for someone's help if you needed it. She didn't want to go to the hospital but she didn't want to disobey the medics orders either, truth be told.

"Okay," she agreed. "Once we finish up with the report I'll go to your place."

"That's fine," Dray told her. "If you'd feel more comfortable at your place I'm willing to pack a bag. I'm off call for the next two days."

"No, your place is fine...unless you don't want me there I mean."

"Oh, no! Not at all. I just want to make sure you get rest."

"Well believe you me, there's little rest at my place. It's kinda noisy."

"Then my place it is...Ready to go talk to the officers?"

"Lead the way," Abby said as she gestured with her hand.

Once the report was finished and Jake was hauled away in handcuffs, Dray carefully walked the blonde out of the café. The Lieutenant and her two buddies were waiting by her Chevy. Pete wore a smile as he watched Dray tending to the small blonde. If Dray noticed it, she pretended that she hadn't. She instructed Abby to lean against the cab of her truck as she fumbled for the keys.

"Hey guys, I wanna thank you for helping me out in there. You guys are the best." The men shrugged and shifted uneasily while Dray settled the blonde into the truck. They weren't sure what to do next. It certainly wasn't the time or place to go introducing themselves, especially since the blonde looked half-dead on her feet. Pete was very pleased that Dray had the next few days off to tend to the woman.

Ted was the one that finally broke the awkward silence by pushing his hand out and giving both women a handshake. "Naw, you woulda done the same. 'Sides, we was just the cavalry while you took on Sitting Bull single handedly."

Dray snorted and ran a hand through her unruly hair. "Heh, well he's gonna be sitting in bull if I've got anything to say about it." The men chuckled a little, gave both women a wave and headed over to Pete's old pick-up. Dray stood watching until the red taillights disappeared down the road.

She waited until Abby was safely buckled up and the passenger side firmly closed before she quickly moved to the driver's side. Abby had to admit it. *I kinda like the special treatment.* But she issued herself a warning. *Just don't get too used to it.* And although having the luscious brunette tending her for a couple of days did sound terribly inviting, Abby knew she'd be feeling better and heading back to her own place in a few hours.

A few seconds later, Dray was buckled in as well. Gripping the wheel with both hands, the firefighter exhaled deeply, leaned her forehead against the backs of her hands and just sat quietly for a moment.

Abby watched, wondering what was going on inside Dray's mind. She was thankful that she didn't have to ask. When Dray began to speak, her voice was raw with emotion.

"I must have been flying because I don't remember anything before I saw that asshole hitting you." She turned and placed trembling fingers against the blonde's damaged lip.

Realizing how forward she must of sounded and acted, Dray began to recoil pulling her hand away. But before it could completely leave Abby reached out and took it in hers, giving Dray an unspoken approval of her actions.

Dray gulped a few times before she could continue to speak. "He hurt you, Abby. God, I'm so sorry I couldn't get here earlier."

"I told you it will be okay, somehow...Why don't we just focus on getting home? To your place I mean," Abby clarified. She didn't want Dray to think she was moving into her world, her home.

The clarification wasn't needed. Dray was more than willing to open up to her. The girl got a busted lip and her bell seriously rung and all because she stood up for someone who couldn't defend herself. Dray enjoyed Abby's company before but she had to confess she was starting to admire the woman on a deeper level.

Dray willed her fingers to stop shaking and turned the key in the ignition. The truck started with a roar and they moved slowly away from the curb.

Twenty minutes later Dray pulled up in front of her apartment. She looked over to find that Abby had fallen asleep and a small grin played on her face as she watched the slumbering woman. She exited and walked around to Abby's side, opening the door.

She looked down at the blonde's crown of messy hair and silently debated whether she should wake the sleeping woman. It would be simple for Dray to carefully ease the woman into her arms and carry her up the two-story walk-up. Dray knew she had the strength and Abby was a slight woman.

Unbuckling Abby's belt before tensing her biceps, Dray girded herself to sweep the slumbering woman into her arms. Making certain that Abby was secure before moving, she began to pick up the light woman. Dray's chivalrous thoughts began to disappear as Abby's small hand came to rest just below her right breast. Dray rethought her strategy. Maybe carrying the young woman was a bad idea. Dray could remove the hand but if it returned while in her arms, she thought she might drop Abby, in her excitement. So instead of picking her up, Dray gently removed her hand.

"Abby?"

The blonde snuggled closer and groaned.

"Just a few seconds more?" she mumbled. Dray could tell by the tone that Abby was obviously still asleep.

"A few more seconds and I might ravish you," Dray muttered before speaking in a louder voice. "Abby, Hon? We're here; time to get upstairs to a comfy bed. Okay?"

Abby snuggled closer, her hand resuming its place just below Dray's breast. Then her body went rigid against Dray's, and the firefighter knew Abby had startled herself awake.

Wondering exactly what she should do, as casually as she could muster Abby removed her hand and slowly opened her eyes, looking around her.

"Oh, I must have fallen asleep." Abby nodded. Even with one eye puffed closed, the firefighter thought the blonde was the sexiest thing she'd ever seen and those hands felt pretty wonderful too.

Dray tried to hide her look of lust she was sure shown on her face. She watched as Abby wet her dry lips with the tip of her tongue, and Dray felt her body ignite. If she wasn't mistaken she could assume that Abby enjoyed her sleep induced fondling as much as she had.

Dray could imagine the blush that must be riding rampantly over Abby's cheekbones, down her neck and across the mounds of her breasts. And then she swallowed a moan, breaking the silence between them.

"Well, let's get upstairs and into bed, huh?" As the words left her mouth, Dray realized the innuendo. "I didn't mean it like that." Pinching the bridge of her nose, she looked at the blonde. The open carnal look was still there. *Well, in for a penny, in for a pound.* "Well, yes I did mean it like that," she confessed. "Just not now. I really meant that I'm tired."

"I know what you meant," Abby grinned, taking great delight that she could make the beautiful woman off balance.

"Come on," Dray answered with a grin, delighted that she hadn't offended her. "I'll help you."

Abby leaned on Dray as they left the truck. She knew she was fine on her own but if Dray was offering her body this close to hers Abby was going to take it. Dray fumbled with her key to gain entrance to the lobby and sighed in relief as the doorman helped her get inside and to the elevator.

Both women were bleary-eyed by the time they got to the fourth floor and moved out of the elevator. A short walk later and another key inserted, they found themselves in Dray's apartment. Abby had no time to take in her surroundings, too intent on finding someplace to lie down and cuddle with the tall woman beside her. She wondered briefly if there would be time for anything before she fell asleep but the thought left her head as soon as Dray helped her onto the bed.

The firefighter stood quietly looking at the drowsy woman before pulling the bedspread up around Abby's shoulders. Easing her jean jacket off and walking stiffly out of the bedroom, she draped it over the back of her recliner. She moved over to the side table and quickly wrote out a note to remember to call the health inspector later. That chore done, she unlaced her boots and kicked them off. Climbing gratefully onto the sofa, Dray pulled the multi-colored afghan down so that it covered half of her face and all of her body, and then quickly slipped into dreamland.

It took every inch of Abby's resolve to get up and out of the firefighter's apartment once she'd dusted the cobwebs from her addled brain. Having lain there soaking up the quiet comforting atmosphere of the Dray's apartment for a good twenty minutes after waking, Abby knew that it would be far too easy to simply roll over and accept the woman's offer to tend to her for a couple of days.

But the thought of it rankled Abby. Her father had always told her that reaching out for help was an indication of weakness. Although she rarely agreed with the man this was one point she had to give him. And she was anything but weak.

She stifled a groan as her swollen cheek and eye came into contact with the pillow. She was a strong woman who made some bad decisions, that's all. She wasn't about to make another misstep by being a burden to this woman who seemed to share a growing attraction.

After carefully dousing her face with cold water, she'd grabbed up her backpack and quietly made her way to the door. She had her hand on the brass doorknob, intending to put a stop to the roller coaster ride she currently felt she was on. But not before gazing intently at the firefighter who was slightly snoring under a bundle of afghan. Abby could feel her pulse race as she inspected every inch, every line, on Dray's face. Her lips were exquisite, and the blonde wondered how it might feel to have those lips sucking hotly on her neck and shoulders.

Giving herself a mental shake, Abby pushed down her thoughts of simply stripping and joining the firefighter under the blanket, waking her up with much more than a simply thank you for what she'd done the night before.

Instead, she picked up the pad and pen on the desk and wrote a very short note and then left the apartment. Out on the street, Abby had decided to take the bus after a couple of harsh innuendos of being a beaten-up streetwalker and questioning glares were hurled her way. It was far too early and she was far too banged up to endure any more agony than she already was so she ceased walking and opted to get home quicker by bus.

Abby willed herself to stay awake as she stood gripping the bus handle. Every now and then she'd unconsciously lick her swollen lip, which caused pain and jolted her awake. A stretch of five consecutive hours of sleep should have made Abby feel rested, but instead she felt she'd been run over once or twice.

The bus dinged, indicating the next stop, and Abby's eyes opened just enough to see whether it was her stop before closing them once again and letting the gentle rocking of the bus lull her back to semi-consciousness.

A young mother and her small child jostled her as the bus slowed to the next stop. Wincing slightly as someone or something nearby pushed against her, Abby jerked into full wakefulness and started as she recognized her stop. The lady pulled her child close as the little girl began to cry and point at Abby.

"Don't stare, Margie." The child's face was pressed tightly against her mother's belly and the woman glared in Abby's direction as they exited the bus. It was obvious by the look of disdain on her face that she figured Abby for a streetwalker, too.

Abby straightened her shoulders and she looked steadily back at the woman. "I'm proof that no good deed ever goes unpunished in this world. Trust me."

Pushing her hair over one shoulder, the blonde smiled briefly at the child who was now peeking curiously at her before she walked down the street to her apartment.

It took her more time than usual to make it to the third floor of the cheap hotel she was staying at, and Abby leaned momentarily against the wall near her door before digging her keys out of the backpack gripped in one hand. Her eyes constantly moved up and down the hallway. In her current state, she knew she was a walking advertisement for 'victim' and had no intentions of living up to it.

The door squeaked open and she kicked it closed before slamming the bolt and locking it. Her fingers unerringly found the switch in the darkness, bringing the dreary room and it's contents into stark brilliance.

Heavy gray blankets had been pinned over the windows in an effort to keep out the noise and the peeping Toms from getting their jollies at her expense. A small single bed that was nothing more than an iron frame with a lumpy mattress sat in one corner. Abby had changed the sheets a few days earlier and she could almost feel their crisp coolness against her cheek.

The floor was stained but well swept, and a few articles hung on a rail meant to act as a closet. The walls looked like a Rorschach experiment gone wrong, and Abby briefly wondered for the umpteenth time exactly what the original color had been. The room was really only a place to crawl into between shifts in order to get some sleep but lately her nightmares had been keeping her from getting any more than a few hours of sleep a night.

Abby adjusted a large safety pin on one of the blankets to allow the morning sun to pour into the room. She clicked off the light, dropped her knapsack on the end of her bed and rubbed the back of her neck. "God, what I wouldn't give for a bucket of aspirin."

She paused briefly in front of the cheap full-length mirror and groaned. No wonder everyone had given her dirty looks. If it was possible, she looked ever worse than she was feeling.

"How am I gonna get a job looking like this?"

She pressed two fingers at her temples in an effort to push away the growing pain. There were two weeks left before the rent was due again, and she still had to pick up a few groceries to last before getting another job. She could still taste the pancakes she'd enjoyed at the café with Dray.

Abby grabbed up an old travel magazine lying on the rickety dresser and pushed thoughts of the firefighter away. Her lips quirked into a lop-sided grin as she remembered the manager explaining why he charged18 dollars a night – this place was far from a palace he told her. She eyed the last six inches of mop handle that acted as one of the dresser's legs. Naturally stressed didn't even begin to describe its condition but it fit the ambiance of the room to a tee.

But it was home, of a sort, anyway. She flipped through the magazine, her fingers caressing well-loved photographs of Key Largo and other well-known dive sites found in Florida. If she just closed her eyes, she could feel the salt crust that naturally dusted her skin after a dive. It had been three years since she'd worked as a dive tour guide. But things had become untenable when a few of the hotel's customers had wanted more of Abby than she was willing to give. She had resisted the temptation of giving up her pride and independence for an easier way of life then and she would continue to do so now. She pushed the magazine back into place on the dresser.

Her thoughts strayed back to the brunette who probably still lay sleeping in her apartment. She yawned at the image dancing in her imagination. "And that's just where I'm gonna be in about two seconds – asleep."

Quickly stripping down to her underwear, Abby carefully pulled out one side of the covers and slipped into bed. Her gaze settled on the beams of light filled with particles that shone through the crack in the blanket and her eyes slowly drifted shut.

Then the shouting started in one of the rooms above her. Abby groaned and pulled the extra pillow over her face. She yowled briefly at the pressure and instead pulled the covers over her damaged face. There was no use trying to get a job looking the way she was so she'd just have to heal up quickly in the next day or so before going out to look for one.

A brief image of ice entered her brain and Abby made a mental list of the things she'd need to hurry the healing time along. Her head had begun to feel like someone was ringing a very large bell inside it and Abby narrowed the list down to ice and aspirin.

Soon, she tumbled down the well into sleep.

Hours later Dray woke up and walked to the bedroom to check on Abby. All she found was a note thanking her for her help the night before and that she was doing much better. Dray checked the piece of paper three times, turning it over, hoping that she'd missed the young woman's phone number but found nothing. The sound of her pre-set clock radio startled her.

Running her fingers roughly through her hair, Dray groaned and made her way into the bathroom to start her day with one thought on her mind. *Who IS Abby Dean?*

# Chapter 4

Dray popped a few peanuts into her mouth and chewed slowly as she removed her jean jacket and placed it on the barstool before sitting down. The number of patrons had increased over the last half hour and now the temperature was that of a sauna. She passed her Heineken back and forth between her hands on the bar, the bottle sliding easily on the thin layer of condensation dribbling down from her beer. It was her second in as many hours.

The jukebox played a slow song with a deep throbbing bass, and although Dray couldn't make head nor tails as to who sang it or even what the words were, it was obviously a torch and twang number currently popular on the radio. It fit her mood perfectly.

Shooters Pub was a middle of the road joint that catered mainly to cops, firefighters and rescue workers. Plaques of distinction lined the walls, along with photos, both color and black and white, of comrades lost in the line of duty. And while it was a noisy place most of the time, it was also a comfortable one where Dray felt she could come and relax.

She took another sip of her beer and sighed heavily. It had felt so natural to have Abby in her apartment, in her bed, and waking up to both being empty made her feel very alone. When had she become so solitary? But being alone didn't mean you were lonely, did it?

Rubbing her tired eyes with both hands, she didn't notice that Pete had entered the bar and was now standing just behind her. She jumped a little as he placed his hand on the back of her neck.

"Hey, Dray. How you doin'?" He patted her shoulder with his other hand. "Nah, don't bother lyin'. I can see by the look in your eyes. You ain't getting any more sleep this week than you got last week, right?" He took the barstool beside her, caught the eye of the bartender and ordered a beer before turning back to his friend. "You still having nightmares?"

Dray took another pull of her beer, rubbed the sweat off her forehead and shrugged. Pete pushed a bill onto the bar and took a swig of his draft beer. "Ah, that's good," he said wearing white froth in his mustache. He took another deep pull of the beer before licking his mustache clean.

"So, what you been up to on your days off, Khalkousa? You took that blonde home last night, right? You two got somethin' planned for the next few days?"

Dray shrugged again but this time a frown appeared at the corners of her mouth. Pete grunted. "Ah, woman trouble."

Dray shot him a dirty look but continued her silence. The Lieutenant unbuttoned the top of his sweat-stained shirt and groaned as a bit of air hit his skin. "God, I'll be glad to get out of this monkey suit. Been a long day, doing up the reports, filing duplicates, yadda yadda." He scratched the bristles that lined his chin. "I took the opportunity to fill out yours early this morning. I don't figure it was gonna be any different than me and Ted's so…"

"Thanks, Pete." The Lieutenant waited for more but Dray seemed to take more interest in the circles forming on the bar from her beer than the company around her.

"Okay, Dray, now listen up. I know this is your life, and I ain't got no right buttin' into it, but Jodi was done and over with, what, 18 months ago? It's time to move on."

Dray nodded and sighed. "Yeah, I know it," she pointed to her head, "in here. But it's hard, you know? How do you get over someone you spent a year with, someone you thought you loved?"

Pete moved closer so that his elbows were against hers. "The operative word here, Dray, is 'thought.' Jodi was a user, always was and probably always will be." He took the hard look she gave him and continued. "She never loved you and you know it. She entered your life when you needed a life preserver."

A tear slipped out from between dark eyelashes, and Dray held a hand to her quivering lips. Pete knew the words were hurting his friend, but she needed to hear them.

"And you can't keep blaming yourself for Ian's death, honey, you just can't. You were working, you had someone minding the boy and you couldn't have known he would hide."

Dray shook her head quickly. "No, I shoulda been there, Pete. I should have known he was in danger. A mother should know that instinctively."

"That's ridiculous and deep down you know it. Mother intuition or not, you couldn't have saved him." Pete took her hand in his and gave it a squeeze. "I'll bet you were a helluva mother, Dray, so don't ever doubt yourself on that account."

Dray gave her friend a little smile and patted his hand. "Thanks, buddy." She stared off into space for a moment before going on. "He was a helluva kid, you know?" Memories of the short life she'd had with her son were like a mosaic against the backs of her eyes, a parade of pleasing images that usually helped coax her to sleep.

"I'm sure he was," Pete told her with a gentle smile. "Especially if he was anything like his momma."

Dray returned the small smile before squaring her shoulders. She turned to look into the solemn brown eyes of her boss. "You're right. I was a damned good mother and there's nothing I could have done." She flexed her hands around the bottle and Pete wondered just how much pressure it would take before the bottle broke. It was time to change the subject.

"I saw how you were talkin' to the blonde and how protective you were at the diner last night. Hell," he scratched his cheek; "you looked like some avenging angel. That freak was lucky you didn't really unleash on him." He chuckled and elbowed the brunette.

Dray harrumphed and took another swig of her beer. "Yeah, well I don't know why but I feel something when I'm with Abby. It's hard to describe, it's like we have this bond or something."

Pete grinned. "Oh, a bond, huh? Couldn't be that she's this hot babe and you're warm for her form, right?"

Dray elbowed him and he could tell by the rising blush that he'd hit the mark. "Well yeah," Dray admitted. "But I don't know anything about her, Pete and she's really secretive." Dray paused a moment considering her words. "Actually it's not secretive. More like mysterious. I mean I can't get a handle on her one way or another."

Both of his bushy eyebrows rose quickly. "What? You spent the night with her and you guys didn't do any talking?" He wiggled his eyebrows. "Ah, too busy with other stuff, huh? You dog."

Blue eyes flashed his way. "Don't talk about Abby like that. She's not some one-night stand, okay? And yeah, you're right – it is my life. I'd appreciate it if you remembered that." Her glare left no doubt that the subject was closed.

"Damn Dray. I'm just teasin' so lighten up okay?"

Dray took a long swig on her beer and sat it down on the bar before facing him again. "I'm sorry. It's not you. It's her actually. I woke up and she was gone, Pete. Sure, she left a thank you note but I don't want her thanks. I want..."

"Her?" Pete asked when Dray hadn't finished the sentence.

Dray didn't have the chance to respond. Both their heads came up though as Ted yelled a greeting from the doorway.

"I got another shift done and the next three days off! Bourbon whisky," he ordered from the bartender, "and leave the bottle, son."

Randy chuckled and pulled down a bottle of Old Granddad from its place on the top shelf. Although he really had no idea how old the man was, he figured he and Ted were close in age. Ted Buchanan was an old regular, just as Pete was, having worked this particular precinct for many years. While Pete was a born and bred Chicagoan, Ted was as deep down Southern as you could get, genteel disposition included. After a particularly tough shift the soft spoken Southerner would come in and buy a couple of doubles of the dark amber liquid and nurse them until the bar closed. That he'd wanted the bottle meant it had been truly a hellish week.

Ted winked as the man placed the bourbon and a glass in front of him. "So, how are my two most favorite people in the whole damned world tonight?" His smile faltered as Pete nodded a greeting and Dray sat silently playing with her beer.

"Hey, hey, what's this, fan club for the lovelorn?" He patted Dray on the arm. "That lady friend of yours alright?"

Pete motioned that Ted should change the subject with a slicing gesture across his neck but the Southerner couldn't catch the hint.

"Pretty little thing like her gettin' all banged up like that, well, it's just a cryin' shame, that's what it is. Oughta horse whip that sumbitch just on principal alone. Bet you tended to her though."

The Lieutenant continued to drag a finger across his throat a few times, but Ted continued to be oblivious to the dark looks both his friends were giving him.

Finally, Dray stood up, downed what was left of her beer and smacked the bottle back on the bar. "She isn't my 'lady friend,' Ted. She's just someone I met, is all."

Ted nodded sagely, and sipped at his bourbon. "And you gettin' all googly-eyed over that sweet package just ain't you, so deny, deny, deny!" He slapped the bar. "Way I see it, she took a shine to you right away. That makes her your lady friend whether you like it or not. You need to settle down, woman." He turned to Pete who was now holding his head in one hand and gulping down the contents of his draft. "That's right, ain't it Lieutenant?" He went on, not caring that Pete was actively ignoring him. Dray narrowed her eyes at the Lieutenant. It was obvious now that she'd been the subject of conversations in the locker room. The thought didn't sit too well with her at all.

"Now look here, Andrea Khalkousa. You listen to your old Uncle Ted. I know you think she's somebody special. Just don't expect the woman to throw herself atcha, like Jodi did."

Pete groaned and covered his face with his hands. "Oh please, God, take me now," he muttered.

Pete's reaction created a sense of levity that Dray needed to cool her nerves. Instead of letting her anger get away from her, Dray rolled her eyes in his direction. She cleared her throat and put a hand on the Southerner's arm. "Hey, thanks for the advice, Ted, I mean it. But please...shut up." As much as she loved both men like brothers, there were times when being with them was just simply mortifying.

"Look Darlin'. You need somebody in your life and this woman could be it. Don't let her get away. She likes you, you like her...go on and do something about it."

"Jesus H. Christ, Ted," the brunette said wearily. "Do you think I'd be in this joint with you two if I thought I had a chance with Abby?" She sat back down on her stool, her back to the men. "Besides, she was gone when I woke up this morning, and I don't have a fucking clue where she lives or what her phone number is."

Both men looked at her slack jawed, as the truth hit them. Although Dray wasn't what you called a Don Juan, she certainly had no trouble getting dates. And there hadn't been anyone special in awhile. To them it was incomprehensible to think of Dray letting some beauty get away without getting her number.

Dray crossed her arms and hooked her feet around the barstool pole. She looked very vulnerable and the guys responded by attacking her from both sides in a large group hug. Pushing them away half-heartedly, Dray rubbed her face and smiled.

"Falling for someone I just met. Pretty sad, huh?" she said with a chuckle. It had felt damned good to actually laugh and let the stress out. It was like a heavy weight had been lifted from her shoulders. She smiled at her friends.

"About damn time is more like it," Pete muttered. He ordered his friend another beer and passed Randy a couple of dollars to cover it.

Dray caught the comment but let it go and continued. "I guess I'm being an idiot, huh? I mean I could catch a fucking clue. Maybe she doesn't feel what I feel, and..."

Pete nodded as he handed her the beer. "Yeah, that's it." He shook his head sadly. "Dumbass woman. Just 'cause she was gone in the morning doesn't mean she won't be back later tonight, right?" Dray blinked deeply. She hadn't thought of that prospect.

"Maybe," was all she said before taking a deep drink of her beer.

Ted threw back the rest of his drink and poured himself another. He wrapped an arm around her shoulders protectively. "Besides, I don't think she's the type to stay away from a good thing when she sees it." He hugged the woman and then ruffled her hair. "I mean, c'mon, Dray," said Ted, his voice beginning to slur. "You, tall strappin' brown-eyed, blue haired..."

Beer shot out of Dray's nose.

"I mean, brown eared, blue eyed, double breasted mattress thrasher..."

Pete spewed beer across the bar, soaking Randy, who gingerly offered the firefighters their own towel.

Ted blinked a few times. "What was I sayin'?"

Pete eyed the bourbon, noting there was only half a bottle left. "I think you was sayin' it's time to go to bed, Ted."

Ted Buchanan lumbered to his feet, a silly smile on his face. "Oh, now I remember. You get that young filly in your bed, Dray, and you..."

Dray's hand was firmly fixed on the man's mouth before he could say another word. A few of the bar's patrons had stopped to listen, the nearest having their mouths hanging open.

"Um. He said he was feeling sick, didn't you, Ted?" She made the Southerner's head nod up and down.

Pete placed a few more bills on the counter, tightened his tie and between him and Dray, they frog-marched Ted out of the bar and into the clear night air. It wasn't that people were shocked at hearing that Dray was gay. Everyone at the precinct knew it, and most of the police force in the area did, too. Some made a big deal about it but most simply took it in stride. Dray's ability combined with her unflinching loyalty and sense of duty to the corps of firefighters and rescue workers took precedence over anything else about her.

However, the very idea of having her sexual proclivities discussed by friends or strangers in a bar in the middle of the night was just not something Dray felt comfortable even contemplating let alone bearing witness to. She kept her private life to herself, thank you, what little there was of it.

Her mood darkened as she thought of going back to her empty apartment that Abby vanished from earlier that day. *What if I never see her again?*

She jumped as a large hand settled on her shoulder and Eddie Marshall walked in stride beside the trio.

"Say, you are as jumpy as a one-eyed cat in a dog pound," Eddie told her. He peered at Ted, noting the way the man's eyes were rolling around. "Had too much bourbon, has he?"

Pete nodded and Dray grunted. She aimed them over towards Pete's truck and sighed gratefully as the large black man hoisted Ted over his shoulder and waited until the truck was opened.

"Look, Dray, I don't want to seem forward, but I couldn't help but overhear some of what you guys were talking' about in there."

Dray groaned. "God, you and half of Chicago." She pinched the Southerner's arm while Pete settled the seatbelt around Ted's slumped form.

"Nah, it ain't as bad as all that. I've got her information from the other night. 'Course, I don't know how accurate it is but I could check it out. You know, official business to make sure the witness is doing okay? Nothing says you can't just happen to be in the neighborhood when it happens," he said with a wily grin.

Dray scratched her chin. "Well..." She thought briefly at how nice it was to have the blonde around, and how good it had felt to feel the dynamics two people experienced as they flirted. "Okay, deal."

The cop held up his hand. "Cool. What was her name again, Dray? Abby something right?" He pulled out a small notebook and pen and began to jot down notes.

"Abby Dean," she told him.

"Any other description?" He waited a full beat. "I mean other than about 5'4", around 120 lbs, long blonde hair, green eyes..."

"Hazel, her eyes are hazel." Dray sighed, a small smile tweaking the corners of her mouth. Then she closed her eyes and pretended she was placing her hands on Abby's hips. "And I'd bet she's about 100, maybe 110."

Eddie's eyebrows went up. "Lady, you have got it bad." Pete slammed the door after settling behind the wheel of his truck and nodded.

"Yeah, hasn't she? Even though Miss Dray here keeps insisting that she just met the woman and there's nothing goin' on," Ted added, finally rejoining the conversation.

Dray reached over and punched his arm. "Hey, I didn't say I didn't want something to be there, just that...Oh, forget it. I'm not arguing with a drunk," she teased before turning to Eddie. "I just want to see her again, find out if maybe..."

Eddie placed a large hand on the brunette's arm. "Well, leave it with me. I'll go over my reports tomorrow and give you a call – let you know what I found out. What's the number to reach you?"

Since Dray knew she'd be off she gave him her home number. Eddie made a note of it along with a promise to call her with a location where they could meet.

Dray nodded and hopped into the back of the truck. "Hey, thanks, Eddie, I owe ya!"

Eddie Marshall just shook his head, both hands on his hips, and chuckled as the truck drove out of sight. "Ah, what we do for love."

Officer Eddie Marshall whistled tunelessly until the elevator dinged and the door opened on the fourth floor. His eyes moved over the small details that indicated this was more than just a regular apartment building: ceiling stucco that had been meticulously painted and kept cobweb free; brass light fixtures dotting the walls; and off-white textured wallpaper that made the hallway seem larger somehow.

He stopped in front of apartment 439, leaned forward and pressed the doorbell. A few seconds later and Dray Khalkousa answered the door.

"Hey, Eddie. Thanks again for doing this."

Eddie smiled and leaned against the door jam. "Not a problem."

The firefighter smiled and welcomed him into her apartment. "C'mon in. You want a beer?"

He looked down at his uniform and shot her a glance.

"Sorry, forgot," Dray apologized. "I'm just a little nervous."

"I could. I'm off duty but since this is a 'working follow-up' it might be bad to have beer breath if hell breaks out for some reason."

"Good point," Dray replied with a grin.

Eddie waved his notebook in his hand.

"You about ready?" he asked.

Dray tried very hard not to run over and grab the big man by his lapels and force him to divulge the information. *Like that's ever gonna happen in my lifetime.* She knew it was just a game to him; he'd give up the information in his own good time, so she decided to play it cool.

"Sure am," she said as she put her shoes on and tied them up in a leisurely fashion.

"Couldn't find a telephone number. Apparently, she doesn't have one." He shoved his hands into his pockets and rocked back and forth on his heels as she read the information on the paper. "You realize this isn't the best part of town and it could be a false address. I just don't want you getting your hopes up too high, Dray."

He read out the address and Dray knew the area well enough. She and the rest of her department had been called to that end of town on several occasions to assist other precincts. Sometimes it was due to druggies freebasing cocaine, and other times it was due to gang warfare, resulting in torched houses and apartment buildings.

"God, I hate even thinking she's in that part of the city, let alone one of those no-tell hotel dives."

Eddie nodded.

"Yup. What's that little thing doing in a nasty place like that? You don't get your butt over there and get her out, then I'm gonna kick your sorry ass, Khalkousa."

Dray was already over at the door, turning the lock on the doorknob. She threw her jean jacket on in seconds flat and blew a kiss in Eddie's direction before sprinting down the hall. Eddie didn't even have a chance to turn close Dray's apartment door before he heard her boots echoing in the stairwell. He wondered whether she was going to take her truck or the cycle. The deep throaty growl of Dray's 1976 custom-made bike answered the question for him.

Although the day was relatively sunny with the temperature being in the low 70s, the wind was picking up. Dray was glad she had her helmet visor down, even though the sweat was running from her hair down the back of her neck. By the time she'd battled the traffic into the south side of the city, Dray felt like she'd just stepped out of a shower.

After locating the right neighborhood, it was just a matter of finding a parking spot close enough so that she could keep an eye on her bike. It took two trips around the block before she spied a likely candidate.

Clutching Abby's address in her teeth, Dray inserted her cable lock through the front wheel of her bike and wrapped it around the pole and then inserted a few coins into the meter.

Eddie arrived just behind her and found a parking space a few places down. With her cycle secure, she tucked her helmet under one arm and checked the address again. She frowned as she realized the worst looking building was the one that Abby lived in.

Eddie walked up with a grin. "I could issue you a speeding citation," he teased.

Dray was in no mood for jokes though. She ignored the comment, making her way inside the building with Eddie following behind her. There was no one at the front desk and Dray figured it was just as well. The desk clerk would probably try and weasel a couple of bucks out of her for information she already had.

Her nostrils flared as Dray made her way up the stairwell to the third floor. The stench of stale urine and vomit was making her glad that she hadn't had time to have dinner when Eddie came by with the information. A couple of men stared at her menacingly, but when they caught sight of her Chicago Fire Department t-shirt and the uniformed officer following her, they turned away and disappeared down the hall.

Checking the information one more time, Dray nodded at the number on the door and knocked. There was no answer after three tries, and she became somewhat concerned. *What if Abby did suffer a concussion but no one was there to care for her?* She didn't think the woman had suffered such an extensive head injury, but her time with Abby had been so brief she couldn't be sure.

Dray looked to Eddie who now began pounding on the door.

"Abby? Abby Dean? It's Officer Marshall from the café. I just wanted to check on you so if you're home open up, please."

When no one came, Eddie shrugged. "Maybe she's not home," he offered.

At that point they both heard a loud groan from the other side of the door and the pair looked at each other.

Dray rattled the doorknob but it was locked.

"Abby?" Dray shouted.

Her nose twitched as the acrid scent of dope came wafting down the hall. Looking up and down the hallway, she was surprised that no one had opened their door to see what the commotion was all about. The more she thought about it the more sense it made that no one would bother to interfere. Sometimes it was safer to turn a blind eye. With what she knew of the neighborhood, it was probably an act of survival to do so.

Dray heard a stream of abuse coming from the end of the hall and then something crashed against a wall somewhere in the building. She spied a used diaper lying in the doorway across the hall and cringed. The very idea of Abby being in such a horrible rabbit warren made her skin crawl.

"Come on, Abby, it's me, Dray. You know, the firefighter?"

Still nothing. Checking the top hinge on the door, Dray could see that it wouldn't take much to simply push the door in, regardless of the amount of locks that might be present on the other side.

She shot a look to Eddie. "Okay, this is your area of expertise," she told him. "Do we have grounds to go in?"

He paused a moment and then nodded toward the door. A moment later they both pressed their shoulder against the door until both hinges gave in.

Once opened, Dray gingerly stepped over the threshold. There was no use having a baseball bat smacked against the back of her head as she came into a room unannounced.

"Abby, it's Dray. Are you here?" she called again.

Her nose wrinkled at the sour smell in the room and Dray realized that Abby must have been sick. A few noises could now be heard in the hallway, so Eddie stepped out to meet them.

"Police business," he told them in his best authoritative voice. Curiosity wasn't enough to make them stay, not when the word 'police' was heard.

Seeing the condition of the room, Dray decided then and there that she'd do whatever it took to get Abby out of the place. She switched on the light and stepped back as a few cockroaches scurried out of sight, reminding her easily of the human inhabitants out in the hallway. The rumpled bed in the corner was empty, and Dray stood in the middle of the room scratching her head. Perhaps Abby had gone out for a bite to eat? She spied the backpack just by the bed and discarded the idea.

Making a quick tour of the room, Dray took in Abby's mean little existence. A few well-worn articles of clothing hung from a rod in the corner, there were some well-worn paperbacks and magazines throughout the room, and two dusty looking wool blankets pinned up over the windows.

"Oh, this is no place for you, Abby, no place at all." She was tempted to sit in the only chair in the room and wait until the blonde returned when she heard the toilet flush.

Dray stood outside the closed door and cleared her throat a few times, hoping that Abby would hear her. She didn't want to scare the woman, as it was now obvious she hadn't heard either the yelling or the breaking down of her door. That was a little strange. She placed her helmet on the table and turned the knob on the bathroom door. When it swung open, Abby lay half crumpled on the floor with her head hanging over the toilet.

"Oh, God, Abby." The blonde only groaned as she continued to dry heave. Dray twisted both faucet handles in an effort to get water into the sink, but the plumbing only groaned and clanked in response.

"Damnit," she shouted. The pipes rattled noisily behind the wall, their pitch increasing, and then a bit of brackish water spurted out of the nozzle and into the sink. Quickly grabbing a small towel that resembled an old rag, Dray sopped up some of the water and then knelt by Abby. Pressing the cool fabric against the back of the blonde's neck made the woman finally realize there was someone else in the room and she looked up in the firefighter's direction.

"Dray? Is that you?"

Eddie stepped back inside and saw the young woman. "Sweet Jesus," he muttered before opening up his cell phone and dialing. "Yeah, it's Marshall. I need an ambulance quick." Eddie stepped back into the hallway to give the women space in the cramped quarters as he called in back up.

Dray's heart was squeezed tightly as she took in the blonde's haggard and beaten condition. The once red marks had now turned an ugly shade of blue and purple. In one quick motion, Dray picked up Abby and carried her in the bed a few steps away. Abby lay shaking on the wrinkled sheets and Dray could tell by her sallow complexion that the woman was well on her way to being dehydrated.

"I don't want you to see me like this," moaned the blonde. Lifting a hand a couple of inches off the bed expended too much energy, and another small groan escaped her lips.

"Never mind about that. You got something decent to drink in here? Some juice or water or something? We gotta get some fluids into you, fast." Dray turned away from the bed and began searching the room. However, a quick inspection didn't turn up anything that resembled food, and Dray suspected the woman hadn't eaten recently, given how weak she appeared.

She turned quickly with both fists bunched and at the ready as the door was pushed open with a shriek. Relaxing slightly when Eddie stuck his face in through the doorway, Dray released her breath.

Eddie came back inside to stand watch. "Medical team's on the way," he told her. "ETA in about 6 minutes."

"Thanks Eddie," she told him.

The blonde was wearing a nightshirt and underwear. Dray picked up what looked to be a bundle of rags and arched an eyebrow. She recognized the torn jeans but they looked in even worse condition from when she'd seen Abby last. After a brief searching for something else, she gave up and packed them in her knap sack along with a shirt she found on a hanger.

"Hey, Eddie, we gotta get her outta here."

"And we will," he stressed to her. "The team's already dispatched, Dray. They'll be here before we can get her to the hospital. Just sit tight."

Frustrated Dray asked, "Will you meet 'em?"

"Sure," he told her, making his leave to stand outside the hotel to lead them direct to Abby.

Dray kept checking Abby's pulse and ended up simply holding the woman's hand. Three minutes later, Dray heard an ambulance roll to a stop outside and she looked out the window as Eddie stopped them from entering immediately, instead instructing them to bring a gurney first. A few moments later, Abby was carefully placed on a stretcher and into the back.

Dray hesitated to move as the ambulance doors closed. Eddie's hand on her shoulder roused her, though, and she blinked at the man.

"I guess I'll meet you at the hospital, right?" she said clearly distracted.

"You okay to drive?" he asked.

Dray realized she had to pull it together. Abby was in safe hands now and she didn't need to wipe out her bike and end up beside her in the emergency room.

"Yeah," she told him with conviction in her voice. "I can take it from here if you wanna cut loose."

"No, Dray," he answered. "At least let me follow behind you to the hospital."

Dray swallowed and nodded before she took a ragged breath. She had the cable lock removed in seconds flat and hopped on the bike. Keeping her word, she made sure Eddie was inside his car and ready to follow as she pulled out into traffic.

Abby felt like she'd been swimming underwater for a very long time. She could hardly move her arms, and even trying to open her eyelids took a momentous effort.

It felt as if she was watching a movie or a dreamscape of some kind. A man pulled on his uniform jacket, tugging on the lapel to put it firmly in place. His insignia glittered dully in the waning afternoon light. He wiped at it, frowned, and then carefully pushed his collar back into place. "It will have to do," he said.

Although the words were spoken in another language, Abby had no problem understanding them perfectly. It was a rather dank office, devoid of any human touch; very Spartan and very typical of military quarters found anywhere.

There was a small stove in the corner, its door gaping open like a hungry maw. Abby wondered why there wasn't anything in it; it was obvious the man was chilled. Then a woman with a hat, which covered her ears, shuffled in. Her threadbare clothing showed her malnutrition, worn like it was some badge of honor.

She stood with shoulders slumped and yet Abby could see a certain rigidity to the woman, a certain defiance that seemed in stark opposition to the image she held up for display. And so did the soldier who clenched his fists in anger as she stood before him.

A full minute slid by quietly, belying the building rage that flowed between the two until every breath the woman took was on fire. Opening her mouth wide, Abby sought only to question the motive for the war between them. And yet, as usual, she knew nothing would come of it; this time would be like the last time, her throat closed, rendering her mute to all she would bear witness to.

Abby ground her teeth in frustration, the bedclothes twisting in her fists. Why couldn't this dream just end? Why did she keep dreaming about this stranger?

Her eyes fluttered and her heartbeat began to slow; the dream would fade, as usual, with the characters in the play standing there, fixing each other with intensity, and would then replay the next night, or if she were lucky, next week. She rolled over into a tight ball and urged the last scene to play out, if only so she could awaken, drag her sweat sodden body over to the hotel window and wait until the dawn painted the sky the same color as the pain in her head.

But it didn't end, not with that scene anyway. Abby's eyes danced feverishly under lids closed tightly, and the dream played on.

"Why is the fire not lit?"

Silence.

"One day you will push too hard, little one. One day I will let them have you."

The small figure lifted her head and Abby could tell by the man's response that she was openly staring at him.

"You promised food if I worked for you. So far you have taken your ease with my body, expecting the fire to be lit within me and here in your office as well? You cannot have one, why should you have the other? You owe me."

With a howl of rage, the man flew across the desk grabbing her up with his large hands fastened around her thin throat.

"You dare to defy me? I let you live, prisoner, be pleased you have my interest," he sneered at her. "It might change before even a crust is thrown your way."

A harsh slap rang out as muscle met bone and a wide spray of blood flew from the figure's nose. Then he shook her and the woman's hat fell crumpled to the ground.

Abby's heart felt pierced as she recognized the bruised face.

It was Zosia and, yet she knew, it was also her own face.

Breaking through an imaginary surface, Abby took a deep ragged breath as she regained consciousness. She lay panting for a couple of seconds as she tried to get her breathing under control. Then she settled on trying to open her eyes.

The first thing she saw was Dray sleeping in a chair in the corner, her head slumped forward. Abby tried to open her mouth but her lips seemed to be glued together. She blinked in surprise when she moved her left hand up to her mouth and saw the IV tube. Her surroundings came into focus quickly and Abby could see that she was in a hospital room. Tilting her head the other way showed that she was the only patient.

*Oh, no. I've got no insurance; who's going to pay for this?* She tried to remember how she'd gotten to the hospital but came up empty. The last thing she remembered was climbing into bed with a very bad headache. *Oh, yeah. And I was sick in the night, I remember that.* And then bits and pieces of what followed bubbled up in her mind and an image of Dray picking her up from the floor and placing her in bed hit her. A total feeling of embarrassment infused her immediately as she remembered throwing up all over herself and crawling into the bathroom.

Small tears formed in the corners of her eyes as she cried softly. The noise roused the firefighter and she was on her feet and over by the bed before she was even fully awake. With very little hesitation, she took up the woman's hand, noticing how very soft and frail it was. "Abby, are you all right?"

A fresh spate of tears followed as Abby looked up into the concerned blue eyes of the firefighter. She was mortified, angry and afraid. What would the woman think of her, having found her in such condition? And what about the state of her apartment? She groaned and covered her face with both hands. "Don't look at me," she croaked. "I'm a mess," she blubbered and then cried harder as her split lip bled a little.

Dray pressed the button to call the nurse and one appeared almost instantly. The firefighter dragged her chair over to the bedside as the nurse fussed over her patient.

"Take it easy, Abby. You're not a mess, you're..." She swallowed and closed her mouth as the nurse started taking her patient's vitals. She didn't want to get too personal in front of the nurse, not if she could help it.

She sat quietly as the woman went about her duties, and only turned as her name was called. A doctor stood in the doorway and motioned her over.

"I'm Dr. Bronson," he told her.

They shook hands, and he pulled her out of the room. "She a friend of yours?" Dray nodded. "She got any family in town?" Dray bit her lip. All that she knew of the blonde was her full name and that she hadn't been in town long.

"None that she's mentioned," Dray offered.

The doctor nodded as if he understood. There were lots of people in the inner city who barely made ends meet. Summertime in Chicago meant that the high temperatures would exacerbate a person's already poor health. He believed that Abby fell into that category and explained it.

"Well, I need to know the particulars if you know of any." He paused and looked at the clipboard he was carrying. "She's suffering from heat exhaustion and dehydration. Judging by her appearance, I'd say that she suffered a mild concussion recently, within 48 hours. You know anything about that?"

Dray explained what had happened at the diner.

Bronson nodded. "She probably hasn't been eating all that well, so that kind of physical trauma would explain her present condition." He closed the clipboard, tucked it under his arm and leaned against the wall.

"She's got no insurance and we can't keep her any longer than a few more hours. I don't want to release her to have her end up back in here."

Dray nodded, having made a decision as the doctor was speaking. "No, she's got friends, Doc. In fact, she was going to come stay with me for a few days." He grunted and walked back into the room, Dray trailing behind him.

"Miss Dean? My name is Dr. Bronson. How are you feeling?"

Abby licked her lips as the nurse pulled the cup of water and straw away from her mouth. It had taken two glasses of water but Abby's thirst was finally quenched.

"I'm okay," she croaked, and it was obvious to Dray that her voice was getting stronger. The six hours of IV therapy was really making a difference, slowly but surely.

"Dray here tells me that you're going to spend a couple of days with her, that right?" Abby shot a look over at the brunette and then back at the doctor. She didn't know what to say.

Dray bit her lip. The doctor looked at both women and tapped his front teeth with the end of his finger. "Okay, I think I'll just let you two talk things over and I'll be right back."

He nodded to the nurse and the two left the room. As soon as they'd gone, Dray held her hands up.

"Okay, I know – short notice. Look, they're not going to let you go unless you've got someone to take care of you. You never gave me a name of someone to call at the diner. You want me to call someone now?"

Abby thought of Arlene but dismissed the idea immediately. The woman had her own problems, why saddle her with more?

"No, but..."

"See, the way I figure it is you come stay at my place for two-three days until you get your feet back under you, and then I'll help you look for another place." She narrowed her eyes at the blonde. "Don't even think about going back to that rat trap you were living in. I've had a buddy pick up your belongings and take them to my place, so don't worry." She ran her hands through her short hair. "God, Abby. When I think of you in that dive, with those cockroaches, and that filthy water..."

Abby clenched her jaw. "That happens to be my home," she answered defensively.

"A home?" Dray countered. "It's barely a dwelling."

"You know where I was three months ago? A shelter on the nights they had room. In the alley when they didn't." Dray tried to hide her surprise at the news as she listened to Abby go on, "That place is all I could afford, okay? But I paid for it with my own money and it was *my* place. You don't have any right to..."

Dray nodded in agreement. "Yeah, you're right. I got no rights when it comes to you. And I admire your independent streak, but with no insurance they have to release you and with no one to watch over you the doc says you'll probably end up back in here. You want that?"

Abby opened her mouth and then closed it again.

"You've got your pride. I get that," Dray told her. "But sometimes the strongest thing to do is to turn to someone for help when you really need it. I'm offering so don't turn me away."

"Why?" Abby asked. "You don't know me. Where I'm from. Who I am. You know absolutely nothing, Dray."

"Then stay with me. Show me who you are without running away in the middle of the night."

"Well, technically it wasn't the middle of the night the last time I left," Abby offered in weak argument. When she heard the comment spoke out loud she began to grin at how ridiculous she sounded. Seeing the resolution on Dray's face Abby knew she wasn't going to win. "Okay, but it's only for a few days, right? Then I'm gone and I get my own place."

She pushed down the realization that she had no money, no job and had lost any hope of keeping a place of her own for quite a while. It had taken six months of saving every nickel she made before she could afford a room at the dumpy hotel. And she'd been living hand to mouth as it was after paying for the room.

Abby bit the inside of her cheek and then stuck out her hand. "Deal?"

Dray shook it solemnly and then brought it to her lips.

"Please don't think of this as being a sentence, okay? Hell, I'll get some of my friends to look around for a place. And if it's too much, I'm sure we can..."

Abby sat up and snatched her hand back. She was feeling stronger by the minute, and whether it was because of the medical intervention or the topic of conversation, she couldn't say.

"Don't even say it, Dray. I've done just fine on my own for years and I'll continue to do so. Every battle I've fought has been won on my terms or not at all." She pinned the brunette with a stern look. "I won't take charity, Dray, so don't offer it."

Dray's lower jaw was askew as she contemplated the blonde's words.

"In the first place, why does life have to be a battle?" Dray asked. "And in the second, who says I was offering charity? I would never disrespect you, Abby. And just so ya know, I'm not in the habit of taking in strays," she added with a smirk.

Abby opened her mouth with a quick rejoinder in mind but Dray stopped her in her tracks as she leaned forward. "Call it a loan, if you wanna. I know you're good for it. Someone like you doesn't come along very often, so don't blame me for wanting you to stick around."

The firefighter's smile was so genuine and warming that Abby had no choice but to respond. She reached up and slowly pulled the brunette down so they were nose to nose. "You want me to stick around?" She brushed the firefighter's lips briefly with her own.

"I want," Dray said softly. Abby didn't miss the hint of desire under the concerned tone and she had to smile.

"It's good to feel wanted," she admitted.

"Does that mean you'll stay?" Dray asked. "At least, until you can get on your feet?"

Abby could hear the concern in Dray's voice and it felt foreign to her. She'd lived alone for so long, wandering through life as a drifter. She never thought she'd be wanted by anyone and it suited her just fine. No commitments, no baggage.

But for the first time in her life she found herself wanting Dray's approval, craving her attention, needing her respect. It excited yet scared her. Could she keep her promise to Dray and stick around? She knew she had to try because if she didn't she might end up regretting it for the rest of her life.

"Okay," Abby said with a growing grin. "You want me then you got me."

Dray tapped the blonde on her pert nose. "Good. Now you go to sleep. I'll be back in a few, all right? I rode my bike to your place but I wanna get my truck before we head out, okay?"

She smiled and winked as she walked over to the door. Abby could hear the woman whistle as Dray walked down the hall.

"Oh my God. Did I just say she could have me?" Abby covered her eyes with both hands. "Oh, I am in so much trouble."

The hospital released Abby into Dray's care a short time later. Dray placed a few pillows and a blanket in the cab in an effort to make the ride a little easier. Dray knew she was being silly but she'd begun thinking of Abby as fragile cargo that needed protecting.

The nursing station had insisted that Abby couldn't leave the hospital unless she was in a wheelchair. The blonde knew it was a lost cause so she simply smiled graciously and let the nurse push her into the lobby. She didn't have to look for Dray to know that the woman was following close behind.

It only took a few minutes to get to Dray's truck and with very little help, she and the nurse eased Abby into the passenger seat. Dray felt a little better about making a fuss over the blonde. She just couldn't help herself. Abby gave her a dirty look as the firefighter tucked the blanket around her knees. "I'm not decrepit, you know."

"Oh, I know it. But indulge me, will ya?" Abby resisted the urge to push the dark hair out of Dray's eyes and ask the woman

Trish Shields

exactly how she'd like to be indulged. Her lips still tingled from the near kiss she'd given her earlier. The thought made her blush. It was going to be a long, hard couple of days.

# Chapter 5

Dray dropped her raglan shorts by the hamper and slowly pulled her shirt up over her head. She glanced at herself in the mirror, grimaced and then leaned in to turn the faucet of the shower on. She went back to the sink and looked at her reflection. The thought of finding Abby's battered and sick body in that dive came back to slap her.

She swallowed deeply, pushing the vision away but images of her son's death swirled around until both were entwined. A sob escaped her lips and both hands grasped the sink until the skin of her knuckles was white and taut. She tried to tell herself that although she hadn't saved her son she managed to save Abby. She was there now, even if only for a few days. And it wasn't just Abby that she had helped. Over the years, many lives were saved thanks to Dray. But no matter how many were saved that loss of her son, her flesh and blood, haunted her.

Her eyes looked blindly into the mirror, watching once more as her visions pulled her back to the night when she fought two men, breaking one's nose in her effort to get back into the inferno of her apartment. Some part of her had known it was a wasted effort; she knew enough about clapboard tenements to know hers was an accident waiting to happen. But with her limited income, what choice did she have?

As the hallway filled with black smoke and the other tenants were herded out, Dray knew by the look on the two men's faces...she was too late. And yet she'd fought like a wild cat, determined to see what no mother should ever see: irrefutable evidence of the death of her child. She could still see the bleak look on their faces, smell the acrid smoke filling her lungs; watch helplessly as the meager mementos of her life were reduced to ash, annihilating everything that she was and any future as a parent she could ever have.

So lost in her torment was Dray that she didn't even notice Abby had entered the room.

The blonde had stopped by the bathroom door and knocked when she thought she heard sobbing on the other side. Not getting an answer she decided to check on Dray.

Now inside Abby took in the sight before her. Through the rising steam she could see the woman was totally rigid, her jaw tight and face expressionless as tears rolled down her face. At first, she thought the firefighter was angry – at what, she didn't know, but upset all the same. Abby turned to leave but stopped as she heard a small escape of breath. It was barely audible and yet the strangled quality to it drew her closer until she stood directly behind the nude woman, her hands moving tentatively to the middle of the firefighter's back.

Dray jerked around placing both hands on Abby's wrists, her eyes still somewhat glazed. The blonde watched as a haunted look came into the tall woman's eyes; she offered no resistance, knowing the woman could easily overpower her without a problem. She found herself looking at the firefighter's biceps as they bunched in barely controlled fury. Abby tried to step back, unsure of what Dray was doing or thinking at the moment. Abby watched carefully as the brunette's eyes seem to focus a bit at the sudden movement. A second later, Abby felt the woman pull her close.

It was as if time had stopped; the familiar smell of the woman assaulted her senses, evoking a rapid array of images, none that seemed to make much sense.

Dray could see her thumb pushing a bit of soot off a small woman's face. It was Zosia's face, the woman in her nightmares. Unable to puzzle through who this woman was to her or why she kept seeing these distorted, strange images, Dray simply released the breath she was holding and let the scene unfold, closing her eyes, trying to concentrate and make some meaning of her recent visions.

"It's nothing that a little soap and water won't fix, Zosia." Dray heard in her mind, still focusing on the vision.

The slender woman looked up at the darkening sky. "It's the middle of the day but it feels like the end of the world." She held out her hand. "It's snowing ash."

It felt as if Dray was on the inside, looking out as the action unfolded around her. Dray brushed the soot from the woman's roughly cropped hair. Zosia was leaning against a broom and the firefighter had a feeling of being surrounded by black snowdrifts.

"When I breathe, I can taste it in the back of my throat. It's inside me, part of me," the woman spoke again.

Dray reached out and watched the tears make a trail down through the dirt on the shorter woman's cheeks. "You are a part of me, Zosia, I can no longer deny it."

The younger woman shrank back away from the touch, and the reaction hit Dray solidly, leaving her feeling somehow guilty. Pulling her hand away, the firefighter struggled with the words she wanted to say to the woman. The feeling was deep concern mixed with total despair and try as she might Dray couldn't get a firm grasp on what her mind was trying to show her.

Giving up on the vision Dray opened her eyes again to find everything was exactly how it had been. She was still in her bathroom and Abby was standing very close to her. But when the blonde lifted her eyes it was Zosia's troubled gaze that Dray saw looking back at her. A deep voice filled her head, echoing endlessly until she opened her mouth, spewing it forth.

"I'm sorry." Dray released the woman's wrists. Her hands looked almost foreign to her and she stood staring at them as she opened and closed her fists.

Abby was totally nonplused, unable to discern exactly what Dray could be sorry for. Then she spied the soot on her wrists.

"Don't be sorry. It's nothing a bit of soap and water won't fix," Abby answered reassuringly with a gentle grin.

Dray stared at the long smudge on the inside of Abby's arm. The phantom image terrified her, and she wondered briefly if she was finally having a mental breakdown.

Out of her own fear and an unexplainable draw she felt for Abby, Dray tucked the blonde head under her chin and began to gently rock back and forth.

Slowly snaking her arms around the tall brunette's waist, Abby snuggled closer, feeling very safe and very comforted as whatever fight Dray was feeling began to leave her.

Why Dray felt she had to do it was a mystery to Abby; it was fairly obvious that the firefighter needed a shoulder to cry on. After a few moments wrapped in Dray's embrace, Abby leaned back and looked into the troubled eyes of her protector.

It was funny, but that's exactly how she was beginning to think of Dray. Visions of her dream at the hospital popped back into her head and she trembled. She didn't know how it could be but this woman had been in her dream, she was sure of it.

Dray frowned a little as she watched a slow tentative smile etch across the shorter woman's face, lighting up her eyes even in the warm mist from the shower. And any of Dray's verbal and thinking skills she might possess came grinding to a halt as she felt two hands moving behind her neck, pulling her down. The soft silkiness of Abby's lips moved against her own and Dray closed her eyes, releasing herself into the feeling. She moaned at the contact, suddenly very aware of her nakedness. But soon any bashfulness she might have felt flew away when the blonde's tongue slip slowly inside her mouth.

So many thoughts swirled inside Abby's brain. Hell, it had been a good three and a half years since she'd been intimate with anyone. It was far easier to just close ranks and not get involved. People always saw what they wanted to, rarely venturing past the outer shell. Everyone except Dray, that is.

The firefighter was more than just muscles on a six-foot frame with blue eyes. She was intuitive with an old soul and for whatever reason Abby knew that Dray saw something within her that pulled them closer. She knew this was where she wanted to be and the person she wanted to be with. Abby sensed the tall woman's hesitation at their physical closeness but longing for that connection, Abby gave into the feelings that washed over her.

She went with the fire she felt spreading from her belly to points south. It made her knees weak and the flesh of her inner thighs tingle. Abby pressed herself closer to the woman, sighing as she felt the rigid body slowly yielding. She took one step and then another, one hand behind the tall woman as she maneuvered them closer to the shower stall.

Dray felt the back of one heel hit the edge of the stall as she watched her own robe that Abby had borrowed slip from the woman's body to pool on the floor, leaving her dressed in one of Dray's oversized T-shirts. Dray put both hands out to grip the frame and steady herself. Her eyes momentarily widened as she discovered what the blonde had in mind. Gently dipping down, she placed one hand under the woman's knees and then straightened back up, taking Abby with her.

"You're kinda banged up, Abby, are you sure?" She felt her tongue being nibbled and every nerve in her body felt stretched tight. Then she stepped over the base, into the shower and slowly lowered the smaller woman back down to her feet.

Abby felt the hot water cascade down her back and pressed her body against the woman's muscular torso. They both groaned as the water trickled between them and Dray let her hands wander down to the edge of Abby's shirt. Not certain just how to proceed, she broke the kiss and then began nibbling at the blonde's neck. She'd let Abby determine where they were going next, having no intentions of scaring the woman off, if she could help it.

The only thing keeping Abby's hands on the woman's hips was uncertainty. She wanted to touch the firm breasts before her, taste the woman's skin. In fact, just the scent of Dray's skin was enough to drive her crazy. It was the woman's hesitancy that played over and over in Abby's mind. Then she felt Dray's hands drop to her sodden shirt and felt the hot flash of teeth on her neck. She tilted her head back and felt the water streaming down her face, a small river flowing between her breasts, joining the one running down the inside of her thighs. The ache she felt was so intense and so very overwhelming. She knew what she wanted, had wanted ever since she'd seen the firefighter remove her helmet and look her way. There was something about those eyes and the earnest look on her face. And then, of course, there was that smile. Yes, she'd felt something then. It felt like coming home.

"Yes, touch me," she murmured, as she slowly moved her hands up to hold the woman's face. "You won't hurt me, really." She licked at the almost healed cut on her lower lip and smiled. "I promise."

The taller woman saw passion and need, yes, but something more. Dray was fairly certain there was no other place she wanted to be than gazing into those eyes. She slowly leaned down and took Abby's mouth gently with her own once more, wrapping her arms around the woman's petite frame. A moan of frustration escaped her lips until she felt two strong hands encompass her own, pulling off the last of the garment before she heard it plop to the floor. Soon those same hands were moving slowly over her shoulders and her upper arms, finally, painstakingly moving to her breasts.

Sometimes it's fairly evident the Fates have a sense of humor and consider mortals to be mere playthings, moving them about on the chessboard of life at their whim. They chose that particular moment to intervene. Both women jumped apart as the temperature of the water changed rapidly from hot and soothing to cold and painful.

"Jesus!" Dray yelped as she scrambled out of the stall, dragging the chuckling blonde behind her. The firefighter got her feet tangled up in her haste to get out of the cold spray and ended up on her butt on the cold, tiled floor.

"That's cold!" Dray lifted her behind a few inches and then her feet slipped in the puddles rapidly spreading around the shower, sending her sprawling once more. Abby stood there, hands clasped tightly over her mouth trying desperately not to laugh harder. It was a losing battle and soon she was bent over, filling the room with laughter. With a growl, Dray grabbed the woman around her knees and then it was Abby that was complaining about the temperature of the floor. The taller woman awkwardly made her way over the blonde's prone body and managed to inch her way up the side of the stall and turn off the water. Grimacing, she plucked the sodden remnants of Abby's shirt out of the drain, wrung it out and then tossed it over the shower bar.

"Ah, so that was pretty funny, huh?" Dray asked with a grin. "You wanna stay on that cold floor or get me a coupla those towels?"

Dray had both hands on her hips and indicated the location of the towel cupboard with her chin. Abby smirked and got to her knees. She wasn't about to have a close encounter with the floor by trying to stand in the puddles that decorated the bathroom floor. She grimaced, noting the beginnings of a bruise on Dray's hip.

"Okay, okay," Abby told her. "...just gimme a few minutes."

Dray smirked as she watched the muscles move across the woman's shoulders, her eyes following the movement down to the base of Abby's tailbone. Caught up in the sight of the woman's shapely buttocks, Dray found herself swallowing deeply, her throat suddenly gone dry. *I'll give you the rest of my life if you want it.*

She walked carefully over to where the woman crouched and just stood there. There was something about the way Abby was tilting her head, hanging over the pile of towels that was so damned familiar. And then she turned her head and everything seemed to be in slow motion.

Abby slowly raised her chin, caressing every part of the woman's body with eyes that glittered like serpentine. It was the way Dray was standing there, legs apart, gaze intent on all before her. She looked both proud and melancholy at the same time. Both saw the desire, the passion rising in their eyes; goose flesh covering their sensitized and heated flesh, less to do with their sudden exposure to frigid water than the realization that something inevitable was happening between them.

Abby watched however as a confused expression took hold on Dray's features.

Images of another woman filled Dray's head again as she looked at Abby. Their features were so similar in nature in her mind. Although the woman before her was crowned with beautiful blonde hair, the person in her mind still wore the telltale signs of having been recently shorn. Her scalp was covered with small scabs, some no more than the diameter of a quarter, all on their way to healing. And yet, Dray could plainly see that the woman was anything but healthy. Her arm shook violently as someone's hand reached out to caress the bruise on the side of the petite woman's face. Peering attentively at the phantom hand, Dray could see that it belonged to a man; large and somewhat gnarly, the nails were clipped very close and the palm was heavy with calluses. Farther up the wrist was a sleeve of heavy gray wool - a uniform.

"You will know better than to look up next time, my Zosia." Dray heard the words as plain as if the person were standing next to her but she was quite aware that she and Abby were alone.

"I will do whatever you want, Ksenka. For food." Dray heard the second voice and looked around the room briefly.

Abby grew increasingly concerned. *Perhaps she hit her head in the fall?* She watched as if Dray was trying her best to concentrate on some unseen force surrounding her.

"Are you okay, Dray?" Abby called out as the woman swayed above her.

It was like the sun was suddenly filling Dray's mind, radiating over every part of her and illuminating every corner of her soul. She could feel her lips stretching into a smile that mirrored the face of the soldier holding the poor woman roughly. It was so real that she could almost feel the torn and threadbare cloth beneath her own fingers.

Abby reached up and placed her hand on Dray's thigh, making that dizzying connection once again and the brunette knew there was nothing she wouldn't do, hadn't done, to and for this woman. It was then, truly, that the firefighter knew the truth; in another time and place they'd known each other. *I'm not crazy*, Dray told herself silently. *This is real.*

"Can you feel it?" Dray asked Abby out loud.

Abby felt her hand being encompassed and a rush of emotions swept over her. Her dream self had had some connection with the soldier that tormented Abby but was it best forgotten? A word floated up before her and although her first impulse was to feel revulsion, there was a sense of peace as well. Abby was on the verge of saying it when Dray spoke. Stumbling to her feet, the blonde stood stock still as the name was stolen from her tongue and hit the air through Dray's.

"Ksenka," Dray whispered. "Does that name mean anything to you?" Abby's fingers curled at the small of Dray's back and she inhaled quickly in surprise. The firefighter heard the sharp intake of breath. "It does, doesn't it?" Dray pushed.

The way the muscles moved beneath Abby's hand was so familiar as was the name but she couldn't place or say how. Resting her cheek against the woman's breast was calming and yet...there was a sense of deep sorrow there.

"I know it. I mean, I've heard it in dreams before but..."

"You can't explain it?" Dray asked.

"No, I can't." Abby admitted. She and Dray still had so much to learn about each other. There had to be some explanation of how they both knew the name. "Maybe we heard it in a film," Abby answered.

"A film?" Dray responded.

"Yeah a movie. Maybe that's why we both know it. If you think about it what other explanation could there be?"

The firefighter wasn't sure how she knew it but, in some tangible way, they were connected. And it wasn't by the same taste in motion pictures. Perhaps they still had unresolved issues and they were destined to repeat their mistakes until they got it right? Perhaps they shared a past that had been so painful, so sad that...Well, maybe she really was just going crazy once and for all. But something gnawed at Dray, telling her it was more than just coincidence and she still had all her mental capacities. Discussing it with Abby seemed pointless until she felt comfortable knowing more.

"A movie," Dray said not entirely convinced but letting it go. "That must be it."

Next she felt soft lips tentatively kiss the base of her neck and all thoughts of uncertainty left her as she focused on the woman before her. *Hell, even if we did share a past connection somehow there's no sense worrying about it. I can't change it.* Dray figured that she could, on the other hand, focus on the woman before her now.

She bent down and rubbed her nose along Abby's cheekbone and smiled at the contented sigh given in response.

Abby laughed a little self-consciously. Her thoughts had mirrored Dray's that something was deeper here. That name was important but she wasn't prepared to start spewing new age, past lives, karma talk in Dray's direction.

She tried to move back but Dray was having none of it and captured the woman's mouth once more. Getting lost in the present, the smaller woman groaned and moved her hands up and down her lover's torso, ceasing her movements as she felt Dray flinch. She pulled away from the kiss and looked up at the suddenly wary firefighter.

"What is it?" she asked uneasily.

Dray looked down and then slowly expelled the breath she'd been holding since the sensitive flesh of her inner arms had been caressed.

"I just...I'm not really comfortable with anyone touching me there. It doesn't hurt, it just brings back some bad memories."

Abby slowly moved her hands back up to touch the faint pink lines of the old burns. Dray flinched again and Abby could tell it was taking all her willpower not to push her away.

"I've seen scars before and they don't bother me, okay? I think you have the most beautiful body I've ever seen in my life. Nothing could ever detract from that. 'Sides, these are a part of you and I wanna know all of you, Dray." She hesitated, biting the corner of her mouth. "I don't know how to say this without sounding like some sort of...dork," she paused, biting her lip.

Abby's reluctance to continue peaked Dray's curiosity. "What is it?" she asked with a cock of her head.

"I...well, I felt this connection between us the first time I saw you but I thought it was your..." She cleared her throat, "...your shoulders and your smile. And, well, there was some sexual attraction going on. At least I sure felt it."

Abby saw the beginnings of a smile play over the decidedly luscious lips of her soon to be lover. Encouraged, she went on. "I don't know if you realize it but you have this animal magnetism thing working for you; it just exudes from every pore. And so I wondered what making love to you would be like. But I was also a bit...um...my life is kinda complicated right now. I don't...I'm not working, I don't really have a place to stay and, well, I don't need someone feeling sorry for me," she tucked a strand of hair behind an ear, "and getting involved didn't feel like the right thing to do right now."

"What changed?"

"You. I've seen the things you've done. Not just for me but for other people and I'd be a fool to throw that chance away. You know where I come from – no place special – but still you see something here in me. I gotta admit I like that feeling, too."

Dray felt the woman's soft fingers tracing her lips and smiled crookedly in acknowledgement. "Kinda scary, huh? But kinda nice."

Abby nodded, somewhat side tracked by the softness of the woman's lips. "I know it sounds strange...but it feels like I've been given a second chance to find something I didn't even know was missing. Like I found..."

Dray kissed the fingers covering her mouth and finished the sentence. "...The missing piece of the puzzle?"

Abby nodded softly.

Dray watched, as Abby's face seemed to light up, then the petite woman hugged her close again and Dray felt as if her heart was going to burst; this simple acknowledgement of their connection seemed to free them both from the latest tendrils of uncertainty.

"Hey you," murmured the firefighter, "you're turning blue. I'm sorry about the hot water. Maybe a bit later..."

Abby smiled and boldly took the woman's hands, leading her back into the main room towards the rumpled bed. "I think I have a way better idea for warming me up," she smirked.

Dray smiled. It amazed the brunette that such a wisp of a woman could have such an effect on her. She smiled ruefully and then felt a catch in her throat as the smaller woman lay back in the middle of the bed. She could see the passion rising in the blonde's eyes, mirroring her own. It seemed as if all of her senses were heightened. She took in the film of moisture covering the woman's soft skin; the faint blush that covered the slightly tanned cheeks; the damp hair swept off the woman's face, the rest hanging in tendrils against the pillow. The fading marks of her recent injury detracted little from the blonde's beauty. Her eyes wandered down the lovely torso and her breath caught tightly in her throat as Abby slowly bent her knees and opened her legs.

"I want you right here, Dray...right where you belong. I want to feel your body moving against mine."

Dray's jaw fell as she experienced the words washing over her. She felt two hands clasp her wrists and wondered how her feet could have moved without her knowing it. She looked deeply into the woman's sparkling eyes and was lost. She hadn't been aware of zoning out but the woman who'd been previously lounging seductively, striking an erotic pose, was now kneeling on the edge of the bed before her, her face inches away.

Her mouth was covered once more as Abby pulled on her wrists until Dray had no choice but to join the woman on the bed.

Abby took the opportunity to run her fingers softly over the reddened flesh of the woman's upper arms. She noticed there wasn't as much flinching this time so she boldly began to massage the muscled biceps. Dray groaned into her mouth, feeling the shivers move up and down her spine, making her nipples pucker and harden.

"Oh, I want you...so much," said Abby as she moved her hands around to the woman's lower back, pulling her closer still. With a slight growl the taller woman began leaning forward, forcing the blonde to lie back, neither one breaking the kiss. Abby groaned with need as she felt Dray settle her weight along the full length of her. At that moment she thought she'd die from want.

The firefighter felt as if she were at the epicenter of a raging inferno; every touch on her body left a trail of molten fire and every kiss elicited such a fiery response that she would soon achieve critical mass. Her breath came quick and shallow, her motions, erratic. She wanted to feel all of Abby, to encompass all of her being, transcending even the physical. Dray propped herself up on trembling arms, one thigh nestled at Abby's center, and looked down into the carnal eyes of her lover. Leaning down she kissed the woman with such passion that both felt their hearts begin to beat in unison. Small hands were searching and exploring, caressing over her heated skin, squeezing her swollen nipples. Dray sighed and closed her eyes in bliss as Abby moved her mouth to the tender flesh where her shoulder met the base of her neck. Abby moved her hand lower, feeling past the damp curls, opening the trembling thighs and then sinking two fingers into the hot, moist, furnace that was Dray.

Dray gasped as she felt a hot tongue trail down and encircle one of her highly sensitized nipples. She raised her thigh so that it pressed hard against Abby's crotch. The smaller woman moaned in response, sucking harder as she rode the muscled thigh. The heat being generated threatened to overwhelm Abby and she began to thrust deeply into the firefighter. Quickly moving her thumb into play she rubbed the hard bundle of nerves. She felt the tendons stand out in the woman's neck and then bit down, causing Dray to groan out her name in ecstasy.

Abby lay there, her skin feeling very tight with every nerve in her body thrumming to an unknown beat. She began a slow path of small kisses up to Dray's jawbone and then kissed the gasping woman as she tried to regain her composure. "I want more, Dray. Give it all to me."

Sliding her tongue deeply in and out of Abby's mouth, Dray opened her legs and straddled her lover's hips. She pushed herself up on her hands and began to slowly undulate against the blonde's questing hand. Abby brought her other hand down and placed two fingers on either side of the woman's swollen nub, making small circles, pushing a little harder. The taller woman squeezed her eyes shut as she felt another powerful orgasm crash over her.

"God Abby, stop. Are you trying to kill me?" She groaned as she felt the last shudder leave her body. Pinning the woman's wrists against the pillow she sank down, burying her face into Abby's golden tresses. The blonde chuckled and wrapped her legs around Dray's buttocks. The two lay there, comfortable in each other's embrace while Dray got her breath back.

"That was fantastic," Dray said with a chuckle getting comfortable with her lover. "I've never experienced that kind of intensity before."

Abby kissed the woman's temple and sighed deeply. "You, too? I'm glad it's not just me."

Dray nuzzled Abby's ear lobe, kissing just below it. "By the way, I dunno what you were doing with your other hand but, wow!" She chuckled as a blush spread across the blonde's cheeks.

"Just something I learned from a book, actually. I really love bookstores and this one was all about the anatomy of lesbian love. Quite interesting, really," replied the blonde.

Dray smirked and then kissed Abby's nose. "Oh, I think I'm gonna like getting back into books. Seems I've missed too much as it is."

The blonde cleared her throat. "About books. I don't mean to pry but I read a few of your poems yesterday – the ones at your coffee table." She paused shyly. "They're really good, Dray."

Dray scrunched her face up and dismissed the compliment.

"I took some classes through a correspondence school." She looked up and saw Abby was not going to buy it. "I wanted to really go back to school, but I didn't have time for any formal training," Dray explained.

"Oh no, I am impressed. That's more than most people ever do, Dray."

Dray shrugged depreciatingly. Abby stroked the woman's scars and then quietly said, "So, you gonna tell me about these?" The firefighter rolled off the woman and lay with her arm over her eyes.

"I thought I'd make love to you, Abby. I want to share what you gave to me."

Abby propped her torso up on one elbow and pushed a wisp of hair off the woman's forehead. She trailed the tip of a finger across her brow and then down the bridge of Dray's nose. Abby smiled as she saw the well-sculpted lips twitch. "I'd love nothing better, Dray. But we have all night and I think you need to talk about this." She paused and then went on, "How come you always flinch when II touch your scars? Most of them look a few years old now."

The room was silent but for the occasional ticking of the water pipes.

Abby laid her head on her arm and watched as the battle was waged; each emotion fought to be seen and yet quickly quelled and submerged once more. She wondered if the firefighter would ever be able to release those inner demons. They'd laid there quietly for what seemed to be hours but was more likely only minutes, neither speaking, bodies seemingly at rest. Abby wanted to take the woman and shake her, force her to confront things. Whatever was tormenting Dray was keeping her from getting inside. Abby seemed to know that wherever Dray was, fire was involved. And then she watched as a single tear slowly made its way down the sharp planes of her lover's face. With a tentative hand, she reached out and touched the droplet. Her hand shook and she felt her own eyes filling.

"Oh god, Dray. Please let me in. I want to be here for you, I want to help you."

Both heels of Dray's hands were pressed into her eyes as she tried vainly to block the flow of tears. A strangled cry was emitted from her throat as she forced the vulnerability away. The woman's words flowed gently over her, soothing the rage, the sorrow; breaking the chains with which she felt herself bound. She steeled herself against the words she knew would come, the pleading, the endless questions, then the tears and denial. It was just too damned painful to open her heart once more. The last person she'd been with had insisted on knowing every part of her and had dredged up memories so painful that her only defense had been withdrawal. As much as she wanted the petite woman in her life it wasn't a certainty that she'd survive the complete baring of her soul. The beginnings of a plan was formulating in the back of her mind, one where both of them could get out of their close encounter with pride intact, and go on living their lives...apart. Such a feeling of sorrow overwhelmed her at that moment that it was as if her whole being was being shattered. The bond that she'd felt, the connection that seemed to grow stronger with every moment, lost forever? Lost again?

Dray rolled over quickly and took the blonde into her arms, holding her very tightly as the tears coursed down her face. *NO!* She wouldn't push this woman out and she wouldn't barricade her emotions anymore. Sure Pete and the other guys could say that Jodi used Dray but in the end Dray knew she did a fair amount of using herself. She cared for Jodi – maybe even loved her on some level but she never once let her in. After it was all said and done Dray realized it was one of the mistakes she made in their relationship.

If it meant tearing her battered heart open to let Abby in, then she'd do her best, one step at a time. The overwhelming feeling of despair began to dissipate as she felt small, strong hands slowly moving over her face and through her unruly hair. She tucked the woman beneath her and just held on. Finally, she became aware of the soft voice in her ear, saying the words of love she had waited a lifetime to hear.

"It's alright, Dray, I'm not going anywhere. You can tell me."

The brunette raised her head and looked down into the open and loving face of Abby and knew whatever horrors she had to tell her would be accepted and they'd work through them together. "If you only knew..."

"Knew what? That you're a woman who risks her life every day or maybe that you're a warm and caring human being who took someone in need off the streets and let her into your home? That was you on that ladder truck almost getting yourself killed saving that woman and kid, wasn't it? I really hate to be flip, Dray, but I don't see what you feel you have to warn me about."

Dray's hand went to the back of her head, absently stroking the small hair on the nape of her neck. She did want to open up to Abby but it was just far too soon for her.

"Let's just not go there, okay?" The tall brunette tried to get up and, finding herself in a tighter embrace, gave up with a harsh sigh. Abby began stroking the woman's sides and lower back very slowly, trying to tame the defiant look in her eyes.

"Now look, Dray...don't be like that. I want to know about you, okay? And why do you keep touching the back of your neck like that? You have a headache or is it another scar?"

Dray tore her willful hand away as if it had been on fire.

"No. It's nothing," she said hesitantly, her voice at odds with the words spoken. She attempted to roll off the blonde but Abby was having none of it. She held on tightly and just began kissing the firefighter's cheek and the line of her jaw. The seduction didn't work and Dray felt herself pulling back.

"You don't understand, Abby. My life...it's been so hard and so damned fucked up. There are things I could tell you that would make you run screaming away." The woman's large hand dragged itself across her face. "And I don't want that...ever." Her voice trailed off and her hand went back up to the back of her head.

Abby's hand quickly shot up and encircled the woman's wrist. "That's it. Whenever you get nervous your hand goes up there. Now let me look." Dray's neck was rigid, the tendons standing out like cords...and then, seeing the pleading look in her lover's eyes she relented and turned her head. "Tell me what's wrong." In final desperation Abby added, "Please?"

Dray rolled over to a sitting position on the side of the bed, her back to Abby, and fell quiet with the exception of a deep sigh. The blonde felt sorry she'd started it all but she also knew it wasn't going to do either one of them any good if she was selfish and allowed Dray to hide.

No, it had to come out now; the wound would reopen and drain and she'd be there to help it heal. She approached the silent figure, knelt behind her and stretched out a tentative hand. She was only inches away from the strong broad shoulders of her lover when Dray startled her by speaking.

"Don't touch me, please...I don't think I can get this out if you do. And you need to hear this, don't you? You want to see me bleed, right?"

She turned and looked at Abby over her right shoulder and it took the blonde every bit of her willpower not to recoil in horror. The look of wild, unbridled, fury that she saw on Dray's face took her breath away.

Abby's lower lip trembled and she shook her head slowly. "No. I'm only trying to help."

She wore a feral look as she turned and regarded Abby on the bed and she noticed that woman had grown scared. "I'm sorry..." Dray paused to collect her thoughts and calm her growing anger, which came more from her inability to answer Abby than with Abby's questioning. "But you have to understand, Abby," she continued, "I'd been in this abusive relationship with the father of my son. Well that's not really true. Things were good until... When Ian, our son, died."

Abby wasn't sure what the choppy, cryptic talk meant but she gave Dray the time she needed and the firefighter continued. "Anyway, my ex-husband got angry one night and broke my nose and a couple ribs. I learned how to hide from his temper and just keep out of the way." Her eyes became hooded with the retelling and Abby could feel her heart breaking.

"But I was determined to leave. And I did. I broke free of that, but I still couldn't help but think maybe things would have been different if our son had survived..." Her voice was strangely cold and distant and it tore gouges into Abby's heart, painting images so horrible that tears again threatened to fall. She sniffed defiantly and blinked them back.

Dray seemed lost in her reverie and her voice took on a dreamy quality, almost as if she were telling a story. "We did everything together, Abby; Ian was my little shadow. He didn't like sleeping alone in the apartment and I can't say I blamed him. Some of the roaches there were as big as fucking mice." A smirk made a brief appearance on her face as she remembered the two of them hunting the nasty bugs around with shoes. "Ian had been quite good at chasing them under the sofa where he used to..." Her face went white and blank for a moment and then the color returned to her cheeks as her rage built over her son's life being taken from her.

"I don't want to talk about this anymore, Abby. I won't. Point is my son died, my relationship with my husband fell apart afterward and here I am."

She abruptly got to her feet and strode over to the window, pressing her forehead against the cool glass. She squeezed her eyes closed as a multitude of images came at her like the very hounds of hell, tearing and snapping, voracious in their attack.

"Dray, you've got to lance this..."

"Don't wanna talk about it any more."

"I'll help you..."

"I don't wanna talk about it Abby...."

"...get through this if.."

"Fucking drop it, okay?" Dray's face was almost purple in her rage.

Abby stood by the side of the bed, mouth hanging open. Then she sat down heavily, almost as if every bone in her body had simply melted away. She watched as Dray's hand went back to absently massaging her neck.

A small voice started in Dray's head. She tried not to listen; she'd kept it at bay for so long, the harsh truth only coming to her in nightmares or when she drank too much. It was the voice of her son.

She could see his face clearly and she squeezed her eyes shut so tightly that motes of light danced behind her eyelids like fireworks. Trying hard to still the insistent voice, she clenched her teeth, her hands bunched into claws and then fists as she brought them parallel to her head. She began hitting the wall softly at first but the ferocity of her pounding increased, making the pictures on the wall rattle and shake.

Lost in her self-made hell, her vision was filled with red-hot images of the fire, the flames licking over her life and everything she'd held dear. Her rage was all consuming like a rapacious beast that had too long been denied and was at last set free. She lifted her head and howled as she watched the image of her sweet son, the boy that would never be a man, the child with her eyes and her very heart, burn and writhe in agony.

These terrible images weren't born of truth but were conjured up with Dray's own tormented imagination. She'd built quite a few virtual photo album of such scenarios and they now ran together, creating a never-ending reel; reality and fantasy merging until the events of that day faded and were replaced by false images making up a story that had little basis in truth. These pictures ran non-stop through her head as she bellowed out her rage.

Dray realized that unlike times past when her demons came calling, she was not alone. She looked over to find Abby sitting, unmoving on the bed. A look of compassion mixed with shock showed on Abby's face. Instantly, Dray felt terrible.

"I'm sorry," Dray told her. "I'm not used to having company here when I have an eruption. That's what Pete calls 'em. He's the master of understatement, huh?" When the attempt at levity failed, Dray watched as Abby stayed stationary unsure of what to do. Dray sensed Abby's concern and fear for both of them and she spoke again. "It's not you, Abby. Honest it's not...And I'm sorry," she said with a slight sob. "It's just hard sometimes."

Deciding that the tremor had passed and feeling safe, Abby moved quietly behind Dray, wanting and needing to touch her, to show her that she wasn't alone and that they could brave the storm and emerge healthy and strong.

Reaching out her hand, Abby could almost feel the fevered heat radiating off the woman's body. In that split second, that hesitation, Dray turned to face her. Not a tear graced her face, only the hard and callous look of someone who had seen all the levels of hell and had been lost there for a very long time. Abby pulled her lover back to the bed.

Dray looked down at the woman beneath her and tried her best to muster a grin.

"You want to see inside, huh?" the firefighter asked. "There's a price, you know. You aren't gonna like what you see, Abby...not one bit."

"It's alright Dray," Abby reassured her. "Do you think you can tell me the story? I mean about how your son died?"

Dray stopped and then, grinding her teeth, closed her eyes and went on.

"My little boy was three years old," Dray began. "It was late at night and one of the apartment's fire alarms went off...the kids were always pulling them." The voice that had heard so strong and confident times before started to waver and Abby could almost hear the frightened and lost woman she must have been that terrible night. "I was at work and my ex-husband's mother was watching him. She didn't pay the alarm any attention and by the time she knew it was real...well, it was too late. We lost both of them that day. Actually," Dray paused, "That's the day I lost my husband, too. He wasn't killed physically but a big part of him died that night."

Abby watched as the detached and somewhat stoic façade of the woman finally crumbled. Dray began to sob uncontrollably, fat tears pouring out from her wild eyes. Abby bravely gazed up into her lover's face and wiped some of the tears away, nodding that she understood when there was no way in hell she ever could.

"He crawled behind the sofa, hiding from the-the flames...the drapes caught fire...the sofa...and the rug..." She cried harder, trying not to face the images; trying not to think; wishing her mouth would stop working so she didn't have to endure the pain, the horrible, gut wrenching, searing pain that threatened to overwhelm her, killing her little by little.

Abby brought her hands around the firefighter's neck and pulled Dray into a fierce embrace, holding tightly as the woman cried and got out the rest of the story. Like a dam breaking, Abby knew she'd not stop until it was all out. She lay there, trying to be Dray's safe harbor; the tears falling freely from her own eyes as she experienced the horrible fire through her lover's eyes. Abby wasn't even aware that she'd been stroking the nape of Dray's neck, trying to sooth her.

## Chapter 6

Abby had managed to steer Dray back to the bed after her story about Ian with only the thoughts of rest on her mind. The hours ticked by and the two women fell into an uneasy sleep. Abby awoke with a start and then resettled her arms around her lover, who murmured piteously in her sleep, burying her face deeper into the smaller woman's shoulder. Lying there with the weight of the other almost totally trapping her, Abby watched as the shadows crept up the wall and across the ceiling.

She glanced at the wall clock, very happy that her lover was getting the sleep she so obviously needed. Dray moved and twitched, digging an elbow into Abby's side. The resulting twinge made her realize her bladder was full. Gently easing herself from the taller woman's embrace, Abby slipped out of bed and made her way toward the bathroom. Her belly grumbled ominously. *First things first.*

The room was totally black when all of Dray's senses came alive. Still befuddled with sleep, she wasn't sure just what had awakened her but her brain told her there was movement in her apartment. Everything was a haze. Slowly she realized why she was lying on the bed nude and remembered making love with...

Her mind filled in the blank and Dray brushed her hands over her face in an effort to shake out the cobwebs. "Abby," she mumbled. Then she felt a cool hand on her thigh as her lover moved up to the headboard and pulled her close in a loving embrace.

"Hey, sleeping beauty. How do you feel?" Abby asked.

"Half asleep," her lover mumbled.

"Well, about earlier. I'm sorry my prying upset you. That wasn't my intention."

Dray hugged the woman closer and shuddered a deep sigh. "I've never told anyone all of that...some of it...but nev-." She paused as her voice caught.

Abby reached down and caressed the woman's face in the darkness. Moving up against the headboard she pulled Dray's head into her lap. "You're an amazing woman, Dray."

Another tear squeezed between the brunette's eyes as she stumbled with her words. "I didn't want you to see...that. Even after all this time it's so raw, you know?"

Abby smiled sadly. Here this woman was, afraid of looking vulnerable and all the while she was just the strongest person Abby had ever met. To live with those images...Abby squeezed her eyes tightly and tried vainly not to get swamped by her emotions again.

Dray nuzzled the top edge of the soft blonde curls and sighed deeply. The shaky hesitation to her voice was gone as she cleared her throat and continued. "I have such a propensity for rage, Abby. It's like this energy in me. Sometime I control it but then sometimes..."

Abby waited for the woman to go on but she didn't. Frowning, she bent down and kissed Dray's head, her crown of hair so dark it couldn't be seen in the black of night. She thought about her lover and all the darkness in her life and knew, somehow, that she was the key. It wasn't going to be easy for Dray to let go of her devastating memories and she knew they would always be somewhere lurking in the shadows. She cupped the woman's face. "C'mon, Dray. Come up here."

Dray curled her body around the blonde and buried her face in the woman's shoulder, quiet as a tomb. She was pondering the safe uncomplicated lives others lived when Abby kissed her mouth. The warmth and acceptance in that kiss gave her the strength to go on.

Abby stroked Dray's hair, lost in thought.

Dray shifted and lay back next to her against the headboard. Both hands went to her temples and she began to slowly work on the tension that was building. She pinched the bridge of her nose, wondering just how much she should reveal. Then she sighed heavily, knowing that although it might not be the right time at least it was the right place.

Never before had she been so happy for the darkness, knowing it would act as both a shield and a comforting embrace. *Hides a multitude of sins,* a condemning voice in her subconscious muttered. *And you have so many, Dray.* She cleared her throat once more and laced her fingers over her tensed stomach.

"There's other stuff Abby; stuff you should know." Shaking her head ruefully and lost in her thoughts, Dray grew quiet again.

Abby pulled the covers up around them and sat biting her lip, determined not to say anything but hoping the firefighter would go on. She knew, by Dray's tense breathing that whatever it was, it was going to be hard to say and equally hard to hear. Biting her lower lip so as not to cry out, she reached out a calm hand and entwined their fingers. *My god, is there no end to what she's endured?*

Dray swallowed deeply and then raised her lover's hand and kissed it.

"I'm not happy about what I became after the divorce. I fell in with a bad group...I did some drugs, taking 'em and dealing 'em; stupid stuff that allowed me to wallow in my self-pity. It probably would have killed me too if I'd kept it up.

"But then I met this woman. You see, a couple gang members wanted to rob this liquor store for kicks. Seems one of the clerks carded them and gave them a hard time. So they wanted a little payback. While they beat up the clerk, I stood by as look out. I didn't want to do it but I was there anyway. That's what you did when you had a gang. You took care of your family.

"As I stood by the entrance one of the customers inside kept staring at me. But it wasn't fear I saw in her eyes, unlike everyone else. She crept over and all she said was 'You need out.' She handed me a business card during all the commotion. She was a guidance councilor with some grass roots, non-profit program in the city.

"Sounds kinda bizarre I know. I couldn't quite believe it when it was happening. I stuffed it in my pocket and then me and the gang ran outta there like Hell. After we got back and they were celebrating I pulled out the card and looked at it again. I did it for over two weeks – pulling it out and putting it back. Finally I decided what the Hell and went to see her.

Her name was Debbie Nang and she was a powerful force. She kinda took me under her wing and taught me to rely on myself again and she got me cleaned up. Not long after that I got into body building and that's where I met Pete." She paused and brought her knees up, resting her chin on them, quietly brooding and lost in the past.

The silence lengthened and Abby wondered how to respond. Then she put her hand out and touched her lover's shoulder. Dray leaned into the touch and then Abby began to speak, the words stumbling as she tried to empathize with what she'd heard. As hard as it was to hear, and as easy as it was to say she understood, the truth was she couldn't.

"I'm really glad you could tell me all this, Dray. I know how hard it must be for you to share something like that, let alone live with it." She heard the woman release a deep sigh and decided it was probably time to just let her alone with her thoughts. The box spring squeaked as Abby moved to get up.

"Do you hate me?" Dray asked. Abby could hear how tense her lover's voice had become with the question.

"I'm not angry with you," Abby told her. "You just got caught up in some pretty nasty circumstance. I don't blame you. What's done is over and you're leading a good life today, Dray. That's all that matters."

Dray planted a kiss on the blonde's crown and they just lay there in the darkness, held fast by equally dark thoughts. "Yeah well," Dray said taking a deep breath. "There's more."

"More?" Abby asked. Sure she wanted Dray to let her in but Abby's mind soon went to the trite expression of being careful what you wish for. She had a hard life too but Abby didn't realize how much Dray had truly gone through in a few short years.

Then the firefighter spoke in low and measured tones. "Debbie helped me in so many ways, Abby; taught me how to protect myself and that my heart wasn't dead after all. I fell in love with her, Abby, and she loved me. But all that love couldn't protect her." A chill ran through Abby's body as a coldness crept back into her lover's voice. "She was shot one night. A drive by. I found out later that one of my former gang members named Holmes did it. Ironic how he had a seriously fatal accident soon after." The silence deepened between them. "They never did find out who did it."

Abby shuddered at the frank indifference her lover showed and felt momentarily lost in the implications of the admission. She couldn't get over the cold quality of Dray's voice. Through it all she had spoken about the horrors as if she were totally detached from them. She peered over at Dray in the darkness and saw the truth in her words.

"Did *you* do it Dray? Did you kill her murderer?" Abby managed to ask.

"Told you I could make you run screaming, didn't I?"

Abby paused considering Dray's words or more accurately how to respond to them. "Well," Abby began. "If you didn't do it then it sounds like fate stepped in. And if you *did* do it then..."

Abby didn't say anything at first and Dray motioned to the chair in the far corner where Abby's duffle bag sat.

"I could always help you pack," Dray told her. "I wouldn't be offended and I wouldn't hunt you down. I'm really not a homicidal maniac."

Abby shook her head. "No Dray, I'm not scared. I'm just, a bit...thrown is all. You spend so much time saving people in your work that...I just can't picture you killing someone. But if pushed to a certain point, I think anyone is capable of murder."

"Well I thought you should know the truth, Abby. The whole truth and yeah, I've got regrets and heartache. I just thought you should know the score before you get involved with me any deeper. That's all."

Abby reached out and kissed Dray's full lips and then hugged the woman tightly. She wasn't too pleased about all she'd heard and felt frustrated thinking of all the anguish Dray had endured, but also felt a rage at what these experiences had done to her. Her past truly was filled with violence, drugs...and murder. Tugging Dray's arm gently, both slipped down beneath the covers. It was a while before either woman could get past their troubled thoughts, relinquish control, and sleep.

It was late morning when Dray slowly came around to opening her eyes. Stretching out both arms and pointing her toes brought the sweet relief that comes from flexing and contracting the muscles around inactive joints. Dray was the type of person who didn't laze around in bed; she was somewhat of an insomniac and got about five hours each night. She preferred to spend her evenings being productive, her poetic inspiration occurring between the wee hours of midnight and 3:00 am.

"You're still here," Dray whispered with a hint of surprise as she stroked Abby's face and trailing down her torso.

Abby felt a hand stroking her belly and smiled like a Cheshire cat as she lazily opened her eyes.

"Still here. We dozed the morning away, Dray. Do you feel better?"

"You didn't sneak out again so yes, I feel better."

Dray moved her face close and began nibbling on the soft breasts of her lover.

"I'll take that as a yes, too," Abby purred, as she moved her hands around the dark crown, running her fingers through the short unruly hair. Although it was thick, Dray's hair was so soft and silky to the touch. Abby felt she could run her fingers through it and never tire of the action.

She gasped as she felt the firefighter's hot mouth envelope her nipple and she scooted down lower, settling the covers back over them both. Dray let the bud go with an auditory pop and nuzzled the woman's chin with her nose as the blonde yawned.

"You still sleepy? Guess it's been a long night, huh?"

Abby nodded and covered her mouth as she yawned. "I think we both needed the sleep. I'm...I'm sorry if I made you say some things you weren't comfortable with, Dray. I don't ever want you to feel...forced." She looked deeply into her lover's eyes and noticed the dark shadows that had been there previously were gone. What she saw looking back at her was the beginning of a quiet acceptance.

Dray watched as the sun streamed through the windows. It seemed brighter, somehow cleaner, than she remembered. She locked eyes with her lover and with a bemused wonder asked, "How come you've done what three years of therapy couldn't?"

Abby felt a truth forming and then grinned hugely.

"I guess what they say is true: finding the other part of your soul is like having the key to it all."

Dray touched the woman's nose gently and then tweaked the end. "'They' say that, do they? Sounds...well, it sounds kinda like the stuff Debbie would say. She was always spouting some oriental mysticism at me. I don't really remember much except the part about everything being interconnected. It took me a long time before I got that, Abby. I guess I'm a 'hands on' kinda person who has to experience things through all the senses. I suppose that's why I...I do what I do. Wanting to do something about the horrors of life is one thing but I needed to really take part. I discovered my niche when I joined the local fire hall; it's like home to me. And I found myself through the physical aspects of my job."

Abby nodded knowingly. "I guess you tend to do that when you voluntarily enter a burning building."

Rich laughter filled the air and Abby relaxed a little more. She hadn't been too sure exactly how the firefighter was going to react once the light of day came. A smile danced across her lips at the sound of this woman's happiness.

She reached over and caressed Dray's cheek. "You are so beautiful, both inside and out."

The firefighter tsked and was about to reply with a flippant comeback when the phone rang. Leaping up from the bed, she quickly padded over to the dresser and answered it. Abby snuggled down beneath the covers and watched the play of muscles as her lover moved across the room.

She thought of her own path to self-discovery and drew in a heavy breath. She remembered the tearful scene she'd had with her parents, her stubborn refusal to live the life they had planned for her had created a chasm so wide that leaving home, at 15, had seemed the only alternative.

Yawning again, Abby lay back against the pillows and began sorting through the information she'd learned in the last day and a half; it was remarkable that Dray had gotten past any of it.

The woman had not only survived it but had risen above it all and made a new life for herself. A feeling of pride washed over her as she watched Dray standing confidently, full of life. Then a small word formed in the back of her mind and her belly did a two and a half gainer before hitting her spine. Murder. No matter how she tried to dismiss it, the truth remained. By Dray's own account she had murdered a man or at least hinted at it. In truth Dray never answered the question. Abby had always felt the taking of a life was just wrong but she herself had never been faced with that decision. She found her morals conflicting with her heart because although murder was an evil in her eyes she knew that Dray was a brave and caring person.

She rolled over onto her belly and rested her chin on her clasped hands. In all the years she had been in and out of shelters, halfway houses, even living on the street, things hadn't gotten to the point where she'd been able to condone the violence. Although after hearing Dray talk about the horrors of her life, Abby had to wonder just how far she could be pushed before she was capable of making the same choices. Abby released a slow breath and counted her blessings. She always found it easy to resist peer pressure so making her way on the streets had been difficult; no one trusted a kid that didn't want to fit in. She had stuck to her own particular code of non-aggression, refusing to fall into a life of random violence and petty crime or prostitution which happened to many young girls out on the streets.

This had resulted in a fair amount of beatings but soon the people who seemed to enjoy tormenting her, faded away when they couldn't elicit the reaction they wanted from her. Another sigh escaped when she thought about just how lucky she was to have managed to sidestep the fate that had befallen her lover. However, she certainly hadn't gotten out unscathed.

She'd built up a hard 'I don't need anyone' attitude by the time she was 19 and had convinced herself that it was true. It was only when she finally acknowledged her sexuality that she could admit she did need someone and wanted someone to share her life. It became a quest for her; knowing that she was missing something – that part of her soul was absent. She had so much to give and, at 24, had set about changing her ways. She'd previously gone from job to job, not really paying attention to anything but the meager paycheck at the end. It was a mystery to her as to why she had found the initiative to finally go out in search of a new life only a few days ago.

Was it providence? Abby glanced over her shoulder at the tall woman who was now a very important part of this new life. Then she noticed Dray rubbing the back of her head and knew something was up.

Dray put the phone down and came to sit by the pensive looking blonde.

"I've gotta get back up to the station. It's nothin' serious but, well, it seems that I didn't quite dot all my 'i's or cross all my t's on my report about those two kids and the fire marshal's got some questions. He's at the station now."

Abby cocked her head and frowned and then it dawned on the firefighter that she hadn't mentioned a single word about the work she'd done in the apartment building, having been so preoccupied with one thing and another.

"Um, well, our team went into the building after two missing kids and, well, we found 'em." She paused and then went on. "It was pretty bad. The boy we couldn't save but the girl's gonna be okay. Well physically anyway. It'll take her some time to get over things."

Abby placed her hand on the woman's thigh and waited, knowing there was more. Dray swallowed and gave the woman a weak smile but her mind was a jumble of images. Just how much info did Abby really need? Patting the small warm hand in her lap, Dray went on. "Yeah, the other kid didn't make it. In my line of work, you come to expect that kinda thing. Hell, the fact that we found 'em at all was an amazing piece of luck so one out of two ain't bad."

The brunette leaned down and planted a soft kiss on the blonde's forehead and then reached for her clothing. "If I'm lucky, I should be able to finish up the paperwork and be back in a few hours. Think you might be able to amuse yourself while I'm gone?"

Abby smirked, "Sure, I'll wait for you."

"Promise? No sneaking out. No two sentence Dear Jane letters?"

"I promise," Abby said holding a hand up while the other one rested across her heart.

"Good because I want to speak to you some more. Nothing too terrible I hope," Dray prefaced herself. "It'd be nice to have a 'clothed' conversation with you is all," she teased.

Abby chuckled. "I think I can manage to get dressed by the time you get back." Abby wound herself around Dray's seated form. "I'll miss you." The firefighter smiled indulgently and tussled Abby's golden hair.

After slipping on a white t-shirt and a pair of jeans, Dray paused by the door. She grabbed her jean jacket and ball cap and sighed contentedly. Shaking her head, she marveled at just how fast things had changed in the span of 36 hours.

# Chapter 7

Dray removed her jacket and casually threw it in the direction of the coat rack. Pete didn't even bother to watch the trajectory, knowing it was going to be the same as it was every day – a perfect bull's eye. He sat at his desk and watched the woman stretch, working the kinks out of her shoulders and neck. *She looks different,* he thought. *Not really rested but somehow more relaxed.* Then he thought of the blonde he'd seen her with the other night.

"So Dray, sorry to get you back in here on your day off but there's a coupla things I need to go over."

"Where's the marshal?" Dray asked as she looked around.

"Just left. It's just you and me." He tapped the loose pages of the report, trying to get them into a neat pile. That was when Dray knew there was more going on than just grammar and punctuation. She sighed and flipped the chair around, straddling it and then waited. A silent game of 'blink' began as they fell into their normal ritual. It always seemed to occur just before some serious head-to-head discussion. Dray wondered what it was this time. She went over the recent incident systematically from beginning to end, finding little fault on anyone's part. They'd been damned lucky the kid had stayed by the open window and then, suddenly, Dray was experiencing a strong flashback of trying to pry the little girl's hand away from the doll, only to discover it was the other missing kid, or what was left of him. She shuddered and then blinked deeply.

Pete sat at the desk and watched a strange look appear on his friend's face; it was the same look she'd had when they'd found the dead kid under the chair. He sighed and shuffled the papers again.

Finally, Dray became aware that not only had she lost the game but that an air of awkwardness was wafting off her buddy. She frowned, wondering why Pete wasn't meeting her eye. She took in the fact that he had about a three day growth of stubble and looked like he'd been dragged threw a keyhole backwards. Whatever it was bugging the man, Dray knew it must be something serious. Pete hated to shave, often letting his beard grow out for one day, maybe two, but three? Nah, the itching drove him crazy.

She blew out a puff of air and crossed her arms over the back of the chair. "Okay Pete, spill it. What's up?"

She watched as his hand came up and scratched furiously at the hair that was threatening to join the rapidly disappearing bare space between neck and chest. Sometimes Dray wondered why he even bothered to wear a shirt; Pete was walking reminder of man's origins. He coughed and then cleared his throat.

"Listen, it's about...ahem, well...you kinda...."

Dray slapped the tabletop and leaned forward. "What? C'mon, Pete, talk to me."

"Well, you kinda zoned out back in the building and....I know you're having flashbacks, about your kid and all."

Dray stood up, pushing the chair roughly away. She walked over to the window and stared out, thinking of the long dialogue she'd had with Abby. The tightness in her shoulders eased a bit just thinking about the blonde and then she turned and faced her friend. "Yeah. Wasn't the first time and probably won't be the last either. But I'm handling it. I'm gonna be okay, Pete."

The Lieutenant placed the report back on the desk and walked over to the window. "What would have happened if you'd completely zoned out, Dray?" A firm hand went to his shoulder and he found himself lost in soft blue eyes. *Funny how warm they are, not the usual cold shards of ice.* He chewed the inside of one cheek and searched the woman's face. She really did look more relaxed, almost as if she'd come to terms with things.

Dray squeezed the man's shoulder and grinned. "Hey Pete, stop being my nursemaid, will ya? I know I've been kinda distracted lately." The cold reality of her life just a few days prior seemed so alien now. "I'm handling things, Pete. I've found someone I can talk to...someone to share things with."

"Abby?" he asked.

Dray gave a slight grin and nodded.

Pete let an easy smile cover his face as he watched a slight pinkish tinge play across the sharp angles of his friend's high cheekbones. He nodded to himself, *Yeah my friend, I think you have.*

It was a genuine pleasure to see how happy Dray was and knowing she'd found someone she could really trust enough to ease her burden meant the world to him. Regardless of how long they'd known each other or the heartache they'd gone through, Pete knew the woman had never shared the things deep inside, where they could do the worst damage.

"You look tired, Dray. You having nightmares again?" Pete thought she was going to deny it and was ready with a response.

"Yeah, the nightmares don't completely go away but that's not really anything different. I don't know why I'm tired; I think I slept most of yesterday." She rubbed her eyes and then expelled a breath. "I guess it's all the talking I'm doing lately. I'm not used to just letting it all hang out, you know? It's like a heavy..."

"Weight's being lifted off your shoulders? Yeah, I kinda noticed that when you came in," he interrupted and then hit her shoulder playfully. "I'm glad those road maps you have for eyeballs are due to too much sleep or I'd hafta give you another day to recoup." He grinned as he watched that thought slowly sink into her brain.

"Well, come to think of it," she yawned dramatically.

"Done."

Dray smiled and then cleared her throat, "So the fire marshal stopped in today?"

Pete nodded. "He knows your history. He's concerned but I told him I'd look into it, which is why we're talking. You're a great point Dray. I just want to make sure your head's screwed on straight," he added with a teasing grin. "But seriously, I wanted to know if you were okay."

"Nah, I'm fine," Dray smiled and then cleared her throat. "So," she pooched her lips out and nodded slowly. "You think the report needs some fine tuning, huh?"

Pete smirked and picked at some non-existent lint on Dray's shoulder. "Um, actually," he murmured.

She poked him playfully in the belly. "Uh huh. I see." She walked over to the door and grabbed her hat and jacket. "I haven't even had breakfast yet. I was in bed, you know." Pete suddenly had a clear image of just what that sentence entailed and it was all Dray could do not to laugh as she watched a blush come up his collar. "I'm goin' home, Pete, and I'll see ya in a couple days?" He nodded and scratched at his fur again.

92

"Oh, two things, bud. One, get the lawnmower out and ditch the 'missing link' look; and two, lay off those hero sandwiches, will ya? I'm pretty sure my finger went in a good half inch when I poked ya. Body hair aside, that's just not you, you know?"

The Lieutenant grinned and made a mental note to stop by the gym after work. They both had made a practice of stopping by three, sometimes four, times a week but Dray stopped going and without her there just didn't seem to be any incentive. "Yeah, yer right. Buffalo belly...." He rubbed both hands over a slight paunch and then let his stomach muscles relax.

Pete smiled, relaxing in the easy banter they used to share. "Believe it or not, I like the insults," he smiled warmly. "I've missed...this. I know it's been hard lately but I want you to know," Pete closed his eyes briefly. "I'm here for you. Any time." Dray came back over to the man and surprised them both by hugging him fiercely.

A moment of awkward silence filled the room and then Dray turned and left, leaving a slightly bemused Lieutenant. He smiled crookedly and then, catching his reflection in the mirror, grimaced. "Lawnmower, huh? Weed whacker's more like it."

Dray balanced both coffees between her chin and hand and inserted her key into the door. A wave of giddiness that had begun to infuse her whole being the closer she got to home finally broke over her and it took every ounce of self-restraint not to go barging into the room, closing the distance from the door to the bed in one giant flying leap. She carefully put the paper cups down on the counter, gazed over at her lover and slowly took off her coat. Setting it on a nearby chair, she proceeded to slowly remove each shoe, her eyes never leaving the blonde's face. *You wear such a lovely grin as you watch me watching you, Abby; knowing how much I want you right now,* Dray mused to herself. *Just what is it that makes all the bells and whistles go off every time I look at you?* She sighed, leaving the easily answered question in her mind. Walking over to the side of the bed the brunette's hand slowly worked its way from Abby's bare toes to mid calf. "Such silky smooth skin."

Abby darted her tongue out as way of response. "Want some?" she purred. Grabbing Dray's hand, she stilled the movement and looked into the firefighter's eyes. "Uh uh. No touching with fingers." Dray tried to move her hand again and Abby smirked. "Nope, just with your eye lashes, to start with."

A smile eased across her face as she contemplated the challenge. *Okay. So she wants to play, huh?* Removing her t- shirt and bra and wearing nothing but jeans, Dray smiled wickedly as she caressed and fondled her own breasts.

"Just my eyelashes? Are ya sure?"

With a cocky grin, Abby nodded. Placing both palms flat on the bed, Dray slowly moved up the woman's bare legs, her lashes barely whispering across ankles, calves and then knees. She relished the muscles dancing and quivering under the onslaught and wondered just how long the game would last. The urge to bring her tongue into play was very strong but she resisted, holding it tightly behind gritted teeth. Straddling Abby's lower thighs, she bent down and fluttered her eyelashes across the firm belly beneath her.

She smiled at Abby's response as the tips of her breasts grazed the woman's ultra sensitive flesh. "Oh, jeez...you said only lashes. I'm so sorry." Placing her fingers loosely over both nipples, Dray took in her lover's rapid breathing and then continued her attack.

Slowly letting her breath caress the silky skin, unsettling the fine hairs that covered the blonde's luscious body, she continued to whisk her lashes up and across the bountiful breasts. A groan was released as she watched the rosy nipple pucker and then harden, wanting only to taste it, savor the flavor and feast until completely sated.

Casually placing both arms on the bed and bracketing either side of Abby's shoulders, she leaned in and, this time, both moaned as the brunette's darker nipples grazed over the slightly smaller ones. She fluttered the lashes once, and then twice, on Abby's cheek. Unable to prolong the agony any further, Dray dipped in and took the ruby lips before her, kissing the blonde resoundingly. Slowly lowering her body until it was mere inches away from full contact, she broke off the kiss, smiling down at her conquest. "Should I stick to lashes or have we moved on?"

The blonde swallowed weakly and nodded. Dray smirked and kissed the woman's pert nose. "Just let me put some music on, babe." The tall brunette sauntered over to the stereo and fumbled through a rather wide selection of music. With a triumphant whoop, Dray held one and then popped it into the player.

Abby smiled, enjoying the playful side of someone she felt she knew and yet, was still beginning to know. Oblivious to anything else, her eyes drank in the sight of the firefighter's shoulders and biceps as the rest of her clothing was slowly removed. It was as if her breath had caught somewhere between exhalations as Dray turned and saw the passion rising in the woman's eyes.

As the brunette resumed her position astride the blonde, Dray smirked and touched the tip of her tongue to the woman's eyebrows. "Now where were we? I think we have some unfinished business." She shuddered, feeling two soft hands on her buttocks. Abby looked up and attempted to pull the woman hard against her. "Moved on, have we?" Dray asked again.

"Eyelashes be damned, Dray, I want to feel you." And then she gasped as the firefighter's mouth latched onto her neck.

"Not yet, no, not yet," she purred teasingly, holding the woman's wrists against the bed. Abby's throat constricted and she heard a snick as she forced down a swallow.

Funny how the short few hours they'd been apart left her feeling as if a raw drug had been introduced directly into her system. Her senses felt alive, her body already hotwired into responding to every nuance of Dray's breathing. Her skin felt on fire, every cell vibrating from the delicate, delicious torture she'd just been subjected to.

Dray felt an urgency building within her as the blonde began to make small mewling noises. She let her hips sway which, in turn, caused her breasts to softly caress the smaller ones beneath her. Releasing the tender skin, Dray moved her mouth across to each clavicle, letting her tongue dance across the bone.

Abby moved her hands up and tangled her fingers in the soft ebony mass of hair. "Oh, I want to make love to you, Dray," she purred. "I want to hear you again, feel you, taste you." Her mouth was taken with a searing kiss, leaving her breathless and trembling with need. Dray slowly inserted her tongue and gently moved along the length of her lover's equally questing muscle, groaning with the contact.

"But it's my turn now," Dray said releasing the tender lips with difficulty.

Closing her eyes tightly, she felt each nipple sucked into Dray's hot mouth, and then the soft breath of her lover moving slowly down the length of her body. It was exquisite; every follicle jumped to attention; each nerve ending tingled.

"I want you to just lay there, Abby. Don't open your eyes and don't move a finger. I want to do it all, okay?" Dray watched as the muscles twitched in the blonde's knees and thighs. A faint blush was creeping up from between the woman's breasts and the brunette delayed any further movement until Abby slowly nodded. She pursed her lips and thought, *Where to begin?*

She slowly moved to the side of the bed, making sure that none of her skin touched Abby's. She lifted the woman's right hand and then slowly sucked in one digit at a time, paying each one the reverence it deserved before going on to the next. As she passed over the pelvic region, Dray slowly blew out a soft breath of heated air, watching as the golden curls moved ever so slightly. The twitch in Abby's legs intensified.

"I'm going to slowly make love to every inch of you so you might as well relax; this might take a while." She said this with a sultry voice and was granted one of the most erotic responses she could have imagined; Abby slowly extended her tongue as far as it could go and then arched her back, presenting her breasts for further inspection.

Dray's nostrils flared and she hissed out a long breath. "Not gonna play fair, huh? Just for that, I'm not going to do your other hand. I think I might just have some of that coffee." Abby felt the mattress shift and slowly peeked out from beneath her eyelashes. Her eyes widened as Dray padded over to the counter.

"You aren't really gonna leave me like this, are you?"

Dray turned away suddenly, covering her mouth with her hand acting as if she was stifling a yawn.

"Why don't you come to bed and we'll do this later tonight?" Abby offered. The statuesque woman turned and threw the blonde a look that indicated the last thing she wanted to do in bed right now was sleep. "You look tired so it's not a problem," she added.

"Nah. Just let me pour some of this coffee into my eyes and I'll be right with ya," Dray remarked before taking a drink.

Abby smirked, thinking of the image Dray had just tossed into her head: Juan Valdez eye drops for those who just can't get their caffeine fix fast enough. Why bother with the stomach lining when you could gain quicker access elsewhere?

"Now where was I?" she purred as she made her way over with both cups in hand.

Abby held up her left hand, wiggling the fingers.

Dray shook her head slowly. "Nope, you lost that one, remember? I've got to change venues now," she said as she set the coffee on the nightstand.

Abby sucked a tooth and slowly arched one of her own eyebrows. Then she very slowly moved her dismissed hand across the pert flesh of her nipples, watching with pride as some of the bravado left the firefighter. Dray leaned over, completely entranced as the skin puckered and pebbled, her throat suddenly dry. Steadying her raging pulse, she pushed herself away from the sight and bent to Abby's right foot.

Her tongue was mere centimeters away from Abby's baby toe when she noticed a slight tremor. She took a quick swipe and grinned. Looking up quickly, Dray saw a worried look cross her lover's face and then it was gone. *Uh huh.* Eyes still locked with those of her prey, she growled and descended once again. The tremor was now more than slightly pronounced.

"Um, Dray?" Abby squeaked.

Dray grinned, slowly extending her tongue.

"No! Um, ahh..." Abby thought of something to delay the inevitable, anything at all. Holding up her left hand, she tried a tease. "You never did get around to this hand. Dray?" When her entreaties were ignored, Abby began turning up the charm. "Come up and show me that wonderful mouth of yours." The dark crown hesitated briefly and then Abby clenched her teeth as her second baby toe was licked. *God give me strength!* she intoned silently.

The firefighter was really enjoying this; none of her lovers had been the least bit ticklish. While she was slightly sensitive in that area, Dray could tell Abby had a full-blown case of it. She smirked again as she placed a hand on the woman's narrow ankle, pinning it to the bed. Then she raised her head and looked at Abby. No longer was the worried look brief and slight; Dray could see that it was taking a lot of effort for Abby to maintain control. Suddenly, the game seemed cruel and she moved the other hand to the opposite ankle and then slowly caressed up and down the trembling flesh.

"Does it tickle here?" she asked.

It became clear to the blonde that Dray had known from the beginning and had been simply toying with her. Evil thoughts of revenge ran through her head and then Abby hesitated and nodded. Dray moved her hands to just below Abby's knees.

"How about here?"

Seeing a negative response, she bent down and let her tongue dance over each knee and then began placing small kisses on her inner thighs. Dray smiled as the legs were parted voluntarily. She licked a slow trail closer and closer to Abby's curls and then popped her head up just before claiming her prize.

"So, about that left hand, still feeling neglected, is it?"

Abby sat up and grabbed the woman's shoulders, pulling her up as she leaned back down. "You brat! You rotten," their forehead's touched, "little," Dray slowly lowered her body so they were belly-to-belly, "brat." And then their mouths connected. As the kiss deepened, Abby wrapped her legs tightly around her lover's middle. "By the heavens, Kazimir, you drive me crazy," she said between kisses.

Dray barely registered the name but upon hearing it she knew – Abby felt a deeper connection too. This name, like the other, was real and not some fictional character they both had heard.

Dray couldn't pinpoint when or where but she knew Abby realized it as well. Instead of making it an issue, Dray got lost in the sensation and then sank her teeth carefully into Abby's shoulder. Her hands came up to massage the sweet breasts. Abby groaned as Dray's hips began to rock against her.

"Yes."

"I guess we have some unfinished business, huh? Now, where was I?" Dray picked up a small hand and began dancing her tongue along a finger. "No, I don't think that was quite where I was..."

"No huh..." Abby began pushing the woman's shoulders lower but stopped her efforts as one nipple was sucked slowly into Dray's mouth. "Oh, yes," she groaned. "Right back where we left off."

Dray inhaled sharply as Abby pushed her breasts together, offering them up as a set so that neither was neglected for long. Sliding her hand under the blonde, she moved slowly down to dance her fingertips at the top of Abby's ass and then moved tantalizingly down the cleft. Now it was Abby's turn to gasp. Dray shifted and Abby's eyes popped open and she promptly fell into a sea of blue.

"You okay? Am I being too rough, too forward, too..." The blonde shook her head and blinked rapidly. "Too slow, maybe." And then she groaned as two fingers danced at her opening. She grunted softly with each stroke, and her hands fell limply to the sheets.

"No, baby, keep those beauties together for me while I feast." Abby blinked up at the brunette and felt her core tighten as Dray's tongue swabbed the tip of one breast and then the other, building a rhythm that was in perfect synch with the motion between her legs. She nodded stupidly, the eyes rolling back in her head and slumped back against the pillows. It took every inch of concentration for Abby to keep her breasts pushed so provocatively together. Her eyes flew open as both nipples were sucked hard into her lover's mouth and Abby groaned loudly. "Oh God, Dray, yes."

Dray grinned wickedly around her mouthful and slowed her thrusts. Abby pushed against her, encouraging the woman to continue the building momentum but Dray had other plans.

"Oh Baby, I love your tits." Dray licked one very engorged nipple and then nipped at the other. Judging by the increased lubrication coating her hand, the brunette knew Abby was close to exploding.

# Inferno

Abby tried to form words between her gasps. She needed the woman to fill her, to increase the momentum and punch through the semi-resistant barrier between frustration and orgasm. Now!

"Oh, Honey, Baby, Dray, sweetie, please now...I need more, faster..."

Dray moved back a little and smiled at the young woman as she protested. "Hey, just wait, Baby. It'll be worth it, I promise."

Abby was thrashing against her lover's hand, the toes on her feet curled around Dray's calf muscles in an effort to drag her closer. When the fingers were slowly withdrawn, she thought she might just die. Or kill Dray first and then die. She moaned in anguish and began pinching her own nipples in an effort to get closer to the brink.

The sight of Abby twisting and pulling at her swollen flesh was almost enough to make Dray lose her mind with desire. Her hips began to undulate slowly against the heel of her hand as she sat cross-legged in front of her lover. Abby's knees were pulled up high and her legs were wide open. Dray played her index finger up and down her lover's slit until neither woman could stand any more torture. And then as the blonde's head began to thrash back and forth, Dray slipped her finger past Abby's ring of muscle and quickly pumped her thumb in and out of the blonde's cunt quickly.

The shocked look on Abby's face was short lived and quickly replaced by a total look of carnality as a multitude of orgasms swamped her.

A short time later after Abby had calmed down and her tremors were rolling across her body at a more manageable rate, Dray moved her hand away and laved the area with the flat of her tongue. Abby groaned piteously and tried to push the brunette's head away until Dray's mouth made contact with the bundle of nerves still throbbing erratically. Then she was holding Dray's face hard against her as another orgasm ripped through her. When she was finally released from her lover's grasp, Dray rolled over, wiped her mouth and sighed contentedly.

"I surely do like having something sweet with my coffee. You know you mentioned a name again. Kaza...something, I can't remember. But it wasn't Ksenka, I know that much."

Abby was as weak as a kitten and could only summon up a noise that sounded remarkably like the bleating of a lamb. When she could form words, they came out as whispers and the brunette had to lean forward to make them out. "Kazimir Ksenka." The blonde shrugged weakly, her eyes still closed and legs splayed open. She coughed as her voice became raspy. Dray chuckled while she crawled up and laid her head on the blonde's shoulder. She fingered the fading bruise on the side of Abby's head. "You must be thirsty, huh? Don't want you getting dehydrated again." The firefighter nodded toward the dresser. "I got two grandes. You want yours now or later?" Abby snuffled a little and rolled over. Stifling a yawn, the brunette shrugged and then curled up around her lover and pulled the covers over them both.

Two hours later and two hazel eyes blinked open. She could hear soft snoring coming from the relaxed form beside her and smiled lazily. Her smile widened as she remembered the intensity of their recent lovemaking. While she hadn't been into anything other than what could be termed 'vanilla sex,' she found that she wasn't opposed to trying anything with Dray and in fact went eagerly down whatever erotic path the firefighter was willing to take her. The skin at the base of her throat turned a rosy color as she remembered how absolutely fantastic it had felt when Dray had inserted a finger slowly into her ass. Two fair colored eyebrows lifted as her clit began to throb again. Would she ever be able to get enough of this woman? She hoped not.

It became apparent to Abby that, although Dray's days were filled with work at the fire hall and their nights filled with the sometimes gentle, and oft times fiery, sexual encounters, that the woman just didn't seem to need as much sleep as the normal person. Many early mornings found her lying in the rumpled bed sheets alone. She knew her lover needed time alone, but Abby felt the need to discover where Dray's nocturnal wanderings took her.

She remembered the first time she'd followed the woman down into the basement work area of the apartment's garage. A brief feeling of jealousy filled her thinking the woman could make love to her so ardently into the wee hours of the morning and then go off to some sort of tryst with another. It was only after watching Dray don a pair of greasy coveralls that Abby could finally push the green eyed monster away and just let the firefighter have some important time alone.

Abby smiled and rolled over onto her belly, the pillow scrunched tightly under her chin. It was truly amazing just how open Dray had become after the initial 'honeymoon' period of their relationship had passed. She wondered for a moment if it could even be considered a 'relationship' since their attraction up to this point had been physical.

Sure they talked about their lives but it usually ended with them tumbling into bed or the sofa or the kitchen table or... No space in Dray's apartment was off limits and they'd managed to 'christen' just about every area imaginable. But by doing so little by little, almost every part of Dray's life was open to her, including her nocturnal forays.

The air had been filled with a noxious odor she always associated with the maintenance crews that put down road tar. While it wasn't an altogether unpleasant smell, it would now be forever associated with a certain grease monkey she'd fallen in love with.

She yawned and stretched, taking a great deal of comfort in that tender, but very pleasant, feeling following an especially intense bout of lovemaking. The apartment creaked with the echoes of people making their way back from the busy interludes of weekend life. Abby rolled back over and stared at the ceiling. Was it the weekend? It was hard to tell because Dray's shift was four days on and then four days off, making the usual concept of a workweek superfluous.

Gazing over at the clock radio, she did a few minor calculations and then grinned. The sunlight danced along the blonde strands of her hair as she padded her way into the bathroom. A somewhat off tune melody filled the apartment as she went through her usual morning ablutions.

A few well-phrased curses could be heard as Abby made her way down the stairwell into the basement. She rolled her eyes and then pushed the smirk off her face. It wouldn't do not to show suitable deference toward the only other thing Dray spent her precious free time on. No, 'baby' was a serious subject and although she hadn't known anyone who took that much time and patience on an inanimate object, she could live with it. She wondered if the tarp would be off or if Dray was almost finished with her masterpiece.

Leaning against the wall looking very dangerous, she waited. Having an air of arrogance about her, it was almost as if she knew the aura surrounding her commanded attention. Her sleek lines, the blatant sexuality and the power that exuded from her very presence electrified the air.

Dray's long tapered fingers twitched as they moved through her dark brown hair. The woman's fierce gaze moved over the dark form and she felt the familiar rush of hedonistic desire. It had taken her the better part of four years to get to the point where she felt comfortable about taking it for a nice, long ride. Dray had anticipated this moment ever since she'd spied the cool lines of what remained on her stripped frame.

Dray had diligently used every hour of every day off cleaning her up, making her respectable and filling her out like she might have been twenty-five years ago. Looking at the motorcycle with cold, objective eyes, she could see that it had all been worth it.

She was black and gold with purple trim and was totally chromed out; her three-inch extended forks, superglide tank and drag pipes positively gleamed under the florescent lighting. She was a 1974 Custom low rider, softail frame engine cases, four speed tranny, single disc front-end, 3 half-gallon fatbobs, tombstone speedo 5 stud clutch, primo belt drive, manual and electric kick-start.

It was the closest thing to heaven Dray had ever been. She sighed and ran her hands lovingly over her prized bike. Images of her lover lying asleep in their bed upstairs filled her vision and she smiled. Arching an eyebrow she amended her previous thought...until Abby. Her forehead creased when she thought of how a symbol of her past was connected with her future. Running a greasy finger over the lines of her jaw, Dray nodded. Although the shared dreams were still felt, their presence was haphazard at best, coming and going with larger periods of time between visitations. Rather than leaving them feeling disoriented and depressed, both women felt settled with the truth of their connection.

*Abby.* Dray tasted the name on her lips again. Didn't seem to matter how many times she said the woman's name, it always made her feel like she'd come home. The brunette ran a hand lovingly over the cold metal of the bike's handlebars and then snapped back to the present and the task at hand.

"Damned petcock," she muttered and dragged black fingers through her hair. She pushed the cycle onto its kickstand and walked slowly around it, rolling her shoulders as she did so. It had been a long five-hour job and the damned petcock was still leaking. Both it and the carb had made Dray feel like pulling her hair out on several occasions.

"Fuel lines, sparks, ignition and carb." She finished checking each item off mentally and then stretched her hands above her head. A nice satisfying pop made Abby wince as she watched unseen from the doorway. The blonde knew her lover had been in the basement parking lot for quite awhile and could see the frustration in the woman's rigid stance. She knew Dray had gotten up at 5:00am, as usual, and had been working on her beloved motorcycle since then. By the looks of it, the leaky carburetor had finally been replaced.

She watched as her lover bent over the manual, checking the specs and then going over to her bike again. Dray scratched her chin, deep in thought, totally oblivious to Abby's presence.

*Okay, throttle response is good. Adjusted the plugs, running her at 2000 rpm. Been there, done that. Set the idle speed. Oh yeah, that was fun. Goddamned idle screw was so flippin' temperamental. Man! Okay, so why the fuck is the petcock still leaking?*

Abby arched an eyebrow as the woman muttered, going from workbench to bike and back again. She'd given up trying to help Dray; it only got them into arguments, as she hadn't a clue as what the devil a petcock was. So, she just stood back and let the woman rant and rave, preferring to give her the love and attention she needed after the tirade and shower.

Dark patches had spread from the firefighter's underarms and almost connected to a dark blotch at the front of the woman's coveralls. Abby made a face thinking of just how sweaty and grimy her lover was. She wondered just how Dray could survive wearing the heavy outfit when Dray's curse filled the air and she unzipped the coverall and stepped out of it. The blonde smiled; there were times when it was almost as if they could read each other's minds.

Appreciative eyes roamed over the broad back and shoulders as the tall brunette bent over the cycle once more. The loose fitting jeans couldn't hide the narrow waist or muscular thighs and the shortie T-shirt really accentuated the firm muscles of Dray's lower back. It had taken Abby at least a month just to get the woman to wear something without long sleeves, even around the house.

Abby closed her eyes and remembered the first time she'd placed a kiss on the red flesh and how Dray had jumped. She wasn't sure why at first but gradually began to understand just how very sensitive the scars were, even after all the skin grafts.

Images of the look on Dray's face as that part of her body was bathed in wet, hot kisses filled her mind. Abby had used her tongue along the ruined flesh and had been gifted with the most exquisite series of moans. It seemed the firefighter had never let anyone touch her there, certain that the nerve endings were so damaged as to render the area numb. But Dray's head was thrown back in ecstasy when they moved together, her hands grasped the brass headboard while Abby's mouth sucked and nibbled on the flesh of the woman's inner arms. Abby was overcome with such intense passion that her body shook with desire.

Then she blinked a few times and swallowed. God, how she wanted Dray! She slowly walked over to where she was working, molding herself tightly against the woman and then slipping her hands around to caress the smooth flat abs of her lover. Her nose twitched with the heady scent of Dray's perspiration.

"Hey, babe," she whispered as she kissed the nape of Dray's neck. Abby could hear just a small, sharp intake of breath, indicating she'd caught the woman slightly off guard.

"Hmmm?" Dray smirked around the screwdriver she held in her teeth but continued on with her work. Bending over to inspect the other side of the gas tank, Dray lifted her other leg off the floor and Abby could feel the tight buttocks against her belly. She moved one hand around and slowly outlined the woman's ass with her fingers.

Dray closed her eyes and a small sigh escaped her mouth. The blonde could see the reaction she was having and moved her hand slowly up and down the inside seam of the jeans. The heat radiating from the woman's crotch was almost scorching in its intensity. She watched with fascination as a bead of sweat slowly made its way down the furrow in Dray's back. Pulling back a little she touched her tongue to the droplet, tasting the saltiness, and the familiarity filled her senses.

Dray's fingers continued securing the connections, each wire just where it was supposed to be, belying the rapid beating of her heart, the quickness of her breath and the tremble of her knees. She couldn't get over it; it never failed to surprise her what the mere proximity of the woman did to her. She leaned her forehead onto the cool contours of the bike, her breath condensing on the cool metal of the gas tank.

She slowly lowered her foot and leaned back into Abby, who in turn, encircled her lover's waist and pulled Dray hard against her. Then the blonde felt the torso beneath her shudder as she moved her hands slowly under the T-shirt, running her delicate fingers along the strong rib cage. Abby moved her mouth to the inside of her lover's arm and slid her tongue across the tender flesh, eliciting a rapid intake of breath. A silent promise was made; one Dray knew the blonde intended to keep.

"You've been down here for a long time, hon. You ready for some breakfast?"

Dray dropped her chin down as she felt the soft mouth on her neck. "Oh, I'm hungry, alright. Can we wait until after a shower?"

Abby moved her hands higher, cupping her lover's breasts, her fingers making slow, maddening circles closer and closer to

Dray's stiffening nipples. She smiled as her hungry mouth trailed kisses across one shoulder and her fingers claimed their prize.

"I can wait. Can you?"

Any thoughts regarding a leaking petcock flew out of Dray's head and were replaced with images inspired by the closeness of Abby's breasts and taut points that brushed against her back. Abby chuckled as her lover turned quickly, kissed her cheek and then made a hasty retreat back to their apartment.

The steam rolled across the ceiling tiles and began filling the room almost immediately, the shower hissing like her rapidly elevating libido. Water cascaded down her chiseled face, washing the grime away and she thought about how good Abby's hands had felt on her body and how excited she became when attention was paid to previously off limit areas.

She lathered her torso and then proceeded to slowly drag the cloth over the taut muscles of her belly and then, lost in thought, began moving her hands over her breasts, moving towards the sensitive areas of her inner arms. Her touch gentled and she imagined Abby's fingers and mouth there. A shudder ran through her frame and she tilted her face back into the hot spray of the shower nozzle.

Humming softly to the music playing on the CD, Abby finished cutting up the raw veggies and scraped them onto a platter. The singer's heart felt voice rolled over the woman and she closed her eyes in response. The song was becoming a favorite of hers.

She thought about the words and about how they seemed to speak of her karmic connection with Dray. "If I lose you," she hummed along and then had this overwhelming need to be with her lover.

Abby crossed quickly over to the other end of the apartment and stood in the doorway, watching Dray through the curtain as she ran soapy hands lazily over her body. She moved closer, and then disrobed and sat cross-legged on the floor and just took in the scene before her. She loved the play of muscles just below the surface of her lover's tanned skin; the way Dray moved – totally unaware of the affect she had on those around her.

Her throat became parched as she watched the woman's strong hands move down to caress the curls between her legs. She closed her eyes briefly and her breath caught as one of Dray's hands plucked at the delicate flesh there while the other traced the outline of one very erect nipple; Abby's own hands slid easily into her lap, fingering the dampness there.

"Oh God, Dray." The blonde refocused and brought her hand up, the smell was intoxicating. Closing her eyes, Abby could just imagine her own hands being those of her lover and moved them to cup her breasts. The thought of Dray's tongue encircling her nipples brought goose bumps to her skin, despite the warmth and humidity in the surrounding air.

Totally oblivious to what was happening outside the curtain, the firefighter went on with the business of making sure each bit of grease and grime was removed from her skin. Running a hand through her dark tresses, she pinched a few strands between her fingertips until they squeaked. Dray sighed audibly and then turned the water off. Inspecting her short nails once more, she nodded and then pulled the curtain open. Her heart leapt into her throat as she stepped out of the stall and looked down into her lover's smirking face.

"Thought you said you could wait," Dray teased as she began to wring her hair out with the towel.

The words were meant as a challenge but Abby could feel Dray's hunger for her in spite of the goading.

"See something you like?" Abby said, running the tip of her finger up the back of Dray's hard calves, the other hand still buried in her own crotch.

Dray confidently and carelessly tossed the towel behind her, leaving the rest of her body dripping wet. The taller woman's nostrils flared as she reached down and pulled the kneeling woman against her. "I like everything I see and I want it all."

The blonde swallowed and nodded, "I know. But I want it to go slowly, Dray." Abby moved her hands up behind the woman's knees and gently caressed the skin there. She could plainly see the lust in Dray's eyes.

The firefighter tangled her fingers in the blonde hair of her lover and shook her head slowly.

"Oh, no babe, not slow because I want you right now." She pulled the woman up and moved them both against the tiled wall. "I want you hard and fast. Face forward, Abby," she told her making the woman turn around, "...yes, like that."

She cupped the shorter woman's buttocks, watching with satisfaction as Abby's breathing changed. She began laying a trail of hot fire across the petite woman's shoulder and neck with her mouth and tongue. When the blonde arched back into her, she moved her hand down to caress the swollen flesh of the woman's labia. The response was immediate. Her free hand was grabbed and brought up to cover one of her lover's rosy nipples and Dray complied, roughly massaging them.

"Oh God, Dray," Abby moaned.

The brunette smirked, "Oh, was that too fast? Should I slow down?" she asked, all the while her fingers continued to pay homage, dipping and caressing until they were soaked with the woman's essence.

Abby gritted her teeth as she fought to stay upright and Dray, feeling the trembling body of her lover, pressed her harder against the wall. "S'okay, Abby, I'm here. I won't let you fall."

The blonde groaned, squeezing her lover's hand. "Dray...don't stop...what you're...doing...oh, God."

The firefighter smirked, removing her fingers and pushing her knee firmly between the thighs of her lover. "But I thought I was going too fast? In fact, I think I'll just slow down a bit...more."

Dray pressed her knee up into the tender, moist flesh and moved her hand up to caress and massage the other breast. Dray began a slow rhythmic movement against Abby, who in turn ground herself against the surface of the cold tiles trying to build a little friction.

"Fuck slow," Abby retorted, reaching behind her to bury her fingers into Dray's thick mane.

Dray grinned as she nibbled a path across one shoulder, finally settling on the sensitive skin near Abby's right ear. The blonde moaned as sharp teeth nipped her neck but it was the combination of Dray's hungry mouth sucking hard on her earlobe along with the pulling and pinching action of her hands that drove Abby's need up another notch.

"Oh God, Dray now. Now!" Abby strained hard against each thrust of her lover's pelvis but it still wasn't enough. She wanted to feel Dray. "Inside," she gasped as she pulled Dray's hair tighter.

Dray growled deeply. "God, you taste so good, you smell so right. You want me to go fast?" the brunette teased, trying to keep her own ragged breathing under control.

Abby panted heavily and nodded her head as Dray picked up her pace. One hand came up and pulled Abby's long hair into a knot and the blonde found her neck fully exposed to her lover's hot mouth.

"You're sure?"

Not waiting for an answer, Dray sank her teeth into the tender flesh just over Abby's pulse point, closing her eyes at the groans of ecstasy coming from her lover. Abby was barely able to nod her as she felt the pressure of Dray's knee lessen and then stop altogether. Abby's eyes fluttered as she was entered.

"I think I might be able to grant your wish." The brunette groaned as she felt a trickle of hot juices run down her hand.

Abby leaned her head back and whispered, "Oh, I love you, Andrea."

In all the days of their sexual escapades Dray never heard Abby confirm what she herself had been feeling yet never voiced. The declaration only fueled Dray's desire even more. The brunette fell against Abby, grinding harder as her heart overflowed.

"Love you too," was all Dray could pant as she felt her orgasm building. "Oh God, Abby," she called out, clutching the woman against her. Abby felt her knees begin to buckle as the fingers twitched spasmodically within her and she almost passed out as her own orgasm slammed into her, full force.

Both women slowly sank to the floor, grateful for its cool surface. Dray cradled the woman against her, slowly regaining control of her breathing.

"How do you do that? With just the sound of your voice, just a certain timbre, you can make me fall to pieces." Dray tried to swallow and grinned lopsidedly as Abby pursed her lips.

"I guess I'm a veritable legend in my own time."

The firefighter nodded and swallowed again. "Yes...yes, you are. But I think you meant, 'in my own mind.'" The blonde chortled. "I've never been what you'd call a confident lover, Dray. I don't know why but with you, everything just fits." The taller woman leaned heavily against the wall and then gathered Abby to her.

"God, I'm glad I found you, Abby. My life's been so..."

A slim hand came up to cover her mouth. "I'm here, we did find each other and I'm glad I can make you let go like that; it's good for my ego," she smiled.

The brunette smiled in agreement. She'd never had such intense love making with anyone else. Ever. She leaned down and kissed Abby passionately. She felt the woman tense and pulled away.

"You okay?" Dray asked.

"I was just thinking."

"About what?"

Abby let out a sigh. She knew this discussion would come up at some point so she considered her words carefully. "About being *here*. I mean, I'm okay now – all healed. And I just think that maybe I should get back on my own again."

Dray's spent, happy expression dropped. "What?"

# Chapter 8

The firefighter brought up both her hands and cupped the blonde's face. "Honest answer time here and I promise not to be offended but...do you wanna leave?"

"Oh no," Abby said quickly, shaking her head. "That's not why I mentioned it at all, Dray!"

"Then why the rush?" she asked, searching Abby's eyes for an answer.

Abby took a deep breath and let it out slowly. "You have to understand. I've been on my own for a long time. I've been self-sufficient and I'm not real big on hand outs."

"You think I want you to stay here because I pity you?" Dray asked.

"Maybe," Abby answered with a shrug.

"Oh Sweetheart," Dray began kissing Abby's forehead. "No, that's not it. And if you want the truth I think the reason I want you here is a bit selfish. Yeah, the sex is fantastic but..."

"But what?'

Dray considered her response. "I like coming home to someone. And I like the fact that *someone* is you. I meant what I said earlier. I love you too, Babe."

Abby grinned and Dray could tell although the words delighted her, Abby still had issues. "Look," she offered, "maybe you could get a job someplace, part time, and get some money saved up. You mentioned school, right?"

"Well yeah..."

"Then stay here and put your money away. You can help buy groceries if you feel like a dead beat, which I assure you you're not," Dray told her giving her an Eskimo kiss. "Save the rest of what you make and maybe this fall you can take some classes, build a career. How's that sound?"

"I don't know what to say," Abby answered dumbfounded.

"Say yes," Dray smiled as she cupped Abby's chin with her thumb and her forefinger, locking the blonde's gaze with her own. Abby grinned and ran her hand along Dray's arm. "Yes."

"Good," Dray said grinning herself. "Now we have all the time in the world, Abby." She brought her legs up suddenly as Abby pounced upon her. "Oooof! Hey, what," and then she felt a small, wet mouth envelope one of her nipples and Dray just lay her head back and smiled as her senses slowly climbed to overload.

The two lay in bed, the blonde sprawling across the larger woman's torso but causing little discomfort. Dray leaned down and planted yet another kiss on her lover's temple and smiled, thinking about the two things that Abby did really well: sleeping and eating. Abby moved her legs and Dray felt a familiar twinge deep within her sex. *Well, three then.*

Dray couldn't get over just how natural and easy their lovemaking was.

It had been a good couple of weeks and although she still had the occasional nightmare, Dray's life with Abby was helping tone them down. No longer was she falling into a fitful sleep, afraid of waking up in a pool of sweat with her sheets tied in knots around her. Oh, the images were still just as strong but now she got out of the burning buildings and there was always someone there to save her from herself.

She hunkered down a bit lower and pulled the single sheet up over them both. Although already coming on 4:00 PM, it was a nice lazy day when neither one of them had anything to do but lie in the comfort of each other's arms. And that was perfectly fine.

Dray found her eyes drifting closed and decided not to fight it. She'd been up the night before with a dream, had taken forever to work it through her head and ended up penning a few pieces of prose before slumber finally claimed her. Not certain just why melancholy had a hold on her; she tried to keep the demons at bay. Sighing heavily, she kissed the blonde again. 'Poetry: cheap therapy, for sure,' she mused. Stroking the blonde tresses softly, Dray briefly opened her eyes and then recited from memory, her voice at first soft and hesitant but soon becoming strong and clear.

The clear bright twinkle of her eyes
Stabs through the gloom enveloping my heart

And I am left speechless,
Unable to wallow in the darkness
That surrounds me.
Her hands caress my stern and serious face,
Calming the lines that grow there
Until I am finally at peace.
Her smile shines through to touch each
Shadowy corner of my being,
Making me smile in spite of myself.
And then I am home, back in the
Comfort of her embrace,
Able to let go of the harsh realities
Of Life and drown in the tranquility
That is she.

Dray's voice wavered on the last word and she took a deep shuddering breath. It was hard for her to look within herself and see that she wasn't an island. She knew she'd been kidding herself. She started as she felt a soft fingertip trace her cheek.

"Hey, sweetie. Penny for your thoughts?" A pair of bright hazel eyes looked up at her and Dray felt her doldrums partially dissipate under the onslaught of a very bewitching gaze

She pondered this briefly until her mouth was occupied with a pair of very soft and sensuous lips. "Oh, it was nothing, really," she whispered between kisses. "Just thinking about you...about us."

Abby stopped to nibble a little on the firefighter's nose before speaking again. "Yeah, I heard your poem...very nice. Is that what you were doing in the wee hours of the morning?"

She'd become accustomed to her lover's insomnia; there were too many past demons to battle for the woman to ever have a good night's sleep on a regular basis.

Dray smiled lazily, stretched and then sighed. "Yeah, being around you has helped my poetry a lot; I think it's 'cause you've got this aura of tranquility."

Abby smiled and kissed her lover sweetly. "I've been called a few things in my life but 'tranquil' was never one of 'em. Pest, irritant, brat..."

Dray scrunched her forehead in mock horror at that. "You don't see yourself as peaceful and serene and a brat? Hell, I sure do." She yelped as sharp teeth nipped the tip of her nose, pushing aside all thoughts of a nap. "But seriously, you...you ground me, Abby."

The blonde dropped her jaw and just stared at her lover. "No...you ground me Dray. I'm a vagabond. I haven't held a steady job until just recently. With you...us...well, I want to make things more permanent in my life."

Dray rolled over, tucking the blonde comfortably beneath her. "You are the most grounded person I know, Ab. You just seem to have this way about you. It's hard to describe, you just seem so confident."

She watched as a smirk played across Abby's lips. "Boy, have I got you fooled. Nothing could be farther from the truth. I'm just this," she stumbled along trying to find the right words.

"This free spirit who loves life and tries her best to make those around her appreciate it," the brunette finished for her. "You once told me I was the strongest person you knew. Well...I think you are." She paused as she tried to organize her thoughts. "You said you left home at, what, fifteen? Man, that had to be fucking hard, babe. I can't imagine it. That takes guts, Abby, and you must have done something right – you survived with your sanity intact."

Abby pushed a dark lock out of her lover's eyes and leaned up, capturing Dray's mouth briefly. "That, my dear woman, is open to conjecture."

"I wanna hear about it. Tell me your story, Abby. All of it." She snuggled the woman closer and began rubbing small circles over the blonde's lower back.

"My story. Well, there isn't really much to tell." She paused, biting her lower lip. She was hesitant to whine about her past; it was nothing compared to what Dray had endured and just seemed so inconsequential. She began making lazy circles around one of her lover's nipples in an attempt to distract her attention.

"Won't work, babe. Although that feels really good." Dray gently took Abby's hand, making her stop. "...I wanna hear about you, the real Abby Dean. You pretty much dragged all the dirty laundry out of my closet."

Abby reached up and covered Dray's lips and sighed. "The real me? Well, I was found under a cabbage leaf..." Dray sucked a tooth. "Okay, okay. Well, my mother's a housewife and my father..." Dray frowned as a look came over her lover. She stilled her hand and ignored the impulse to comfort the young woman. She knew once they got started she'd get sidetracked again. Finally Abby continued.

"Martin, my father, works as a used car dealer." She shrugged and began to pick at the sheets. Biting her lip with indecision,

Dray finally gave into her impulse and ran her fingers through the hair at her lover's temple. "Tell me."

Abby shook her head, offering up a weak smile. "S'nothing really. See, my father and I never really got on. Well, okay we probably did, once upon a time, probably when I was five, but after that – nothing." Dray nodded but said nothing. It was obviously painful to go through her past. She really didn't know what to say and so she reached out and entwined her fingers with Abby's. It seemed to help and after a brief moment of introspection, the blonde continued.

"I have a sister, Diane, who's younger than me." A smile twitched at the corners of her mouth. "We did everything together, a real dynamic duo." Her smile slipped suddenly and Dray squeezed the small hand in reassurance. Abby blinked a few times, her eyes bright with unshed tears. "Things happen, you know? You think you know someone and...boom, surprise, you don't know them at all."

She sniffled a little as Dray rolled them over and pulled her into an embrace. "It's nothing, really. We had a fight, my parents and me, and I left, that's all."

Dray soothed the woman by softly rubbing her back. "It must have been something pretty rough to get you to leave home at fifteen, though, right?" Abby shrugged. "Not really. Oh, I guess my parents were the typically dysfunctional parents everyone has. You know, their kids are never smart enough, pretty enough, or got good enough grades, that sort of thing. At fifteen, I guess I just had enough of all the negative bullshit. I mean, there's only so much you can put up with, am I right?" Abby continued, not waiting for any response from the firefighter. "And so I hitched my way from Portola, California to Florida."

Dray pushed herself up and gazed down at her lover. "At fifteen you hitched a ride across the whole damned country?" She shook her head at Abby's cavalier shrug. "That's just nuts, Ab. Geez, you coulda gotten robbed, or beaten or..."

Abby touched her lover's nose. "But I didn't. It took awhile to get to Florida, but hey, I had nothing but time on my hands anyway." Dray rubbed her jaw, contemplating the treacherous journey across the country. "God, what did you do? You stay with family along the way?"

Abby curled closer to her lover, suddenly weary of the twenty questions. It was hard to tell the truth while busily skirting any 'real' truth. "Suffice it to say, I bummed around a lot, got some temporary jobs here and there and ended up in Florida." A smile creased her lips again. "Hey, think of it this way – it was an

Trish Shields

adventure few kids my age would ever have dreamed of let alone go ahead and do." She brought up her left hand and began counting. "I learned how to make a twenty dollar bill last a month, that you can go for quite a while without going to the Laundromat if you wear your clothes inside out, and learned that I was a natural when it comes to water sports."

Dray's eyebrows shot up. "While I'm sure we'll be able to use some of your skills at making every penny count, I don't think I want to know any details about your previous methods of hygiene, okay?" Abby pushed Dray's shoulder. "Well, hey, when all you've got is one set of clothing, you learn to make it last, and washing them often wears them out." Dray held up her hand. "Okay, that's enough detail, don't wanna hear any more." She tweaked her lover's nose. "But I do want to hear about the water sports." She trailed her fingers down Abby's neck, making a pattern at the top of the blonde's breasts. "I think you're very good at getting wet." Abby chuckled. "I'll have you know that I'm a certified diver; got my card working at a resort in the Keys one summer."

Dray leaned down and kissed her lover sweetly. "Hey, that's another thing we have in common then. I love diving." She leered and waggled her eyebrows. Abby squealed as the firefighter's fingers played at the tender flesh on her sides. "Oh, no fair! No tickling, please!" They rolled a little until Abby sat straddling the brunette. "You sure you aren't ticklish? Not anywhere?" Running her fingers through Dray's hair rhythmically, she waited until the brunette had closed her eyes with enjoyment. Then she quickly leaned down and inserted her tongue into her lover's left ear. "Ack!" Dray sat up quickly, grabbing the blonde by her wrists and then slowly pushed her back onto the bed. When she was positioned between Abby's legs, she looked down, a solemn look on her face. "I don't guess you've been in touch with your family lately, huh?" She nodded as the blonde gazed off into the distance. "Yeah, that's what I thought. Wanna tell me why you hate your Dad so much?"

Abby pursed her lips in thought. "Nah, not really. Besides," she poked Dray in the ribs, "doesn't sound like you keep in touch with your family either, am I right?"

Dray rolled her eyes, having been so easily out maneuvered. "Why when I have all the family I need right here?"

"Jeez, I love you. C'mere woman," Abby murmured.

Dray chuckled and snuggled the woman back into her position on top. "Hey, I get any closer... woman...and I'll be inside you."

114

Abby sniggled a leg between the strong muscular ones, and smirked at the firefighter. Wearing that come hither look Dray knew only too well, she slowly leaned in and kissed her deeply. "Just what I had in mind."

Dray chortled as she dragged the sheet up over their heads. "You are so good at getting me side tracked, Abby. You win this time...again...But we are going to talk about it. Right?" She gasped as the blonde avoided yet another question, her mouth otherwise occupied.

Pete sat scratching the bristles at the base of his neck, his attention a million miles away. Dray and Abby stood by the café's entrance.

"God, is he deaf today or what? Pete?" Dray called out.

The Lieutenant continued to zone even when the two women made their way through the busy café and stood next to his table. Dray elbowed her lover and pointed to the open newspaper still clutched in the man's hand and the travel brochures scattered over the tabletop. The destinations varied from dives sites found in North America to those found in Hawaii and Australia. Abby tried to read the article upside down but gave up and moved behind Pete to continue reading the article. She sighed once or twice and picked up a brochure for a holiday in Hawaii. Dray smirked and waggled her brows at her lover. "You did say you loved getting wet, right?"

The blonde pursed her lips in though. "Hmm, it's been awhile since I've been scuba diving." Dray motioned her to sit and gave her boss a poke in the ribs. "What? Who? Oh, hi ladies."

Dray smirked. "So, you zone here often or just today?" Pete brought the napkin to his lips. "Just taking a breather from work is all. My stomach can only take so much of that kettle rust that passes for coffee." He grimaced and belched softly. His head turned as Abby's finger trailed over the article he'd been reading earlier.

"Where's Howe Sound? I haven't done any diving outside the Keys but I don't think I remember that name around the Great Lakes area."

Pete shook his head. "Nah, it's in British Columbia." Abby's eyebrows shot up. "British Columbia as in Canada? Wow. Sounds like they have some premium diving up that way, according to this article. You trying to pick a place to go for a vacation?" The Lieutenant nodded. "Yeah, I've been thinking about it for awhile and since I've got some time banked up..." Dray's head leaned back as he banged the top of the table with his open palm.

"Say, why don't we all take a trip up to Canada? These other destinations cost an arm and a leg." He grinned at the brunette. "You and me been talking about doing a dive trip on and off for about three years. Could be a blast." Dark brown eyes danced as the Lieutenant thought of all the dives he could log. He'd promised himself a new dry suit after he'd logged 150 dives and he only had eight to go. His enthusiasm waned slightly as he contemplated spending most of the time teaching Abby how to dive. "Jeez, I'm sorry Abby. I mean, you're welcome to come along but how much fun would it be, you sitting on the sand while Dray and I do a coupla dives every day?"

Dray gave the man a look. "And why would Abby sit around twiddling her beautiful thumbs when she's a certified diver?"

Pete's eyes widened. "Well, hot damn!" He turned to the blonde. "Yeah? You're not just pulling my leg, right?" When Abby nodded, her eyes beginning to twinkle as the man's excitement grew, Pete rubbed his hands together, picked up the other brochures and piled them back into his briefcase. "That settles it!"

Dray looked at Abby, who shrugged back and smiled. "It's not like I've got anything better to do. You got some time off, Dray?"

Pete smirked. "Time off? Dray? Jeezo, woman. Dray has vacation time banked up the wazoo 'cause she never takes any time off. She's just this workaholic that has a very slender grasp on the definition of 'fun.'"

Abby covered her mouth as giggles burst forth. Her face was a lovely pink as she took Dray's hand into her own. "Oh brother, have you got that wrong."

Pete cleared his throat as his friend growled at the blonde in response. "Ahem, so I guess that's a yes?"

Dray glanced quickly over at her boss, nodded, and then locked eyes with Abby. "Be nice to go away. Do a coupla dives during the day..."

"And do some at night..." Dray's crooked smile was mirrored by Abby's while Pete sat oblivious to the undercurrent of erotic tension.

A waitress came by to top up his coffee but he shooed her away. Dropping a ten-dollar bill onto the table, he folded up the newspaper and dropped it into his briefcase. Smoothing his uniform, Pete smiled at the ladies. "So, you comin'?"

Dray and Abby exchanged another look and the firefighter chortled as her lover blushed crimson.

It had taken the trio better part of a week to drive out to the west coast and after settling their gear in a fairly decent hotel they'd made their way across to Vancouver Island and the nice sleepy town of Mill Bay by way of the ferry. Hours had been spent checking out local scuba dive shops for information and Dray and Pete decided Henderson Point would be the best site for the day.

"So, you did your check out dives and what, about thirty dives total? That about right?" Abby nodded as she pulled her long hair into a ponytail. "When was your last dive, babe?" asked the Lieutenant dragging some equipment down to the water's edge.

The blonde briefly closed her eyes, calculated, and then spoke. "Almost ten months ago, give or take. The Florida Keys. Most of them were at about 80 feet."

Pete smiled and nodded reassuringly. "Good, good; this should just be a refresher then. Sorry I couldn't rent a boat; shore dives are okay, though. Kinda hard dragging your gear back up the beach but hey, you look strong enough."

Abby smirked and made a muscle. "I am woman!"

Dray walked over with two tanks, one over each shoulder. "Yeah, my woman." She gave the blonde a quick kiss. "Here ya go. I'll be right back; got to get the rest of it." She plunked the tanks down in the sand and then laid them side-by-side. Pete stroked his chin, idly scratching on the stubble he seemed to wear permanently as of late. He watched as Dray walked back up the beach, her aqua colored suit clinging in all the right places. He jumped as he felt a hand on his shoulder. "Jeez...sorry. I must have been wool gathering."

Abby smiled knowingly, her eyes taking in the very same sight. "Yeah, nice wool, huh?"

Pete wiped his hand across his mouth, barely concealing the smile on his lips.

"Aha...Yeah, well. You know," he stammered.

And Abby did truly understand; Dray Khalkousa was a thing of beauty, a living breathing goddess of fire. She watched the play of tanned muscles as the tall brunette walked towards her, the weight belts over one shoulder, BCs looped through one arm and a large dive bag on her back. She was truly a walking ad for better living through exercise.

Her two friends continued their conversation and Dray jumped through a few mental hoops as she thought of them both. Pete was a good friend, a damned good firefighter, too, but they could never have the kind of relationship he wanted when they had first met.

They'd been through a lot and probably would go through more before their time together was over. She didn't have any illusions on the normal life span of a firefighter. They usually developed heart problems due to the stress, those that didn't die in fires, that is. Abby was Dray's fail safe; there was no way she was going to let either one befall her.

She walked closer, openly admiring the luscious blonde waiting for her. While her suit was a Speedo one piece, Abby's was a nice amber-colored bikini. She basked in the admiring gaze of her lover and tried not to think just where Pete's eyes would be.

Abby watched the muscles clenching slightly in her lover's jaw and went to greet her, throwing both arms around Dray's waist.

"S'okay, Babe. I think you look lovely. And his eyes are on your boobs, not your scars." she said, planting a brief kiss on the woman's neck. A dark eyebrow shot up.

"Yeah? Well I still wish I'd brought that damned wind breaker," she whispered back while Abby rolled her eyes.

"It's 90 degrees out here, Dray. Besides, you look so damned sexy I could eat you up." Her breath hitched as she felt a skilled tongue outline her lower lip. Acting decisively, she held the muscle between her teeth and then slowly sucked it into her mouth. Abby groaned as she felt a strong hand cup her ass.

"Ahem!"

Dray arched both eyebrows towards the man while Abby pulled away from their embrace, her eyes wide and cheeks crimson. "Oh...I, um...forgot you were there, Pete; I'm sorry."

Holding both hands up, Pete shook his head, giving them both his version of a lecher.

"No, no...don't mind me. I'm lovin' every minute of it. Just pretend I'm not here." Abby narrowed her eyes, a mischievous look on her face, "After all, two luscious babes," he began backing up, "hanging all over each other, and me with a front row seat." Abby launched herself, knocking into him, "Ooof...and I get to spend the whole day...ooohhhh!" Then he stumbled back on the tanks and went down hard, falling squarely on his belly. He began laughing as two fingers dug into his side. "Ahhhh.... Stop...stop..."

Abby pursed her lips and looked over at her lover. "Whatcha think, Stretch, should I make him holler 'Uncle'?"

Pete grabbed the woman's wrists and sat up.

"What? Why, I'm crushed. I was just gonna say that I get to spend the whole day with two people in love – two very nice people – that I consider good friends."

He glanced over at Abby, checking her reaction. Dray rolled her eyes, knowing full well what was coming. Abby was too busy being conned to notice anything, buying his puppy dog look hook, line and sinker. Pete watched as her face softened and then pushed her back into the sand and grinned. "Now it's my turn." He lowered his face and began softly rubbing his stubble across her cheeks.

"Ack....stop...stop...Dray, help!"

The brunette bent down and softly tapped her buddy on the shoulder. "All done? I think we'd better get going if we wanna make this tide."

"Aw, you...what a spoil sport. Okay, okay."

He slowly got to his feet, dusting himself off and chuckled as Dray began checking her partner out, paying close attention to just how much sand she seemed to be covered in. Each grain of the stuff would be removed expediently if the brunette's attentions were any indication. Giving them a private moment, he turned and began sorting out regulators, bottom timers and compasses.

He snuck a quick look and found the two kissing and grinned to himself. *Yup, life is good. Now, if I can just find someone.* His mind locked as a small dog went barreling past him. He looked up and had a few seconds to register what was happening before he was knocked down into the sand again. This time his vision filled with black and white of his Dalmatian who was giving chase but now decide to pay tribute to his master.

"Jeez Dave. Get off!" Pete gave up and just succumbed to the wet attentions of the fire hall's mascot. The Dalmatian made a thorough inspection of the man's face and then started in on Pete's neck area. "Ack! That tickles, you silly mutt!" Dave whined as his collar was grabbed and he was pulled away.

"What have you been up to, ya fool? Bet there was some female down the beach, huh?" The dog wagged his tail fiercely. "Yeah, love's in the air, alright." Reaching over, Pete found a piece of driftwood and heaved it over his shoulder. Dave bounded off and the Lieutenant got to his feet. "Goddamned mutt."

Abby smiled and patted the man on his shoulder. "Oh, you know you love all that nice unconditional love, not to mention the face cleaning." She sighed appreciatively as a wet tongue flicked behind her right ear.

"Everyone needs some of that nice, wet, unconditional love, right Abby?"

The blonde tried not to grin but thinking about her lover's ardent advances made it difficult. Her eyes lit up as she contemplated making slow love on the beach at sunset. "C'mon, time's a wasting." Dray's teeth nipped her earlobe.

Giving herself a small shake, Abby grinned and patted the taller woman's behind. "I'd follow you anywhere, honey."

Dray opened her dive bag and dragged out two wet suits. Both were blue quarter inch neoprene; plenty of protection for the waters in the area. Tossing her lover the suit, Dray grinned widely. "Good. Then let's get wet!"

Abby held the suit up against her chest. "You think this is gonna fit? I think it's way too big."

The taller woman tugged hard on her wetsuit, wiggling her butt as the groin area snuggled in tighter. "Do me a favor, will ya? Just try it on."

Dray knew the woman had only previously worn a short-legged suit since she'd done all of her diving in warm water. She eased the straps down over her shoulders and then reached for the boots. A few minutes later, she stood all suited up and Pete helped to check her gauges.

Abby grumbled with exasperation. "Dray? Could you help?" Dropping her mask/snorkel, Dray smirked and came up behind the woman, grabbing the material at Abby's waist and pulling hard, grinning as the woman's feet left the sand. "Whoa...give a girl some warning, will ya?"

"There ya go. Help you with anything else?" She moved her hands to the front, smoothing the neoprene before fastening the strap. Abby arched an eyebrow and wondered just how long their dive would be and how long it would take to ditch Pete and Dave, leaving them alone on the deserted beach.

Within another five minutes, they were both suited up and walking slowly backwards into the waters of the Saanich Inlet. Pete shoved his hands into his pockets and smiled at Dave's antics as the dog leapt high into the air and then landed with legs straight. As he watched, both women adjusted their masks, gave him the thumbs up and then jackknifed into the water.

Dray had regaled her about the joys of West Coast diving; the area was rich in marine life, a veritable smorgasbord, with ocean gardens to rival anything she could see on land. Having done most of her dives in warm water, Abby was somewhat skeptical. Having close encounters with reef sharks had made her very aware of her underwater surroundings. She didn't know whether she was disappointed or relieved when Dray had told her that the only denizens of the deep she might be lucky to see were giant sea skates.

She went on further to point out that the chances of that were rather remote, unless they wanted to do another dive at Kelsey Bay. Even Pete was interested in that one. He bragged about the dive he and Dray had done with a large basking shark and the conversation naturally turned to the types of shark attacks they'd heard about. None of the grisly details were enough to dissuade either diver from the day's plans. Abby had always looked at diving as being a very intense and rewarding experience and because it would be another first for them as a couple, she couldn't wait to get started.

They descended slowly, pausing every now and again to equalize. At one point, Abby found her mask flooding and entertained her companion with facial expressions as she removed it, crossed her eyes, replaced the object and then blew a steady stream of bubbles up under it and forcing the air out of the small space. Dray found herself wanting to take the silly woman into her arms; so she did. They floated at about 35 feet, adjusting their BCs, and then Abby smiled around her regulator as Dray removed hers and mouthed the words 'I love you.' Mask to mask, Dray took another breath and let her reg fall. Abby copied the action and they watched each other, slowly moving closer until their lips touched. The blonde wrinkled her nose as small bubbles made their way between them and then felt her mouth completely covered. The kiss deepened and she felt lightheaded as her body began starving for oxygen.

Opening her eyes, she found blue ones somberly gazing back at her and then air was being pushed into her mouth. She inhaled slowly and then her body felt aflame as Dray's tongue made a brief appearance. As the kiss ended Abby reached down and placed her reg near her lover's mouth and pressed the purge button. Dray nodded and inhaled carefully; there was such a feeling of trust between them. Then both women replaced their regulators and just floated, eyes locked. Dray brought her hands up, making a heart sign while Abby moved her legs up to wrap around the backs of Dray's calves and they just basked in the total feeling of contentment.

The brunette tapped her shoulder and pointed to the gauge. Abby's 3000lb tank was now down a third and they'd only been underwater for 15 minutes. Dray wanted to show Abby the bounty that awaited them and indicated further descent. Nodding happily, the smaller woman let some air out of her buoyancy compensator and began heading for the bottom. Dray was pleased with the woman's enthusiasm and slowly kicked after her.

Checking her own gauge, she tapped the compass, checked the amount of air remaining and nodded as a few ocean mounts came into view. Visibility was very clear, between 15 and 20 feet. They hit a thermo cline at about 40 feet but it was almost imperceptible; the one they hit at 60 feet, however, wasn't. Abby came up short, hugging herself tightly as Dray came behind her and briskly rubbed her arms. The temp had just dropped from 50 degrees down to 43. Not a big change but certainly noticeable to someone who'd been out of diving for a while. She gained eye contact and then put thumbs up. Abby nodded and they were off again.

They followed the sandy bottom and there before them was the sea wall at Thomson Cove. Dray smiled happily as Abby's eyes grew wide at the spectacle of marine life. Standing at about 60 feet, the wall looked to be at least another 30 or 40 feet down.

She pointed to Abby's eyes, then to her own and pointed out over the precipice, nodding when she got the thumbs up. Placing her arms out and parallel to her shoulders, the taller woman closed her eyes and then just fell. Abby watched as Dray assumed the free fall position, admiring the clear lines on the woman's body. It seemed like a long way down as Abby watched and then, finally, Dray flipped over quickly and just lay there on the ocean floor.

Abby hesitated, added a bit to her BC and then jumped off, doing an admirable job at the beginning of a swan dive in slow motion. The added air made her fall very slowly and so she had time to watch as she fell towards the waiting arms of her lover. Dray reached up and caught the woman by her fins as she overcompensated, almost missing her mark.

Pulling the smaller woman down into her arms made her feel so alive. Abby removed her reg and kissed her lover's cheek, grinning as she felt her legs lifted and wrapped around her lover's thighs. Dray took a breath from her reg, let it fall and just smiled as she felt small even teeth nibbling at her chin and jaw. *This*, she thought wistfully, *is almost as good as sex. Almost.*

Abby pulled slightly away and replaced her reg, looking deeply into the eyes of her lover; their connection was so strong. She could feel the total love, knowing that Dray would be there for her in every way, shape and form.

She smiled around her reg as the larger woman rolled her carefully over. Dray tapped the woman's facemask and then gestured outwardly. Abby followed Dray's hand and saw a veritable garden before her. They made their way over to the sea wall and the blonde watched her companion pick up two small alabaster nudibranchs, offering them up for inspection. Abby took the small sea slugs and turned them over, admiring them as they twisted and turned, their tentacle-like appendages waving in the current. Dray reached over and took one of the small creatures and lifted it high, letting it fall as if in slow motion. Both watched with total fascination as the creature's body undulated back and forth, looking like a small leaf caught in a whirlwind. Dray pointed out further marine life and Abby smiled in appreciation as the sea pens gently rocked in the slight current and the tall stalks of white and pink sea anemones stood proud, looking very much like bunches of cauliflower. They'd seen the occasional rockfish but Dray pointed at a long black lingcod and Abby nodded vigorously.

The fish darted in amongst some of the larger rocks and both women followed it with their eyes. It looked to be a good two feet in length at least. Dray unhooked the spear gun at her belt and made sure the line was untangled before she pulled back on the rubber band, fully arming it. They moved a bit closer and the cod darted quickly away. Abby shook her head and stopped. She was feeling frustrated until she felt a hand on her shoulder. Crouching down so they were parallel to the ocean floor, Dray motioned forward and they slowly made their way closer to the fish. The cod, meanwhile, had decided that staying perfectly still might dissuade any predators from guessing it was food. It was sadly mistaken.

Dray brought the gun up to chest level, inhaled quickly and then squeezed the trigger. Abby watched as the spear cut threw the water and then imbedded itself in the fish's body. It began to thrash and the line grew taut. Abby lay transfixed watching Dray's biceps stretch and bulge as she fought with the line, and then Dray was off after the fish before it could pull free.

It was only a matter of seconds after she had gone to tackle the fish that Abby was hit with such a sense of déjà vu that she lay frozen with fear. She could remember a darkened figure pursuing her with cunning and determination, every bone in his body taut as he stalked his prey. She had a sense of claustrophobia when the dark walls of her dream began to close in on her. Something or someone horrible was waiting for her just at the end of it. In the darkness, waiting.

She blinked and then readjusted her reg between lips that had all but gone slack. Who was this man and why did he seem so familiar? Bits of the dream floated up and a sense of cold foreboding settled over her. Although there seemed no way that she could know the strange man in her brief vision, he did have an air of danger to him that brought Dray immediately to mind.

Knowing her lover to be a caring and loving woman made it very hard for Abby to wrap her head around the past violence; things just didn't quite mesh. As the woman grabbed and twisted the spear, wrenching it from the body of the fish, she wondered just how Dray had become a killer.

Abby found her breathing labored and slowly got it back under control. She shook her head, casting the dark thoughts away and watched as her lover held the fish under one arm and made her way back, her strong strokes eating the distance up easily. There was such power and grace in the woman's movements.

It was obvious something wasn't quite right as Dray swam back to her lover; Abby had a small worried look on her face leaving her to wonder just what was going through her head. Filing the questions away for another time, she picked up her gauge, noted the information and then glanced quickly at Abby's console and saw, with some alarm, that her tank was now down to just above 800lbs. They still had at least another 15 minutes of strenuous traveling time unless they wanted to do an arduous surface swim.

Even given Abby's good shape it just didn't seem a viable option. Tapping Abby's lenses and then the gauge, she pointed back the way they'd come and jerked her head in that direction. Dray waited as the woman registered the amount left in her tank and then smiled around her mouthpiece as Abby slowly nodded her head. Dray put her hand around the smaller woman's waist and they slowly kicked their way back to the edge of the wall and then upwards, leaving the cod for the decorator crabs and other opportunistic denizens of the deep.

The firefighter was worried; she'd lost track of time and although there was plenty of air left in her own tank, she hadn't taken into consideration Abby's. She kept checking the woman's instrument and then stopped, pulling the woman close. Abby responded by lacing their fingers together and Dray felt a lump in her throat as she saw the total faith in her lover's eyes. She checked her compass and altered their course a bit.

Abby's gauge was now down to the red mark, making the airflow slower, wearing the woman down as she fought to drag what remained out of the tank. This part was going to be interesting, Dray knew, for although she'd seen Abby's dive log and was aware of her past experience, it was the first dive they had made as buddies and Dray wasn't too sure how Abby would react.

Reaching down, Dray lifted her orange octopus second stage and held it up between them. Abby's gaze was totally focused, her face serious as she tried to understand what Dray wanted her to see. Pressing the purge button, a silvery flow of bubbles leaked out and she watched as the taller woman offered it to her. She tilted her head in question and watched as Dray's eyebrow movement made her mask wiggle. Then it dawned on her and she grabbed her gauge; it was well past the red mark. Panic enveloped her and she looked up at the lighted motes that danced on the surface, so near yet so far away. It was 60 feet...she could do a swimming ascent and be back safe and sound, if only...

Dray watched the look of cold panic hit Abby's eyes and grabbed hold of her waist. Abby made the signal across her throat as the air got harder and harder to suck on. Dray held up the safety second again and took her own reg out, replacing it with the orange one. Abby reluctantly removed her own reg as Dray passed hers over. Taking a few breaths, she held a thumb up. This time there was an almost immediate response and brunette sighed with great relief. She really didn't want to end up dragging Abby to the surface and then endure a long swim back to shore. That would not only be physically challenging but also mentally demoralizing.

Once Abby was somewhat settled, Dray removed her orange reg and indicated they should trade. Abby hesitated briefly but then nodded. Dray used hand gestures to show that the hose on the octopus was much longer and she wouldn't have to be clinging onto Dray the whole way. Then they set off, Dray's one hand looped through the back of her buddy's weight belt.

Pete threw the stick again and checked his watch. Scanning the horizon, he snorted. *Must be havin' a great time at that wall.* Dave returned, a roughly mangled bit of driftwood clenched in his jaws. His chest heaved with the exertion yet his tail was still wagging madly. The Lieutenant made his way over to the rocks and started to drag fixings out of the backpack. Lunch would be a simple fare but he figured the girls wouldn't care.

He remembered the last time he and Dray had been diving together. It had been a while ago and while she was well aware of just how stupid it was to go diving alone it hadn't stopped her. He opened her dive log and scanned the past five or six entries; at least she'd limited her dives to shore entries and a depth ranging from 40 to 60 feet. Dray was a very experienced diver, having gotten her Specialty Diver certificate and dragging him along when they were in their 'fitness craze' days. Hell, she'd done it all; everything but go for Diving Instructor.

She wasn't into that but had at least taken the course on Master Diver, a subject that came easily for her since she loved the organized and controlled way of things. He smiled at that, knowing it to be very true. She was spontaneous but didn't much like the characteristic in those around her. Structure was a real problem; she thrived on it and yet it was a love/hate relationship, causing her to rebel whenever the mood struck her.

He glanced at his watch again. *Shoulda been up a good ten minutes ago.* He frowned and looked at the Dalmatian who'd walked over to water's edge and sat looking out into the distance. *Hmmm....*' He set his jaw and then began repackaging the picnic. He wasn't too sure exactly what he had in mind but began taking his sneakers and socks off. Then he rummaged through the dive bag for an extra mask, fins and snorkel.

"Goddamnit...where's that pony bottle? There's the extra reg. Okay, first stage hose connected, yup." He wiped a forearm across his forehead and tried to formulate a plan.

His head came up as he heard Dave barking wildly and he stared intently out at the vast blue of the ocean trying to see something.... Anything. There! Two dark heads bobbing at the surface. *Oh, thank God!* Dropping his equipment he ran forward, wading out to about mid chest before stopping. "Dray!" he yelled in a worried voice, waving his hands frantically over his head. There was a brief pause and then one hand waved back. Pete let out a tight breath he wasn't even aware he'd been holding. He closed his eyes briefly, saying a very fervent prayer when a smaller hand also waved in his direction.

The two women made their way to shore and plunked themselves down in the shallow water. Abby removed her mask and then wearily pulled her hood off before lying back in the sand with a contented sigh. Pete squatted next to his partner and cocked an eyebrow in her direction. Dray smiled weakly. "Ah, the joys of buddy breathing, Pete. I kinda got carried away, showing Abby the Thomson Cove sea wall and the time got away from me."

He said nothing as he noted the worry lines around Dray's mouth. "Sumpin' happen out there, babe?" Abby cleared her throat and looked away.

"No. No, not really. Abby just went through her air supply kinda quick is all. I wasn't expecting it." She smiled tightly when her companion hugged her.

Abby wiped her nose with a shaky hand. "I got a bit rattled, Pete. I let myself get distracted and kinda inhaled most of my air at one sitting."

Pete nodded slowly. "Air hog. Hey, it happens. So, you guys enjoy your dive, other than that?"

Dray began removing her fins and weight belt and then turned to help Abby. "Yeah, actually. It was an okay dive."

Abby scoffed as she pushed her lover's shoulder. "Oh brother, if that was just an okay dive then I don't know if I could survive a great one." Pete watched as the blonde animatedly described how they'd come upon the wall and all of the rich marine life they had encountered. "Yeah, it was a blast right up until my gauge went into the red," she said wistfully. "I want to do another one. Can we?" She looked imploringly over at the other woman who was slowly peeling the wet suit from her body. Pete noted the tension in Dray's shoulders and got up.

"Hey, I'll just take the gear and stow it in the truck, okay? It might take me a while, so," his voice trailed off unnoticed and he watched his two friends holding each other closely.

Just then, Dave came bounding down the beach with the remains of what appeared to be a good-sized crab. He dropped it at his master's feet and wagged his tail fiercely. "Oh, for me...why Dave, you shouldna."

He turned and began making his way back to where the truck was parked, then whistled sharply, nodding with satisfaction as the dog dropped his prize and heeled immediately.

Dray hugged the smaller woman tightly. "I'm so sorry."

Abby shook her head and buried her face in the front of her lover's suit. "No, Dray. I got distracted, it wasn't you."

Blowing her lips out, the taller woman lifted the smaller chin and gazed into her eyes. "Wanna talk about it? I know something was bothering you down there."

Abby thought briefly about telling her that it had been a momentary lapse, that she'd let her mind wander and had just screwed up. While it was true there was no way she wanted to start lying just when they were getting so close. She took a breath and stepped back, pulling the last of the wet suit off before she went on.

"I was thinking about...stuff. Things you told me about your life...before," she began hesitatingly. Her lover's eyes darkened and then Dray turned and looked out at the horizon.

"You mean my propensity for violence; my fiery temper, my..."

Abby leapt up and took her lover's arms. "No. That's who you were, not who you are now, Dray. It's just that the woman I see

127

here before me, the woman I wake up to and who makes love to me just doesn't jibe with the images of you...I don't know...ganging around and..."

"Killing?" Dray finished in a low voice.

Abby could only nod at first until she found her voice. "I saw you kill the fish and I started to think how you killed someone. Did you shoot them? Did you stab them? Did you do it with your bare hands? Did you-."

"Yeah, I have a pretty dark past, Babe." Dray's hand moved up to her damp hair and she slowly massaged her neck. She sat down heavily in the sand and gingerly took one of her lover's smaller hands into her own. "Are you worried I'd hurt you?" she asked.

"No," Abby said reassuringly. "It's just hard to get a mental picture of you being that way."

Dray took a deep breath. "How can I explain this? I had a choice, Ab. I had to do what I did to survive. But it's more than that. I had to become stronger or I'd be lost. I tried to resist, Abby, really I did. But it got easier to give in to the shit around me, becoming just like they were. Worse than they were."

Abby shook her head quickly and swallowed the lump that was forming in the back of her throat. She blinked back the tears that threatened to fall and began pondering what her lover was saying.

"I'm not proud of what I did, just giving into the rage," Dray went on, in a voice filled with self-hatred.

Abby could almost see the woman enveloped in a dark and mournful cloud; the resulting silence was almost deafening. Letting her damp suit fall, Abby quickly pulled on a pair of shorts and an oversized T-shirt, took her place on the sand beside her lover and waited.

Her somber eyes took in the ritual Dray performed when worried – rubbing her neck – almost without knowing she was doing it. Suddenly, as if her hand was on fire, Dray pulled away and scowled. Her fingers came away with a few strands of hair and Abby watched as the woman stared at her own hands as if they belonged to another. "These Goddamned things have done such damage, Abby."

Abby wanted to rail at the world for causing such a wonderful person such pain and torment. She reached over and pulled the woman against her. "These hands," she said, "are capable of such tenderness, such loving care, Dray. They've saved lives and they've saved me. Don't ever forget that."

She turned the large, rough hands over, admiring the well-formed and tapered fingers. She traced the lines on each palm and then continued.

"You are the strongest person I know, Dray Khalkousa. You risk your life every day being a firefighter; you pour your heart out in poetry and prose. That past you say you despise...well, I've been thinking about that. I can't condone what you did but I can understand why you had to act the way you did. Everything that happens to us makes us who we are. Without that past you wouldn't be the woman you are today. And I love this woman," she finished tightening her hold on Dray's hands.

Dray put her face in her hands and just cradled her forehead for a moment. Then she dragged a hand wearily over her features, almost as if she were trying to erase the images and emotions being evoked. "Do we hafta talk about this now? I mean, shit Abby, I just put your life in danger being so fucking stupid down there."

Abby hugged her tightly. "Look, I understand that we both got kinda sidetracked. Being down there with you, well," she paused. Dray looked over, afraid she would see the disappointment in her lover's eyes. She couldn't bear that.

"I...um, found it to be...um, very erotic," Abby finished with a light chuckle.

Dray blinked as a faint blush came to the woman's fair cheeks. "You did?" A small grin momentarily inched its way across her lips. "I found it very exciting, too, Abby. But that doesn't excuse me being an idiot and completely losing track of time. What if-."

The blonde snaked her hand around her lover's waist and hugged her close.

"How come you always 'what if'? I know without a doubt that you could get us out of anything. Truly, Dray. And besides, I have been diving before; I could have made that free ascent. It wasn't really that far."

Dray pursed her lips, "Yeah, you coulda but you were also a bit freaked out down there. When people panic sometimes they forget what to do."

"Wouldn't be the first time I was in trouble you know?" Abby answered with a grin. "I've managed to get myself out of a few scrapes over the years and that one was the least of 'em, let me tell ya," she added with a chuckle.

"Like what?" Dray prompted. "I know you don't really talk much about your life before I came along either but...I'd like to hear about it."

The blonde squirmed a bit in the sand and then leaned back, propping herself up by the elbows. Dray reached over and pulled her ball cap from the side pouch on her dive bag and placed it on Abby's head.

"There. Now the sun won't bake your brain, you won't get sunburned and there won't be any more excuses. Right?" Abby bit her lower lip and then nodded quickly. She knew it had just been a matter of time before Dray would weed more information out of her so she relented.

"Well, it's not much, really. I mean it's just..." Her throat went dry suddenly and Abby swallowed with a click. "Well, my Dad and I never really got along, as you know. He was always so critical of me. Didn't matter what it was. My effort was just never good enough. Mom tried..." Abby snorted at the image of her mother shaking her head slowly, mouth zipped as usual, as her husband laid another verbal barrage against her and her sister. She couldn't remember exactly how old she had been when the truth of her parent's 'good marriage' became crystal clear for her.

Dray took the woman's small hands in her own and just began tracing each finger, waiting for her to continue. Even though Abby was adamant her story was not worth the telling, Dray was fairly sure by the way she changed the subject that not only was it serious, it was still bothering her.

"Go on," Dray coached, giving the hands a squeeze.

"I don't think I was ever happy at home, not really. I guess Lydia and I learned at an early age that it was really just the two of us. Lydia's my sister, by the way," Abby added with a sheepish grin to which Dray just nodded for her to continue. "My father ruled the house like a prison warden and if we were lucky, we got time off for good behavior. I think he was always afraid of losing control of us girls. He spent quite a lot of time on the road drumming up business for Bruno's Auto Sales and Services.

"He decided that he'd start bringing his bigger clients over for dinner in the evenings. It became a regular thing; Father thought it was a good career move and for the most part the clients were decent people. But this one guy," Abby said shaking her head as she remembered, "I guess it was around my fifteenth birthday when he brought one business owner by for supper. I hated this guy and the way he had charm and finesse in front of my parents didn't sit well with me. There was something underneath, you know? But all Father could see was the 10 vans he talked about ordering. I found out soon enough why I shouldn't trust him."

Abby trailed off and Dray touched her arm. "Did he hurt you, Abby?" the brunette asked.

Abby took a deep breath. "He offered to take me out for a root beer float instead of waiting for my father to get home. He was smarmy – a slippery weasel type of guy," Abby added with a knowing grin. "I figured I'd be safer in public than letting him into the house alone." Dray's forehead furrowed in concern as a look of desperation moved slowly over her lover's face. "We got to the drive-in concession stand and he tried to touch me. And I just lost it."

"What did you do?" Dray asked.

Abby gave a said grin. "Anything any 15 year old would do. I called 'Daddy.' I told him where I was and what happened...About 10 minutes later he showed up. Weasel denied it; my father believed him and then he blamed me for losing one of his biggest sales of the year. I left not long after. Figured if my father wouldn't protect me, why should I stay? I've been on my own ever since."

Dray let her breath out slowly, her teeth tightly clenched thinking about a father who would put his young, innocent daughter in that kind of position, just for business favors. She squeezed her eyes shut and then swallowed.

*Breathe...center...relax,* Dray told herself. It didn't work. Images of some guy pawing this sweet and trusting kid forced their way into her heart, making her blood boil.

Abby moved her hands to rub the raised goose bumps on her arms and Dray snapped out of her haze, grabbing the dive bag and pulling it closer. She knew the tone of her voice would give her feelings away instantly but she also knew that Abby was hardly in any shape to notice.

"Hey, you must be cold, huh?" Dray offered instead.

Quickly rummaging through things, she sighed gratefully when her fingers closed around the heavy beach towel she usually kept there. Her head whipped around as she heard a cough.

"Um...sorry to interrupt," Pete said quietly, feeling as if he walked into a very private conversation. He shifted his weight from foot to foot, both hands jammed into the pockets of his jeans. Neither woman would meet his eye. He coughed again and then went on. "It's gettin' late. You guys want to head back to the hotel?"

He jangled his keys from one hand to the other, looking very awkward. Dray draped the towel around her lover before getting to her feet. Abby pulled it close and then just sat, looking off into the distance.

"Look Pete, I think you should just go ahead and go back to the hotel, alright? Ab and I have some things to do."

Pete smiled, "And I should take a hint and get going. Okay, I can pick ya up tomorrow, and maybe do another dive or two? Listen, I've got coupla sleeping bags in the back. You want 'em? It might not get much cooler than this but that sand is gonna cool down once the sun really hits the water."

Abby registered them talking and even managed a weak smile when Dray kissed her neck and said she'd be right back. Then she was lost to her past once more, oblivious to the glory of the fading sunset.

## Chapter 9

Dray gathered the last of the driftwood and heard Pete's truck misfire again and then sputter hesitantly to life. She raised herself to her full height and took one step in his direction before smiling as the truck backfired and then took off. Placing the wood by the fire pit Dray felt the anger building up inside.

Abby blinked slowly, finally taking in her surroundings. She noted the tense posture, the clenched jaw and the almost palpable feeling of rage coming off her lover.

"I wasn't...I mean he would have if we were alone...but he didn't, Dray." The dark head rose, steely blue eyes locked onto hazel and then Abby watched the tension slowly leak out of the woman.

Dray pulled some matches from her pocket and lit the fire with shaking hands. All the images of her lover being taken by force blew away like wisps of smoke. As her vision cleared she looked across the fire and saw the worried, small face of a woman who had endured something that, while not being actual physical rape, was nonetheless harrowing.

"Are you upset with me?" Abby asked quietly. Abby bit her lower lip and then held out her trembling hand. "Come and sit with me, please?"

Dray could see in the red glow of sunset just how upset Abby was and felt her heart wrench at the small vulnerable voice of her lover. She dropped what remained of her match into the fire pit and slowly stood up, feeling her thighs and calves flex and contract after being so tense.

The blonde pushed at the tears that began to fall with the heel of her hand, and then she smiled as Dray snuggled in behind her, pulling her closely against her strong form. Abby felt her lover's comforting arms stretch tightly around her and closed her eyes. Dray's hot breath at her neck, at her ear, made her shiver raising a faint row of goose bumps covering her skin.

"Abby, you can tell me anything. I'm here to listen and accept anything you have to say. I'm angry with the worm that touched you. I'm angry with your father who didn't have the balls to stand up to that jerk. But I'm not angry with you, Baby. Not at all." The blonde bobbed her head quickly and then grew silent. "I just needed a minute to calm myself down so I don't go on some damn fool seek and destroy mission. I'm not sure who I should be more angry at this very moment – the slime ball or your father for not sticking up for you."

Both women sat there in the sand watching as the impossibly large ball of fire dipped lower in the sky, finally kissing the emerald waters of the Pacific. Dray pulled the towel more closely around her lover as she felt the woman begin to shiver.

Many images filled Abby's mind as she sat in the haven of her lover's arms like the one of her father who stood at that little drive-in, making excuse for his daughter's behavior in order to win a sale lost to a pedophile. She remembered trying to talk to her father about how his client made her uneasy but he hadn't listened. He'd said the dinners were good for his career and that Abby was 'just being silly.' During the confrontation at the drive-in she'd gone from being silly to being called a slut and a tease.

She also remembered the drunken rage that her father had fallen into after they returned home that night. Acrimonious words flew back and forth between them as her mother dragged her to her room.

"God, Dray. He took the word of a pedophile over me!" She snorted derisively, gritting her teeth as the memory of her father's harsh words of condemnation filled her ears, hitting just as hard as they had the first time. "I couldn't believe the hateful things he began spouting at me from the driveway, cursing the day I was ever conceived. He ranted and raved about how selfish I was, how ungrateful I was being, that I was unwilling to pull my own weight and do what was right for the family. God." Dray tightened her embrace and began whispering small words of endearment against the cooling skin of her lover.

"You know, that was bad but it was nothing compared to the disappointing stare of my mother. God, she just stood there. I tried to talk to her, explain how it had been with Mr. Bruno, but I could see it was a lost cause. No matter what I said, it was all just going to fall on deaf ears."

"He was drunk, Babe. Maybe she didn't feel safe..." Dray drew a heavy sigh and then shut her mouth with a snap. What the hell was she doing, making up excuses for Abby's low-life parents? Abby turned in her embrace and stared into the brunette's eyes.

"Yes, he was drunk. Yes, he said some things I don't suppose he would have ever voiced, but you know what? Right there and then I could see my future. Lydia and I were just 'things' to them. Sure, I suppose they both loved us in their fashion but I could see my life if I stayed." Pulling her hair back from her face, Abby blinked a few tears away, turned and buried her face into her lover's shoulder. Dray cringed as the muffled words were spoken against the skin of her neck. "I ran to my room and slammed the door. I can't remember much about packing or hugging my sister and darting out into the street."

Dray put her hands up to Abby's face and gently cupped it. "Where did you go? Did you have any money, any friends? God, Ab...you were a child." She hugged the blonde close to her, hooking her chin over the woman's shoulder. It was a miracle that Abby had ever survived life on the street, avoiding gang pressure, drugs and crime. She took a deep breath, inhaling the soft fragrance of her lover's hair. "How did you ever survive?"

Abby rubbed her hands up and down her lover's back and snuggled closer, finally moving her cramping legs into a more comfortable position around Dray's hips. The brunette moved her hands slowly and pulled the towel around the two of them and then slowly rocked back and forth, a silent lullaby playing in her head.

Rummaging briefly in her pocket, Dray sighed with relief and then handed the blonde a couple of crushed tissues. A few mournful cries floated down to them from the seagulls overhead as Abby cleaned off her face and blew her nose.

"S'okay, Dray. I did survive. I spent my first night in the park under some bushes. I must have looked pretty sorry the next morning because a few people dropped coins into my jean jacket as I sat on one of the benches trying to get organized. I made a few bucks there that day. I'd heard a few comments about a halfway house throughout the day and that's where I spent my second night. I told them I was 18. Not sure if they bought it but I knew if they realized I was a minor they'd report it to the cops or social services and I'd be right back where I started. But things got easier after that."

The taller woman pondered the last statement, biting the inside of her cheek. *Easier...yeah, like life on the streets going from one halfway house to the next and living from hand to mouth could be easy.*

"So, just how did you manage to avoid the usual consequences of a woman living on the streets?"

Abby rested her cheek on the strong shoulder of her lover and sighed deeply, lost in her memories.

"Well, I've always been a loner, not fitting into any particular group. Lydia was pretty much my only friend growing up. We sure did get into some trouble." She laughed a little as Dray's eyebrow shot up. "Yes, trouble. I might have looked like Sandra Dee but I felt like Natalie Wood, ready to stand up for what I believed. You know, like in that movie with James Dean."

Dray smiled and then drew her lover's face up for a sweet kiss. "My little rebel without a clue? Classic movie fan, huh?"

Abby smirked and kissed the taller woman's nose. "Hey," she grumbled playfully at her companion. "I had to have some place I could call sanctuary, didn't I? I must have spent at least half the day at either the library or a movie theater – a double feature for two bucks kept you warm for four hours or more during the winter. I even worked as an usher when I was 17, though cleaning up after some movies used to make me gag. Some of the other workers and I conned the manager over at the Palace to help out on clean up detail. All it took was once. We got rubber gloves after that. So yeah, I was a rebel."

Dray tried hard not to roll her eyes and succeeded, for the time being.

"Man, when I was still home Lydia and I would while away the weekends watching the old movies that came on after midnight. Our parents didn't really seem to care as long as we didn't make a mess and had our chores done without complaint. I guess, come to think of it, we were pretty low maintenance kids. Okay, so we never really did get into what you might call 'real trouble.' I mean, we did do the usual pranks: toilet papering the neighbor's trees on Halloween and soaping their car and stuff. That was as mischievous as we got, I guess."

"Ah, so the truth comes out; you were Little Miss Goodie-Two-Shoes, huh? Well, I gotta tell you a secret: I was pretty quiet when I was growing up, too. In fact, I spent most of my time with my nose in one book or another. Used to drive my mother crazy; she was sure I'd need soda bottle lenses before I reached the age of twenty."

Abby settled herself a bit more. "So. Now you know more about me. Are *you* ready to run screaming to the hills?"

Dray touched the woman's nose. "Hmm. Don't count on it." She paused and then cleared her throat. "So, when did you know?"

"Know what?" Abby said with an exaggeration, both of them fully aware of the question being asked.

"Are you gonna make me say it?" Dray said nibbling on Abby's earlobe.

"Well, I suppose my father pretty much gave me a clue about that." Abby lay her head on Dray's shoulder. "I started thinking about how uncomfortable I was around all the boys in school. At first, I thought it was just because I knew my parents wouldn't approve of me dragging any friends home." Dray moved her arms around and rubbed Abby's sides, the woman's body language immediately giving her emotions away. "They really frowned on 'outsiders.' When I was older and away from their control I began to think and do what I wanted. I didn't like being around guys. They just seemed so crass and alien to me. I remember an incident one night in the women's shelter when I was about seventeen. I suppose that particular hole in the wall could be called home as it was the first place that I'd stayed in the longest. Anyway, there were two girls there that said they were sisters or cousins or something. They used to spend a lot of time holding hands and hugging and such. Folks pretty much gave them a wide berth. I wasn't too sure why so I took it upon myself to make friends with them. After hanging out with them for a couple of days, I realized they really weren't cousins or anything; just really close friends." She stopped to push her hair back from her face as the wind began changing direction.

"So, this one night I was just kinda lying in bed waiting for sleep and I saw them together. Jolee kinda crept into Moira's bed and at first, I didn't really think too much about it. I couldn't see much because of the darkness but I could tell something was going on."

Dray watched as a faint blush began up her lover's neck and throat. "Oh, you could, huh?"

Abby smirked and replied, "Yeah, I could. The kissing was fairly easy to figure out but it was really the terms of endearment between them that cinched it for me. They were really good to each other. My folks were certainly not what you'd call 'loving' towards each other. No public displays of affection or anything. I think Lydia and I found out about sex on PBS."

Dray snorted, thinking of the documentaries that depicted animal sexuality and shuddered. It was amazing this woman hadn't ended up on a therapist's couch for extended periods of time.

"So, a healthy sex life to you is watching two dung beetles going at it?" She yelped as two fingers were dug into her side. "Stop...stop...okay, I give." She pushed the blonde away gently. "Why do you keep trying to see if I'm ticklish? I'm not, you know. All you're doing is digging between my ribs." She grabbed Abby's wrists and then leaned in for a smoldering kiss. "So, little rebel mine, just how did you learn about human sexuality then?"

"Heh, well...they kinda took me aside and introduced me to kissing."

Dray's eyebrows shot up. "Both of 'em...taught you at the same time? My oh my...you are a wild one."

Abby got a hand free and swatted her again. "No. Jeez, Dray. I was curious and they...well, they helped me answer some questions. I do have a really good imagination, you know. And I began having some pretty good dreams and fantasies. By the time I was twenty I'd answered most of the questions I had on sex with women."

"Twenty? Slow learner, huh Abby?" Dray smirked as a dangerous glint came into Abby's eyes. She let herself be pushed back into the sand until the woman was stretched out on top of her.

"I might have been a slow learner, Dray my love, but I sure made up for lost time. Dung beetles aside, of course. Wouldn't you agree?"

That was it; the brunette just couldn't stop either the laughter bubbling up or the rolling of her eyes any more than she could have stopped the sun from sinking below the horizon. Abby tried to keep a straight face but soon the two of them were rolling around in the sand, hooting with childish abandon.

"God, I'm sorry. I just had this image of you...this wanton woman acting out what she'd seen on a fuckin' documentary...oh, God...then applying it on hapless women by pouncing on them and dragging them into the bushes!" The images threw the taller woman into further gales of laughter. Abby watched in amusement until her lover drew quiet. Tracing her fingertip along the planes of Dray's face, Abby watched with a sense of fascination as a fine dusting of white sand seemed to highlight the woman's burnished skin, making Dray look every inch a goddess.

"I love you, Dray. I love the way you can make me laugh, poke fun at myself and just not be so serious. And I'm really glad that I told you about Mr. Bruno."

Inferno

Dray pushed her long fingers through her lover's golden hair and gave Abby a very passionate kiss. "I'm glad you did too, babe. Just remember there isn't anything you can't tell me, okay?" Abby nodded and their mouths brushed softly against each other again, their ardor rising.

"Well, there is one thing, but..."

Dray arched an eyebrow at the suddenly quiet blonde. "Yes?"

Abby smiled gently and then propped herself up on either side of her lover's shoulders. "Well, it's like this. You know how I feel about you, right?" Dray nodded. "And you know that I'd do anything for you. Any time and any place?" The darker woman scrunched her forehead.

"Yeah, that goes double for me." The blonde moved a few errant wisps of hair out of her lover's eyes and then smirked.

"Well, I guess we know how we feel but I gotta tell ya, if I don't get into a sleeping bag or someplace warm I won't be able to put into action this good imagination I have 'cause I won't be able to feel anything pretty soon."

Dray chuckled and then rolled the woman beneath her. Getting to her hands and knees, she leaned down and kissed Abby and then quickly got to her feet and grabbed one of the bags. "Well, that's easily rectified. Hold on..." She fumbled with one duffel bag and pulled out two sleeping bags and a couple of poncho liners. "This oughta do the job nicely." Abby lay in the sand clutching the towel. The stars twinkled overhead and the gusting wind made her eyes tear up.

Walking down the beach a little, Dray picked up a few of the dryer pierces of driftwood and piled them close to the fire pit. Abby watched her with loving eyes and wondered just how strange fate was. As the brunette fed pieces of wood into the fire, the flames rose and both women watched as cinders floated up into the dark sky. Dray's thoughts went back to the night they met and she glanced across at the wistful look on her lover's face.

Abby sighed contentedly as the taller woman began to set up a small lean to using some of the larger pieces of timber that littered the beach. She closed her eyes and could suddenly see clear images of just how it was in the dreams she had of the camp. She remembered huddling under the scratchy blanket as her lover fed pieces of broken furniture into the small stove in the room. Taking a slow breath Abby imagined the tangy smell of their love making that permeated the blanket and the air surrounding them and sighed happily. It felt so right, so much like ... "Home", she murmured.

Although it seemed that a large chunk of time had passed, she noticed Abby was still smiling up at the stars, lost in her own reverie. Clearing her throat, she dragged the sleeping bags into position by the fire.

"There ya go. We shouldn't put the sleeping bags too close to the pit just in case but the lean to will help keep the wind off us and reflect some of the heat from the fire. C'mon, you. Let's get you into some heavier sweats and warm again."

Abby nodded her eyes twinkling and a grin just playing at the corners of her mouth. "Well, I suppose we could get me warmed up like that but I thought we'd do it the old fashioned way."

Dray zipped the two sleeping bags together, a sly smile playing over her lips. "There...plenty of room for both of us."

Abby watched as her lover draped the open ponchos over the lean to and then grinned as Dray began to strip. "Oh, I'm feeling warmer already."

She could feel her arousal rising like a burning fever as the play of light and shadows accentuated Dray's curves. Even the woman's dark hair seemed to be interlaced with flames as gusts of wind made the short tresses dance and undulate, moving to some primal symphony.

Abby blinked slowly, the spell broken as Dray rubbed her arms and threw another couple of logs on the fire.

"C'mere you," Abby instructed bewitchingly.

Dray stood and turned, her eyes flashing with desire. She slowly dropped to her knees.

"Warm enough?" Dray asked.

A gentle smirk played on her lips as she felt the waves of desire roll off her lover. Abby nodded slowly and reached out from under her blanket and pulled the woman closer.

"Uh huh, much warmer. But I still have this sense, this desire to be warmer still. Think you can help me out, Stretch?" Without waiting for a reply she grabbed Dray's hands and placed them under her T-shirt against her firm breasts. The large hands began tentative exploration. Abby groaned as each rosy bud was brushed and tantalized.

Abby made room as Dray slid her large frame into the bag and settled between her satiny smooth thighs. Moving to entwine one of their hands, she opened her legs wider and then crossed them over her lover's taut buttocks.

"I want you, Dray. I need to feel you." A dark head nodded in response and Abby grunted as she felt the tender flesh of her shoulder taken between sharp teeth. She felt herself sliding wetly against the firefighter's belly, a jolt searing through her each time her clit came into contact.

Dray felt the woman's need rising to a fevered pitch. She looked into eyes darkened with lust and knew this would not be a night of lovemaking but one of primal lust, an encounter where both parties felt the need to excise demons.

"Do you feel me, Abby? Do you feel what I do to you and what you create within me? Do you?" Abby nodded and placed both hands on Dray's biceps, holding on for dear life as she felt her lover begin to rock strongly against her. The woman's mouth descended and began exploring every inch of her mouth with expert strokes and deepening kisses. She felt her breath taken away as the waves of passion created between them began to roll back and forth, rising like a tidal wave.

Dray gasped as she felt the liquid fire of her lover paint the surface of her lower abdomen, feeling her muscles clench and spasm as the volume increased.

"God, I love how wet you get for me, Abby. I love how responsive you are," she whispered as she trailed her tongue and lips up and down the blonde's exposed neck. Her hand moved to cup the firm breasts against her, tweaking the nipples before moving her hand quickly over the woman's lower back, pulling the woman's buttocks hard against her.

Abby gasped as the first jolt of her building orgasm came on suddenly. She felt the zipper give as Dray locked her elbows and began thrusting against her.

"Oh God...oh.... Oh God, Andrea!" She leaned in and buried her teeth in her lover's flexed forearm, muffling her scream against its quivering surface.

Dray shuddered as she felt her flesh claimed, the pain mingling with intense pleasure and cried out as the teeth moved from forearm to breast.

Instead of relaxing against the sand in release, Abby tightened her legs, trapping her lover hard against her. Dray's arms gave out and then she found herself looking up with surprise as the stars glistened overhead.

"I know what you do to me, Dray. I've always known. I want...to see...what I do to...you. All of it," she panted between nips upon her lover's breasts and neck area, leaving small red welts in her wake.

Gritting her teeth, the firefighter tried to focus on what her lover was doing but found her mind wandering. She never liked to be made love to in this fashion, finding it more enjoyable, and much safer, when the control was hers. "Oh God," she whimpered as digits were slowly pushed inside.

Abby began thrusting against her, all the while whispering softly. She watched as Dray's eyes fluttered closed and she bent to her task. One of her hands came up and caressed her lover's face, the softness of the skin too difficult to resist. She ran her fingers over Dray's lower lip and then her throat went dry as her thumb was taken into the hot wet depths of her lover's mouth.

Abby understood how hard it was for her lover to just let go. Removing her fingers, she pressed her pelvis hard against her lover's groin and grabbed the woman's shoulders. "I want to see what I do to you, Dray. I want to look down into your eyes, knowing I made you happy and set you free."

Dray gasped as she felt herself give in. "I...I can't let...go...Abby."

"Yes you can. I'm here and I won't ever leave you, Dray. I never will again, I promise."

Dray couldn't believe just how fast her orgasm was building. She'd never been able to achieve orgasm this way and yet there she was, being taken, giving up her control. While she found the experience a bit unnerving she was caught up in the throes of it all. A compassionate look came into Abby's eyes and Dray could have wept with joy at the total acceptance she found there.

"I want it all, Dray. I want your love, your desire, and your total trust. I want all of it. Let me in, Dray...all the way."

Grabbing her lover's hips, the blonde moved her upper thigh between Dray's legs and began pounding against the tender heated flesh. "God but I love you, Dray...oh so very much. Trust in me, Dray. I won't let you fall."

Dray opened her mouth and roared as she felt her heart dash against her breastbone countless times before it just seemed to explode.

She gathered the blonde to her and buried her face in a curtain of burnished gold as she fought to keep the tears at bay. New areas were being discovered and walls were being breached each time they made love. Dray was constantly overwhelmed with what she'd been able to give this vibrant and caring woman, and yet part of her wondered how worthy she truly was. Why she was the object of Abby's unconditional love was a mystery. Small teeth gnawed at her as she remembered the afternoon's events and just how stupid she'd been. *I can't be trusted with this love...sooner or later I'm going to fuck it up.*

Abby frowned as she felt her lover shuddering briefly against her and then grow quiet. She wasn't sure just what going on.

*Could I have asked too much of her, of us?* Each woman retreated a little, trying to sort out the ramifications of Dray's silence.

"I love you, Dray."

The brunette pulled the blonde down beside her and snuggled her back into the sleeping bag. "I know."

"I'm glad you do, Babe, 'cause it's never going to change...Thank you."

Dray tilted her lover's face up. "For what?"

"For letting me in."

"I guess I was a bit surprised at just how powerful and," she paused, "and how liberating that experience was for me."

Abby slowly released the breath she was holding and then leaned in for a quick kiss. "So, did I do okay? I mean I've never made love to anyone like that either. Being totally dominant like that was kinda...well, thrilling. You know?"

Dray smiled. "Well, Woman of National Geographic, don't get too used to it." She held her hand up and watched as the tremors slowly eased off and stopped all together. "Whoa."

Abby raised her brows as she saw her lover gain back all of the control she imposed on herself. Then she eased back down onto the woman's shoulder and both gazed up at the clear western sky, pointing out one twinkling constellation after another and going over the events of the day.

"What the heck was that gross orange stuff I saw against the wall near the bottom?"

Dray rubbed her chin in silence and then grinned. "Oh, you mean the stuff that looked like snot?"

Abby made slow little circles over her lover's warm belly. "Now there's an image. Yeah, and that weird thing that looked like a walking branch. What was that?"

"Well, the first one was an egg sack from a Rockfish. The other one was a Clown Jellyfish. And yeah, it does kinda look like a branch. Good thing that sucker isn't bigger. Those creatures prey on shrimp and those branch-like appendages could be really scary if they were any bigger. I've watched them in action and they are tenacious in tracking down their prey."

A shudder ran through her companion's frame and Abby eased up onto one elbow. "What is it?" Dray held her breath and then Abby felt the woman's hand resume its methodic perusal of her willing and very responsive flesh.

The brunette had a hard time suppressing a grin as she watched Abby fall into a swoon. Hissing demonically, she slowly pushed the blonde's chin aside and began to close her hand around Abby's throat. Abby felt a shudder run through her as Dray gasped and pushed herself away.

"What is it?"

A feeling of hopelessness surrounded her as people were poked and prodded relentlessly forward, an end to their suffering finally at hand. Dray felt pulled along with the crowd, searching each face and still not finding who she was looking for. Her heartbeat resounded through her like the trip hammer of a Gatling gun, its staccato beat of one word endlessly repeated: Zosia. She had to stop it, couldn't let it happen, not now. She spotted a petite figure just ahead, the woman's blonde hair partially grown out.

Reaching out in real life, mirroring her movements in the dream, Dray saw herself grabbing the smaller woman and pulling her close. Dray felt her arms come up in defense as the blonde tried to break away. She mouthed something but there was no sound, the abject fear in the stranger's face making her recoil in horror. Why would some one ever look at her in that way? *Don't leave me!* she wanted to scream. Hands pushed at her and her fingers began to lose their purchase around Zosia's shoulders, making her grip all the harder. The woman twisted in her efforts to get away and two strong hands settled around her thin boned neck. And then the dingy hallway was whisked away and the night sky slammed into her head.

She wore a look of horror as she stared at her fists, still seeing the large masculine hands closing around Zosia's throat.

"Nothing, it's nothing," she lied; the words dry in her throat. "I'll never let anything happen to you. Never. I love you so much, Abby."

The blonde tilted her head in question and then sighed as Dray's lips brushed her temple. "I know that," she smiled, feeling her toes positively curling and then she sighed deeply as Dray's love washed over her in a blanket of warmth. The somewhat solemn expression in her lover's eyes twinkled with intensity and Abby mentally compared them to the stars that dotted the sky above them. There really was no contest, none whatsoever.

"Dray, you can be a relentless predator all you want just as long as I'm your very own personal prey."

The brunette smiled awkwardly and pulled the blonde down on top of her. "Oh, you can count on it, lover." Dray leaned in, a lecherous grin on her face and then felt a fist gently poke her in the stomach.

"But first...well, it's not silver or a cross but maybe," Abby narrowed her eyes conspiratorially, "just maybe this will get me in good with the head fiend."

Dray looked at the small brown jewelry box in panic and quickly looked up into her lover's eyes. Abby took her other hand and smoothed the frown lines blossoming in the woman's forehead. "Oh please, it's just a necklace, not a ring or anything." Dray wasn't sure whether she was disappointed or relieved. Not that a ring wasn't a good idea but that she'd thought perhaps the proposal would be her idea.

Abby smirked as a thoughtful look came into her lover's eyes. *Ah ha. So, she's thought about it, too.* She cleared her throat, reminding herself that they'd only been together for a short while, not a great span of time in itself but a benchmark for her when it came to relationships. No, she decided, it was far too soon. All the silly jokes of U-Hauls aside, Abby was well aware of just how easy it would be to go with her emotions and totally commit. It was a foregone conclusion that Dray was her destiny but how many times had they gone through different lives before they'd ended up in this one?

She firmly believed that a soul had to pass through many existences before the learning requirements were met and a state of inner peace was achieved bringing the soul finally at rest. Abby didn't think they were that far along but didn't want to do anything without really thinking of all the ramifications, thus preventing them from making some sort of cosmic mistake. What if they were supposed to be married and because Abby didn't feel she was ready they missed their chance and somehow changed their future? It hurt her head the more she thought about it.

"So, you gonna open it?" She poked Dray with the box again and then smiled as a lovely gold chain was pulled from the case. Dangling at the end was a St. George's medallion. She held it up and the flames seemed to make it come alive.

Abby's smile slipped a little and she wondered if she'd made a blunder. "If...if you don't like the medallion..."

Dray shook her head and held it out to the blonde. "No, I love it."

Abby bit back her disappointment as the necklace went back into the box. She'd hoped to see the firefighter wearing that as a symbol of their bond and yet it seemed destined to remain in a box deep in some drawer. Deciding this wasn't really the time to get into just why Dray wasn't going to wear her present, she lifted the woman's chin with her forefinger and gazed deeply into endless blue.

"I got you St. George because he slays dragons and I think you do, too. We can exchange it if you want."

Dray reached over and captured her lover's lips in a gentle kiss that seemed to last forever. "Oh God, I love you Abby," she said between kisses. "I'll treasure it forever."

# Chapter 10

Both women sat sunning themselves on the beach, fingers entwined, when Pete appeared beside them. He'd shaved and was wearing his swimming trunks. Dray turned her head briefly, noting he'd brought the dive gear back down to the beach. They were to head back home in the next few days and she felt a little uneasy about doing another dive.

"Oh come on, Dray. I know you want to," Abby prodded. "Tell you what, why don't you and Pete just do this great dive you've been talking about...Hundred Mile Point...or whatever...and Dave and I'll hold down the fort. Whadya say?"

She smirked as Pete's face lit up. Dray's fingers twitched and then she sat up and smiled. Abby would be more than pleased to see that shining face every day of her life forever – and beyond.

"I don't know, Ab."

"We've both had a good night's sleep and," she bit her lower lip, "had a good breakfast hours ago and..."

Dark eyebrows shot up. "Oh, so you're telling me that a good night's sleep consists of about two hours and the stale rations from months ago are enough to satisfy your appetite?"

Pete smiled. "Heh. I thought you might be hungry. I'll be right back."

He wasn't gone for more than ten minutes before both women could smell a combination of coffee and bacon and egg sandwiches.

"You brought me greasy food to chow down on before a dive?"

Pete grinned. "Yeah, great idea, huh?"

Getting to her feet, Dray punched her partner in the shoulder and smirked. "Yeah, ya done good." She searched Abby's face for any tell tale sign of regret and found none. Abby just grinned at her and waved her hands toward the ocean. "Well okay, if you insist. It won't take us long. Say, Pete...race ya to get all the equipment back in the truck."

Pete's eyes danced with merriment. It was like old times. "Sounds like a plan, Stan. Dave's in the cab and the loser gets a face licking. Deal?"

Dray nodded and shook her friend's hand. "You got it. But how come he's stuck in the cab?"

Abby got to her feet and began dragging some of their camping equipment closer to the dive gear. "The poor thing must be beside himself, wanting to race up and down the beach. Like I said, I'll watch him while you two dive."

Pete scratched his neck. "Well, it's like this, I spent almost all night picking little marine life outta that dog's fur, not to mention the sand fleas he now grants residence to. Forget that. Had to buy some special flea powder from the local vet in Victoria and it cost me a Goddamned fortune, regardless of the rate of exchange. So he ain't getting out on this beach for a while."

He turned as Abby made to protest his decision. "Tell ya what – you could take him for a nice walk down Government Street. Heh, not only do they have this great tea place but chocolate..."

Abby groaned. "Tea and chocolate? God, Dray...I think he just described your heaven." Dray smirked. "They sell coffee too, right?"

Pete nodded and then picked a bottle out of his gear. "Here's some of that flea powder and his leash, too. He won't like the dousing but he's gonna be a nice clean mutt for the drive back to Chicago."

Dray shook her head sadly, her empathy rising at the plight Dave was enduring. Dave was an animal that reveled in the freedom of racing up and down the beach and she'd never seen a dog that took more readily to the sea. Most dogs didn't like the taste of fish or other seafood delicacies but Dave sure did. The crabs didn't scare him and after a close encounter with a stinging jellyfish he knew enough to mind them.

The worried look that creased her face didn't go unnoticed. "Honey, I'll take Dave for a nice long walk. Maybe we'll find a playground or a park and he can run around until he drops."

She smiled at the wink her lover gave her and then clicked her teeth at the Lieutenant. "I don't have to give him a bath first, right?"

Pete frowned. "Like Dave'd let ya give him a bath and be subjected to flea powder? That cruel I ain't."

Abby sighed gratefully. "Well, all right then. So, unless you two want to keep yapping..."

It had taken them only five or ten minutes to get all the gear loaded back into the truck. It was Dray's speed that enabled her to make more trips and have most of the gear packed away, thereby winning the contest.

They drove in companionable silence and then made their way over the rocks down to the entry at Ten Mile Point. Abby played with the dog as the two went over the dive tables and factored in slack tide. The Dalmatian groaned dejectedly as Abby held up his leash, causing Pete more than a little concern.

"You wanna go for a walk, Dave? Walkies?" The dog hid his eyes under both paws. "Huh. Well, he didn't get too much sleep last night because of all the scratching. I guess you two will just have to do without tea and chocolate."

Abby grabbed her bottle of suntan lotion. "You know, that works for me, too. Besides, there's always mail order shopping."

The dog yawned again as Pete ruffled his ears before slamming the truck door. "So...gonna suntan in the nude?" Pete yelped as a pinecone bounced off the back of his head. "Hey! I was just askin'." Two blue eyes glittered in his direction.

"We could both be buck naked and given a choice you'd still pick this dive," Dray quipped.

Pete rubbed his jaw thinking about the image Dray had just painted, opened his mouth and then hung his head. "Yeah, you're right. Sad, huh?"

Sidling up behind him, she snapped the waist of his bathing suit. "Yep. Hey, Blondie? We gotta get a girlfriend for this guy. Then we can watch them make out." A pink blush started to flare across his face, beginning at his earlobes. Mumbling something incoherent, Pete grabbed some of the gear and then told Abby about the dog biscuit stash he had in the toolbox in the back of the truck.

Dray snickered as the man quickly made his way down to the cliffs. Then with a quick kiss on the end of her lover's nose, Abby wished both friends a good dive and they were off. Abby spent a good ten minutes getting the blankets and such exactly how she wanted them and then grabbed up her paperback and got comfortable.

An hour went by quickly. She was just in the midst of dozing off when the Dalmatian pushed his way through the back window of the truck to sit in the bed. Feeling two very soulful eyes gazing her way, Abby yawned and stretched and then rummaged through the tools and offered the dog two biscuits. Dave's tail wagged slightly, making a drumming noise against the metal side of the truck.

"Come on, boy." She held up another biscuit and the dog gave one small backward glance at the truck cab and bounded out beside her on the blanket. Grabbing up a rubber ball, Abby looked toward the small thicket of trees by the parking lot and then threw the ball. "Go get it, Dave!"

The dog hesitated for half a second and then scampered after the ball, his close encounter with the vet and flea powder a distant memory.

Dray and Pete did back-to-back dives that afternoon and Abby managed to talk her companion into a brief shore dive at the breakwater in Victoria before the end of the day. Abby found it rather sweet when her lover doted on her while suiting up. Things were different while diving however, and Dray's demeanor was very serious as she focused on the task at hand. That lasted for all of about twenty minutes, until Abby pulled her lover into a heated embrace, kissing the woman soundly. After replacing their regs, Abby held up her gauge and smiled.

A weight seemed to be lifted off of Dray's shoulders after that final dive and she began to mentally set the blonde up in some night courses in Advanced Diving given at the local university back home.

*Home*, she thought longingly.

It had been a relaxing couple of days on the West Coast but both Pete and Dray seemed very keen to get back to work. The drive home was relatively uneventful, the three of them opting to drive straight through from Billings, Montana with each of them taking a shift driving. It was during Dray's time at the wheel that Pete began to notice a sense of withdrawal coming from his partner, at first putting it down to a lack of sleep. After all, three adults and a dog that preferred the company of humans to a lonely truck's bed certainly made for a cramped living space. However, before too long the woman's moodiness was more than apparent and Pete sat silently, his efforts to draw her out dwindling down to nothing.

Dray absently stroked her lover's temple as she cradled Abby's head in her lap. Pete was surprised at how easy it was to get her to relinquish the wheel at the last gas station. He noted the new necklace she wore and tried to engage his friend in some easy banter. It all fell on deaf ears and Pete felt the woman withdraw a little further behind her walls.

Dave rumbled low in the back of his throat and seemed to be watching the woman with trepidation, almost as if she were an oncoming storm. Bolts of electricity seemed ready to fly from her blazing eyes and his flanks quivered with anticipation. Pete kept glancing his way, offering a word or two to calm the dog but nothing seemed to relieve the tension as they pushed on toward home.

Pete offered to help get Abby upstairs as they finally rolled in front of Dray's apartment building. But a curt shake of Dray's head stopped him in his tracks. While he'd been through Dray's darker moods and lived to tell the tale, this one seemed deeper than the others and he couldn't help but wonder just what was going on inside the woman's head, especially after the wonderful vacation they all shared.

Abby had awakened enough to stumble up the stairs leading to the entranceway of their building, but Pete could see she'd be asleep as soon as her head hit the pillow. Although there were dark circles under the woman's eyes, she'd gotten quite a bit of sun, bronzing up nicely beneath the clear western sky.

The man sat in his truck, scratching the tender area behind his dog's ears, wondering just what had transpired between the two women. There had been some tension after the Henderson dive but things had seemed much better the past couple of days.

He shook his head, muttering nonsensically to his adoring companion, who seemed more than willing to be soothed by his master's voice. The sense of foreboding had lessened for the dog as soon as Dray had left the cab. The dog whined and Pete threw the stick into gear. A couple of backfires later and they were on their way.

Abby had stood mutely, eyes closed, as her lover removed all of the rumpled clothing she'd been wearing for the last 24 hours. Even though they'd both gotten into bed, it was a long while before the brunette's eyes fluttered closed and she dropped into an uneasy slumber.

Once asleep, Dray pictured a man as he pulled on his uniform jacket. His insignia glittered dully in the waning afternoon light. He wiped at it, frowned, and then carefully pushed his collar back into place. *It will have to do.* Although the words were spoken in another language, Dray had no problem understanding them. She looked around the area of the dreamscape where she stood as an unnoticed observer. It was a rather dank office, devoid of any human touch; very Spartan and very typical of military quarters found anywhere.

There was a small stove in the corner, its door gaping open like a hungry maw. Dray wondered why there wasn't anything in it; it was obvious the man was chilled. Then a woman with a hat pulled down to cover her ears shuffled in, her threadbare clothing showing her malnutrition.

Her posture lent a certain defiance that seemed in stark opposition to the image she held up for display. It was obvious that the soldier could see past the façade easily and Dray watched as his temper escalated.

Dray ground her teeth in frustration, the bedclothes twisting in her fists. Why couldn't this dream just end? Why did it have to repeat over and over with nothing put to rest?

Her eyes fluttered and her heartbeat began to slow; the dream would fade, as usual, and she'd wake up soaked to the skin and wondering why the dream wouldn't resolve itself. What was it trying to tell her? Well, if she couldn't control the dream she could control how she would respond. Instead of twisting the sheets around her, Dray forced her body to unclench and relax. When she felt like her body was melting into the mattress, she released a breath and fell back into a deep sleep. This time when the dream began to take up where it had left off, Dray felt less harried and dragged unwillingly along.

Dray's eyes danced feverishly under lids closed tightly as the scene continued.

"Why is the fire not lit?" the man asked.

Silence.

"One day you will push too hard, little one. One day I will let them have you, and then where will you be?"

The small figure lifted her head and Dray could tell by the man's response that she was openly staring at him.

"You promised food if I worked for you. So far you have taken what you want from my body without giving anything in return. Now you expect me to be your personal slave, too? You owe me."

With a howl of rage, the man flew across the desk grabbing her up with a large hand fastened around her thin throat.

"You dare to dictate to me? I let you live, prisoner, be pleased you have my interest," he sneered at her. "It might change before too long, when your worthiness comes to an end. Already I am becoming bored with a creature such as you. Continue to please me and continue to live."

A harsh slap rang out as the soldier's temper got the best of him. It was obvious to Dray that the man wasn't used to defiance, and certainly not from a wisp of a girl who by rights should be treating him with respect born of fear if nothing else. As the soldier shook the woman her hat fell crumpled to the ground.

Dray's heart felt pierced as she recognized the bruised face.

*Zosia.*

At some time during the night, Dray got up and went out onto the balcony, pen and paper in hand. Lightening began flashing in the distance across the darkened sky and the surrounding air became super charged with positive ions as she began to write furiously. Crumpled paper sat under and around her lawn chair, but Dray remained undaunted as she squinted in the lantern's glow and continued to write.

Abby slept soundly, oblivious to the approaching storm.

The next morning was dull and gray with the promise of rain and while the humidity rose, it was kept at bay until late afternoon.

Dray stood looking out the window as the heavens finally opened up, splattering the panes with cold rivulets of rain. Although it was now into autumn, the days were still comfortable with the heat of a late Indian summer. The rain was a welcomed respite and Dray pressed her forehead against the cool glass gratefully. She started as a small hand moved up the small of her back.

"Hey, sweets. You're a million miles away, huh? Wanna talk?" Dray stilled her own hand as it moved up the back of her neck.

"Been thinking is all." She said, dismissing any further talk on the subject.

Abby had been aware of her lover's moodiness but knew it would pass. She seriously doubted whether Dray had ever taken two weeks off for a vacation. Pete had basked in the time away from their hazardous job but Dray seemed preoccupied after the first three days.

"Think a bad storm is comin'. I can almost feel the electricity across my skin." The taller woman turned and pinned Abby with a fervent gaze. "You can feel it, right? The energy? It feels like being underwater, caught in a rip tide."

Abby frowned and then placed both hands on Dray's upper arms. "What's the matter, baby? You seem really jumpy. You having those nightmares again?"

Dray dropped her gaze and turned back to the window. Abby frowned as the woman's shoulders slumped and then had to lean forward in an effort to hear the soft muttering of her lover.

"Yeah, but I don't want to talk about it, okay? Not now."

Abby nodded once but wasn't willing to let the woman completely off the hook. She knew something was bothering Dray and decided then and there that if she didn't want the woman's mood to get any worse she'd have to do some probing.

The same dream had plagued the firefighter for as long as she could remember. Sometimes days, even weeks passed and Dray would be free of her nightmares. Then it would begin again. Abby had gotten somewhat used to the midnight wanderings of her lover after the first few months but it still bothered her that Dray didn't feel comfortable enough to talk about them.

"Is it the same dream or do they change from night to night?" Getting no reply, she turned and went to put the kettle on for another pot of tea. "Hey, Dray? Why don't we have some of that tea we got in Victoria? You game? And chocolate, too. I mean, what the heck, let's live dangerously." Dray didn't answer and continued to stare out at the gathering storm.

Abby sighed deeply and decided to just keep her distance for a while until Dray gave her some sort of clue that she was ready to resume their lives. It was times like this that Abby felt the most vulnerable. Dray was the strong one, the protector with more than capable shoulders, and her shelter from whatever life would throw at them.

A few hours went by and still Dray stood by the window. Abby tried to entice the woman with a nice fresh salad, and had even waved a hero sandwich nearby but Dray was having nothing to do with either. The silence was making the blonde uneasy

"C'mon, Dray, you've got to talk to me. Tell me what's going on. You've been like this before but never for so long. Is there," she frowned and then went on, "have I done something..."

"S'okay. I'll be fine, just need some time alone is all." She frowned as Abby grabbed her by the arm and dragged her away from the fading daylight. Sighing heavily, Dray allowed her lover to remove both sneakers and socks. She lay back against the headboard, lost in thought, totally oblivious to the young woman who was quietly disrobing before her.

Abby ground her teeth a little and then pushed onward. If she was going to help Dray out of this funk she was in, well, it was going to take a lot of patience and even a seduction scene or two.

As the brunette laid there, every fiber in her body felt as if it were twitching. She felt an overwhelming sense of foreboding, almost as if an anvil were sitting on her chest making each breath a Herculean labor.

Slowly removing her shirt and pants, Abby added a wiggle here and a grind there, doing her best burlesque imitation. She remembered watching a great old movie with Shirley Somebody or other doing the bump and grind. She thought it was sexy and had filed the info away for another time. Right now seemed perfect. Hearing the squeak of the bed she zoned back in, her mouth agape as the taller woman just got off the bed and walked away. "Dray?" She stood there in total dismay as the woman grabbed her coveralls and toolbox.

Dray ducked once as the thunder crashed directly overhead. She punched the elevator for the basement and stood impatiently, drumming her fingers against her thigh.

Abby appeared in the hallway wearing a short bathrobe. "Honey? What's wrong?"

Dray looked up but found it hard to meet her lover's eyes. Just what was up? All she knew was there was something coming, something bad. That little voice inside was all but screaming and had been ever since the last day of their vacation. *Vacation...more like enforced exile,* she thought in a fit of pique. Oh, the first few days had been good; sleeping under the stars had been the best. It had always been hard for her to sit still and just relax for long periods of time. Inactivity made her antsy and moody, and regardless of how much she loved being with Abby it was just hard to step away from the mindset that was needed to be a firefighter and slow everything down. While some of the guys really looked forward to time off, she couldn't be counted in their company, preferring the high tension and rigid focus that the job required.

The brunette thought back to that night under the stars, that wonderful moment when she'd truly felt happy, relaxed and at peace. Learning that Abby had been strong enough to not only fend off that pedophile but also flee her home had clarified a few things for Dray; she couldn't look at the young woman as being vulnerable or dependant any more.

Anyone could hide in the shelters and curry favors with the dominant gangs. It hadn't been a path that Abby could follow, however. She'd shunned that and had simply made a niche for herself, using good intuition to make friends that would help instead of use, refusing to get caught up in violence and crime.

It was quite an amazing feat and Dray admired her all the more because of it. She wasn't sure why but it was shortly thereafter when the nightmares started to come back. This time, though, there was a different feel to them, almost as if Dray could sense them reaching out to her, pulling her into the action instead of letting her merely bear witness.

She shook her head slowly, pushing away the sinking feeling that something or someone was coming.

"Why are you pushing me away, Dray? Why are you running? Have you...I thought you were – we were happy."

Suddenly Abby felt disjointed as if the world had just shifted. She closed her eyes and could almost smell the cold gray air, the groan of the other prisoners, and the overwhelming certainty that death awaited them all. She began to hyperventilate, the air somehow poisoned and closing in on her.

Dray's eyes widened and she snapped out of her fog as Abby stumbled, blindly stretching a hand out. A cold feeling of fear and guilt hit her squarely and she suddenly felt the enormity of her actions: when she should have been pulling her lover closer, she'd been pushing her away. Dray rushed forward and then embraced Abby, holding her very close. "I'm sorry, so sorry, baby. I...I haven't been honest with you...or myself. God."

Abby blinked up at the solemn expression on her lover's face and felt fear clutching at her belly. Finally, the room stopped pitching and the tears began to fall. Turning away she reached back and pulled Dray towards their apartment and then carefully closed the door.

The firefighter placed her equipment on the floor and then slowly stood up. How was she going to explain something that she didn't understand herself? She took a breath and then opened her mouth to speak. Her jaw snapped closed as she noticed the pallor in Abby's face. And then the blonde began to speak and she felt her guts twist into tight knots.

"When do you want me to...leave? It won't," she wiped her runny nose on the back of her trembling hand, "take me long to pack up."

Dray's heart wrenched painfully as Abby's face crumbled and she felt hot tears spring to her own blind eyes. Her lack of explanation left Abby open to the only conclusion she could think of – she wasn't wanted. *Good going, Dray.*

"Oh God, Abby, no. Look at me." It broke Dray's heart to think she had caused her to question their love and their life together. Cradling the woman's tearful face, Dray locked eyes with her and then, in a trembling voice spoke from her heart. "This isn't about 'us' or about 'you.' This is...the dream is back but it's something more this time. I can't put my finger on it. Oh God." Suddenly Abby's fears about being rejected, about being parted from the only person she'd ever loved, vanished and all she could see was Dray's need for her right now. She pulled the woman over to the couch and they sat holding each other close. Abby placed her head over Dray's heart and just stayed there, waiting for the staccato thumping to slow and even out. Finally, she looked up and watched as two gloriously blue eyes met her own.

"Everything we've ever done, Dray, in our lives has brought us to this moment in time. All the pain and horrors we've been through have helped shape who and what we are. I couldn't imagine going through what you have and still be sane. That takes strength. Living on the streets was hard, yes, but I never had the kind of loss you've had. And I'm not too sure just what kind of relationship you had with Debbie Nang, but I think she gave you a gift you couldn't appreciate then but can understand now. Am I right? She could sense your strengths, Dray, and she utilized them but also fortified them, giving you a sense of your own worth."

Dray looked at the blonde, her mouth hanging open. "Where the heck did that come from?"

Abby bit her lower lip self-consciously and ran her hand along Dray's arm. "Well, I've had some time to think about this the past few days. I thought you might be comparing what we have to, I dunno, her and you discovered that I didn't measure up. Maybe you'd made a mistake by asking me to stay."

The firefighter tilted her head back, blinking the hot tears that began forming and shut her eyes tightly.

"God, Ab...no. Debbie was important – she made an impact on my life. I think...I know I loved her but," she reached down and grabbed Abby's hands, "I loved her the only way I could back then and with what little I had. She taught me how to love myself, Abby, and because of that I could begin to open my own heart and share something of myself with another human being."

She let her lover's hands fall, paused and then pulled shaking fingers through her hair before she continued. "I was so fucked up, babe. I didn't want to give myself to anyone, knowing that in a fraction of a second they could be taken away from me. Love was an investment; something I felt had to be measured out carefully. I gave her what I had but I can see now that it was just a small fragment of the bigger picture. I think she sensed that, too. Although we were rather close in age, she always made me feel like a young punk, someone she had to nurture and care for. And I guess she was right."

"But don't you see Dray, she could sense what you had inside. I'm just glad she was there to offer the nurturing you so desperately needed and that you were strong enough to accept it."

Dray nodded and then cleared her throat roughly. "I think maybe I could use a little time and something to drink." She looked down, seeing her lover's robe falling open. "And why are you dressed like that? Not that I'm complaining but you were just in clothes not two seconds ago, right?" Running a hand over the back of her neck, she narrowed her eyes. "Did I miss something?"

The blonde smiled and patted the firefighter's hand. "You just stay right here and I'll put the kettle on." She got up and cinched the belt around her robe as she moved about the kitchen. "You've been kinda preoccupied, Dray. You tend to zone out when something is bothering you and you've been gone most of the day. You know? Really gone. I kinda thought if I distracted you a bit you'd relax and tell me what was going on. Hence the robe." She turned and loosened the belt, letting the robe fall open, revealing some of her many charms.

"I figured it must be pretty bad, whatever was bothering you, because you didn't even notice me. I mean, Dray...just where were you going with your stuff?"

Dray looked over to the door and frowned at her toolbox and coveralls. Arching an eyebrow she gazed up at Abby and smiled.

"Ah...well, when I really get zonked I tend to go and work on something. I guess it was my bike. That damned petcock has me all but spitting nickels. I don't know what the fuck is going on with her."

"Ah hah...so there is another female in your life. You and that motorcycle, tsk tsk."

Dray smirked at the woman's pretense at jealousy. "Yeah, we do so many hot things together. I love to get down and dirty with her whenever I can. And she moves me, babe. Like no one else can. Someday we'll both take her for a spin and I can test that theory."

Abby reached up and swatted the woman's shoulder and then moved into the kitchen. She hummed softly while scooping the fresh grounds into the machine, pressed the button and then cranked the stove up to high for hot water. Passing a hand over her forehead she sighed and then plunked herself back down on the couch. Soon the apartment was filled with the gurgling of the coffee maker and a whistle announcing water was ready for tea.

# Chapter 11

"Look, I gotta go. That was Ted. Pete and a couple of other squads went into this warehouse just before lunch today and," Dray grabbed up her beeper and checked her watch, "some of the others have been located but not Pete and his crew."

"Is he alright?" Abby asked.

"That's what I'm gonna find out. I'm officially on leave for another coupla days but," she grabbed up her jacket and pulled the door open, "I have to go down there, Abby. Another pair of hands can't hurt and besides, it's my squad."

"Dray, I want to come." The firefighter flashed the blonde a doubtful look. "No, really. I want to know Pete's okay and I promise not to get in the way."

She saw the determined look on her lover's face and Dray knew she'd be wasting her breath. "Alright," she said as she checked the battery life on the beeper and left the apartment. "Get your shoes on."

The brunette took the stairs two at a time and then raced to the underground parking lot. Casting a brief look at her bike, she jumped into her truck and sat revving the engine, praying Pete would be all right and that she'd be in time to help. Blood red fire began coursing through her veins as she felt her own motor begin to rev. Just when she thought she couldn't possibly wait another second, the side door was thrown open and Abby jumped into the cab.

"Let's go!"

It was half past three in the afternoon when they arrived. The cordons were already in place and both women could see throngs of police and firefighters working together around the industrial park.

Dray stepped out of her truck and climbed into the back, shielding her eyes she surveyed the destruction before her. Two smaller buildings had already been reduced to blackened hulls and another larger one was slowly being consumed despite the efforts of the fire crews.

Dray counted the pumper trucks and other vehicles and whistled. The area was dense with billowing gray smoke and, for a moment, she wondered what all the fuss was about; there were far too many fire trucks involved for a normal run of the mill industrial fire. She felt Abby slip an arm around her waist and then tore her eyes away from the scene.

"Dray?" The brunette bent down closer in order to hear over the roar of the fire and the general garble of onlookers and service personnel. "It seems the cops and firefighters have everything under control. Any sign of your team?" Abby asked.

The wind shifted and there, sitting like a giant malignant spider, was a very large charred-looking building. It almost seemed to pulse with energy and Dray could feel something slowly creep over her heart.

"Abby, you can't stay here."

"Dray?"

"Look, the fire marshal is getting the area clear of folks who'll just be in the way." She jumped down and then helped the blonde back into the cab. She grabbed her gear and pressed her keys into the woman's hands, then stood back and began searching the crowd. Abby could see the mind-shift in her lover; she was already gone, focusing on the task at hand.

A policeman came up and began yelling instructions. Dray removed her wallet and showed her ID and Abby watched him wildly gesticulating in her direction. She watched the man's mouth and could almost hear his words.

"You gotta get that fuckin' truck outta here. I don't care who you are. And she's a fuckin' civilian! You know the procedure. Get her outta here. Now!"

Hearing the tail end of the discussion Abby made her way to the driver's seat. Dray ran back over and hopped back inside pointing down the block. "Drive," she ordered.

Seeing a parking space, Dray motioned Abby over and she stopped the vehicle.

"Dray?"

"Okay Ab, keep the scanner on the police frequency," Dray reached in and dialed in the correct bandwidth, "right here. You keep it on that one and you should stay up to date, right? Now, you get going and I'll catch you later. Can't say when, though." She removed her watch and then paused for a second before removing her necklace. "Could be a little bit hot in there if I wear these. You keep 'em for me, alright?"

Abby looked at the items and nodded, swallowing back a sob as Dray exited the cab. Dray never took off the necklace she had given her...she'd bought it for the firefighter because, somehow, it connected them. A nice, small, box link chain, it just seemed to be the kind of thing Dray would wear. She knew that if Dray was taking it off now then it was a dangerous situation. She searched her lover's face and saw past Dray's stoic façade and into the shadows just behind her eyes. Her belly clenched tightly as she picked through the jumble of emotions and found what she least expected: fear.

Abby's hand reached out of the window, clutching at her lover's sleeve. "Is it bad, Dray?" The brunette swiveled her gaze back from the crowd and Abby could tell she wanted to say something. However, Dray was distracted as she heard her name being yelled and Ted pushed through the crowd, rushing over, helmet in hand.

"Thank god. I was hoping you'd get down here quick. Listen...oh, s'cuse me, hiya Abby," his head bobbed once in deference. "Look, we got us a problem. The Lieutenant, he was in one group and me and a coupla others was in another. One of the Lieutenants from another station had gone in earlier but," he wiped the soot and perspiration from his cheek, "the radio's been patchy for awhile now." Abby sat, mouth agape as Ted seemed to just ramble on and on in a nervous rush until he ran out of spit. After a deep swallow, he continued. "I was a headin' the group that was doing the back exits and we found some victims – serious third-degree damage." Dray darted a quick look at her lover, elbowing the man before gripping the hand at her sleeve.

Dray waved a hand frantically. "Okay, okay. Jeez Ted, don't start getting too graphic on Abby, will ya?" She released Abby's hand. "Stay here," she said addressing Abby. "I've gotta get inside," she said before she moved a short distance away. "Just how many body bags we lookin' at here? And where's Pete?" Dray asked her team member.

Abby watched as the two firefighters began going into rather descriptive detail, her presence forgotten. The two tall forms only stopped their conversation when another policeman started yelling in their direction.

Abby could see that very familiar far away look her lover got and knew she wasn't even really there anymore but inside the burning warehouse, figuring things out. She opened her mouth to tell them both to be careful but Dray had already turned and was running through the crowd, Ted hot on her heels.

Abby sat gripping the steering wheel, watching the two of them disappear into the crowd without a backward glance or any words of endearment before she'd left.

"I love you too, Dray."

The two firefighters moved carefully forward, poking at the timbers as they went by in an effort to make a path for the two others bringing up the rear. Johnson hefted one of the large hoses, checking to see that neither one of them got tangled while Peters did a periodic inspection of each joint to see that the hoses were still firmly secured to the hydrants outside. They'd gone to the back of the warehouse but could see the flames licking through the doorframe, the metal door already blackened and bulging in several spots. Dragging their equipment around to the side of the building, they found the office area still intact. Lieutenant Pete Melrose looked at the available information on the building's structure – a combination of metal and wood, new material and old – and could see this fire wasn't going to be as straight-forward as initially thought. He quickly relayed the information on the small radio and then the four of them began to work the area.

The offices were empty, the floor littered with papers and books that lay curled in drying puddles caused by the now defunct sprinklers. Pete and the other firefighters were just beginning to think the fire might be confinable and there'd be a very low body count when Rodriguez had tried to push open the door leading to the other offices. Putting their backs to it, they'd finally gotten the door opened only to find the hallway filled with smoke and half a dozen dead bodies. It hadn't taken the Lieutenant long to realize the people had panicked and had become lost and disoriented in the smoke. The majority of the victims inside had probably become trampled in the stampede of people.

It had taken them a good ten minutes to move through the carnage into the main corridor of the office complex. They'd split off into two teams, each equipped with fire axes and a flame-retardant hose.

The Lieutenant began juggling the odds, factoring in probable survivor ratios along with worst-case scenarios and came out with an analysis he really wasn't prepared to face. The statement from the warehouse owner had the employee count at 89 working that day and the body count had already hit seven – the other fatality radioed in by Lieutenant Rick Bobbec before he went silent. Both team leaders had decided any chance of success would be determined by how quickly the people could be found. With a flip of a coin, Pete had taken the back door with Bobbec heading out to the far side of the building and entering through a side exit clearly marked on the floor plans. He'd given Rick a quick handshake and watched as the last man on the team had dragged the hose out of sight. Pete checked his watch – it had been a good forty minutes since they'd split up and he wondered what had befallen the other team.

At this point, with a good chance of getting the rest of the survivors out, the fire marshal was reluctant to just contain the area and let the fire burn itself out. However, an uneasy ripple effect had hit the squad when Bobbec hadn't checked in. At this point they had to assume the worst and add seven more bodies to the count.

Pete hitched the tank on his back and gave his crew the thumbs up, watching as Rodriguez and Peters disappeared into the billowing smoke, fervently hoping they'd have better luck finding survivors. He blinked the sweat out of his eyes and noticed the temperature was beginning to climb. He motioned to Johnson and watched as the man doused the area with a blast of water and then both men grabbed the hose and pushed on.

Parts of the hallway were so thick with smoke that each man stood as close as he could to the other, moving in tandem. The Lieutenant began noticing a slight itching to his wrist where the skin was exposed and wondered about the type of chemicals hanging in the air around them, bathing them in a cloying embrace. He heard static and reached once more for the radio.

"Lieut...co...across...total o...fi..." Pete increased the volume on the radio and tried to find another channel. The garbled transmission ended in a hiss and then...nothing. He'd recognized Mark Rodriguez's worried voice and figured they'd found more bodies. He checked his wristband, noting they were still headed south. He felt a tug on his sleeve as they rounded a bend and nodded as the other firefighter pointed at a few flames licking the ceiling. Opening the hose in a few short controlled bursts, Matt Johnson grinned as he watched part of the beast die.

Both men proceeded carefully around the corner, feeling the increase in temperature, and Johnson quickly opened the hose again. This part of the rabbit warren was much closer to where the storage area was and Pete tried to figure out just what kind of chemicals they'd be dealing with. Not that it mattered; it was all toxic and highly flammable. He prayed none of them would interact to create a deadly combination that would eat through their protective gear.

They watched as black, thick sludge dripped down the walls and then stepped back as one area of drywall collapsed upon itself, part of the ceiling falling in as well. Pete cast his partner a somber look as part of the room next door was exposed.

Making their way through the damaged wall, the Lieutenant stopped suddenly, their way blocked by the partially charred remains of what used to be people. He closed his eyes tightly at the sight, feeling his belly turn over. Not taking in too much of the grisly remains as they became visible, Johnson held up three fingers and cocked his head. Pete nodded and mentally added them to the growing tally. It was apparent they'd tried to get out one of the small windows in the lavatory and had been overcome by fumes. He kicked what was left of the wooden door closed and poked Johnson with his axe handle.

"C'mon," he yelled, "let's keep moving."

"Rodriguez?" Silence greeted his transmission. He gave the radio a hard shake and received a loud hiss for his efforts. Johnson used the axe to make sure they were at the farthest firewall and then both men began walking back the way they had come. They finally came to the juncture where the main group had split up and Pete tried to use the radio once more. Nothing. The Lieutenant switched to the main channel.

"Melrose here. We've lost contact with Rodriguez and Peters. Wally, can you raise them on your end?" He paused, listening to the somewhat garbled message, and then pounded his thigh. He distinctively heard the word 'No' and had to assume their fellow firefighters were still missing. "Okay, out." He returned the radio to its pouch and then took a deep breath.

"We gotta go find 'em, Matt." Matt Johnson nodded and then each man prepared himself for the gauntlet. Walking through the bodies had been hard once; having to pick through and untangle the hose was going to be sheer hell.

Johnson tried not to pay close attention as he bent to untangle the hose but his mind picked out the things his eyes refused to see; each melted and blackened body part analyzed and catalogued for future use, the main attraction in the nightmares he'd have for months afterwards.

Pete steadied his breathing, repeatedly reminding himself to get a grip; he'd been in hundreds of fires and had seen this sort of thing before. But still...he fought the urge to look closer and then reeled back in horror as parts of the bodies began to be recognizable in the lump of God's clay before them. He fought the urge to vomit, his subconscious recording the images of blistered bodies, their tight skin bursting in some areas as the coarse canvass hose dragged across like 80 grit sandpaper.

Johnson made a move to take off his mask, his eyes wide as his state of panic accelerated. Grabbing him firmly about the shoulders, Pete pressed his face against the man's mask, willing the man to meet his gaze. Finally, Johnson nodded slowly and swallowed. It was then that Pete noticed the small blisters forming on his left wrist where his glove hadn't quite covered the skin. Then he reached up and pushed the other man's helmet up, noticing the chemical burn spreading across the man's forehead and temples. He hadn't noticed Johnson had removed his helmet insert and cursed. Lifting a trembling hand, he noticed his own neck snaps had come undone, exposing a small rectangle of flesh.

He swallowed and noticed his tongue felt swollen. Closing his eyes briefly, the Lieutenant dragged out the radio.

"Dispatch...we have an injured firefighter here," he breathed, his heartbeat thumping in his ears. "I'm gonna get him over by the far firewall."

Johnson's eyes went wide with terror. "Lieutenant," his voice rose, "what about the other crew?"

Pete blinked a few times and shook his head. "I gotta get you out, buddy." Then he spoke into the radio again. "There's a small bathroom window there." He cleared his throat again. "You'll have to get a coupla guys to start widening the frame, and do it quick. It's Johnson and it looks like he's showing some of the signs of poisoning." He paused, darting a quick look at the other red patches that seemed to be spreading. "I've got a tally of the dead; the list is growing." The radio crackled and Pete struggled to concentrate on the dispatcher. "No, I haven't been able to reach the others but I'm at the junction now so they can't be too much farther...yeah...I'm fine. Take us five – ten minutes to get there. Out."

The Lieutenant took the man by the shoulders and gave him a reassuring squeeze. "Listen bud, I'm gonna get you outta here, okay? You're pretty well wasted and you got some chem burns, Matt." He patted the man's shoulder confidently. "You'll be fine, trust me. But you can't stay here any longer or I'll be draggin' your sorry butt as well as the others," he coughed, "when I find 'em. Ok?"

165

Matt tilted his head back against the wall and swore silently. This was only his second year as a firefighter and his first encounter with a chem fire. Even after all the preparations he discovered he had been woefully lacking in just what was going to be expected – of him and the fire itself. He took a few steps and then nodded, taking the Lieutenant's hand in his own. A firm grip later, both men were on their way back through the carnage. This time, the hose was left behind and they made better time than either expected.

They got to the last corner and Pete yanked the lavatory door open, easing both of them by the bodies. Matt could see the window frame begin to splinter and then Pete held him back as they both watched cinder blocks being hammered out of the way. Both men felt the urge to hurry into the arms of safety but stood silently until two heavily gloved hands reached through.

"I'm sorry but you can't go in. Look here," Captain Dougherty paused until he could make out Ted's name and station number, "Monson is it? Well, you can't just barge in here and go off half-cocked. I know you got crew in there and yes, two teams are not responding to radio hails but until we know what we're dealing with we don't wanna send in any more crews."

Dray elbowed her way around Ted and reached out a friendly hand to the fire marshal. The man frowned and then peered closely at the firefighter before him. Under all that equipment were two very blue and familiar eyes staring back at him.

"Dray?" He pulled her into a bear hug and then stood back, gazing at her like a long lost daughter.

James Dougherty was a bull of a man and had been a firefighter himself for almost fifteen years before being booted so far up the ladder that he'd had to take his present job or end up flying a desk. He loved the life of a fireman, the danger, excitement, and the glory. He'd been one of the trainers when an angry young spitfire had taken her basic training. He knew quality when he saw it and took pride in taking the woman under his wing, coaching her and teaching her after hours when all the rest of the recruits had finished for the evening.

"So, how are ya, stranger? You here as back up?" He gave Ted the once over, noting the smudged face. "Say, you from the other team? With Bobbec? You reported in, right?"

Dray smiled winningly, distracting the man immediately. "Well, Jim...you know how it is? Can't resist the call of the siren, now can I? You know Pete's in there, right? Well see, I'm just off this course dealing primarily with chemical fires and I was supposed to be in there advising him. But, well, duty calls. All right?"

She tapped Ted on the shoulder and pushed the man ahead of her through the cordon. She grabbed Dougherty's hand again and pumped it vigorously.

"Really great to see ya, Jim. You're looking pretty fit even if you got a desk job now," she teased. "Listen, you and Marilyn come over to my place for pasta one night this week, huh? We'll catch up!"

The man smiled and sucked in his gut, a faint blush coming up his collar. He opened his mouth to reply, suddenly noticing that both firefighters were moving quickly away through the crowd towards the building, and then it hit him.

"Dray! Aw, shit...goddamnittohell! How does she do that?" He muttered under his breath and then picked up his radio and spoke quickly into it.

All but running around the side of the building, the two firefighters finally came to a halt and ran through equipment checks as quick as possible before Jim could get out a warning to stop them. "Close yer mouth, Ted – you'll catch flies," Dray ribbed.

Ted blinked a couple of times and then shut his mouth. "How'n hell did we get past the cordons, Dray? One minute this guy's givin' me grief and then," he chuckled knowingly.

"Well we're not in yet," Dray said looking around her from someone that might come by and thwart their efforts.

Ted chuckled. "Why, you opened that pretty mouth, dincha, and sweet talked your way past?"

Dray grinned briefly, the look on Jim's face still fresh in her mind. "Yeah, well, whatever. I'm gonna end up payin' for that in the end. Hell, I might even have to get Abby to make vegetarian pasta and actually have them over to the apartment."

Ted grimaced at the mere thought of vegetarian anything. Green squiggly noodles just didn't sit well with his southern upbringing. "Ack, no sir. Gimme turnip greens, collards cooked with ham and some hot corn bread."

"And of course, don't forget the grits," Dray added.

Ted just chuckled as Dray spun him around and checked his tank. She tapped him on the helmet and he took a couple of breaths, nodding once.

"You sure you wanna go back in, Ted? I mean..."

Ted looked at her. "Wull, yeah. Pete's in there, ain't he? You'd do the same. 'Sides, I was only in long enough for that blaze to scare the fool outta me. I figure I'll be just fine now," he chortled.

Dray smirked. "How long was long enough, Ted? You and Bobbec got split up and then what? When did you decide to get the hell out?"

Ted scratched his cheek where he could still feel the warmth of the woman's hand. "Well, I figure about fifteen minutes. Couldn't be more than that. The bunch of us kinda split up almost immediately, figuring we'd have better luck finding survivors. But we got lost in there where the offices are coverin' the back exit and Lieutenant Bobbec sent me out. I think he figured I'd find the others and join up with Pete somehow. But in that smoke we all got turned around and," Ted swallowed a few times, remembering the panic that had gripped him when he realized the other firefighter he'd been paired with were nowhere to be found. Guilt sat in his belly like some carnivorous beast, eating at him from the inside. There was no way he was not going back in there...he had to. "We gotta go back in, Dray. We just gotta."

There had been many a night when Dray had found herself caught in the throws of guilt over what she'd done or not done in a crisis situation. Lives had been lost. While it was a harsh reality, being a firefighter had some truths that were undeniable; not being able to save a fellow firefighter or not being at the right place at the right time to prevent a death were just a few of them.

Dray snugged on her mask and took a few breaths. Satisfied, she got a little closer to the man and said in a loud voice, "S'okay, Ted. I know you did your best. You always do. Don't beat yourself up too much buddy, 'cause deep down you know just how fucking lucky you are to have gotten out of there unscathed." She gripped his shoulder hard. "Right now we're Pete's only chance. We'll find him. And with any luck, maybe some of the others, too."

He gave her a weak smile and two thumbs up. Dray winked and tried to think positively. Things were never good when firefighters got lost. It was probably some sort of miracle that Ted had found his way out in the first place, let alone tempting the Fates by going back in. However, she knew he was her best chance of retracing the path the others had taken.

"Ok, let's give me the once over and get movin'."

Dray made sure everything was tight and secure, did a few deep knee bends and then looked back down the street where her lover sat parked.

*Love you, Abby.*

Wordlessly she followed Ted.

Abby sat in the truck fiddling with the keys wondering just what Dray was up to at that very moment. She felt a blanket of tension settle around her shoulders and wished she'd kissed her lover, or at least hugged her once more, before letting her walk away. Her mind began playing the old 'If only' game as she detached the radio from the bracket and angrily pulled the keys from the steering column.

The walk upstairs was painful; she just didn't want to go into the apartment alone. Feeling as if she should have stayed back at the warehouse fire, Abby thought briefly about just going back to the truck and, "Then what?" She sighed, resigned to another lonely evening.

Oh, they weren't too bad for the most part, and she was getting used to them but she really felt differently about this one. Why had Dray taken off that necklace? What did she know and she wasn't telling her?

"She never even kissed me goodbye."

She wasn't sure how she got down the hall and opened the door and was quite surprised to be standing in the kitchen without memories of any of it. She placed the radio on the table and slipped into a chair, her hands fisted tightly in her lap.

The clock ticked loudly as she stared at the radio. Finally, she got up and turned the coffee maker on, staring blankly off into space. The hour chimed on the clock and she jumped a little. After fidgeting with the cup and spoon, her thoughts dragged her back over to the table where the radio sat like a fat beetle, all black and shiny.

She looked away and tried to concentrate on each drip that ran through the coffee filter. Closing her eyes, she could almost hear Dray lifting her weights in the other room. Finally, the coffee forgotten, she crossed over to the table and switched on the radio. At first there was nothing but static but then she heard someone ask a question about the squad that just went in and she thought of Dray and Ted. Grabbing the radio and pulling it closer, Abby turned the volume up and sat with her mouth dry and heart pounding. She squeezed her eyes shut as Pete said a firefighter was injured.

"Oh, please no...Dray...anyone but her...please." And then a mixture of relief and guilt struck her hard when she heard Johnson's name mentioned. She remembered seeing him at one of the station's barbecues. She had brief images of a man of average height and weight, smiling and whistling at the Dalmatian. How could she wish anything to happen to that nice guy, trading Dray's fate for his?

Suddenly, she heard the words 'chemical poisoning' and felt the blood drain from her face. "Dray."

Although it wasn't the first chemical fire she'd been in, Dray felt an uneasy and foreboding feeling settle over her. She wondered whether Rodriguez and his team had gotten out all right. They'd gone quiet a good twenty-five minutes ago and Dray put the radio to her ear, trying to ascertain any further info on either the missing firefighters or the victims they'd gone in after. She cursed under her breath, thinking of the loss of life this had cost already. One firefighter had been removed because of chemical poisoning and almost a dozen bodies had been pulled from the blaze. Then Ted discovered three more.

It broke her heart listening as he retold of the carnage he'd witnessed in his brief bout with the blaze and his account was so vivid that she could almost see the grisly scene play out before her. They'd barricaded themselves in a room, mistakenly thinking they could hold the fire at bay until help came. *Things never work out that way*, Dray thought sadly and pushed the images away.

She moved her helmet flap aside and listened closely to the static on the radio and then heard Pete check in. His voice was somewhat garbled but she could tell it was him. Then silence.

"Melrose? You hear anything from Bobbec, over? Do you copy?" Static was the only reply she got. Dray punched the send key and spoke quickly into the radio.

"Hey, Melrose? Come back." Silence again. She clicked the button once more. "Pete? You there?"

Ted put the hose down and came over to listen. "Y'all getting anything on that, Dray?" he asked, nodding to the radio in her hand.

She shushed him and pressed the radio hard against her ear, the volume already up to its maximum setting. "Something's wrong with this piece of shit."

"Been like that all day," Ted told her. "Gotta be this location, maybe lots of electrical wires interferin'," he offered.

She rattled it once and then sighed, putting it back in its case. "They can't be too far ahead but there's no tellin' where they are, Ted. I mean, without the frikkin' radio we could be dancing in circles and never know it." The tall southerner turned back for the hose. Adjusting her equipment and axe, Dray took another look at the plans and then they walked deeper into the unknown.

## Chapter 12

Pete adjusted his SCBA, making sure the mask was positioned fairly close to where he felt the swelling was on his neck. It wasn't as blistered as Matt's forehead or cheek area was but the lieutenant knew that given time, it would be. The sooner he found Rodriguez, the better off they'd all be.

He kicked a burning chair out of the way and took a firmer grip on the hose, dragging it farther into the office complex. Wiping the soot and grime from his mask, Pete could see evidence that the two firemen had been in the area. A feeling of hope flickered inside and he prayed they weren't too far ahead. He looked at his tank gauge and saw he'd have another twenty minutes, providing he didn't have to do much in the way of strenuous activity.

The heat prickled his neck area and rivulets of sweat meandered down between his shoulder blades and lower back, causing him to shudder. *God, what I wouldn't give for a nice cold brew,* he sighed, and then groaned, *while sitting up to my ears in a cold bath with the air conditioner on full blast. Yeahhh.*

He was just starting to grin at the thought when the door handle he was grasping was yanked open. He stared in surprise as another firefighter stumbled through, falling hard against him.

"Shit! Is that you, Bobbec?" A shake of the head made his heart lurch. Oh, there'd be damage, for certain, Pete realized. But he couldn't give up hope they'd find the leader and his squad relatively intact.

He pulled back the man's slumped shoulders and gazed into the black facemask. "Rodriguez? Well, thank god, man. I was just comin' to look for you and Peters." He shook the man's shoulders.

"Where is he?" A look of horror came into Rodriguez's eyes and Melrose knew the body count had just risen by at least one more.

"Did you see any of the other firefighters on Bobbec's team? Anybody?"

Rodriguez shook his head again and Pete could see the man was having trouble breathing. "Is there an exit out that way? What's the fire look like? I need to know the status of the fire!"

Mark Rodriguez swallowed what little moisture was in his parched, swollen throat and managed to croak out "no exit."

"Relax Buddy," Pete said trying to calm him. "Relax and tell me what's happened."

Rodriguez gave a nod of understanding and motioned Pete closer. "The fire was moving too quickly," he told the lieutenant, "I had to abandon the hose when the wall collapsed on Peters."

Silently Melrose told himself to relax as he heard the news.

"I tried to pull him out Lieutenant," Rodriguez continued, "but it was so hot. He was pinned and...I tried to...he was...Oh, mi dios que...él fue quemado antes de mis mismos ojos...la bestia, él le consiguió... oh, mi Jesús dulce." The man tried to wrench the mask from his face, his features twisted with remorse. "Me intenté... intenté salvar..." Pete batted the man's hands away and hugged him briefly; all too familiar with the torment a person could feel when confronted with the voracious and unforgiving nature of a blaze.

"C'mon, let's get you the hell out of here." There had to be another way around the office area. Grabbing up the man's discarded axe and hefting the man by his waist, Pete half dragged the injured firefighter back the way he'd come.

Abby raced down the stairs, her heart in her throat and her mind clouded over with images conjured up from the dispatch updates. *Chem fire...chemical poisoning, a firefighter already removed, firefighters missing, Dray...Goddamnit...did I bring the damn keys?* She stopped dead and began searching her pockets. Finally, her frantic fingers closed around Dray's tangle of keys and she nearly sobbed with relief.

After almost ripping the truck door off its hinges, Abby jumped inside and jammed the key into the ignition. The smell of her lover assaulted her senses as she settled into the cab and stretched her feet forward to tap the gas pedal twice. She pumped the gas again, absently rubbing the leather wheel cover as if coaxing the truck to start. Satisfied she turned the key. The motor made a funny growling noise but wouldn't turn over. She tried again and was rewarded by a deeper rasp and then nothing.

"Damn it!" she said slapping the steering wheel.

She snapped out of her frustrated haze and peered closely at the gas tank. There appeared to be enough gas. Putting the truck back into neutral and then shifting it into first, Abby could see everything seemed right.

"Shit. Come on, you." The blonde gave it a quick few taps on the gas pedal and tried to turn it over. There was nothing this time, not even a click. She banged the steering wheel in aggravation. The bright numbers on the clock in the dash screamed out, reminding her that time was wasting.

Quickly removing the keys, checking all the dials and then taking a deep breath, Abby tried to just calm down and start the truck just like Dray would. But still the temperamental truck wouldn't start. Stepping out and slamming the door, Abby wrestled the hood open and was immediately assaulted with the smell of gasoline fumes.

"Damn!" She looked outside the garage to see if anyone was around. Even if she could manage to catch a lift back to the warehouse, just close to where it was, she could run the rest of the way. Abby ran out to the sidewalk, looking for a cab. When no cab was to be found she started to try to flag down traffic heading in that direction. But it was no use; no one was stopping.

*Think, Abby. How can I get back there?* She wondered as she walked back into the garage.

They'd had almost three wonderful months together and she was damned if she was just going sit at home and twiddle her thumbs while her lover perished in some damned warehouse fire. It wasn't going to happen. She slammed her fist against the saddle of Dray's motorcycle and the bike moved an inch. Abby blinked and then looked down at the chrome and steel and smiled.

"I'm coming, Dray," she said with a grin, "and you'd better be okay or I'll..." she thought briefly of her usual ending of 'I'll kill you.' Instead she left the sentence unfinished.

Ted and Dray came across a few pockets where the blaze still had something to consume and both firefighters took their time methodically dousing every flame they ran across. So far they hadn't run across anyone, dead or alive, and Dray was beginning to wonder if the fire was centrally located, this back exit being a good safe way to get any survivors out. She kept a mental tally on exactly how many turns it had taken to get to where the back offices were. Although the building plans indicated a certain floor plan, much had been modified throughout most of the building with the main area broken into two hanger-like warehouses. It was the far right hand one that had sustained most of the damage, the fire spreading and consuming most of the office complex on that side of the building.

They came around the corner into an open area and Ted pointed up to a metal staircase that led to a few more offices and supply rooms. The owner had mentioned to dispatch that the area was temporarily closed off due to renovations. Dray looked up the stairs and across the walkways. "Renovations my ass. This place hasn't seen an honest building inspector in ages."

Ted snorted once and they moved down into another area of the complex. She and Ted worked through every room, making sure there were no last minute surprises, when they heard the first evidence that the second story was going to come down around them if they weren't prudent with their time.

"C'mon, Ted...we have about another ten minutes tops before this section of the warehouse starts to come down. Look...we're gonna have to kick this fire door down leading to the main area and then get the hell outta here, okay?"

Ted nodded. They counted three and then slammed their heavy boots against the reinforced door. Nothing. Ted pivoted the head on his axe and then motioned the brunette to stand back. Dray smirked and with a flourish indicated he could be her guest. He brought the blunt end of the tool hard across the handle a few times and nodded with satisfaction as it fell to the floor. Giving the thumbs up, Dray began the count again, the outcome being much more favorable this second time around.

They both looked upon the area with a sense of awe. Dray watched the bright red flames dance across the ceiling, casting an almost iridescent glow on everything around them. And then the smoke snaked around their ankles like tentacles and the woman was brought back from her brief trepidation. She nodded once and they slowly made their way around the burning debris.

They moved deeper into the darkness and Dray could feel the heat of the blaze leeching the moisture from her body, making her vision blur with its intensity. She poked the timber with the head of her axe and then stepped back as it creaked in protest. Taking a breath of air, she lifted the axe and swung, catching the column halfway, and then jumped to the left expecting the trajectory of the beam to swing to the right. However, the butt end of the heavy timber popped up and hit her squarely in the side, pushing her hard over towards the nearby flames. She stumbled on the debris scattered around her and went down, holding her hands out in front of her. Dray stifled a cry as the bare flesh of her neck was exposed to the hungry fire and began rolling out of harm's way. Ted ran to where she was and began pulling her to safety as the roof above them began to crackle and creak.

"Gotta get outta here, Dray!"

Dray winced and holding her side, slowly got to her knees with Ted's help. She could feel her burned skin tightening; the familiar sensation of live hornets just beneath her flesh grew with intensity and she bit down hard on the inside of her mouth, trying to suppress the pain and refocus on the task at hand.

Once she was standing on her own, Ted grabbed the axe and began pushing the debris out of the way. When there was a small area finally cleared, he helped her through and they both worked their way forward, mindful of the voracious flames.

They could feel the heat but because of the billowing black smoke neither one knew exactly where they were. Ted turned on his flashlight but gave up as the glare only bounced back.

He turned and motioned to Dray; two index fingers pushed together meaning 'stick tight.' Dray nodded and gave the man a weak smile. He frowned, suddenly aware of the woman's careful gait. His heart began pounding; although their survival was already in doubt it would be almost impossible if one of them were more seriously injured. Another part of the upper catwalk came down with a crash, the twisted metal barring their way back. He bit his lip and then turned, grabbing the woman by the shoulders.

"All right, straight up. How bad you hurt, Dray?" he yelled in choppy sentences, pressing his mask against hers, willing eye contact. Dray paused for a split second and then tried to take a deep breath. She attempted to keep a game face as he moved his hands over her rib cage.

Catching her wince, Ted nodded once and then grabbed her sleeve. "Look, we gotta stick together so I'm gonna lead and you're gonna follow me, nice an' close, right?"

Dray thought briefly of just pushing the man aside and taking point, thereby proving she was fine. But Dray knew that Ted wasn't being misogynistic and it would be up to him to lead them out, for both their sakes. She nodded once and they settled themselves into a slow but steady pace, inching forward carefully.

Abby felt like kicking the damn bike as she tried to will the Harley the last hundred yards into the gas station. Everything had gone so right, up until there were a few sputters and the engine quit.

The attendant, spying the low rider, hurried out of one of the bays and wiped his hands clean of grease. The man was in his late twenties and had the look of someone who was far more at ease with mechanical objects than human beings.

"Hey there. Can I h..."

Abby cut him off with a raised hand and a dire look. "Just...get me some gas. I'm kinda in a hurry, okay?" The crestfallen look on his eager face made her stop and then, "I'm sorry but I'm in a hurry and this damned-."

"Yeah, nice bike," he said taking it from her and pushing it up to the pump. "Like, I mean, I'd kill just to sit on it, ya know?"

Abby arched an eyebrow, fists on her hips. "What the...?" *What was it about this damn bike?* "Look, can you fill it with," she took the helmet off, pulling her hair free and then continued in a rush, looking at the grade options. "You know, I have absolutely no idea what this thing takes."

The young man slowly got to his feet, his jaw slack, and just stared at the goddess before him. Needless to say, the bike was all but forgotten.

Abby, totally unaware of her effect on the man, continued to run her fingers hastily through her long golden hair, and then pulled at her blouse in an effort to dislodge the sweaty material from her overheated body. "God, it's hot today."

The guy started, coming out of his haze. "Hot...yeah. Well shit...oh, scuse me, Ma'am." A faint blush began creeping up his neck. "Um, can I get you a soda?"

"Wha-No, just the gas," Abby answered, drumming her fingers on the gas tank as the man eagerly went about granting her request.

*Stupid motorcycle, I could be there by now.*

As he pumped, images of Dray paraded across her eyes; the woman taking off her helmet that first time, looking at her with the most intense blue eyes Abby had ever seen; throwing her head back and laughing whole-heartedly when the mood struck her; and of them making love, Dray's form rising and falling above her. She glanced at the mechanic's bay once more, the few seconds the guy had been gone felt like an hour. She peered in hoping that perhaps it was only gas that was needed after all.

He closed it back up and she handed him a five-dollar bill. "Keep the change," she told him as she slipped the helmet back on and tried to start the bike again. Try as she may, the engine wouldn't turn over.

"Son of a bitch," she cursed under her breath.

"Maybe I can work on this baby," he told her. "It'd be worth it just to take it for a test drive after I was done." He dropped to his haunches and checked out the frame.

A smile came to Abby's face.

"If you can get me down to industrial park in the next 15 minutes," Abby offered. "I'll have my girlfriend take you out cruising someday, all day long. Sound good?"

The man smiled toothily and nodded. "You betcha, lady." He pushed the bike into his garage and ran back into his office, flipping the 'Closed' sign before locking up.

"This here's my truck," he said with some pride and Abby put on a brave face. It was a rust-colored, 1998 Ford F10 and while the exterior was in fairly good shape the interior looked like a cyclone had been through it. It was apparent, by the remnants inside, that the man was a connoisseur of fast food. She arched an eyebrow at him and steeled herself for a ride that would certainly provide a test for her olfactory senses. She gingerly worked her way through the debris and found a relatively bare spot to sit in.

"Think we can get there in 15?" Abby asked.

The young man smiled. "Honey, for a day of riding on that baby I'll make it in under five."

Abby held onto the hoist bar as he squealed out of the parking lot and onto the street.

Pete watched as the ambulance's lights were turned on and the vehicle sped away, throwing loose gravel in its wake. He began to take a deep, cleansing breath, trying to ease the gnawing he felt inside. He'd gone in to find Rick and his crew and had failed miserably, almost losing his own life in the process. He would also be responsible for any injuries Dray and Ted sustain going in after him, the missing workers, all of it. He shook his head miserably, the loss of life horrendous, and all of it sitting squarely on his broad shoulders.

He wiped his face unhappily. In his current state he completely glossed over the things he had achieved and only centered on what he perceived to be major flaws in his skills as a firefighter.

Pete let himself be led over to a brownish patch of grass, lost in his own twisted maze of self-doubt and recriminations. He suddenly became aware of a bright light all but blinding him. Blinking a few times, he was surprised to see himself being tended to by a total stranger, and a very nice looking total stranger at that.

The paramedic flashed the light into the lieutenant's eyes again and sighed. "Man, you are one lucky mother, lieutenant. You know that? Here, let me look at that arm."

She gently pushed up Pete's shirt and gazed at the chemical burns that seemed to snake across his right wrist.

"Shit, you get splashed with something in there, or what?"

Pete shook his head and brought his hand up to scratch as his throat. "No," he croaked, "Something in the air." He coughed and tried to clear his throat. The woman reached across and handed him a bottle of water and then lifted his chin.

"Ah, I see. Well, you got another spot here," she pulled his hand away. "I can see where you had your mask...just a perfect line. You are damned lucky that stuff only affected your skin."

The lieutenant looked at her and took a deep drink, wincing as he swallowed.

"Yeah, I know you have a sore throat, that's usual with chemical fires. And at least this stuff wasn't so toxic that it ate through your skin like phosphorus would." Pete reached over and handed her both his mask and jacket, pointing to the seal on one and the sleeve on the other.

"Holy shit." She whistled. "Damn, that stuff is brutal. How long were you exposed to it?" Pete opened his mouth to talk and she put a hand to his lips. "Shit, I'm sorry, don't bother to talk. Give it a few hours, a few days; I'm sure you'll feel better." She peered down his throat. "It looks a bit inflamed but on the whole, not too bad but you might wanna check in with your physician by end of week. Ok?" He nodded and began to scratch at his neck again. She grabbed his hand and gave him a look. "And no scratchin', got it?"

Pete grinned and then stuck his hand out.

"Pete Melrose," he said, his voice sounding like he'd gargled with straight razors. The woman winced and pushed the bottle back to his lips. He smiled and guzzled three quarters of the contents before sighing in relief.

"Rachel," she said, sticking her hand out. "Rachel Cummings. Glad to meet ya." She found herself gazing into the man's soft brown eyes and realized she was staring. With a slight shake of her head she looked away. "I could come by the station next week to make sure you're doing okay." She dipped her head down and studied her fingers.

Pete's brows knit together and his eyes widened in surprise when he realized the tone in her voice changed from professional to somewhat casual. He smiled weakly, thinking twice – maybe he was just her good deed for the day so he nodded, patting her hand.

"Sure," he squeaked.

The woman lifted her chin and there was a smile on her face and a twinkle in her eyes. "That'd be great, Lieutenant Melrose."

Pete immediately began rethinking his previous take on things and smiled toothily back at her. "Heh, and you can call me Pete."

"Well," she began with a flirty smile, "Let's get you finished up." She grabbed his hand gently and began spreading a clear ointment over the blistered flesh. The two sat silently as she finished wrapping his wrist. She reached out and slowly lifted his chin and Pete thought for a moment that she might kiss him. He sighed, when the moment passed and she was all business, pushing his jaw to the side and gently prodding his reddened flesh. "This one isn't too bad and shouldn't leave any scarring. Like I said, you got off easy...um, Pete."

"Yeah," he answered absently, thinking of Rodriguez's story. He just stared as she packed up her case and headed back to the ambulance, giving him an over the shoulder look that said 'I'll be back.' He snorted at the turn of events. *All this time I've been fixin' myself up and wearin' smelly stuff to catch a dame and all I had to do is get fricasseed,* he thought, shaking his head. He looked at his watch and then back at the building.

"Where are ya, Dray?" he wondered out loud.

As the fire rose at the rear of the warehouse, the paint on the outside of the drums began to peel and burn. The metal containers creaked and groaned as their contents expanded. A loud bang was heard and both heads turned as one of the barrels rose high in the air spreading its toxic contents before bursting into flames. As the loud crack reached them, both figures ducked, wincing against the sudden attack on their eardrums. As a blanket of rolling black smoke edged ever closer, Ted steadied his axe and they both picked up the pace.

Dray felt her heart rate increase as a feeling of dread came over her and she put her hand in the middle of Ted's back, tapping twice. She watched as his helmet dipped twice. And then they ran.

She could feel the heat rushing towards them as she fell. The next sensation she had was being dragged to her feet. Clutching her hand to her side, she knew by the pain she'd broken something. Not being able to see, she shut her eyes, blocking out the wispy tendrils of billowing smoke. While she had been in some pretty tough spots in her years as a firefighter, there had never been such a feeling of hopelessness before. "Abby," she whispered with a tinge of regret.

The idea of never seeing the petite blonde again was like a physical blow and she pushed the thought away. Grabbing tightly to the coat in front of her, she ran, hoping Ted knew where the hell he was going; that, perhaps he could see a way out. Suddenly, Ted went down and Dray fell heavily on top of him, barely stifling a scream as she felt bones grind against each other.

Ted could feel his pulse racing, the sweat coming down in rivers from his hairline and his hands feeling as if his gloves have somehow become a second skin. Running on instinct only he tried to dart his eyes back and forth, hoping to see a glimpse of anything that would give him hope they might find a way out of the inferno. He saw a glimmer of light and he steered them towards it. But not more than a few paces and he came to a stand still.

He'd run hard into a utility cart at mid thigh level and ended up ass over teakettle, sprawled in the debris. The air was pushed out of him as Dray landed squarely on his chest. He lay there momentarily dazed and then started to crawl.

Dray opened her eyes. The air was thinner down on the floor and there was light – and a possible way out of the Hell that surrounded them. She grabbed Ted's arm and tugged in the opposite direction he was trying to take them. The man resisted and then Dray used all of her strength to tug him along.

He stopped and put his face close to hers. Barely able to take a deep breath, Dray tried to tell him but it was no use and she just nodded her head in the direction she wanted them to go. He shook his head vehemently but soon relented and nodded. Her intuition had gotten their crew out of some pretty horrific situations. He just hoped she was right again.

Pete sat on the grass, his helmet and mask lying forgotten beside him. His eyes were glazed and he wheezed as he gulped down another pint of bottled water. Dave lay beside him, head on paws. The man finally looked over and they both locked eyes. Pete reached out a bandaged, shaky hand and patted the Dalmatian's head. Dave weakly wagged his tail, uncertain of the emotions rolling off his master.

"I got a bad feelin' about this one, Dave. Shoulda gone in teams bigger than four." He coughed and wiped his mouth with the back of a grimy hand. He thought of Rodriguez lying in the ambulance, overcome by fumes. It'd been a hard job dragging the man out the side entrance, barely making it before they both collapsed with exhaustion. A pallet of barrels had suddenly begun to roll off as the wood caught fire and Pete knew they could be lying under it but for the grace of God. He closed his eyes again and thanked Him for sparing their lives.

A few of the other firefighters wandered over and tried to get the dog to play with them. Dave just looked at them morosely and whined. "You can sense it, too, can't ya boy?" muttered the lieutenant as he softly patted the animal's side.

He jumped to his feet as he heard the first barrel explode, running back to the warehouse, gear in hand. The fire marshal was telling each squadron to back off.

Pete ran over to Captain Dougherty, trying to talk him into letting him and a few of the others go back inside, they had crew still trapped in there. The captain grabbed him hard and refused straight out because of the highly toxic fumes. There was just no way he could, in all good conscience, let anyone go back in there. It would mean certain death. The lieutenant banged his fists frustratingly against his hips and turned his back to the fire. There had to be something he could do.

Dray felt as if her legs were being wrapped in barbed wire – razor sharp, barbed wire. She pushed Ted ahead of her and found herself silently crying, the pain in her side so intense that each breath was a little death in itself. Somewhere along the way she'd lost a glove and could feel the temperature of the surrounding air; it felt like touching the surface of the sun.

A crack filled her ears as she heard a timber begin to give way and she rolled, dragging the other firefighter with her. Ted shouted in surprise and then he was up and moving them both, the burning wood somehow illuminating a way through the cloying darkness, allowing hope to blossom. He took hold of Dray's sleeve and yanked, pulling her a little more towards what he hoped was a way out of their death trap, and then stopped to place her over his shoulder before taking off again. Dray grunted as her damaged ribs came into contact with his shoulder with every step that he took. She closed her eyes tightly, fighting against the black silence that threatened her. Then a cloak of noise rushed up suddenly, leaving her only a moment to contemplate their dismal chances of survival before she passed out.

Ted felt as if the top of his head was going to blow off; the pressure of carrying his partner combined with the pain in his legs and the fear that had taken hold of him was exhausting.

Finally, his knees just buckled and they went down. He cried out in frustration, using words his Momma would have tanned his hide for. He thought briefly of just giving up, the inevitability of their deaths so close.

But suddenly, he felt a sharp pain in his hand and turned to see Dave tugging at his glove. He could have kissed the mutt. Taking hold of the dog's collar, he swore there would be a fat, juicy steak in Dave's future. He could barely make out the shouting and followed the dog, dragging the inert form of his friend behind him.

"Now listen, Goddamnit! I got crew still in there and I ain't just leavin' them to die." Pete ground his teeth and tried again. "Can't you just give me five minutes, just five measly minutes? If we can't locate 'em, then," Pete squeaked the last word out and then squeezed his eyes shut. *She can't be gone, she just can't. Not like this.* Pete passed a hand wearily over his face and turned away, leaving the Captain to stroke his mustache in thought.

"Look here Melrose, I'm not heartless, I know Dray's in there and I'd do anything to go in myself and find her. But we have to face the facts. The chances of her, or anyone, surviving that inferno are," he wiped a moist hand across his brow, "remote." Melrose turned and pinned him with a beseeching look. He tried to remain dispassionate, and realistic, but seeing the determined look on the lieutenant's face, Dougherty knew beyond a shadow of a doubt that if anyone could find the crew it would be this man.

He rubbed his jaw, peered over his shoulder at the billowing smoke, and then cursed quietly. Pete leaned in, praying to hear the words that sang like a litany in his soul, *say yes, say yes, say yes.*

"Five minutes, but you don't enter the building," the Captain said grudgingly. "This is against my better judgment, you know." He turned, his fists bunched at his side. Parental feelings for Dray swamped any resistance he still had and he gripped the lieutenant's shoulder. "You'll have to wear a mask the whole time. No way I'm losing any more men."

Pete nodded enthusiastically and turned to ask for volunteers. What he saw before him was every person in his own squad plus quite a generous amount from the other halls.

"Okay," he took another swig from the water bottle. "I'll take O'Brien and Martins. The rest of you, check the perimeter to see if anyone is trying to get out, but no going into the building – marshal's orders." His throat tightened as he felt dozens of hands pat his back before he settled into the routine of check out. No sooner had O'Brien been verified as being good to go than Dave returned at his master's side, desperately trying to get his attention. Pete looked down to watch Dave run toward the burning building.

"Shit! Dave," he called painfully while rubbing his sore throat. "Dave!"

Pete hurriedly put on his mask and waited two full seconds before making a dash in the same direction his dog was leading him.

Approaching a section of the warehouse that had collapsed, the trio of men poked and prodded at the timbers, trying to widen the gaping hole they found. Billowing smoke belched from the building and glass was blown out the top floor windows.

Pete ducked and then leaned into his task with a vengeance. Both men watched their lieutenant as the man began waging personal war on whatever stood in his way. O'Brien began praying as the three of them went to work trying to open an escape route. They both knew the chances were pretty slim that anyone else would be pulled from the fire alive.

Pete stopped in mid-stroke, cocking an ear as he heard a sharp noise. "Hold it! Stop...stop! Dave? C'mere, boy," he coaxed.

He whistled once and waited. Straining his ears, hoping against hope that he really had heard a noise, Pete leaned towards the dark gaping maw of the fire. He jumped back as another explosion ripped through the building, the flames reflecting off his mask. He watched in horror as part of the roof at the back of the warehouse began to fall.

"Where are you, Dray?" he muttered to himself. He stared transfixed as a barrel flew up and exploded in mid air, spreading arcs of liquid fire 50 feet from where they stood. He felt a hand on his shoulder as O'Brien tried to pull him away.

He half-heartedly resisted although he knew the truth – there was no way anything could survive those flames. He turned to look at the other two men and found neither one could look him in the eye. He swallowed hard, letting out a slow painful breath.

He had to face facts. No way anyone could have survived that inferno.

"What'll I tell Abby? Oh God, Dray."

Pete seemed to lose the ability to stand up right then, leaning into the taller man as the enormity of the situation hit him. All the good people he worked with: Ted, Dray, Rodriguez, Johnson, Peters, Bobbec and his whole team – injured or dead.

James Dougherty tried very hard to keep his face as stoic as he could, knowing that it wouldn't help Melrose or the others in his district by falling apart. Inside, however, he was waging a losing battle as all the images of Dray as a young brash recruit assaulted his senses leaving him feeling as destroyed as the man he held.

"Wroof!" Pete's head whipped around and he broke away from the confining embrace of the older man and rushed forward. There, out of the black smoke bounded his dog, sneezing and coughing. He strained to see the crawling figure of a lone firefighter.

"Oh, thank God, thank God," murmured the lieutenant, praying the firefighter wasn't injured too badly.

Reaching down, he grabbed the figure just under his armpits and pulled up. Face to face, Pete recognized Ted and gave the man a brief hug. Ted winced as he found his bare and badly burned hand trapped between them.

"Stop...no....it's Dray...gotta get..." Pete thought the man was out of his head, attempting to turn and go back into the flames. Then he felt a hand weakly pulling on his leg and looked down. There she was, curled up, hat askew and mask almost pulled down to her neck. But he could tell that she was alive.

Alive!

Before he could say a word, the other two firefighters grabbed the injured pair and the five of them quickly moved as far away from the fire as possible. Two EMT's took over for the firefighters, leaving the three men to watch as the fire continued to burn out of control.

"Here," Abby said ripping the section of the fast food bag she'd just written on. She handing her escort the piece of paper. "My part of the deal."

As soon as the truck pulled into the back lot, Abby had the door wrenched open and was running pell-mell through the crowds, looking left and right. The driver sat in his truck scratching his chin. Then he shrugged his shoulders and looked at the paper the blonde had given him. "Abby Dean, 555-3459." He put the Ford in reverse wearing a smile as visions of chrome danced in his head. "Cool!" he said stuffing it into his breast pocket.

Abby pushed her way forward in the crowd of onlookers only to be told, in no uncertain terms, to just go home and not get in the way.

"Now look, I don't know who you are but I've gotta find out about," she swallowed, thinking about just what Dray meant to her. She choked back a sob and squeezed her eyes shut as tears coursed down her flushed cheeks. "I've got to find Dray Khalkousa."

The captain could see just how upset the woman was and figured her mother or sister worked at the warehouse. He stepped closer upon seeing how adamant the woman was getting with the man holding up the barricade.

"Look, just tell me where she's at!" Abby said addressing the man in front of her. "I would have felt something if she was," her voice trailed off unable to finish the sentence. "Just tell me where Dray Khalkousa's team is at?"

Captain Dougherty walked closer at the sound of the name. "You a friend of Dray's?"

Abby sniffed and laughed weakly at the description. Hope flooded her soul as she realized that this man knew Dray and might help her.

"Yes, she's my...my entire world. Can you help me or not?"

Before he could answer, Pete pushed through to her, croaking her name. Both heads came up and Abby ran into the man's arms. Captain Dougherty silently asked Pete for the skinny on the situation and was caught between feeling relieved that yes, Dray had survived and doubtful as to the severity of her condition. By the look in the lieutenant's eyes, the news wasn't good.

Pete held up a finger to the captain, silently telling him to wait until he could speak to the woman he held. Quietly he led the woman away but Dougherty followed anyway. He felt a cold hand grip his heart as the blonde stopped dead in her tracks refusing to move any further.

"Oh, my God, she's not dead, is she? Pete, tell me she's not dead!"

Pete shook his head wearily, only a faint croaking sound coming from his throat. He looked behind them and Abby turned to see they weren't alone. Dougherty was listening too.

"No...no, she's alive Abby, but..."

"But what? Tell me what happened," the blonde insisted.

"The EMTs took her away." He stopped to clear his throat and then went on. "She's been burned, Abby, bad, and I dunno about her lungs. She didn't have a good seal on her mask," Pete added more for Dougherty's benefit than Abby's.

Dougherty ground his teeth thinking about the ramifications. A fire could do horrible things to the human body but the damage chemicals could inflict were many and their effects long term.

Abby paused a moment and looked at Pete's condition. "How are you?" she asked sincerely.

He gave a half smile, touched by her concern for him as well.

"I'll be okay," Pete reassured her. Before he could add anything more Dougherty spoke up.

"About those burns, Melrose; you're gonna have to take some time off and I want a full report on just what the doc says about it, okay?" He took his cap off and scratched his sparse, gray hair. "Just who is she to Khalkousa?" he added nodding toward Abby.

Pete paused a moment and looked at Abby.

"Her name is Abby Dean, sir, and they've been together for, gee...a few months now I think...I've never seen Dray happier."

He smiled at Abby and she in return gave him a lopsided grin.

"Well, just keep her outta the way lieutenant," Dougherty said. "I don't want anyone else hurt here today."

Pete gave a respectful nod as the captain replaced his hat and then looked over at the fire brigade spraying foam and a deactivating chemical powder on what was left of the blaze.

"I've got to see her, Pete. Where did they take her?"

Captain Dougherty surprised them both by placing both fingers into his mouth and whistling shrilly. The response was almost immediate as two firefighters came running up.

"Sir?" The two men nodded as the older man detailed exactly what he wanted.

"You," he pointed to one of them, "Get my car." He turned to the other man, "You – find out which hospital Dray Khalkousa was taken to."

"Yes sir," he stated briskly before hurrying away.

Not long after a four-door sedan, complete with siren and flashing lights pulled up. Captain Dougherty gave Pete's shoulder a swat and winked at Abby as the two climbed into the back seat.

"Make sure they do another check on you too, Pete, and call if you get news on the team members, okay? I'll keep an eye on things here."

Pete nodded as the other two men jumped into the front seat and soon the vehicle slowly made its way around the barricades.

Pete looked behind him and saw the Captain heading back towards the mop-up job in progress. He felt a little strange leaving the scene, feeling that he should be doing something.

Bobbec's face popped up into his head, as did those of Ted, Johnson, Peters and Rodriguez. He bit the inside of one cheek and then thought about Dray. Yeah, he'd leave the scene for her...and Abby.

Pete raised his bandaged hand and carefully pulled his collar away from the reddened flesh of his neck. Abby winced at the thought of the condition her lover might be in since Pete claimed to be 'okay.'

She desperately wanted to ask how badly Dray appeared, along with a sea of other questions – what had happened, did she find Pete or did Pete find her, how badly was she burned? But more than anything she wanted some assurance that Dray would recover. Surely, a woman as indestructible as her lover would be able to take whatever life threw at her in stride, bracing herself for more. She had in the past and there was no reason to believe this would be any different. But still the doubt was there. Abby knew first had the trite expression, *That which does not kill us...* But somewhere in her worried mind she wondered if Dray would live to be stronger in the end.

Instead of pushing Pete for answers she simply looked out the window, praying that Dray would survive.

# Chapter 13

Abby and Pete quickly walked into the crowded hospital.

"Busy day for them," he said, trying to keep his hands away from the bandage at his throat. "I wonder how long it'll take to get through the red tape?"

"You should be getting yourself taken care of, Pete. I'll be fine."

"Oh, don't worry about me. I'm as strong as an ox and almost as smart," he told her, his self-depreciating humor an attempt to keep her calm. "You sure you don't want me to stick around and flash my badge?"

Abby winced with every syllable the man spoke. It sounded like he had a mouthful of broken glass. "Pete, you really don't look very well. Maybe you should-."

"I'll be just...fine." He cut in, swallowing back the bile that was rising in his throat. "So. You want me to divide and conquer that line over there?"

He mopped a line of sweat from his forehead and tried to still his shaking hands. *Must be shock,* he thought to himself. And then his stomach lurched one way while his equilibrium wobbled the other. He suddenly became grateful that he was standing in a hospital.

Abby noticed the sway of his body and lead him to a vacant seat.

"I'm suddenly not feelin' too good." A pasty look had begun creeping up the man's neck and Abby's forehead dimpled with concern.

"Promise me you'll stay right here," she told him.

Abby didn't wait for him to answer. She immediately ran up to the emergency station cutting her way to the head of the line.

"Hey," she said calling over getting a workers attention. "I've got an injured firefighter from the factory fire out here."

"We'll be with you in a moment," a clerk told her.

"No," Abby insisted. "Get a nurse out here, now." Another worker, who overheard them, peeked out from behind a filing cabinet and walked over.

"Where?" she asked as she began to follow Abby. The clerk saw Pete as they approached and didn't bother finishing the journey. "I'll get someone now," she told Abby before dashing back the direction they came. In a matter of seconds later they helped the lieutenant onto a gurney.

"We came here to find out about another firefighter – Dray Khalkousa?"

The clerk nodded. "I'll check for you, just wait here, okay? It might take awhile. We've got lots of rescue workers here today," she explained.

Abby gave a polite nod. "I understand. Thank you."

The clerk gave her a nod and a comforting grin before pointing back to the waiting area.

Making her way back, Abby found herself looking at two impossibly long lines of people either waiting to be admitted or, like her, trying to find out about loved ones who were already patients of the hospital.

Abby scrunched herself down into one of the vacant seats.

She waited.

And waited.

While the drive to the hospital was somewhat of a blur, Abby was becoming only too conscious of the long hours alone in her little corner of hell with only a very vivid imagination to keep her company. Hours had ticked by and no one seemed to be able to answer her inquiries each time she went back to the desk.

"Melrose?" a voice called out. Abby shot to her feet to see a doctor taking a roster from the nurse.

He ran his finger down the clipboard. "Yes, here we are. Well, it could have been worse. There are some rather nasty burns on one hand and what looks to be a puncture wound or two from a dog on the other. His lungs are fair considering what he's been through, all in all, the prognosis is good for a full recovery."

The young blonde stood there with a smile spreading over her face. 'Prognosis is good...full recovery' was all she heard.

"Would you like to see your husband," he asked.

Abby found herself totally flummoxed. "Who me? I don't...We're not married. I just brought him in to see our friend, his co-worker, Dray, I mean Andrea Khalkousa. I'm still waiting for word on her condition."

"Oh...Hmm...Well, I don't see anything else here."

"Look, her name's Andrea Khalkousa," Abby said before spelling out the last name. "Tall brunette, wide shoulders?"

"How many firefighters were brought in today, nurse?" interrupted the doctor as he stepped away from the apparently transient blonde.

The nurse's jaw twitched but she squinted at the screen for a minute.

"Well, at least 12 have come in requiring serious attention, five have been treated and released, and one is being kept for observation. Then there's the Lieutenant Melrose finishing up in out-patients right now and two in the burn unit."

Abby remembered Pete saying his entire team had been hurt so that left three people unaccounted for. "Where are the others?" Abby asked. "There should be 3 others," she added.

The doctor pointed to the waiting room with a firm voice. "Have a seat Miss and we'll call-."

"Look, I'm done sitting. I need to see Dray," Abby said, her tone almost matching his.

"Now, now; just relax, I understand."

"The Hell you do!" Abby countered. "If she's not here then where would she be?"

The nurse went back to typing again, continuing to search as the doctor held up a finger to make a call.

"Look, she's got to be here. Wait! I remember; she's with Firehouse #73. Does that help?"

Pete came trudging down the hall from the treatment room with his coat over one arm, and carrying a sheaf of papers in the other. He looked remarkably better than the last time she'd seen him.

"Try and have me admitted, will they? Ha!" Pete rubbed his hand where they'd stuck in an IV and grumbled. "Dehydrated, my ass. So I was a little shocked...nothing serious, it'll pass. Nothing keeps me away from my crew...ever."

Even though he'd tried to be as gruff as possible with the nurses treating him, or trying to, he was grateful for the medication given for his throat. He could almost swallow without tears coming to his eyes. The anesthetic throat spray had done wonders, and he had a fist full of prescriptions to fill.

*Later*, he thought as images of Ted and Dray filled his mind again. He'd badgered the nurses for information about the two but had only gotten a vague update on Ted. He wasn't pleased about that at all. Well, at least Ted was doing better than when they'd first brought him in.

The nurses said the man had been damned lucky he'd been able to keep his mask on, thereby avoiding dangerous smoke inhalation. However, he did have some chemical burns, severe back pain and a greenstick fracture on one of his legs. They'd keep him for a few days. Melrose mentally added another two or three weeks of home convalescence, even though he knew Ted would balk.

*Tough shit buddy, you saved Dray's ass and if I could, you'd be lying on a beach in Waikiki.*

Pete had just pushed open the double doors when he was almost knocked to the ground as Abby all but flung herself into his arms.

"Pete!" He felt himself being spun around and his belly lurched.

"Whoa...what the..."

Abby clutched at him fiercely and he moved them both over to the waiting area. "Have you heard anything about Dray?"

"S'okay Abby, just sit for a minute." He peered around the room and frowned as his gaze settled on a man looking belligerently their way. "You still haven't heard anything?"

"They say she's not here, Pete, but she has to be!" Pete clenched his jaw as Abby went on. "There are three firefighters not listed on that roster and-."

The doctor cleared his throat and walked over, stopping her in mid sentence. "As we've explained to her, we haven't found anyone by that name in our records here in the E.R. She's getting irrational and perhaps it's best if you move her along."

Pete's jaw turned to granite and then he slowly put the articles he was holding on the table. Abby saw the warning look in his eye and pulled at his sleeve.

"Pete, it's not worth it, really. We both know that Dray's gotta be here. It's just a matter of where they put her. We've waited this long..."

The doctor smoothed his tie a little and addressed the fire marshal, or whatever position this little man held, with blatant condescension.

"If this Dray person is on your payroll, and she was in that fire, then you've both been waiting a very long time for someone who's quite obviously dead. We have three bodies in the morgue right now and the nurse is checking..."

The bespectacled doctor found himself propelled across the room and up against the nearest wall before he had much time to do more than merely gurgle a response.

"Listen here, you sonuvabitch," said the lieutenant in a low, menacing voice. "I don't know who the fuck you think you are and quite frankly, I don't care. You ever treat someone like this again and I'm gonna show you my limited knowledge on how to do a rectal examination, you got it? Work on that bedside manner. And for your information, it's lieutenant."

Then he released the man's lab coat and dismissed him with a wave of his hand. "C'mon, Abby. If we have to look through every damned room then that's what we'll do 'til we'll find her."

"Nurse," the doctor called over to her. "Call security."

"Please do," Pete remarked flippantly. "And while you're at it call the police down here. How much you wanna bet I got more friends on the force than you do?" he taunted the doctor.

The nurse gave the stunned resident a wry look and then motioned to the two visitors. "I don't think that will be necessary, doctor," she added nodding them to follow her.

It took them a while to ascertain just where a certain tall, dark firefighter had been put. Seeing the worried look on Abby's face had the nurse checking the computer records with a fine-toothed comb, ruling out the morgue straight away. The air whooshed out of Abby's lungs the minute the three bodies had been identified. Although she really did think she would have known had Dray died, a part of her knew there was just no way she ever could. It didn't stop her from voicing exactly what she knew the lieutenant wanted to hear. "Well, we knew that," she said as Pete gripped her shoulder gently in camaraderie.

They talked briefly while the nurse delved deeper in the computer files. Not finding anything she motioned them to follow her. "Let's take a trip up to the burn unit. Maybe they haven't had the chance to put her file into the system," she offered.

The three of them walked along in relative silence until they came to the nurse's station and the clerk addressed the attendee.

"Hey, Gorchyk? We've got some people looking for somebody. Came in from that fire down in the industrial sector. You have a Khalkousa, Andrea Khalkousa?" the clerk asked.

The attending nurse stood about 6'5", had the darkest skin Abby had ever seen, and seemed to be constantly pushing a pair of metal framed glasses up the bridge of his nose.

He pursed his lips and sighed deeply.

"You talkin' about that hard case we had to put in isolation? Yeah, we got her. Had to tie her down when she came to and freaked. Wasn't doin' any good screamin' and fightin' and just being a bad ass. None of that nonsense is going on in my unit." He pushed his glasses up again. "You ladies want walk down this way," he smiled at Pete and patted his shoulder. "And you can come, too."

Pete rolled his eyes at Abby in mock disdain but automatically felt a kinship with the large man.

"You her husband or what? 'Cause I got to tell you, she's really in no shape to be gawked at, ya know?"

"Uh, no...I'm her lieutenant, have been for years. Abby here, she's her..." he stopped. A crease lined his brow as he mentally perused the typical labels and came up empty. Abby bumped into his back as he stopped walking.

"I know she ain't your sister, honey," the dark nurse told Abby. "Not the slightest bit of a resemblance. You just a friend, too?"

Abby tilted her head a little. "Yes. I'm a friend, well, more than a friend actually."

The mountain of black flesh hunkered down a bit so they were at eye level and he waited until the smaller woman's eyes cleared.

"I can't let you see my patient unless you're family."

Abby felt a tear seep out of the corner of her left eye and pushed it away with trembling fingertips. "She's not just a friend," was all Abby could manage.

The nurse understood and gave her a reassuring smile. "Well, all right then; family it is. Mr. Man here," he said motioning to Pete, "he's gotta wait in the hallway, but you can follow me, Hon."

Abby swallowed deeply and then wiped a shaky hand over her face. The head nurse peered at her out of the corner of his eye. Being a pretty good judge of character he could tell right off that the blonde wasn't going to go to pieces, at least not in front of strangers.

"I'm not gonna lie to you, sweetheart," the nurse continued. "This isn't gonna be a pretty sight so you better be someone that loves her a whole lot. She's gonna need whatever strength she has left and all that you have to give her in order to get through this." He hunkered down again and pulled the woman's hands up against his belly. "You understand I'm not asking 'cause I have any axe to grind, you know?" Abby nodded and gripped the man's large hands tightly.

Nurse Gorchyk pushed his glasses up and smiled softly, finally getting the confirmation he knew all along. He patted the blonde's hand and then began his trek down the hall once more.

"Well then, come along. I think she's been waiting for you."

Abby nodded and then put her hand on the lieutenant's wrinkled sleeve. "I'm sorry you have to stay here, Pete. I'll tell her you're here," she said, her voice choking the last words off with emotion.

Pete inspected the end of his shoe and nodded. "I'll wait for you," he muttered.

As Abby, the ward nurse and the emergency room nurse moved down the hall, Pete felt such a sense of loneliness sweep over him that he had to fight down his urge not to just run after them and insist he go along. Memories of his close encounters with fire returned. There wasn't a firefighter he ever knew that didn't know the inside of a burn unit up close and personal.

As they walked along the look on the blonde's face must have registered shock because the black nurse turned and then pulled the older woman to the side.

"Danielle, don't tell me that skinny assed intern didn't tell her anything about the patient's condition?"

Danielle Winchell sighed. The new intern she'd been saddled with the last two days was, quite frankly, a waste of good skin and brain tissue.

"We didn't know we had the patient," Winchell said softly. "Doctor Wiseass Intern had this poor woman thinking she was in the morgue."

Herman Gorchyk moved his glasses up to their rightful position and frowned. He knew exactly which intern Danielle was referring to but said nothing. He'd seen his fair share of moron doctors and nurses, in his 15 years, but that new intern, well he did take the prize.

Danielle interrupted Herman's thoughts as she spoke. "Ms. Khalkousa had been logged in as being one of the John Doe's brought in today."

"Damn," Herman muttered. "I'm sorry, Danielle. I asked Rosa to change it before she went off shift after we found discovered our John was a Jane during our examination. I shoulda double checked myself."

"Well good help is hard to find," Danielle joked, showing forgiveness.

"I'll have a detailed talk with her tomorrow. Trust me."

As they continued to walk slowly, Herman turned to Abby. "Now just so you know she's got a lot of tissue damage, like I said. But we also had to restrain her so she couldn't leave. She gave us a tough time and she's one strong lady, but I probably don't have to tell you that, do I?"

Abby simply nodded.

"Oh, don't you worry, she'll be fine. She's on morphine so she should be out of it for a few hours at least." He patted the woman's shoulder and waited until the blonde had mopped her face a little. Then he went on. "The prelim lab work showed some high levels of toxins in her blood, so that explains her psychotic behavior. But I think there might be some head trauma as well."

Abby could see the genuine concern in the larger man's eyes. He was only doing his job but there was more to it; he really cared. It made her feel better to think that her lover was in the very large and capable hands of this medical professional.

He peered over the rim of his glasses and shook his head. "That woman is a hellfire, isn't she?"

"She's the strongest person I've ever met," Abby told him.

He gave her a ghost of a smile. The glasses went back up the man's nose and then he proceeded.

"Well, she's got three broken ribs right side, a fracture of her right radius, and three broken fingers right hand. She's also got second-degree burns to her left hand, and third-degree burns to her upper chest, and throat areas. There are also some lacerations, second-degree burns and singed areas on her face. As for her lungs we're waiting on lab work. By the rasp of her voice, and the wheezing, it's not good."

Abby wiped her face with her sleeve and then swallowed deeply. "Anything else you haven't told me?"

Nurse Winchell looked at her associate and then down at the clipboard. "These toxicity levels are very high, Miss Dean. They've done some fairly extensive damage to the patient's nervous system, and there's no telling how long the effects will last."

Abby nodded and put a shaky hand on the nurse's arm. "Effects? What kind of effects are you talking about?"

Herman rubbed his face in thought.

"Well, according to the information released by the Center for Disease Control, there can be some pretty weird, paranoiac episodes. The patient can drop between fifteen and twenty pounds because of the intense nausea and can experience fierce headaches, too."

"Are these the kinds of symptoms you think Dray might have?"

Herman sighed. "Oh, she's had some episodes, that's for damned sure, but it's the blindness that has me worried."

Suddenly Abby lost all ability to speak.

## Chapter 14

"Blindness?" Abby felt the room tilt and tried desperately to remain focused.

"Yeah," he said, drawing the word out slowly, "but I'm betting it's temporary. I checked her face for flash burns and such. The eyes themselves seem fine, and without any apparent damage. That leaves chemical poisoning."

A gasp left the blonde as 'poisoning' and 'chemicals' accompanied the word 'blindness.' She wasn't too sure about the types of chemicals involved, but poisoning wasn't a good word to have associated with them.

"How...how long do you...?" Abby sputtered as she wondered about her lover's recovery.

Herman put his large hand gently on her shoulder.

"Tough to say," he told her. He acted as if he was going to continue but suddenly stopped when he heard shouting from inside the room.

"Wy gttupi! B' b' zabijac was! Sonuvabitch, get your hands off me!"

Both stood in stunned horror as the barrage of epithets and mumbo jumbo continued unabated.

Abby seemed to move in slow motion as she crept closer to the isolation room. She stood with her head against the metal door, trying to get past the verbal garbage coming from her lover. It just didn't seem possible. Abby opened her eyes and peered in through the safety glass window and felt like screaming. She didn't know what she'd been expecting but it wasn't this.

Dray lay in a narrow bed equipped with restraints, most of which were totally ineffectual, biting and trying to claw at the cast on her right arm.

Hearing enough, Herman walked inside the room and caught Dray's attention. With calculated precision, she aimed and hit the male nurse with a bedpan.

"Ha ha! I didn't miss you this time, did I Holmes?" the brunette croaked. "You can run, but you can't hide! Come on a little bit closer, I got something for ya."

Herman rubbed his shoulder and moved closer.

"Okay, Missy. I don't know who Holmes is but you and me's gonna have a talk. There's somebody here to see ya but you gotta be good or I'm not letting her in." He reached out, carefully snagging a leg restraint and buckling it before Dray had a chance to kick him.

"Was gttupia kobieta! You just come close enough and leg tied or not, I'll fuckin' beat you three ways 'til Thursday. Whatcha say? Just you and me? I bet a man like you is into pain. You like to hold women down so they feel defenseless, huh? Well, tough shit. I got outta these straps once and I'll do it again so let's get it over with once and for all, right? Just come a little bit closer."

Abby shook her head, her jaw agape as the big man skillfully managed to get both legs back into the restraints. The blonde watched as her lover's biceps bulged and a thin sweat covered her bruised body. Dray thrashed back and forth in a mad effort to escape her tormentor, and her rage escalated with each handful of air purchased.

"Goddamn you to hell!" Dray bellowed hoarsely as she mashed her cast against the side rail of her bed.

"Now, now...Khalkousa. Just calm down, I ain't here to make your life miserable. I don't wanna tie you down, woman. Look, you got a visitor and I wanna make sure you ain't gonna hurt her or yourself. Now c'mon and play nice."

With a roar of sheer malice she launched herself at the man, legs straining horribly. Abby was sure they would break so she pushed her way through the half-opened door. She wasn't sure what she was going to do but she couldn't just stand by and see Dray in such torment.

Herman cast a look over his shoulder, silently pleading for the blonde to just leave until he had things under control. Nurse Winchell who heard the commotion from down the hall, darted forward, hypo in hand, and poised to do battle.

"I'm not a Goddamned victim! I'm not, I tell you! Never again. Never!"

Abby stepped closer as the nurse emptied the last of the tranquilizer into the firefighter's hip and watched them carefully push the hysterical woman back down on the bed.

It was as if all the air had slowly been removed from the room as Abby looked down at the contorted face of her lover. A snarl painted Dray's lips and an angry welt framed her face where the SCBA mask had been. Her usually sparkling blue eyes were glassy and somehow alien, as if they belonged to someone else.

Abby moved even closer to the bed as Dray began thrashing once more. She watched as the blank look her lover wore was replaced by a look of unbridled fury.

"Get your stinking hands off me, syn psa!" she growled in a low raspy voice.

Herman frowned and looked at the nurse. "Say what? Am I losing my mind or is she speaking in tongues?"

Nurse Winchell shrugged. "I dunno, kinda sounds Polish to me." She looked pointedly at the man. "Maybe I'd best take missy here back to reception 'til the patient gets settled down. I don't know why that hypo hasn't kicked in yet but this one should do the job."

"Beats the Hell outta me but yeah, ain't no time for her to be seein' this hellion in action."

Nurse Winchell motioned for Abby to follow her but the blonde didn't notice. Her heart hammered loudly in her chest as she witnessed the vapid look on her lover's face. It was so very unlike the woman she knew and she felt the first twinges of real fear seep into her heart. *Dear Lord, where's Dray gone.*

Her lover seemed charged with electricity and Abby felt herself drawn closer. Her eyes saw the bunching muscles, the curled talons clenching and unclenching as if to some unheard pagan melody, but her heart saw something else. It was as if she were observing some wild animal caught in a snare and felt unable to resist the urge to soothe the beast before her.

Her body moved as if in slow motion until she was looking into the raging blue eyes of a familiar stranger. And then, for just one split second, the lines on the beast's face smoothed out and it was Dray, lost and helpless, who was caught in some terrible space where she was alone and terrified.

"Dray?"

Herman's expression went from shock to disbelief, as Abby's voice seemed to gentle his patient. Closing his mouth with a snap, he began talking in soothing tones as the woman's jaw slowly relaxed.

"You might not want to be getting that close," Herman offered.

Abby ignored the warning and moved in closer. She couldn't put her finger on it but something, some haunted look, seemed to permeate every inch of Dray's noble features until there was very little resemblance to the woman she knew and loved.

"Oh Baby, where did you go?" Abby questioned softly.

"Ona jest moja."

Abby's brow creased and she wondered what the words meant.

"Pomagajà mnie?" Dray seemed to ask. Again, Abby was confused.

Dray's closed eyes moved back and forth rapidly as her labored breath began to even out and then her harsh features relaxed into a drug-induced slumber. Abby leaned over and kissed her sweaty brow.

Herman nodded to the nurse and they slipped outside, taking a spot in the hallway outside the door. They spoke quietly about what they just witnessed. Nodding, Nurse Winchell walked back down the hall as Herman returned to the room.

He opened his mouth to say something but stopped dead in his tracks. The young woman had removed all the restraints and was in the midst of climbing up beside one of the most unpredictable patients he'd ever seen.

"What the...? No way, little girl. You can't be thinking of climbin' in with that wild child. And even if you was, no way am I lettin' you."

Abby brushed the short dark hair from her lover's eyes and then used a corner of the sheet to wipe a bit of pink drool forming at the corner of Dray's mouth. She locked eyes with the man and spoke in a very calm, matter-of-fact voice.

"I don't think I'm in any danger whatsoever, Herman. And I don't much like you referring to my girlfriend as a 'wild child' either. She's a human being first and foremost, and a patient second. And just how much stuff did you give her? All told, I mean?"

The nurse pulled his eyes away from the purity of the open and frank look. Her words cut deep and he felt a twinge of guilt for the offhanded comment.

"Okay, I'm sorry. That didn't come out just like I wanted it to. Let's start again." He cleared his throat. "First off, you ain't getting into that bed without restraints on her, no way. It's against the rules for one thing and just plain foolishness for another."

Abby opened her mouth but closed it with a weary sigh as Herman's hand went up.

"I gave her enough Morphine to pull down a bull moose, that's the God's honest truth, but enough without hurting her. I don't rightly know why it didn't pull her down and have her out for the count. Might have somethin' to do with the chemicals in her system right now, I don't know. I'm a nurse, not a doctor."

Abby sat back a little, her hand still touching Dray's face. It wasn't going to do either of them any good if she and the nurse were at each other's throats.

The blonde looked down at the puffy eyes and the spread of blue and purple across Dray's nose and cheekbones. Yes, it was quite a harrowing experience. She remembered just how afraid she'd been back in their apartment that night. Just the look in Dray's eyes, how terribly cold they were, when she had recounted the horrible circumstances in the death of her son had been enough to freeze her blood and take her breath away. She looked down as her lover exhaled a raspy breath and could almost feel herself transported back to that moment when the image she'd had of this pristine hero had begun to splinter and fracture. Reality was never more real than that instant.

"Why don't you climb down from there and we'll set to getting her all cleaned up. I'm sorry but we're gonna have to put them restraints on her, okay? It really is for our safety," the nurse told Abby.

Abby bit the inside of her cheek and then quickly bent down and brushed Dray's lips with her own. *Come back to me, honey*, she prayed and then climbed back over the bed railing.

Two other nurses came into the room and the taller of the two spoke quietly with Herman.

"You'll come with me, okay? Herman's got some work to do with our patient and by the looks of ya, you could probably use some down time at the cafeteria. 'Sides, there's a big guy just outside wants to speak with ya."

Pete took that moment to poke his head from around the corner.

"Hey Abby, you okay?" He wore a tentative smile, which quickly left his face as he caught sight of Herman lifting the nude form of his friend carefully out of the bed. He tried not to look at the damage done to the beautiful body but was unable to.

Pete found his breath trapped in a cold fist as he took in the angry burns that seemed to radiate from just under Dray's chin down to the area between her breasts. One eyebrow looked patchy in places, though Pete couldn't tell whether it was due to fire or chemicals. Her face wore pit marks and red slashes, testaments to the trouble the medical team had gone to in removing the congealed mess her SCBA seal had been reduced to. The Lieutenant closed his eyes tightly. Didn't matter what the doctor's said; a person was never ready for the realities of a burn unit.

He remembered the vacation the three of them had taken and how carefree the days were on the beaches of Henderson Point. Swallowing convulsively as he thought about the pain Dray must be enduring, he tried to focus on anything to keep from screaming. The other nurse began to strip the linen off the bed and Melrose found a small hand grasping his as they were both led out of the room.

The Lieutenant sat with his back against the wall of the hospital cafeteria and sighed as the petite blonde went through the articles he'd been prescribed.

*Just like a mother hen*, he thought to himself.

She reached over a hand and poked his neck gingerly. He briefly wondered how a person like Dray stood it. Dray was no more demonstrative than he was and the idea of anyone, including a good friend like Abby, touching him in such a personal way in broad daylight in front of people was really ...well, irritating. He knew she meant well...thoughts of the nice paramedic floated past his eyes.

Pete winced as more lotion was smeared across the front of his neck.

"Jeez! Ya got hands like a sailor."

Abby arched an eyebrow and sighed.

"Don't move around so much and I won't have to be so rough with you then. And, while you're at it, you can stop being such a baby."

She dabbed the last part onto the inflamed skin and then carefully worked it through the course hair of the man's upper chest.

"Not a baby," he said with a touch of petulance, making her bite the inside of her cheek but Abby said nothing, choosing to focus on the task at hand instead.

"You gonna tell me about Dray? What happened in there, Ab? I...I heard some yelling."

Abby swallowed deeply and shook her head. She had to process what had happened first. Then maybe she could talk about it. Briefly. The condensed version, sanitized just for Pete's sake, would be the best all the way around.

Abby looked down at the man's hands and sighed. They were so big and hairy and...so very unlike Dray's. Dray had large hands, too, but they were like pieces of art. They were so well sculpted and the way they flitted about when she was trying to express something important was akin to some sort of ballet. Visions of the burns radiating across Dray's chest, lower right arm and hand suddenly swamped her and she inwardly cringed.

"You nice folks mind if I join you?" Herman asked.

Pete looked up to see the large man towering over the table. "Sure! Have a seat," he answered.

The silence from Abby was deafening. The nurse shrugged his shoulders and took a seat, placing his cup squarely in front of him. It was his second cup and he was determined to get this one down before the first could do much complaining. His tongue felt furry and he was glad for the antacid in his pocket.

"So. Um," the blonde grabbed a napkin to wipe the ointment from her fingers and then just looked back at the nurse with an open gaze. The nurse continued to sip at his coffee and just looked back at both her and Pete.

Pete cleared his painful throat, "Yeah, you have any more news for us about Dray?"

"Yes, about the blindness," Abby began, "What's the duration and is it permanent? And when do you think the chemicals will be out of her system? And what kind of rehab will we be looking at?" she blurted out her questions at a rapid-fire pace.

Herman held one hand up, downed the rest of his coffee and placed it carefully on his tray.

"First off, I guess you better tell me a bit about our mysterious Dray Khalkousa."

Abby opened her mouth but closed it as the nurse pointed one finger at Pete.

"You start, if you don't mind."

He smiled over at the Lieutenant and waited. Pete took a long, refreshing swig of his iced tea and then settled back in his chair.

"Ah...well, lessee. Dray's been a firefighter for about four years now. She's pretty much been at the top of her class in both written and practical. She does point real well and is one helluva fireman."

"Firefighter," said the nurse as he removed a small scratch pad from his front vest pocket and began to make notes.

"Huh? Oh. Yeah, thanks. It's taken me a while to get used to that term, 'cause I guess I don't think of it as being particularly labeling."

Herman grunted. "According to the x-rays she's had lots of broken bones over the years. I'd wager she's been in more than one bad scrape."

Both friends nodded and Herman relaxed, doing the same.

202

"Has she had any counseling? I'd imagine that was a regular requirement in this field?"

Pete mumbled something incoherent.

"So, no therapy?" He placed the pad and pen on the table and pressed the tips of his fingers together under his chin. "And why is that, Lieutenant? With her history and all?"

Pete bit his lip and then sighed. "Well see, it's like this. Yeah, she's been in a coupla really big blazes and she's had her share of mishaps in that area, too; things falling on her, getting trapped in warehouse fires, that kinda thing." He saw the look on Abby's face and cleared his throat. "There have been times when she was unable to save kids, had folks jumping out of windows before she could save 'em. Stuff. But she's handled it, ya know? She's been in therapy when the department has requested it. It's not all that unusual for firefighters to do that. Some events are more stressful than others and yeah, Dray's seen her share. She has," he finished rather lamely.

"Yes? Go on."

Pete was beginning to feel he had to justify himself and Dray. Why should he have to stick up for his friend or his job as her supervisor? He'd done the very best he could for Dray, always had. His belly lurched.

Herman noticed the emotion that swept over the firefighter. "Look Lieutenant Melrose. I'm not making judgments here. I'm just tryin' to find out everything I can that might help us care for Dray. The more I know, the better."

Herman leaned forward, waiting for Pete to at least answer his direct questions and was rather surprised when the blonde began to speak.

"She was in therapy before."

The nurse picked up his pen again and jotted down a few notes. He looked up and nodded towards Abby, indicating she should continue but Pete spoke first as he leaned back in his chair.

"Her son died in an apartment fire about six years ago. She tried to save him. But...".

Herman closed his note pad. He waited until he had Pete's undivided attention and then began.

"All right. She's been in a number of really intense situations and has come close to death a few times. I'm assuming she's very much a risk taker if she usually takes the front position when a team is sent in." He pursed his lips and then looked directly at the blonde. Holding up his fingers, Herman began to tick each one off.

"She has a penchant for extreme violence but has had no serious therapy since working as a firefighter. She's obviously made some positive choices in her life and tried to move past the pain. But I wouldn't say she's been entirely successful in that area."

Pete bit the inside of his cheek and then stared belligerently at the head nurse. "Look, why d'you have to know this anyway? You're treating her injuries, right? You're a nurse not a shrink."

Herman's lips moved into a cruel smirk.

"Yeah, I'm just working on the outside of Ms. Khalkousa, but I gotta see the inside, too. Being a nurse, it really helps me see what's going on upstairs," he said tapping his temple. "I'm not gonna mince words – take your friend upstairs, she's in a world of pain right now. It goes beyond just the chemicals or the drugs administered. If Dray is ever gonna heal properly it's gotta be inside and out."

Pete pursed his lips and gazed out the window as Abby played with the napkin in her hand.

"So," Herman stated in a matter of fact tone. "You two gonna see her through this?"

# Chapter 15

Herman Gorchyk yawned as he twirled the combination on his locker. It had been one trying shift but, finally, it was time to go home. He scratched his prickly chin and cheeks absently and then removed his glasses. Pinching the bridge of his nose and then rubbing the exhaustion from his eyes, Herman sighed as he tried to process all the new information on his patient.

Gorchyk yawned painfully as he passed the front desk and fumbled in his pants pocket for his car keys. Mumbling a curse under his breath, he slapped his forehead as his search came up empty and then turned on his heels and headed back towards the Burn Unit.

Around that time, the duty nurse was checking Dray's vitals when her patient began to choke. She jumped and then leaned forward with her flashlight as the patient's eyes flew open. The woman's pupils were still unresponsive and yet the nurse could see by her patient's rapid eye movement that she was seeing something, if only in her mind.

"Now, now...it's okay," the nurse told her. "You're in the hospital but you'll be fine. Just settle down, now." Taylor cringed as the sound of straining leather filled the air. Leaning down onto her patient as quickly as she could, she tried in vain to keep her charge from ripping the leather restraints off the sidebar. Her biceps bulged in effort and she gritted her teeth as the body beneath her pulsed forward. With her face inches from the woman, Taylor knew exactly why she'd been warned and why she'd been advised to report any indications of consciousness to the nurse's station.

It was all a moot point, however, as the call button usually clipped to the patient's pillow slipped off the bed and out of reach.

The nurse grunted with effort when the leather snapped and her patient's large left hand began forcing her off and to the side.

"I'll kill you...fucking...kill...you..."

Muscles bunched and strained as the two levered for power. As the next buckle gave the nurse began to shout out for help. There was a brief popping noise as the brass rivets sprang their connection between the two pieces of leather, and then the nurse found herself in an all out, no holds barred war with a woman who's both hands were now free and inching towards her throat.

Dray bolted up in bed, holding the nurse by the neck as all the pain and torment of her dead son screamed through her mind, the memories as fresh as when they occurred. "Let me go!" Dray screamed. "I need to save my son!"

A voice called out to Dray somewhere in her hysteria.

"You know you can tell me anything, right?"

The small, tiny voice penetrated through the rage that was enveloping her heart and she was suddenly aware that her hands were shaking. She'd been dreaming. What was it – something about...? She tried to focus on the dream but it faded into wisps and was gone.

Then she felt the skin beneath her fingers, felt the soft flesh giving way, and drew her hands away quickly.

"Wha...who?"

She reached forward blindly, trying to find out who was making that rasping noise in front of her. If only she could get the damned lights on. Where the Hell was she?

The nurse fell back onto the bed gasping and crying as she tried to draw in a burning breath. Her eyes flew open as she felt a warm hand on her leg, and she stared in disbelief at the patients shift in demeanor.

She blinked in total confusion as her mind tried to grasp just what had happened. She'd been manhandled and shaken as if she were nothing more than a child's rag doll by someone who, by all rights, should have been unable to even pull against her restraints, let alone break them. The nurse knew by reading the woman's chart the extent of her injuries, and wondered just what kind of powerhouse she was when healthy.

Dray's fingers moved across her left hand and she frowned. An eyebrow shot up as IV tubing was detected. Flinching with effort, she wrapped the tube around whatever it was on her right hand, and pulled. A soft, insistent beeping began on the monitors above her head.

*Sedation...she should have been well sedated.* The nurse swallowed painfully as she tried hard to remember what the chart had indicated. Wasn't she supposed to have been given Morphine during the last shift? She wiped the tears from her eyes and peered closer at her patient. She didn't look drugged at all. In fact she looked quite lucid.

"Where...where am I?" Dray asked as she attempted to clear her throat. She tried to take a deep breath but the ensuing pain had her gasping and clutching her side.

"What the...?" Dray's fingertips played over the bandages securing her broken ribs, and then her mouth hung open.

"A fire, I was in the warehouse and," her eyes shifted from side to side as fear gripped her. "Oh my God, where's Ted? And Pete? Did they get out?" Dray flinched as her raspy voice pierced her hearing and she wondered just how badly off she was this time. She shuddered in memory and struggled to swallow again.

The nurse leaned in and patted the woman's arm. "It's all right now," she croaked. "Just stay calm and I'll find out. I don't know anything about the other firemen, but..."

"Firefighters."

Herman stood in the doorway. He arched an eyebrow at the nurse sitting on the patient's bed, a perplexed look on his face as she crawled slowly to the side and grabbed the clipboard.

"I was on my way out when I heard the monitor sound off."

His eyebrows knit together as he caught sight of the reddening flesh around the woman's neck. And then he noticed the broken leather restraints.

"Oh, my God!" Herman mentally went through just how much he could increase the patient's dose without causing permanent injury.

The other nurse smiled weakly. "It seems someone on the last shift neglected to sedate the patient. It says here in the chart that she was exposed to some chemical poisoning. I don't know but she seems fine now."

"Nurse Taylor, page Dr. Harrington immediately." Any exhaustion Herman felt evaporated as his brain tried to wrap around the strength needed to break the restraints.

The nurse rubbed her neck and swallowed painfully.

"Yes, Herman. It's no big deal, really. We...experienced a nightmare."

"So, this is the infamous Khalkousa, the fireman? I'm Dr. Harrington," he said in introduction. "You were in a warehouse fire and..."

207

"Yeah, yeah; I got that part. What, you guys have a power outage or something?"

Harrington turned to Herman. "Doesn't she know she's...?" He was interrupted as the nurse cleared his throat.

"Ahem!" Herman rolled his eyes and grimaced. He put his hand on the doctor's shoulder and gave him a warning look. The doctor shrugged off the large man's hands and approached the patient.

"The lights are on, Ms. Khalkousa. It's your eyes, there seems to be a side effect from the chemicals you were exposed to. But it should only be temporary," the doctor explained

Dray blinked stupidly, her mouth still open. "My eyes? I'm partially blind?"

"Yes, your sight has been affected, Dray. Oh, you don't mind if I call you that, do you?" The patient nodded absently and he went on. "We won't know the extent of your injuries until we get the complete lab work back."

"My injuries." Dray swallowed and tried hard to focus on what the man was saying instead of the terror that threatened to overtake her. *Blind...I can't be a firefighter...I can't...what kind of life would I be able to live without my eyes?*

Suddenly Dray remembered the others at the fire. "Did anyone bring me in? Was there someone...?"

Herman nodded again. "Yes, you and another fella came via an ambulance and your friends came a few minutes later."

"Was there a woman?"

Harrington rolled his eyes thinking of the altercation he'd had earlier with a certain blonde and decided it was time for a coffee break.

"Yeah, short blonde woman," he answered with little outward emotion before going back to the chart. "I think everything's under control now."

He graced them all with a toothy smile. "Other than her eyes, the patient seems well on the way to recovery, yes?"

Herman gave a nod.

"I think we can reduce her sedation," the doctor told them. "As long as Andrea here behaves herself, that is. Try not to give the nurses a hard time," he warned, handing the chart back to Herman.

Herman sighed in relief and as the resident left Nurse Taylor cleared her throat and smiled, giving the woman's shoulder a reassuring pat. Dray jumped a little at the touch, having been too preoccupied with thoughts of Abby to notice the nurse's close proximity.

"It might take a while before you get your senses back, Ms. Khalkousa. Your body is too used to relying on sight but that'll change and you won't get surprised very often. Just takes time and practice."

Dray felt a wave of nausea hit and it seemed as if her head were slowly being immersed in a bath of molten syrup. What was it the doctor said? She couldn't remember everything the doctor had told her but she did remember one thing.

"The small blonde," Dray asked, "is she here?"

"Ms. Dean came in shortly after the ambulance arrived. She was with your lieutenant. I've been in touch with 'em both on and off all evening."

"Pete Melrose? He's okay?" she croaked.

It was beginning to feel very warm in the room. She tried to brush a line of sweat from her brow and only succeeded in scratching the cast across her flush skin. She winced and tried not to notice the tightening of the flesh around her neck and face; it was a sure indication that she'd sustained damage there, too.

The head nurse cleared his throat and nodded towards the door. Taylor sighed, and still rubbing her throat, left for a well needed break. She stopped at the door and gave them both a tired smile.

"Your girlfriend is asleep in the nurse's lounge right now," Herman told her. "Stubborn one she is," he added with a slight chuckle. "We tried to send her home with a promise to call her but she wouldn't hear of it."

"And Pete?"

"The Lieutenant was released and just got called back to the stationhouse. I expect he'll be back sometime this afternoon. As for the fella brought in with you, hmm Ted I think, we'll just keep him for observation for another day or two. He's got a leg fracture and will be sporting a pretty good rash, plus some wrinkly red skin for a while, much like the Lieutenant."

Dray breathed a sigh of relief, nodded and began to pick at her cast. Herman pushed his glasses back up and just sat quietly. He had hoped for at least a shadow of a smile. Finally the patient cleared her throat and then smiled gratefully as he placed a paper cup of water into her hands. His eyebrows shot up as the woman's fingers began to worry what remained of the leather straps around her wrist.

"Here, let me get those off you. You're gonna behave like the doctor asked, right?" She nodded painfully as he worked each wrist free of the restraints and then moved down to the ones on her ankles.

"You mind telling me why I was tied down?" she mumbled between painful swallows.

Herman shook his head slowly. "Well, Dray. Oh, you don't mind if I call you Dray, do you?"

"Dray is good. And you're Herman, right?"

He sat back and placed a foot against the bar near the bottom of the bed.

"What do you remember?" Herman asked. The firefighter eased back self consciously as he adjusted her pillow and Herman thought she might just avoid the question all together. "Look, if it's too painful..."

Dray shook her head, and then rolled a little to face him.

"More broken ribs, huh? How many, and what are the other injuries?"

"Hey, why don't you just rest a while? Sitting up like that, expending all that energy fighting with one of my nurses...well, you are gonna find you pay for such things when you're dealing with lung injuries. Trust me."

He watched as the woman's cold, frank look was aimed in his general direction.

He sighed. This was always the tricky part. Sometimes it was best if the patient didn't know the extent of their injuries because the knowledge hampered their recovery rate. However, judging by her manner the patient seemed to be the type that rose to the challenge. When he finished the list that included a number of broken bones, poisoning and possible blindness, Herman noticed that she'd slid a little farther down in her bed.

"Now look, I know it sounds bad. But it isn't, not really. You're a strong woman, Dray, and God knows every nurse on this damned floor has seen you in action at one time or another."

"Look Pal, just cut the crap and give me the bottom line, will ya?"

Herman scratched his chin and then removed his glasses. He was getting way too old for this, and it was way past his bedtime.

"First off, I am not a doctor. What I am is the supervisor of the Burn Unit."

"Supervisor, huh? Is that a fancy way of saying you're a glorified charge nurse?"

Herman smiled. "Yup, that it is."

"So that means you can read that chart," she took a deep wheezing breath, and then went on. "So spill it. I can take it, you know?"

"Well, it might not be something you really want to hear...at least not quite yet."

"Hey, I'm a firefighter...I can take the heat, okay?"

Dray's honesty and forthrightness was like a breath of fresh air. Herman was beginning to like this woman more and more. He was fond of folks who didn't like to beat around the bush and said what they meant, and more importantly, meant what they said.

"All right. Well, you might incur some scarring on your hand and neck, but I think the damage done to your face will be minimal, but we'll have to wait and see about that." He paused, noting a quick intake of air.

"Shall I go on?"

Dray nodded, finding her throat dry making the act of swallowing all but impossible.

"You might have some involuntary movements due to your nervous system being ravaged by the chemicals. That might continue for some time. Truth is, we won't know anything concrete about the damage to the rest of your system for a while. That could take days," he admitted hesitantly and then went on, "or weeks."

Fear gripped the brunette as she thought of the worst-case scenarios. She could be rendered incapacitated for brief periods of time or completely destroyed as the effects of the poisons continued to ravage her body. Would it be permanent? She wasn't too sure whether she'd just want to go out in a blaze in glory rather than waste away in some ward with Abby watching her die, inch by bloody inch.

Dray blinked deeply as a fuzzy feeling seemed to spread throughout her body. Her breath became somewhat labored as she tried to find another comfortable position. Every muscle seemed to protest as she tried to roll over. And then she felt a tickle in her throat that rapidly became a rattle.

"Oh, God."

"Dray?"

The nurse became somewhat alarmed as his patient turned a dusky color fighting the urge to cough. He took hold of a wrist, and quietly monitored the patient's pulse.

Tears sprang to Dray's eyes as she felt a wetness spreading between her legs, and then begin to soak the sheets beneath her.

Herman gripped her shoulder as a painful bout of coughing ensued. She clutched at her damaged throat, forgetting the pain, and just focused on keeping the airway clear as panic threatened to swell it shut. A horrible feeling of drowning swamped her as the coughing dislodged what seemed to be a river of thick fluid.

"Don't fight it...just go with it...that's right. Don't fight your body's response to the gathering fluid in your lungs. I'll see about getting a bronchodilator prescribed in just a minute." He rushed back to the bedside just in time to place the emesis basin beneath the patient's chin before she threw up.

He watched as the brunette lay there gasping, then she curled up into a tight ball and he felt his heart breaking. All the information Pete had told him had fleshed out the woman to the point that he felt he had a real handle on who she was and what was more that he respected her.

"I can help that. Give me two seconds, and I'll give you a shot of Morphine."

"No," Dray gasped. "No painkillers."

Herman stood totally immobilized as he fought with his instinct to just give the injection or give in to his patient's wishes.

"Why? It'll help you relax and be able to get rid of more of that phlegm. You will have to, Dray, sooner or later. It's part of the side effect of those chemicals. The really good part is that the increase of saliva will help soothe your throat some." He reached back to the nightstand, and grabbed a face cloth from the drawer. Quickly making his way over to the sink, Herman soaked it, and then pressed it against the back of the woman's neck.

"You are getting way too hot, Dray. Gotta cool you down. These temp fluctuations are bound to happen for a while, too."

Finally, she lay gasping and only barely released a groan from tight lips as the nurse took the basin away and rolled her onto her back.

"Stay put," Herman told her.

A few involuntary tremors ran through the firefighter as she briefly pondered exactly what mischief she could possibly get into during the nurse's absence. It certainly wasn't as if she'd be going anywhere any time soon. Another deep coughing spell seized her and left her gasping from weakness.

# Chapter 16

It had taken all of Abby's nerve to just stand and listen to the night nurse as she rattled off the improvements first and then the warnings afterwards before being granted entry to Dray's room.

*Yeah, yeah – whatever. Just get the Hell out of my way!* she wanted to scream.

Abby followed the nurse and quietly crept inside Dray's room.

Climbing carefully onto the end of the bed, Abby settled herself so that her head rested just by her lover's tailbone, and began the arduous task of settling her nerves.

Dray woke to a presence just behind her and knew instinctively that it was Abby. She lay there, feeling the bond they shared, and thanked whoever it was that had allowed her to survive the fire.

*The fire.* Fear gripped the firefighter as the list of her injuries sprang to mind. Herman said Abby had been asleep in the nurse's lounge. Perhaps she hadn't seen the damage.

Dray felt a slight movement behind her and self-consciously brought her arms up to shield her face. Every other breath was punctuated with sharp pains that seemed to sap every bit of her waning strength.

"Don't...don't move, Abby...please. Just stay there."

Abby winced as her lover's gravelly voice grated against her nerves, and she wiped her nose with a trembling hand.

"What's wrong, Dray? Are you in pain? Should I get the nurse?" Abby asked in a rush.

Dray seemed so weak and so very pale.

Ignoring the brunette's request, Abby moved up off the bed and over to the other side. She took one look at her lover and quickly looked around. She went to the sink and retrieved the basin and a cloth.

Abby quickly placed the chrome beneath Dray's chin and put a hand out to pull the woman's damp hair out of her eyes.

"Don't," Dray's body was racked with spasms as she fought the urge to vomit. *Not with Abby here, no!* Her mind however had no control over the bodily function.

Dray began to cough and Abby wiped Dray's face before taking the basin away.

Moments later, Abby returned to Dray's bedside with the rinsed basin. She looked down as a bandaged hand closed around her wrist.

"You can't stay...just go."

A few tears were blinked back as the brunette fought with her weakened state. She glared defiantly in the direction of her lover, her body shaking.

"I'm not gonna leave Dray. I have to help you," Abby answered, taking the hand from her wrist and placing it in her own.

"Not like this." Dray ground the words out through clenched teeth as she willed Abby away, until she was in better shape and not some horrible freak show. "Go away."

Dray's head felt as if it were on fire and the room had begun to spin giving her the impression that she was falling, falling. Dray reached for the basin again. "I said go!" Dray shouted.

The nurse who was standing outside walked into the doorway and motioned Abby outside. Reluctantly she moved to meet her in the hallway.

"Oh, honey. Please don't take whatever your friend said to heart. She seems like a proud woman so let us handle it, okay?"

Abby sniffed, and made a quick nod.

Nurse Taylor rubbed the small of the woman's back, and then eased Abby into a chair.

"Your friend is a very strong woman, Abby. It has to be hard for her to be seen like this. Do you understand?"

"She's been through fires before, and she's always been okay. This time," she stopped and shook her head.

"You've seen her like this before then?" She peered closer at the woman. "Has she been this extensively burned and traumatized before?"

Abby blinked and her vision cleared. "I don't know about the injuries but she has some scars," she motioned with her hands up the inside of her arms. "Here and there but nothing really extensive," she fumbled, shaking her hands in frustration.

"Well, how did she react last time?"

Abby shook her head. "I don't know. It was before we..."

The nurse nodded her head knowingly.

"I see. Well, I think your friend is afraid of how you'll react. My guess is she thinks you'll bolt because she's not this big, strong, butch fireman."

Abby looked up at the word.

"Oh come on, sweetie. I spotted it the first time I saw you looking at her," the nurse grinned. She patted the blonde's shoulder. "Don't you worry, she'll come around. But you are gonna have to be really strong and not take any guff from her. She needs to know you'll stand by her..."

"...For better or worse." Abby completed the redhead's sentence and then nodded, gratefully accepting a tissue. "We've been together for almost three months but it seems like forever."

"Been married 17 years myself and that IS forever," she retorted.

Abby gave a brief smile. "Well, when I said forever I didn't mean it in a bad way, like it's tedious. It's quite the opposite really."

The nurse walked to the counter and poured two steaming cups of coffee.

"That kind of love shows; it's hard to hide."

"Hard to find, too...I've been waiting all my life for Dray. And now that I've found her, I can't believe I almost lost..." Abby trailed off unable to complete the sentence. Instead she added, "I don't know what I'd do if I lost her. I really don't. And what if it happens again? What if the next fire is the one? Or what if she doesn't recover from this one?"

Taylor took a seat next to the woman, and moved close enough to have their elbows touch.

"She's been a firem...firefighter for a few of years so she's well acquainted with the dangers associated with it. You'd better accept that if you're gonna stick around. Unless you think you can change her...but you gotta ask yourself. Do you want to change her?"

Abby shook her head quickly. "No. I love her for who she is right now. What she does for a living is very much the person she is. I could never expect her to just...give that up. Not for anything. Not for me."

Taylor smiled and then took another sip of her coffee.

"Bleck. This stuff is horrible. You want some sugar with that? I think ten or eleven spoonfuls oughta do the trick."

Abby uttered a short laugh and then placed her hand over that of the nurse's.

"Thank you. You're very kind."

Taylor shook her head.

"Naw, just doing my job. Just like you're gonna do, too. Oh, don't you worry; she's in good hands. Herman will be working closely with her and then she'll be moved out into the burn ward where Doctor Matheson will attend her. He's a decent guy, too. And nothing like the one you ran into in the E.R the other night."

She looked closely at the blonde and decided not to pull any punches.

"Look, I've seen the patient's chart, and while it's not as bad as I've seen, it's pretty serious. Ms. Khalkousa," she stopped mid sentence as the blonde held a hand up.

"Call her Dray, alright? And I'm Abby, Abby Dean."

Nurse Taylor took another sip of her brew and then nodded. It looked like they were going to be interacting on a personal basis for a couple of weeks at least – might as well be on a first-name basis. "Yeah, sure. I'm Janelle, okay?" The nurse glanced at her watch and then pushed a few red strands behind her ears. "Look, I have to get back, but remember this honey...she'll have some pretty fierce mood swings with her body betraying her on more than one occasion. Are you ready for that?"

"I am," Abby answered nodding confidently.

"Now, you said you've been together for three months so realize quick, the honeymoon is over. You're going to have to forget the role you played in her life before and move into position as a teacher, nurse, and a confidant. It's gonna be hard, make no mistake about that, but don't lose faith."

Abby nodded again. "I won't leave her."

"Good," Nurse Taylor nodded. "Because you'll need the strength for both of you now more than ever."

The next few weeks passed in a blur as each woman was pushed to the limit of her endurance. The attending psychologist had begun sessions that left Dray feeling as if she were in free fall.

By the fourth week, Dray's sight had gradually improved and then returned to normal. While both Abby and Herman had expected this to better the brunette's frame of mind, it seemed to have the opposite effect. A good dose of insomnia had arrived and had continued, unabated, leaving her both sullen and withdrawn.

Herman Gorchyk groaned aloud as he threw himself into the chair behind his desk. It had been a long afternoon of rounds, emergencies and Dray. Although he was loathed to admit it, he was getting nowhere with the firefighter and had decided the time had come to ease off a little. He could tell from her records that her body mass had been reduced by at least 2 inches and her weight was off by about 20 pounds.

Herman made a few notes on the patient's file and decided to ask the doctor in charge if they could muster up some dietary supplements. After all, if Dray felt better about herself then maybe she'd be more inclined to co-operate.

As Herman compiled his reports Abby sat in Dray's room when he heard Dray's voice boom yet again.

"You had no right. You knew the bike wasn't road worthy. Hell, how many fucking nights did I spend down there in that fucking basement?"

Abby had tried to reason with her and make Dray understand that when the truck hadn't started and the feeling of danger had welled up inside her, that she had no other choice but to take the bike.

"There was nothing wrong with the truck," Dray continued. "I'd just given the fucking thing a Goddamned tune-up, for Christ's sake," she said, her voice scratching like barbed wire down a long, lonely road. Abby could see the veins and tendons standing out in the woman's neck as she fought to keep herself under control.

Everything had erupted in response to Nurse Taylor's comment about a ride on her 550. Dray's head had lifted with interest and the two had begun a lively conversation about motorbikes in general.

It was only when Abby had mentioned that she'd had to use the bike to get to the warehouse fire that the proverbial shit had hit the fan, although Abby explained that someone was working on it, free of charge. Abby could almost feel the dip in temperature as Dray's demeanor had changed. So could the nurse, who rapidly went in search of meds.

"What made you think you could just jump on my bike and go for a joy ride? Who gave you the fucking right?"

"Dray, the truck wouldn't..."

Dray had clutched her arms tightly around her middle and Abby could see the pain clearly written on the woman's face.

Part of Abby was afraid of this new version of her lover. She'd never seen the woman flip-flop so quickly, going from mood swing to mood swing. And although Herman and the psychologist had tried to prepare her for just this kind of manic behavior, Abby was not handling it well. It was almost as if she were walking on a tight rope, a dizzy height above the ground, with no hope of a safety net below.

"Honey? I was just worried. I'd had this horrible feeling when I was listening to the police scanner, and..."

"You jumped to conclusions and then jumped on my bike." Dray's ravaged face had twisted with rage and any pretense she'd had of keeping a grip on her temper vanished.

"Goddamnit, Abby! You might have fucking wrecked my bike! You could have blown the motor! The fucking petcock was jamming and the whole engine coulda seized up! If you don't know anything about a motorcycle, then you have no business being on one!"

Abby set her jaw definitely. "I said I was sorry. What more do you want?"

Taylor had walked in carrying Dray's medication and the brunette had hit the roof.

"I'm not taking that. I don't need that shit."

Taylor had glanced at her watch. "Doesn't matter whether you want it or not. That's beside the point; it's time for your meds."

"I told you – I'm not taking them."

Taylor had been on the verge of arguing with the firefighter some more when she noticed tears in Abby's eyes.

"Oh, why is she crying like that?" the nurse said obviously frustrated.

"It's none of your Goddamned business what I say to Abby, is it? She's my girlfriend and..."

Green eyes flashed dangerously. "Oh, nice way to treat your girlfriend," she interrupted snidely. "You get your jollies out of pushing Abby around, treating her like garbage?"

"I never touched her."

"No, you'd rather destroy her with your cutting remarks and charming manner. She's been here through thick and thin right from the beginning. If it weren't for Abby, Hell, Herman would have strapped you down in a good old-fashioned straight jacket and waited out your reaction to the meds."

"Oh, you're breaking my heart." Dray pulled away as soon as Abby stretched out her hand.

"Dray, just stop."

"And who do you think sat in a cold, hard chair all night long every night for a week in the ICU?" the nurse pointed out. "She could have gone home anytime and no one would have held it against her. She's put up with your ranting and raving..."

"Are you finished, 'cause this story is getting old. Every fucking time little Abby gets a cross word said to her, you all jump on me and make me feel like shit. Did I ask her to tend to me? Did I ask any of you for your Goddamned help? No, I didn't; I don't need anybody's help, see? I'm just fine...I can handle things myself."

Dray had tried to ignore the growing signals of a pending attack but both women could see just how the stressful situation was affecting her.

"Oh, forget it!"

Taylor had pushed her hand forward, the meds in plain sight and Dray had shoved the woman back, scattering the pills in every direction.

"I'm not gonna take 'em," she rasped between coughs.

It was as if Abby's heart had frozen solid as cobalt blue eyes pinned her where she stood, trying to make her feel worthless. It was almost like that wild child, as Herman called her, was back, but in full force. The only difference this time was that Dray was not only fully conscious but could see exactly who she was hurting.

*God, I don't think I can take this any more.* Abby had stumbled back in shock and the only thing that had saved her from just running away was the pained look that momentarily replaced the dead one in Dray's eyes.

"Dray?" And then she flinched as the scars on her lover's face turned a purple hue and the transformation was complete: this wasn't someone she knew – this was a complete stranger. As Dray moved in her direction, Abby began her retreat.

"Look, just take your meds the easy way or I'll have to get help and we can do it the hard way." Taylor advanced from the side carefully, a new dose clutched in her hand.

"Get the fuck away from me!" The patient's glare swiveled back onto the advancing nurse. "I don't need any Goddamned meds, any Goddamned nurses, any Goddamned keepers!" She glared at Taylor and then her gaze resettled on Abby. "Why can't you understand, Ab? You of all people. But you don't want to understand, do you?"

"We're only trying to help, Dray," was what the nurse had said but it was a condescending tone that Dray heard. Breaking off eye contact with the blonde once more, she turned, her fists balled at her side.

"What I need is silence and to be left alone." She had punctuated the sentence by pushing over a chair.

Something snapped inside of Abby. She'd tried for weeks to be the tender caregiver but she realized it wasn't getting her, or Dray, anywhere.

"That's it, Dray!"

The brunette's head swung around at the firm tone from her lover.

"Excuse me?"

Abby stepped closer, getting inches away from Dray. She looked up and pointed a finger. "You're gonna sit down. You're gonna shut up and you're gonna take that medicine or so help me God-."

"You'll what?" Dray prodded. "Leave? Hell, I've been trying to get you out of here for weeks!"

"Oh no," Abby smirked. "You don't get off that easy, Sweetheart. You're stuck with me whether you like it or not."

The sarcastic tone was one that Dray hadn't heard before and it caught her off guard. She turned to Nurse Taylor to find she wore an equally surprised gesture.

"I'd do what she says," the nurse outstretching a glass of water and a small paper cup of medicine.

With a sigh Dray emptied the cup in her mouth and took a big drink of water.

For good measure Abby looked up and said, "Open your mouth and stick out your tongue." Confused at first Dray did as she was asked and Abby gave an approving nod seeing that the pills indeed were gone. "Now that this mini-apocalypse is over I'm going to get some coffee."

Without waiting for a reply, Abby left the room with Nurse Taylor following behind her. Once they were walking down the hallway the nurse turned to Abby with a grin.

"Good work," she commended.

"Really?"

"Absolutely!"

"Then why do I feel like I'm gonna throw up," Abby quipped.

Nurse Taylor just grinned. "Because you need a break, Sweetie...Tell you what, Abby – why don't you head home for a little while, relax? She'll be fine since she's had her meds."

Abby simply nodded and continued to walk down the hall as Taylor gave her a pat on the arm. "Call if you need me," Abby told her.

"Will do."

Abby got home and collapsed on the couch, not even making it to the bed. After a few hours she woke with a start, unsure of her surroundings.

She went to the phone and began to search through the yellow pages, Abby sighed in relief, finding the number she wanted and then proceeded to dial.

It had been a brief conversation but when Abby had finally hung up the receiver, she was feeling a lot better. Not only had the mechanic remembered her, but had said he'd left a couple messages on her answering machine for a good week.

Yes, the bike had been fixed. It had been a relatively easy procedure to just replace the gas tank. The man had been amazed while retelling that part of the story. Parts for old bikes were really hard to find. As luck would have it, the contact had been able to locate one the same afternoon.

Abby had listened carefully, trying to memorize each bit of information. She wanted all the facts and figures when she went in to see Dray again.

At the hospital, Herman noted Dray's vitals and motioned for Abby to come in.

"She's gonna be groggy for a bit. You know the routine. You might want to..." he paused as the blonde held up her hand.

"Yeah, I know." Abby retrieved the basin and cloth from the nearby sink and took her place in the chair by the bed.

"You sure you don't want me to stick around?"

"For what?" came a gravelly voice as Dray fought to keep both eyes from remaining shut.

Abby shook her head quickly and waited until the nurse had left.

"Hi, honey."

She watched as the firefighter dragged a weary hand over her face. "And a howdy to you, too." Dray repositioned herself a bit higher on the pillow and then gave the blonde a weak smile.

"I shouldn't have torn your head off, Abby. I guess...the pain was getting away from me. I don't like to take all the meds, Babe. They really mess with my mind. I don't like the way..." she paused, her tongue suddenly two sizes too big.

"They make you feel like you have no control, huh? I can relate. But I meant what I said. I'm not letting you go that easily."

"Stop it."

Abby's eyebrows shot up quizzically.

Dray settled herself over onto her left side and just looked at Abby.

"You do it all the time now. And I hate it."

When she didn't get a response other than stunned silence, the firefighter went on.

"Between you and that asshole Masterson, I feel like I have 'fragile' written on my forehead. I'm not some baby, or some mental case, either. I can take care of myself, Abby. I have been for years. Way before you entered the scene."

"But I'm only trying to help you. I love you."

Abby blinked as her lover snorted. "Yeah, I know you love me, Ab. There's never been any doubt in my mind. It's just...well, I don't need you to love me to death, ya know? I can do things by myself. And even though you don't believe me, I will ask for help when I need it."

Abby cringed at the condescending tone but pushed it aside. "No Dray, you won't. You said it yourself – it's a loss of control and that's something you can't do."

Khalkousa pushed a breath out from between sandpaper lips and tried to push off the lingering effects of the drugs. They must have given her a barbiturate, judging by the way the room was spinning.

She cleared her throat and grimaced. *God, not another attack!*

"Can you hand me that basin on your way out? Thanks."

"But I wanted to apologize for taking your motorcycle. I know you were right. I didn't realize just how important that thing is to you."

"Thing?" she croaked. "That 'thing' is a '74 Custom low rider. It's a piece of precision machinery, Abby, not just some toy to go toddling around on. Did you at least remember to put the tarp on it? Pete help you get it home?"

Abby bit her lip, knowing full well the wrath awaiting her.

"Um, actually, it's not due to come back from the shop until next week."

Dangerous silence filled the room as Dray's jaw all but hit the floor.

"What?" she sputtered.

"There was a problem."

"What the fuck did you do to my bike?" The last part of the word was squeaked off as the phlegm began gurgling up. "Where is it? What shop? Goddamn it, Abby! What the hell did you think you were doing? I work on my bike. Me. No one else, just me!"

And then the coughing began in earnest.

"How could you? I've worked so hard," she rasped out, "I've built that engine from the spark plugs up. I've put my whole heart and soul into that," she wheezed out from between tight lips as another bout of coughing ensued and then Dray barely managed to choke out the last, "and it's all destroyed because of you."

"No, Dray."

But it was no use. The coughing fit was gaining momentum, leaving Dray trying desperately to position the basin under her chin, and keeping Abby at arm's length, all while trying very hard not to fall out of bed.

Abby knew she wasn't wanted at that particular moment but she was damned if she was just going to leave Dray to the pain. And she knew, without a shadow of a doubt, that there was no way her lover was going to ask for help. So, being the stubborn woman she was, she just pushed Dray down, rolled her over to the side and held the basin until the spasms settled and then died down completely.

She flinched as the blue eyes of her lover looked up at her accusingly. Abby sighed and then set about cleaning things up and disposing of the basin.

"It's probably the meds that are making you sick right now. You've had some coughing but that's due to you lying on your back when you were asleep. If you can stay rolled over on your left side then it should help drain things."

Dray's nostrils flared as she fought to keep her mouth shut.

"If you'd work with the nurses then we'd be able to go home, go back to our lives and get on with things."

*Our lives. What fucking lives? Everything's changed now.*

"And just what do you expect me to do? The Goddamned physiotherapy is killing me, my body's already so damned wasted I can hardly recognize myself in the mirror any more. I just wanna be left alone, left to heal."

"Left to heal or left to die? Be honest."

Without a second glance Abby just shook her head, turned heel and left the room. The nurses were right: she needed to go home. They both needed more time apart.

Dray lay in the bed with both arms across her face. *Why do I keep doing that? Damnit, I really am gonna fuck this up.*

Abby tossed and turned most of the night, their large bed a very lonely place. Holding her lover's pillow close to her all night, Abby thought that the scent might be enough to allay some of her fears and keep her mounting depression at bay. She couldn't afford to wallow in self-pity. Not only was it counter-productive but also a few of their friends were coming to see Dray in the morning and she had to keep her focus.

The clock ticked on morosely as the dawn came up through the blinds. She sipped at her coffee, not really tasting it but needing its warmth nonetheless. The short wave radio sat on the kitchen table, and Abby remembered hearing bits and pieces of Pete's conversation at the warehouse fire, the premonition that Dray was in danger so strong and clear.

Pete and Ted came by a few hours later to give her a lift to the hospital with the promise that the lieutenant would see to Dray's truck. Abby hadn't wanted to worsen things by even getting into the vehicle, preferring to either walk or get a taxi.

She waited in the patient's lounge, not trusting herself to be subjected to the cold set to her lover's eyes, and let the two men follow Herman down the hall. However, both men had returned downcast when Dray had refused to see them. The brunette had told the nurses she was too tired, but Abby could tell that doubts about her current physical appearance were eating at the woman's self esteem.

Both Matheson and Gorchyk, unbeknownst to Dray, had made arrangements to have a transplant team look at her case. The leaps and bounds in skin graft technologies had Abby very excited. Now, the only hurdle left was getting the recalcitrant firefighter to accept the help offered.

Two days had passed very slowly for the blonde, and she found herself filled with frustration. If Dray could just get past things then they could begin the arduous journey of getting their lives back.

She removed the keys and slid out of the cab, groaning as her feet hit the ground. It had been a long day already as she waited for Dray to get her release papers. The doctors had told her to expect some moodiness. The combination of medication and what the psychologist termed as Post-Traumatic Syndrome was taking its toll on the normally stoic firefighter. Now the damage was done and feelings of anger, frustration and self-pity were all that held the woman together.

Abby feared her lover would continue the spiral she'd begun even before coming around in the ICU ward. She'd been present when Dray had thrashed around in her delirium, ranting about flames and death; lost in hopelessness and despair. A feeling of helplessness had pierced her heart after reading the notes about Dray's hallucinations. Were they ever to be free of their shared dreams? Although Abby truly believed in reincarnation, there were times now when she could almost convince herself they were nothing but pain induced nightmares that had no bearing on who they were or the past failed lessons they'd endured.

Pushing slowly up into a standing position Abby arched her back, easing some of the weariness from her body. She didn't have to even look in Dray's direction to know the woman was shooting daggers at her. After hastily grabbing her purse, she walked over to the lobby, leaving the stubborn firefighter behind.

Although the classes she had started weeks ago were only introductory courses on psychology and family mediation, they had gone a long way to shore up Abby's flagging self-esteem, giving her more confidence than she thought possible.

Thoughts of how Dray had constantly fought with the doctors and nurses, complaining about the lack of medical care and skill they displayed filled her mind. With sudden insight Abby could see that, by constantly pushing everyone away, Dray was protecting herself from admitting just how vulnerable she had become. She wasn't mad at everyone around her, she was mad at herself.

The more she tried to help, the worse things seemed to be. And as much as Abby needed to go to her, to help her from the cab, she knew it was precisely the wrong thing to do. As hard as it was going to be for Dray to ask for help, she was going to have to. That way she'd be in control of exactly what was offered and what would be accepted.

Moving as carefully as she could, Dray eased out of the car and then winced. Grabbing her travel bag in the front seat, she tried to stand tall, rising to her full height, but found that just induced another bout of pain and coughing.

Abby unlocked their apartment and dropped off the bags she had before returning downstairs. When she returned to the landing she saw that Dray had finally made it inside the building. Despite the argument that might ensue Abby took Dray's bag and walked to the elevator ahead of Dray, pushing the button.

Once upstairs and in their home Abby turned to Dray.

"Just leave that stuff there," she told her. "We'll get it after I get back with Chinese." Before Dray could issue a protest Abby turned heel and left the apartment.

Dray looked around the empty apartment and gave a sigh. Deciding on getting a real bath, and not just a sponge treatment, she made her way to the bathroom.

Dray bent carefully and turned the faucets until the temperature was just right. The mirror began clouding over with steam and that was just fine with the firefighter. She had no desire to see how her body had been ravaged. A shudder ran through her body as she recalled the image of the flames closing in on her, reaching out for her in a deadly embrace.

She struggled but the T-shirt finally came off but not before rubbing painfully against the gauzed, raw flesh of her neck and upper chest area. Dray breathed slow steady breaths, trying to calm the rage that threatened to overtake her again. When she was able, she took a few agonizing moments to unwrap the special tensor bandage from around her ribs and then groaned as the pressure was released. The room tilted crazily as the firefighter bent over to fix a plastic bag over her cast, causing her to knock a bottle of lotion to the floor. Feelings of frustration welled up hotly as even the easiest of tasks seemed impossible to master.

"Goddamnittohell!" she shouted, sending the contents of the counter flying. Clenching her jaw tightly, Dray began counting slowly until her heart rate had lessened. It seemed as if everything was conspiring against her. Even the button to her jeans wouldn't cooperate and she winced as her mending fingers fumbled ineffectually at the button.

Tears of hopelessness threatened to fall but the firefighter blinked them savagely away, determined not to let the situation get to her. She decided to just pull the pants down and be done with it, worrying about the button later.

"Can't...even...get my damned pants off...for...cryin' out loud! Goddamnit, leave off!" She wrenched the pants one way while her torso went the other, causing her sense of balance to shift. Before she knew it, Dray was looking up at the stained ceiling of the bathroom, both elbows and backside screaming their reminders that she couldn't care for herself. Trickle of tears became a torrent, the resulting wail almost inhuman in it's suffering.

Abby thanked the woman at the counter and then began to carry her purchases back across the street.

She hoped her lover was lying on the bed fast asleep but knew that was a remote possibility. For one, Dray hadn't had her medication and would be in a great deal of pain before too much longer. For another, she'd seen the state the woman was in and knew a nice bath or shower...Her head popped up sharply as she thought of Dray trying to get undressed without her help.

"Oh, God...shit, shit, shit!"

A horn blasted and Abby jumped back, clutching the small boxes of Chinese food to her as her heart hammered painfully in her chest. Carefully peering up and down the street in the fading light, the blonde finally saw a break in the traffic and quickly made her way back to their apartment.

Abby wasn't too sure what she expected to see but it wasn't the calm woman sitting in the chair before her. Despite the cold weather, Dray had simply changed into another light shirt.

Their bags lay exactly where the blonde had placed them but their jackets had been hung up and both kits lay on the counter in the bathroom. Abby could just see a corner of the T-shirt Dray had been wearing draped over the shower curtain bar.

"I...I see you've been busy, sweetheart. You could have waited for..." Blue eyes pierced her where she stood.

"I don't need a nursemaid, Abby. I am an adult who is perfectly capable of taking care of myself despite what the friggin' doctors would have you believe."

Abby felt a hot flush creep up her face and she willed herself to be calm. "No, I know that, Dray. What," her eyes darted back and forth as she thought of something to say, "what I meant was...I could have done this, you didn't need to bother."

"Don't patronize me, woman. I'm not an invalid," Dray spat through gritted teeth. The shorter woman blinked slowly at the coldness in the woman's voice. Abby swallowed deeply again and then noticed the tremor in the other woman's hands as they gripped the armrest.

She began noticing a few other things as well, things that were minute and easily missed with a cursory first glance. She could tell that Dray hadn't had a shower, despite the towel that lay on the floor in the bathroom. And her pants were slightly damp on the side and looked to be unbuttoned at the top.

She suddenly had a clear idea of just what had happened in her absence. She bit her lip again and then took a deep breath.

"Okay, I get it. I know you aren't an invalid and that you aren't a happy camper, either. I also know you're not comfortable with asking for help."

"I don't need anyone's help, Ab. Can't you get that? I didn't need anyone's help before you came into my life and I sure as Hell don't need it now. Nothing's changed."

"But," Abby snapped her jaws shut and then placed their food on the table. "Fine. If that's what you want, fine. We've been through this before, over and over again. You just wanna argue and I'm not going there, so forget it."

Dray felt a bead of sweat start to trickle down from her temple and her hands gripped the chair painfully. It had taken every bit of strength she possessed to pick things up in the bathroom and get her clothes back to where they looked semi normal.

The pain inside her was like a raging inferno that had been birthed from the very depths of Hell and every second was a torment. She could feel the icy cold grip of fear welling up and her valiant efforts to keep the pain at bay crumbling before its onslaught. But she was damned if she'd give in to it. Just a little bit of time alone to get back the control she felt slipping away was all she needed. How was she going to get the woman out of the room so she could really clean herself up?

"Getting tired. Gonna have a nap. I'm not hungry and you can eat later." It wasn't a request and Abby knew judging by the set of Dray's jaw that the woman needed to save face right now; her battle to hide the pain was tenuous at best.

"Yeah, I could go for a walk. Maybe visit the bookstore just around the corner. How about if I-?"

"Whatever. Just...go."

Abby pushed away the hurt that sat like a large grinning beast on her chest. She refused to let it gain purchase within her heart.

She went over to one of the bags and removed two small vials. Extracting the proper dosage, she set them aside, grabbed a jacket and moved to the door. It took all her willpower not to stop and hug her lover. It killed her that she'd been shut out once again, but Dray's current shape might have made such an action a total embarrassment for both of them.

"I've set out your meds, Dray. I'll be back in about an hour. Okay?"

A mumbled "Okay" was her brief response. Feeling hurt and bewildered, she tried hard to focus on what the psychologist had said. Dr. Masterson had dealt with control issues extensively and had cautioned Abby not to confront Dray because the woman's emotions were all so close to the surface.

He'd gone over the firefighter's past in as much detail as Dray would allow and each incident, as small and isolated as it may have seemed, was bringing Dray closer and closer to a meltdown. Dray, he said, was like a flammable substance that only required the right catalyst to achieve flashpoint. Abby didn't want to be that catalyst.

But it was getting extremely difficult to just let things continue, just be some observer, instead of a partner. How long had it been since they'd even shared a warm embrace?

She picked up keys and carefully walked to the door. Abby opened her mouth to say something, anything, but took a trembling breath instead, and eased the door shut behind her.

*...six, seven, eight, nine...ten!*

Squeezing her eyes tightly shut, Dray finally let the moan escape from behind lips drawn into a thin line by almost unbearable pain. Her head felt like someone had used it to play a rousing game of soccer and then had left it, partially misshapen, out in the sun for a few days. Everything felt too close, too tight, in her body; even her skin felt that it was being stretched beyond its normal elasticity, and that at any moment she'd either fold in upon herself like some black hole or blow apart in a supernova. Either way, she felt out of control and very afraid.

Terrible thoughts began seeping into her brain, binding with the fear and feeding the voracious pain that grew steadily. Gasping with the effort to regain some bit of control, if only over her trembling hands, Dray began to inch herself forward out of the chair.

Sweating profusely, she tried to ease her weight onto her uninjured side, thereby avoiding the coughing spasm that was bound to occur at any moment.

Every second crept slowly by despite her fervent prayers, and it was all she could do to just focus on the bathroom door and not pass out as she walked. Her hair and body were drenched with perspiration and the impossibly heavy clothes she wore clung to her, making it feel as if she were submerged in thick syrup, working her way back towards the surface.

*Almost there...just a little more.*

She staggered into the bathroom, and barely made it to the sink before throwing up. It was a good five minutes before she could straighten up and begin the arduous job of getting her clothes off for the second time. While the pain of having her ribs unbound had been almost unbearable, she took solace from the fact that at least she didn't have to go through its removal again. No, she was in a hurry – she needed a shower badly, if for no other reason than to wash the stink of failure from her body.

After two months of being confined either to the Burn Unit or the Rehab Center, she was more than happy to just kiss the whole field of medicine off. Dray cringed thinking back on the sessions she'd had with the unit's psychologist as he tried to figure her out. "Or judge me as incompetent," Dray muttered to herself.

Finally standing in front of the mirror, the firefighter lifted a shaky hand to the front of her bangs, checking to see how her face looked now that some of the scabs had fallen off and her eyebrow had grown back in. Tiny crimson fingers seemed to be spreading out, racing across the side of her face and up to her temples.

Pulling her hands away from her face, Dray recoiled. She was a monster. She had ceased to be anything but a freak. She hadn't wanted to admit it but it had hurt her pride deeply to think that losing something as superficial as beauty had impacted on her in any way. She had never paid much attention to what genetics had given her in the area of physical beauty. Now that the image she had of herself was damaged, she felt divorced from who she was on the inside and what the rest of the world saw on the outside.

Although Dr. Masterson had suggested that in order to get over the scarring done on the inside she would have to do something about the scarring on the outside, she couldn't face that yet. The fire hall had generously offered to pick up the tab not covered by insurance but there was no way that she was going to be beholden to anyone. Ever.

A sharp gasp was wrenched from her throat as the spray hit the skin on her face and neck. The temp had to be somewhat tepid as the burns were still raw in most places. Dray felt her right biceps strain as she tried to keep her cast from getting wet.

She pressed her forehead against the tile as another ripping jolt of pain went through her body, leaving her knees shaking and she suddenly wondered whether she'd make it back out to the bed before falling again.

Switching the water off, she quickly grabbed a towel and did the best one-handed effort she could muster on the mess of tangles her hair had become. She sighed, wondering just when the luster had disappeared leaving the dull mat she now wore.

As she stood there dripping, the firefighter had a good look at her body for the first time since the incident. Scars and burns aside, she was still in pretty good shape, she surmised. All the more reason she didn't need anyone to wait on her hand and foot. *A little under weight but I could build that back up,* she considered.

What concerned her most though was just how long it was going to take to get back into tip-top shape and then convince Pete she could come back to work sooner than the doctors had proposed.

"If those dumb jerk have their way I'll be out for a good five or six months."

She wiped the condensation off the mirror and frowned. And she knew that would kill her. Even taking the two weeks off last summer had been a difficult chore. "What the Hell am I supposed to do with half a year, just sitting around twiddling my fingers?" Her shoulders slumped as she lifted her chin and began to closely examine her face.

"And what the Hell do I do with Abby? She's not gonna want to stick around with me looking this way. Not for long." She pointed a shaky finger at her reflection. "You know it won't take long before she splits. And you can't blame her, Dray. Why would anyone that young and beautiful want to be saddled with a monster?"

A wave of nausea hit her and it took three or four shuddering breaths before she was able to tamp down the feeling. "I can't lose her, not this time, not after finding each other."

Inferno

Carefully weaving her way back towards the bed, Dray sat gingerly on the side of the mattress and contemplated what she considered to be a corset. She detested the article of torture but knew any relief she thought she'd get by not wearing it was only an illusion – until the damage to her ribcage was repaired, she really had no choice. Gasping from the pain as her ribs were cinched back into place, the brunette got the last strap adjusted and pulled a sheet over her trembling body. It was a long time before she slept.

Dray resettled the seal on her mask after pushing out a few strands of hair. She tapped Ted on the shoulder and then tried the door. It wouldn't give. The air woofed out of her lungs as the door threatened to shatter the bones in her shoulder and she muttered under her breath.

"Damned door must have warped in the heat."

Ted nodded and then motioned the woman to stand back. Taking a moment to line up his sights, the man smiled darkly and then swung his axe, hitting the handle dead on.

"All right! Let's go."

"Lead on, MacDuff," he said bowing.

Dray could feel the heat from the metal through her gloves and hunched her chin down in preparation. Sure enough, there was a backdraft that pulled on her, almost as if the blaze were inviting her in.

"Okay, Ted...you stick close, okay?" She turned around but the man was gone.

"Ted?" She spun around in every direction, trying to catch sight of where her partner had gone. Flames licked up the walls and began rolling across the ceiling.

"Shit! Ted! Goddamnit! Ted!" Black smoke rose up, obscuring the firefighter's vision, and then she watched in horror as one of the wooden beams began toppling in her direction. The butt end started an upward swing and Dray knew she wouldn't be able to dodge the blow. Moving as far back as she dared, the flames licking at her coat, she braced herself for the brutality barreling down towards her.

Then at the last minute, the pillar seemed to roll in mid air and then crash down not four feet from where she was standing. Dray moved to the side and was surrounded by pockets of flame. She hesitated as she thought about her next move.

*Where the hell is Ted?* she wondered. *The guy couldn't have just disappeared...*

And then, through the smoke the firefighter could see an image. It was dark, and hard to make out, the outline shimmering in the heat waves, but she could see it was a person.

"Ted?"

There was no answer, and she moved closer, mindful of the flames but trying to gauge just how to get to the man unharmed.

Where the Hell had he gone? Was he hurt? It made no sense that the silhouetted form remained obscured by the smoke. The brunette waited, calculating the seemingly random pattern of the flames. Right before the next flare occurred she rushed forward, shielding her face with her heavily protective sleeves and rolled through the fire to safety.

"Ted, are ya hurt?" She walked forward, hand outstretched, and then the smoke parted and it wasn't her partner standing there but her lover, Abby Dean.

"But...how?"

Abby stood there, her face bathed in a soft light that seemed almost iridescent.

A crash sounded just off to the right as the ceiling began to fall in. It was as if the air surrounding her was being sucked out and replaced with flame, leaving her gasping and disoriented.

"Where's Ted? We gotta get outta here, Abby. If we don't leave now we might not be able to." A patch of the roof yawned dangerously and then the area exploded as an influx of air whooshed into the building. A roar of flames rushed towards them, feeding on the influx, leaving the air surrounding them quivering with heat waves. The resulting blast left Dray tumbling head over heels, her body coming into contact with hard, blunt surfaces as she was battered by the raging fire bent on her destruction.

"Abby!" she shouted, images of the unprotected woman causing her imagination to run wild.

Finally coming to a halt, her right shoulder jutting out at a wrong angle, Dray lay dazed and confused. Pushing herself forward, she found her legs trapped under what remained of a back wall.

"Gotta get up...get Abby...Ted." She burned with every breath as the heated air scorched her unprotected lungs. A bitter taste threatened to overwhelm her and she wondered when she'd lost her mask. She tried to push the rubble from her lower torso, and then watched in horror as the exposed skin on her hands began to blister and peel. Then her trousers seemed to deflate as her legs withered and shrank to half their body mass. Instead of the strong vibrant woman that she had been all of her life, she was reduced to a vulnerable pile of disfigured flesh, no good to any body.

"Oh gods," she moaned as her hands moved quickly over her face. Her helmet fell off and Dray lay there, gasping.

"You're nothing but a stupid, good for nothing bitch, Khalkousa. You never were no good. You are the reason that Debbie Nang was killed. It was your fault."

Dray shook her head slowly as the form morphed into Holmes. He stood there, hitting the palm of his hand with a truncheon. She reeled in shock as the man lifted his chin to adjust the tie he always wore, exposing a narrow gaping wound that extended from ear to ear. The wound began to seep small rivulets of crimson and he laughed, releasing a torrent of gore from his throat.

"No...no...oh my God, no!" Pinned to the ground and helpless, Dray covered her face and then shrank from her own alien touch.

The laughter faded and was replaced by a calming voice that all at once soothed her soul. Peering from behind her thick soot covered sleeves, Dray moaned as the image of Holmes shimmered and then became her past lover, Debbie Nang.

A sob rose in her throat as she remembered the woman's soft touch and how very intricate the patterns had been upon her body.

She screamed her torment and rage as the image twisted in agony, and then Debbie reached out to her silently begging for help. She hadn't been there, and hadn't been able to save the first person that had ever truly loved her unconditionally. Debbie had offered everything and had asked nothing in return, nothing but total fealty, freely given by someone who had very little to lose and everything to gain.

Hot tears etched through the grime covering her face and wave upon wave of self-pity and torment rushed through her. A small girl, eyes blank with horror, appeared before her, and the firefighter sobbed uncontrollably as the child embraced the burnt remains of her younger brother. The figure of the small boy morphed and it was Dray's own son lying there, eyes open and filled with pain.

Abby appeared again, reaching out to her, and then instead of a hand it was an accusing finger pointed her way.

"You fucked up again, didn't you, Dray? You always said you would. But what else could I have expected from someone who has failed everyone who meant anything in her life?"

Nurse Taylor appeared beside her, a smug look on her face.

"Why would she stick around a bitch like you, Khalkousa?" She snuggled closer to the blonde, who, while not accepting the redhead's advances wasn't spurning her, either.

"I won't push her away, Dray."

"No Abby, I won't fail you," Dray pled. "I can't...not again."

Every failure in her life became magnified, effectively blotting out any heroic deed she'd ever done, and she felt her heart begin to whither.

Abby quietly closed the door behind her and slipped her coat off onto the back of a chair. The bit of snow still clinging to her boots made a squeaking sound and she winced with every step. Finally struggling out of them, she stretched in the darkness and then made her way into the bathroom.

Although she couldn't hear the usual sleep noises Dray made, it was obvious the woman was asleep. Abby rubbed her tired eyes, their reflection dull by the light of the neon sign across the street. A funny rattling sound began as the tap was turned and the basin slowly filled with hot water and Abby sighed with pleasure as soon as the washcloth hit her face. A groan came from the other room and Abby's fingers settled on the pills beside the sink. A few incoherent words were mumbled and she knew the pain was working overtime. Gripping the doorframe tightly her eyes picked out the huddled form balled up under the sheets.

"Oh, Dray, you can't continue do this. You have to have your meds."

Abby sat heavily on the chair close to the bed. *God, why does she do this? Now I have to wake her up and...*

Abby cringed thinking of the fight she knew would ensue; it was a never-ending battle. Frustration etched lines across her brow and she buried her face in her hands, wishing there were some way to reach her lover.

In her dreamscape, Dray continued to thrash about.

With a brief shimmer Abby became Zosia, dressed in prison rags but standing tall and unafraid.

"I don't fear you, you must know that by now. You try to hide the truth, but I can see inside you."

The phantom woman shuffled forward, her eyes hard orbs of green fire.

"You never even tried to save me, did you? You simply let me die."

Dray's face was bathed in sweat as she tried to escape. And then Zosia reached out her hand.

On the plane of reality Abby sat forward, her hand inches away from Dray's upper arm. Should she wake her from the nightmare or just let her find a way out?

"Damnit, I should have insisted you take those damned pills before I left. God, I'm sorry, Dray."

"Zo...nie pozostawia ja tutaj..."

Ksenka reached out his hand and although every fiber of his body tried to deny the bond he was feeling he refused to voice the truth, for both their sakes. It would be his fate: forever damned to a life filled with tormented nightmares and periods of intense shame and self-hatred. Placing his hand against the glass window, he silently urged the woman to meet his gaze. A sharp smell of burning flesh filled the air and he knew the furnace had been turned on. And he did nothing to stop it.

"JA b´d´ kochąc was na zawsze."

Abby stood over her lover who was tangled in their bed sheets.

"Honey, I don't know what you're saying."

Unable to endure Dray's painful wheezing any longer Abby placed her hand against the pallid skin of her lover. Even knowing that verbal abuse was probably her reward, she couldn't shirk her duty and let the woman continue in her torment alone.

Dray startled awake, feeling frightened and disoriented. There in the semi-darkness was the form in her dream. Was it Debbie, or Holmes, or...?

Abby smiled weakly, her face filled with concern.

"I'm sorry to wake you, Dray, but..."

"What? Zosia?" Dray blinked stupidly, her head still filled with images. And then the image began to clear as her eyes adapted to the darkness to the lover she knew today. "Abby? Oh, God...don't...don't look at me. I'm a monster, just a brutal, good for nothing monster. I'll let you down just like I did them...all of them. How can you even bear to look at me?" She covered her face with both hands.

Abby bit her lip, choking back the sob that threatened to burst from her throat. Did Dray have to endure these terrible feelings of guilt for the rest of her life?

She wiped the corners of her eyes with the heel of her hand and blinked furiously as she struggled with her frustration. It certainly wasn't what Dray needed right then. No, she needed a rock, something to ground her.

"You were just having a nightmare, honey. That's all, just a nightmare." She reached over and picked up the pills, offering them and a glass of water.

"No, no...it was my life...my whole fucking, sordid, hate-filled life – past and present. I just want to die. You'd be better off without me." Dray pulled farther away from the blonde, afraid to see the truth mirrored in her eyes.

Abby smoothed Dray's hair away from eyes that were filled with a haunting sorrow and wanted to rage at the heavens. *Did she have to relive every heartbreaking moment of her existence over and over again?*

And then Abby could see clearly, her second epiphany of the day. These incidents in Dray's life weren't something she had to endure alone. Not any more – Dray's suffering was now her own. And she would help share the load.

"Dray?"

The firefighter watched as a single, perfect tear fell from her lover's eye and quietly made its way down until finally slipping off the woman's chin.

"I love you. Don't you get that? In any way, shape or form, I'll take you. I fell in love with you – the woman who took pride in her job, the woman who took a stranger in off the street. It's not about skin Dray, it's about what's underneath it. Now, we can either both drown in self-pity or we can accept the pain and learn from it."

Dray's eyes filled with tears and a sob escaped her lips. "I'm sorry."

Pressing a hand against her lover's temple, Abby whispered, "I know you haven't been yourself, Dray. But as soon as you understand that I'm not here to judge you and that I can and will help you, then it'll be okay. Don't be sorry Dray. Be accepting."

She offered the water and pills again and felt absolute relief wash over her as Dray reached out a hand and finally accepting the medication without argument.

"It hurts, Ab. It hurts so bad."

Tears dripped unnoticed onto the bedspread as Abby nodded her head, unable to speak.

A couple of minutes passed and then she tried again.

"I know you don't want to, Dray, but we have to talk about this. We have to get past it."

Dray sipped a bit more of the water and then handed it back. She nodded, then lay back gingerly and wrapped a protective arm around her mending ribs.

"It's so hard..."

Easing herself down beside the firefighter, Abby carefully laid her head on the woman's right shoulder. Dray drew her legs up, easing the small of her back, and then moved her other hand slowly to caress her lover's tear stained face.

"I'm sorry I've been such a bitch, Abby. I wouldn't blame you if," Dray clutched the woman tighter, "if you found someone else."

Abby squeezed her eyes shut and began to cry quietly. "How could you ever think there'd be anyone for me but you?"

Tears began to seep from between the firefighter's eyes too as she thought of just how far apart they'd grown. The life they shared before the accident seemed a lifetime away. "That nurse back at Memorial..." A hard look was aimed her way and Dray flinched.

"I've loved you from the first moment I met you. And I always will," Abby murmured.

Dray uttered a shuddering sob and willed her lungs not to spasm.

"But why...how can you stand being anywhere near me? If I'm not this miserable bitch, then I'm a big, old crybaby."

"Because I always have, silly. You think you're weak, that somehow asking for help makes you less than who you are. Can't you see how strong it is to reach out and accept help? I know how hard it is for you to appear vulnerable, I do, but..." Abby stopped talking and just kissed her lover's forehead. "Consider this, Dray: Where would we be if I hadn't taken your offer of help when you gave it? Do you think I'm weak for agreeing to move in here?"

Dray snorted. "It's not the same."

"Why? Because I'm Abby Dean, homeless wench, and you're Andrea Khalkousa, civil servant extraordinaire?"

"No," Dray insisted. "I don't think that and you know it."

"Do I?" Abby insisted. She paused but when Dray said nothing she continued. "You think it didn't take a lot for me to put my pride on the shelf and say, I could use some help here? Look, I know what you're doing. You push me away so you don't have to deal with things. Haven't we done this enough?"

She sighed again as Dray's chin stiffened.

"You must think I'm treating you like a child right now. Well, I'm not. I just want you to stop for a moment and see the bigger picture – what this life lesson has taught you."

"Life lesson, huh? You mean this whole ordeal wasn't just Murphy's Law playing havoc with my life? Listen, I'm used to being in Hell, Honey, and it just never ends."

Abby could sense a cold rigidity come over the woman's body and carefully pulled Dray's chin to face her, forcing her to re-connect.

"You're missing the point, Dray. You don't have to live in Hell."

Dray rolled her eyes but Abby continued.

"You don't. You've paid your dues and the sooner you realize that, and accept it, the better off you'll be; we'll be. You can't save everyone; you can't be the hero 24/7. And here's a newsflash for you, Dray – you're human. And with that comes frailties and emotions. I say this with unconditional love – deal with it, Sweetie."

The brunette's jaw clenched and her breath was held behind tight lips as the words stabbed at her. Abby watched anger roll across her lover's face and a steel blue tint emerged as Dray brought her eyes up and their gazes locked.

"I can do anything, Abby. I've done more things that anyone should be able to. I've always been able to run faster, climb higher, and fight harder-."

"Anything, huh?" Abby asked rhetorically cutting Dray off. "So I guess that means from now on you'll take your meds, stop fighting me about helping you *when* you need it, not all the time, and making life more bearable for both of us?"

"Don't you see, Ab? Everything that's ever happened to me, every minute of the bullshit that I've had to endure, it's all prepared me to be the person I am. Right here, and right now. You can call it karma, or fundamentalism, or whatever; it doesn't matter. All I know is I'm the sum of my past and I have a purpose, Abby, I know it."

Abby dragged her eyes away from the play of her lover's hands and sat up.

"We all have a purpose, Dray. I don't think most of us discover what that is, no matter how long we live, but we just struggle along doing the best we can." Abby pulled her legs under her and sat with her hands resting gently on her knees.

Dray expelled a breath but said nothing.

"What is your purpose, Dray, and how do you know that it won't change somewhere down the line?"

The brunette's face creased in momentary pain as she eased herself back down onto the pillows. She was beginning to feel quite light-headed. *Must be those damned pills*, she thought.

"So many people have tried to make me stray from my course. I was never sure of the path, only the final destination. I'm the best damned firefighter this city has ever seen. I have this ability to understand fire."

A jolt of uneasiness swept through the blonde as Dray's face changed, making her seem much older than she really was, somehow inscrutable. She'd never heard the woman talking like this. Part of her knew it must be the painkillers – it had to be. But still, she found herself leaning forward when Dray's voice had dropped another octave.

"But life is about the journey, Dray. It's not about the destination because we already know that – it's death. We all die and reach our destination. But the joy of being here, the journey we take before we die is what matters. How the Hell do you think I survived on the streets as long as I did? I took simple pleasures and didn't look for huge victories. Yes, you've done amazing things Dray, but for the time being lower the bar, dear."

"What do you mean?" Dray asked. She wasn't sure if it was Abby or the drugs that were confusing her.

"I mean quit judging yourself by what you could do before and focus on rebuilding your body. You want to be a firefighter again. You want a clean bill of health. A good start is by doing what the doctors say – letting me help you with things so you can rest and get strong again. This macho, pride bullshit is hurting both of us. The sooner you accept help, the sooner you'll heal, Dray."

Dray didn't say anything but she did seem to be considering Abby's words seriously for the first time.

"You go to sleep," Abby said stroking her hair. "Maybe I'll go out for another walk, but I'll be here when you wake up."

Dray slowly shook her head.

"No...don't wanna sleep. And I want you here, Babe. I do. But..."

The firefighter's face lolled to the side and she stared blankly at the wall directly behind Abby's head. "I wanna tell you about..." her hand muffled the next words but Abby would not be deterred.

"About what, Dray?"

Dray blinked deeply and then refocused on the blonde. "What?"

Abby suppressed a snort and then patted the woman's cheek. "You were going to tell me about something." She nodded her head encouragingly and then waited.

"Oh yeah. About the visions."

It was almost comical the way Abby felt at that moment. If anyone had been in the room with them they'd have sworn that her jaw had just fallen right off her face. She blinked slowly.

"Visions? What sort of visions, Dray?"

"You know, about that Kazimir guy. He's the guy that works in the camp, remember? I told you about him lots of times," her voice trailed off.

"You mean you're still having those dreams, Dray? I thought you told me they'd gone away?"

Dray wiped her mouth and looked away.

"I see."

With her chin resting gently on her chest, Dray looked every inch the innocent child she was hoping Abby would see and accept. "You pissed off, Babe? Mad that I didn't tell you?"

"No, hon. I'll admit that the idea of you still having nightmares or dreams or visions worries me, but you've had plenty of time to tell me about everything else."

Dray's eyebrows moved in response. "Yeah, 'spose so, but I'm a chicken at heart, ya know? Don't like to go tiltin' at windmills."

Abby shook her head, thinking about the short shrift the firefighter always gave herself. *Chicken, my ass, you just don't like to lose control and go ape shit on someone anymore than you have to.*

"I'll let that one go right now, Dray, but tell me when you're more alert. Okay Sweetheart?"

"Just wanna cuddle with ya...for a bit...okay?"

"Yeah, we can do that but I want you to sleep."

"Don't go, baby, 'cause when I close my eyes, Abby, he's there, just waiting for me."

"Who? Kazimir?"

A small frown appeared on the firefighter's sculpted lips and then air was pushed through them as Dray struggled to say more.

"It's those dreams I keep having."

Abby moved closer as Dray's voice began to slur. She felt almost embarrassed as the drugs began to work and the walls came slowly down.

"He had it all, all the fear, the torment, the lonely despair. He was Ruler of the Damned and I took it all away. All away. Dark place, prison camp." Her eyes rolled and a worried expression moved across her face. "Or is it prison? In my dreams it's a concentration camp, Abby, but you aren't you and I'm...I'm not there. Am I? There's this guy in my dreams, Abby, but every time I think I have a handle on who he is, it just slips away."

"Don't worry about it now Dray, okay? I'll stay here with you – I promise."

Dray rolled carefully over to face her and then put both fists under her chin and snuggled down into the covers. She blinked once or twice but remained conscious.

"I love you, Abby. I always have, and I always will. I know together, together we can do anything. To...gether," she slurred.

Then it seemed as if she noticed just how heavy her eyelids were becoming. She remembered the calming methods of Debbie Nang, and felt herself disengage from the pain and fear and just floated.

# Chapter 17

Abby hadn't realized just how much she'd needed to hear those words until right at that moment as she lay next to her lover. A tear squeezed past her dark lashes as she pondered the woman's words. It meant the firefighter could still see a future for them, and right now that meant everything.

She smiled and moved to the side of the bed. It was clear that Dray needed sleep and Abby only hoped it would be a good seven or eight hours. Just as she pulled the covers up over her lover's chest Dray's hand closed around hers. "I think they're more than dreams, Abby," Dray whispered to her.

Abby closed her eyes just as she did the day months before in the bathroom when she experienced the first flash of what Dray had been seeing repeatedly.

"Zosia," Dray slurred. "Your name was Zosia, and although you were a pain in the ass, there was something about you that called to me. I tried to keep the camp running smoothly but you always found a way to get around the rules." Dray pursed her lips and frowned. "It was my duty as an officer to break this stubborn streak you had and to stop you from helping the other prisoners. They didn't need hope, Zosia; they just needed to do their jobs. The war would end one day and then you would all be free, free as a bird."

Abby's face drained of all color as her lover went on in a voice that was becoming slightly deeper. Abby knew she could write it off as the drugs talking but inside she knew it was much more meaningful – not just to Dray but to both of them.

"Such a feisty thing you were," Dray continued. "JA b´d´ kochaç was na zawsze mój kochany. I remember the first time I saw you – your long golden hair blowing in the breeze as you stood out in the freezing weather. Before it was cut. Many of the women cried that day, but not you. I think it started then, my Zosia."

Abby's mouth hung open and although bits and pieces of memories long since suppressed kept surfacing she tried to ignore their hold on her. It didn't matter who she was before or the type of relationship they had then...this was now and they had each other and that was everything. But even as she tried to keep the memories at bay they began to surface full force and Abby realized she made a promise to take care of Dray. She realized instantly this was part of her promise as well – facing all of Dray's demons, present as well as past.

"Your defiance set you apart and, although we shared many a brutal encounter, the battle you waged was a strong one. You had my heart before springtime."

A small spark of anger welled up in the blonde, and although she knew it was neither the time nor the place, she couldn't stop the memories from pushing her onwards.

"You never spoke of love, not in the thirteen months I was at the camp," Abby muttered in remembrance. "I knew there was affection, but love?"

Dray began to drag her impossibly heavy hand up to touch her lover's face, and then her long fingers seemed to change. *What's wrong with my hand?* The fingers became meatier, her palm fatter, and then her wrist broadened. And then it wasn't Abby's face she was reaching for any more – it was Zosia's. Instead of pushing the illusion aside or trying to run from it, Dray decided to take Abby's advice. Abby would see her through this dreamscape and they would move forward.

"You would have run screaming into the night if I said I loved you, Zosia." Dray paused and licked her lips. "You know it and so did I. There was no way you were ready for that truth. What could we do with the future we were facing? Even now, after all is said and done, with this second chance we have been handed...what can we do about love?" Her hand fell back onto the bed.

Abby snorted softly at her other name, the anger easing back a little. Her skin turned to goose bumps as she thought about the life lived in another time. She had almost divorced herself from those long ago dreams. But why did they keep bedeviling Dray? Just like Dray, Abby was determined to find out and allowed her lover to pull her further into the dreamscape.

"You shouldn't worry," Abby told her.

Suddenly Abby felt as though she were standing and a large hand encircled her wrist.

"Yes, I worry," the voice behind her said. "They are pressing for more production. If we are to fulfill our quota then we must work harder."

Abby's jaws tightened. She was confused. It was as if Dray was speaking in tongues and the conversation shifted so dramatically that she had to keep up. Realizing that Dray was talking of quotas and not love any longer, Abby remembered the same conversation from decades past and uttered the same response as she had then.

"Then give us more food, Kazimir."

"More food? Do you know that I was caught stealing food from stores? I lost my ration of vodka for you, Zosia, but it didn't matter. Not then. It was a small thing, you see? Call it a payment for the company you give to me. Or perhaps selfishness."

The grip on her wrist lessened and Abby eased carefully down beside her lover. Closing her eyes tightly, Abby settled her breathing and then curled her hand over her belly. She could almost feel the constant pain chronic hunger instilled in a person.

Abby knew without a doubt now – Dray was Kazimir Ksenka and she was Zosia, his mistress and prisoner. Fearing what might lay ahead, Abby swallowed hard and took a deep breath before she continued.

"Why was stealing food selfish?" she asked.

"I did it so I could have you to myself, if only for a little longer; your fate was already sealed, my Zosia. How will I ever live with that truth? How can I face you knowing I did nothing to save you?" Dray mumbled something else and then groaned as she moved into a different position.

A tear dripped slowly down her cheek pulling Abby back to reality.

"You did what you could, Dray. And we'll make it this time. Together."

Abby stroked the woman's cheekbones and jaw before kissing her strong nose. The break had healed nicely. She ran her finger carefully up and down the slight bump and smiled. The bond that had been stretched but never broken began to ease back into its original shape, wrapping them tightly together once more.

"You sleep, Babe." She kissed her lover's brow again and then pulled the bedspread up to cover them. "We have things to talk about and specialists to see. And we will. You are going to have to trust that we know what's best for you."

She smiled as Dray snuggled closer.

Dray's cheek began to twitch just as the early morning light was beginning to show through the Venetian blinds. Her breath, previously slow and deep, picked up its pace, making her slumber more than a little restless. Abby moved off the woman's shoulder and curled warmly at her side.

Behind closed eyelids Dray could see Zosia and Kazimir speaking to each other. The pair wore melancholy looks as they spoke.

"Yes, these past few weeks have been wonderful," Zosia admitted. "More than I ever expected to have. I thank you for it. Perhaps after the Allies come...?"

Kazimir shook his head and handed her a piece of paper. She looked at it and pursed her lips before handing it back to him.

A cold hand seemed to close over Dray's heart; it wasn't a dream but another of the visions. Squeezing her eyes shut, subconsciously knowing she was alone this time, no Abby to help guide her. Dray steeled herself for yet another kernel of truth to be offered up. Dray could feel Kazimir's worry underneath his apparent calm demeanor.

"I know the production has been less than expected but honestly, what other outcome can there be? We must have food in order to do the job. They must know that?" Zosia argued.

Kazimir walked over to Zosia, holding what looked like a clothes bundle.

"I have the list we spoke about," he told her.

The woman began snatching up pieces of her clothing and then, after dressing, walked over to the window. Dray's nostrils fluttered as the woman passed right through her. A small tear appeared in both sets of eyes and then the woman turned to face the man.

"How long have you known?" she asked.

The man sat down heavily on the bed and placed his head in his hands.

"I have known for a few days only." Then he opened the bundle, producing a small amount of food. Dray cringed as bits of moldy cheese and bread were brought out.

"See?" he continued. "We can have a feast tonight. You needn't leave right now. I'll give you a pass."

The woman snorted and placed her cold hands against the wall behind her.

"You eat it, it will do me no good now. They'll be coming for me soon."

Dray could feel the anguish rolling off the man in waves. She felt such a sense of sorrow for these two people. The crisp outline of the man's face was suddenly visible and she recognized the guard immediately, somewhat surprised at his behavior towards the woman she now knew must be Zosia.

Getting slowly to his feet, Ksenka made his way over to the petite woman.

"I was hoping to spend the night with you in my arms, little Zosia. After all this time would you deny me this final wish?"

Zosia snorted softly. "I remember the first time I denied you, Kazimir." She rubbed her cheek in memory.

"But everyone has to have the numbers, Zosia, you know that."

"Yes, everyone has to endure that last little rape of individuality. Do you know how much it hurt me?"

"I was there," he interrupted her, "remember? It was also a better job that I did than any of the other guards would have."

His large hand reached out to stroke the blonde's thin wrist and she moved willingly into his arms.

"It wasn't so much that it hurt me physically, Kazimir, but to be reduced to merely a number."

He rubbed the pad of his thumb across the tattooed numbers on the inside of her arm. "I didn't know you then, Zosia. Every prisoner at the camp was just a faceless stranger, someone I had no intention of becoming familiar with. You did your job then you got to eat, you didn't and you were gone. There was a steady stream of faceless strangers. I never planned on..."

Zosia tried to push away from the man's embrace.

"You never planned on finding a bit of entertainment with one of the numbers? I can't believe I am the only one, Kazimir, not with your appetite and reputation."

The guard pulled her hard against him and she struggled for a moment.

"No, you were not the only one, Zosia. But you were the first one I ever loved. And no one will come after you."

The woman resisted for only a moment more and then laid her head against his chest and cried. "Why have we found each other now, Kazimir?"

Ksenka lifted his head and for a moment, Dray could have sworn he was looking directly at her.

Feelings of confusion pricked at her and she looked away. This was hardly the brute of a man she supposed the officer to be. The other images had painted him as being violent and cruel, very unlike the caring man she saw before her.

"Come lie with me. Your last moments will be as beautiful as I can make them."

"Please tell me there is some wine? Or perhaps a little vodka?" Zosia huffed sadly and was led over to the rumpled bed.

"I wish," he started and then fell silent.

Zosia began removing her clothing and then the man lifted her right arm and placed a soft kiss over the numbers. For some reason Dray could see them clearly. She wasn't even aware that her hand had strayed to the back of her neck.

She tried to look away, the creaking of the bed a clear indication of the intimacies to come. With tenderness and care, the officer helped the blonde remove the rest of her clothing and then began to disrobe.

"Will you let me love you, Kazimir?"

Ksenka shook his head and pushed himself down onto the prisoner. "You always ask and I always answer the same way."

"But Kazimir, please? I just want you to feel what I feel."

With a roar of disapproval, the guard jumped to his feet. "Why must you be so demanding? Why can't you just enjoy these past few moments together without asking this question over and over again?"

Dray frowned as the two began to quarrel.

"You are the one who demands, Ksenka, not me. You must have everything just the way you like it. You, you, you! This will be the last time; I will come to you no more!" Then she grabbed up a bit of the food and threw it back in his face.

"Your offering is not acceptable! If you want a whore then you will pay for one."

Ksenka began to dress, pulling his clothing on and cursing loudly when each article seemed to defy him. Finally, in total frustration he spun on the woman.

"Here I have been so worried about how you would react, seeing your name on the list. I was almost caught today stealing what you have just discarded! It will be me alongside you in the furnace! Do you want that?" And then he grabbed his jacket. "I must have been just fooling myself to think you were something more than just a number, Zosia. Well, never again!"

With a shout of temper, the blonde threw herself at the man, beating him ineffectually about his chest and face.

"Don't you say such things to me! You will never know the pain and sorrow of walking those last few steps to your death! Even a condemned man is given a last meal. But not us; we are discarded like rotting cordwood when we have outlived our usefulness! Oh, how I hate you!" She grabbed up the man's hat

247

and then spat on his insignia. "I thought you had changed over these past months! What a fool I am!"

Ksenka grabbed his hat, wiped the spittle from it and then stood staring at the woman as she burst into tears. The evening had gone so terribly wrong.

"All I wanted to do was show you a little pleasure, a little..." Dray could see a look of panic cross his face as he skittered away from the raw emotions that bubbled up.

She watched as he opened his mouth to voice these new feelings but then shut it silently. Her heart lurched as the truth was seen clearly in his eyes: he truly loved her.

He walked over to the mirror, settled the cap so that the swastika was over one eyebrow, and then silently pleaded for the woman to open her arms to him, not to let them leave things the way they were. But she only threw herself back onto the bed and began to cry in earnest. The officer wiped at his face angrily and then left, slamming the door behind him.

The scene changed and images of her life at the hospital flitted past in a never-ending parade of spiteful words, shameful actions, and petty fury. All aimed at the one person she had ever fully loved: Abby.

Dray felt ripped in two as she viewed each scene. There was Abby, reaching out to her, only to be slapped down with hateful words calculated to hurt and maim. Another showed her standing in the hospital, watching in horror and tears as two orderlies held her down while she screamed obscenities at everyone around her. When had things gone so terribly wrong?

Ksenka materialized before her, screaming obscenities and pulling at his hair in frustration.

"Why did I let you go?" he bellowed. She could see him slamming his hand against the small window of the shower house. "I should have taken you. We could have run. You mentioned the Allies approaching...I could have..." Kazimir sighed and ran his hands over his face. "I love you and I will find you again someday, Zosia!"

His form began to shimmer and it was her reflection staring back at her in all its twisted glory. Dray's bottom lip trembled as she saw exactly what others did: the cold and distant woman she'd become coupled with the true evidence of the monster that lay just beneath the layers of her skin. Now she looked just as horrific on the outside as she felt deep inside, and that truth hit her with such a terrible blow that all she wanted was an end to her misery.

She thrashed back and forth, both fists tightly curled around sweaty sheets as she tried to wake up.

"You're the best thing in my life and I will find you. I will always find you."

Was it her own voice ringing in her ears?

A steady noise began breaking its way through Dray's subconscious and she groaned and rolled away from the light that was becoming just as insistent as the growing noise.

"Alright, alright; I'm up."

Abby swept into the room, a small bag tucked under her chin and both hands clutching two cups of steaming coffee.

"Hey, you're up! How did you sleep, honey? Sorry if my banging woke you but I thought you'd have been up and in the shower before I had a chance to even get back with breakfast. I'm kinda glad; it means you probably slept well."

Dray groaned as she carefully moved up into a sitting position.

"Actually, my night was filled with an endless series of nightmares. I don't feel like I even caught one wink the whole time." She ground a fist into her eye and then yawned, her jaw snapping painfully.

"Oh Dray, I'm sorry. I wish those damned dreams would just quit."

Dray pushed up into a semi-standing position and then slowly removed the special bandage from around her rib cage. She glanced over as Abby set the cup down and then noticed a rash on Abby's inner arm.

"Say, whatcha do, spill some of that coffee on you?"

Abby pushed her sleeve all the way up and then rubbed the redness. "No, actually it was there when I woke up this morning. You don't think we have bed bugs, do you?"

An image of blue ink filled Abby's head as she began to pick at the rash. She blinked a few times almost certain that she could see numbers appearing on her skin.

"What...what was your dream?"

"Do you remember what happened last night?" Dray asked. "I mean after you gave me the meds."

Abby sighed and took a seat at the foot of the bed. "It wasn't just my imagination, was it?"

Dray shook her head. "Come here," Dray motioned her closer. "I want to try something."

Abby moved up and took the open hands that Dray offered. She settled herself and watched as Dray began to take small calming breaths.

Trish Shields

They locked eyes and it was as if the room was filled with the light of a billion stars. Although Abby was aware of her surroundings, it was like there was an overlay of another existence. She could sense the dingy room packed with stick-like figures; the air filled with pain and death, and each face either blank with the horror of what his life had become, or pinched and haunted, wishing only to reawaken from the nightmare he found himself in.

And then the scene changed again and she was looking out a window. The sky was dark and dreary, the trees bare and gray, and although there was an expanse of land between her and the ever present barbed wire, there was no hint of green; none whatsoever. She could see her torn and fragile looking hands curled on the windowsill. They looked so small and careworn although Abby didn't feel she had lived a long life at all; she had no sense of having had a husband or children. And yet there was no overwhelming sadness she could detect, only peace. And then she could feel someone holding her, enveloping her in a warm and loving embrace, and she felt safe.

Then her mind was filled with an image so clear that she could actually experience the pain as the fire ripped across her body. The pain was all encompassing; filling her with a cold, deadly fear until she felt no pain at all as if her heart stopped beating. With her vision darkening, Abby clutched blindly at anything and then felt...nothing.

She was floating high above the ground. She smiled, feeling the peace envelop and protect her. *It's over at last.*

She felt a small tinge of disappointment as a long tunnel opened in front of her. *What? No angels to speed me to my rest?* She sighed sadly. *And certainly no white light to guide me, either.* With a small shrug, she closed her eyes and felt an insistent tugging towards the tunnel.

Just before the opening winked closed behind her, there was a small chuckle, deep, warm and beautiful in its tone and expanse.

*It is only the beginning.*

Suddenly aware of a heartbeat that seemed to surround her, Abby slowly came back into herself. Her extremities tingled and then her eyes fluttered and she was looking up into the very worried face of her lover.

"Hey...what...what happened?" Abby said realizing she was laying on the bed now.

Dray released a heavy breath and sat back on her haunches. "Shit, you scared me. You passed out, Babe. You called me Kazimir, and then boom, you fell over."

250

Abby paused a moment and remembered. "I died, Dray. I mean, not just now. I was in that room with Kazimir."

A shudder ran through the woman as more images assaulted her from her memory. There had been others in the room with her, clutching at her, wailing in fear and pain.

She remembered stretching a hand out, trying to reach her friend but there was a barrier between them. And it didn't matter how hard she screamed, it just didn't seem to matter because no one cared, and there was no rescue, only pain. Her heart felt so heavy as the memories pushed their way into her psyche, forcing her to remember more than she could ever process. Had her friend died in the room with her, too? Somehow she didn't think so. And then everything became clear.

"I guess I should have known you were Kazimir months ago," Abby confessed. A look of horror stared back at her.

"No, Abby. No. I can't be him. I won't be him!"

She reached up and held the taller woman's face gently between her two hands.

"You're not him," Abby insisted. "You're Dray Khalkousa. It was only one life out of perhaps thousands."

Dray shook her head in disbelief. "How can I be a man so cold hearted, so totally beyond redemption? How?" Dray pressed her fingers hard against her temples. "No...no, I can't be Ksenka, I just can't!" Her fingers pulled at the dark wisps at the side of her head. "If it's true then I did so many horrible things, Abby. If it's true, then I was a monster in that life and...all the lives I took. Yours, too...No..."

Abby smiled and carefully pushed the woman back against the box spring. Dray's raspy breathing eased and the feeling of hysteria began to lessen as the blonde's nimble fingers worked at her temples, forehead and neck.

"You are not a monster, Dray."

"I am. I sent you to the furnace," she whimpered.

"No, you save people from the furnace," Abby pointed out. "You risk your life every day so others can live. You couldn't have saved me in that life and we both know it. We were just two people who met under horrible circumstances. Who knows what our lives might have been if the Allies had come a month, or even a week, earlier than they did?"

"I could have tried," Dray told her. "I loved you more than anything – more than the Reich but...I did nothing. I just let them take you." A tear dripped down Abby's cheek and was captured by a large, rough hand that Abby knew belonged to the most gentle of souls. "But I didn't save you, don't you see?" cried Dray, shaking in earnest.

"I don't remember much but you saved me from many more horrible fates because of your personal interest in my well-being."

Dray closed her eyes tightly. "My personal interest? God, Abby. I took you by force; I made you prostitute yourself for food. How can you even stand to be near me?"

"Because I knew then what I know now – you are a good soul, Dray." Abby closed her eyes momentarily, knowing the truth, very aware of the bond that had begun when brutality turned into friendship, and then years later, in another lifetime, to love.

"I forgive you. But you have to forgive yourself."

She held the woman in a firm but gentle embrace as Dray's body was wracked with terrible pain and anguish.

"You did what you had to then and I'll do what I have to now," Abby told her. "I won't lose you again and this time I know exactly how you feel. I love you so much, Dray."

The tight body beneath her touch stiffened and she helped Dray roll over as a coughing fit began. Abby looked down into the troubled eyes of her lover, knowing that there were some things the woman might never forgive herself for but she'd be damned if it would be because of something that happened a lifetime ago. And Abby knew they'd work towards redemption together.

"It's okay, it's gonna be fine. It's not all completely clear to me yet but I don't care. All I know is how I feel here and now."

A fresh torrent of tears overcame Dray and she clutched at the woman tightly. "I tried to stop it, Abby," she sobbed, "and I couldn't."

"Oh God, Dray. I felt it – the pain, the regret and the sorrow." The blonde swallowed deeply as she saw the hot tears of her lover overflow. "But it's done, Sweetheart. It's over."

# Chapter 18

Pete sat in the waiting room, one of his feet tapping incessantly against a chair leg. He chewed off another fingernail, sighed, and then picked up a Reader's Digest from the magazine rack.

"Nope, already read this one."

Glancing at the dwindling pile of magazines he hadn't read, he sighed heavily – his sainthood all but guaranteed – and picked up a Harper's Bazaar.

"Hate these damned things."

Giving the cover of Martha Stewart a pinched look, he glanced quickly about the room and then picked through the pages.

"Lessee; Perfect Peach Cobbler." He scribbled a few notes down and then pushed the loose paper into his pant's pocket. It had been a long eight weeks since he'd spent any large amount of time with his two friends. Demands at the station house and the knowledge that Dray probably needed rest more than visitors kept him away. Maybe he could talk them into dinner at his place. And the good Martha Stewart was going to help him out, too. Rachel might even lend a hand as well.

He smiled thinking about his girlfriend.

Things between him and Rachel had progressed slowly over the last few months to the point where they talked of getting a place together. And while Pete had never been in that position before it wasn't as uncomfortable as he'd expected it to be. His attention began to wander as he contemplated a future filled with love and, perhaps, children.

Eventually his thoughts turned back to his friend and partner, Dray. Nearly a year of physical therapy, operations and psychological evaluations proved the resiliency of the stubborn woman, but clandestine conversations with Abby had proven that Dray wasn't fully up to speed yet. He nervously bit the ragged skin on his thumb. Today's visit with the psychologist would determine if Dray would ever be able to return to work. Pete wasn't sure which outcome he wanted most and he shuffled through the aging magazines yet another time hoping against hope of finding something new.

Abby sat in the large office and tried not to worry. Her fingers tapped erratically on the armrest while she bit her lip to the same nonsensical beat, one that only she could hear.

Dray had been in the bathroom for a good half hour now, adjusting this, applying salve to that, and was pretty much being her usual single-minded, stoic self. The blonde bit her cheek but the pain did little to change her mind about what needed to be said.

"Honey?"

Expelling a large breath of air, Abby pushed out of the chair and moved a little closer to the closed door. *I know you can do this stuff by yourself, and I'm sure you'd rather I didn't see what's under those bandages until everything is healed up, but...*

"Dray? I'd like to help." She took another step toward the door. "And I know you're uncomfortable with that but...look, I'm just going to open the door slowly and just stand by the frame, okay?"

Something dropped and Abby could hear a quiet stream of expletives coming from behind the door.

"You can't expect me to just...Look, I'm your life mate, right, your partner, the love of your life...and I'm not sure what kind of response you think I'll give you when you show me..."

"No," came the muffled response.

"But Dray. Honey, please. I'm not going to go running from the room, okay?" The silence continued. "And it doesn't really matter what you look like, I'll love you anyway. You know that, right?"

The door was yanked open and Abby stumbled back in surprise. "Yes, I do."

"Then why won't you...?"

"Leave it alone, Abby. Some things are best left alone, you know?"

Dray pushed the gauze a little farther out of her way, finished dabbing a bit of ointment on the skin framing her mouth, and continued walking past the comfortable chairs and over to the leather couch.

Having already scanned the room for the most comfortable area to be in for the two or possibly three-hour session, she had decided that the reclining position would probably enable her to put off taking pain meds for at least another hour past her usual dose.

Now that her body was truly on the mend, she'd been slowly weaning herself off the painkillers. Abby hadn't been easily duped and had figured what was going on. However, seeing the stubborn look to her lover's face, the blonde had decided that it wasn't a battle that was worth fighting, considering the firefighter's rate of recuperation. She was now wearing that very same expression.

Checking her watch, Abby nodded and surreptitiously watched the brunette's movements. It was obvious that Dray was still experiencing a bit of pain from the long drive up earlier in the day. For Dray the pain was secondary. For Abby, the pain was ever present, making her feel somewhat antsy. She checked her watch again and wondered if she shouldn't broach the subject of an early dose.

"Hey, Babe. Come and sit beside me, will ya?" Dray asked. And with that simple question, the early dose was forgotten.

Pulling the long blonde hair away from her shoulders, Abby smiled and pushed a chair next to the divan. Its shiny, burgundy leather coaxed her fingers into caressing its surface.

"The Doc will be here in a few minutes, so..." Dray cocked her head towards the door and then took Abby's hand into her own. "I'm glad this'll be the last one, you know? I really hate these fishing trips Dr. Birk goes on, trying to get me to tell him all sorts of deep, dark secrets." She snorted. "He ain't no fisherman, Ab, I can tell you that."

Abby frowned at her lover's rather smug demeanor. "He's only trying to help you. Why do you always have to be at odds with the man, Dray?"

Even with most of her face obscured, it wasn't too hard for the blonde to see that set to the jaw Dray affected when playing the game, a smirk firmly in place, and blue eyes flashing. Dray loved pulling the wool over Dr. Birk's eyes and she knew it. Although the firefighter always made light of things, Abby knew it was more than just a test of wills. She also knew that if this truly was to be the final session, then they had their work cut out for them.

She scratched her chin in thought and then glanced over as her hand ran slowly up and down the leg of Dray's jeans. Her eyes traveled slowly up the woman's thighs, snagged on the belt buckle and then meandered up over the swell of cotton where the slightly puckering flesh was a fresh reminder that secrets always came at a price. *One day I'll see everything inside, Andrea Khalkousa, and there'll be no place for you to hide.*

A blue station wagon pulled into the parking lot two spaces from the door. Waves of heat rose from every inch of the automobile and Herman Gorchyk knew the summer was going to be at least as hot as it was last year, if not worse. *And it's only half way through June.*

"So, this'll be the last session for Dray?"

Herman smiled as he turned the engine off and faced Nurse Taylor.

"Yeah, it's been a long haul for them but apparently Abby's made some real headway the last couple of weeks."

Janelle yawned and then unbuckled her seat belt. She reached into the back seat and pulled the take-out tray into her lap. "Which one's mine?"

Herman took each tall container and sniffed appreciatively. "Ahhh. Gotta love coffee." Popping the lid off one, he inhaled the fresh aroma and smiled. "Double Mocha, double cream, double sugar grande. This one's mine."

Janelle stretched as she got out of the station wagon and did a couple of deep knee bends before glancing over at her friend. Herman was still trying to extract himself from behind the steering wheel. She shook her head and laughed. "Say, you look like those clowns..."

Herman held up a hand. "Don't say it, not if you want another lift to work tomorrow."

The redhead wiped the smile from her face, but was unable to erase the look in her eyes.

"Your green eyes sure are pretty when they dance like that."

The nurse rolled her eyes. "Does this constitute sexual harassment?"

"Only if I meant it," he said with a grin.

Grabbing his coffee cup, he eased up into a standing position and then, placing the coffee on the roof of the car, pushed the metal frames up on the bridge of his nose. His fingers drummed slowly on the metal as he openly gazed at the woman.

"Motor cross is coming next month. Wanna go?" He paused momentarily and then quickly went on. "I think Dray would get a kick out of it, too. I hear she's been pretty busy with fine-tuning that bike of hers. You know she used to race two years ago? Won a cup or two is what I heard."

Taylor was surprised at the new information. While the taciturn firefighter's interest in motorcycles was common knowledge on the floor, she just never figured the woman would volunteer any information on her likes or needs, and certainly not to Herman.

There was a time shortly after the woman had been released when the only updates they received were from Abby but with Dray coming back for check ups they often saw her around the hospital and as a result grew to be friends.

She really liked the woman, and although she figured Abby could have done a lot better relationship wise, Janelle was willing to accept that Abby knew best in this situation. Herman's eyebrows rose at the perplexed look on Janelle's face.

"Coffee disagreeing with you?"

Jan blinked and shook her head. "Just thinking of Abby and Dray. You know, I'd like to think Abby's right and the woman we saw back at the ward isn't a true representation of the person she knows and loves. If she is Abby should be canonized."

Herman scratched his chin as they pushed through the doors to the hospital. "Can't imagine Missy Dean stickin' around if she wasn't a saint."

Pete had just turned the final page of the last remaining magazine when Janelle walked into the room. He stood up and extended a hand.

"Nurse Taylor, right?" he asked and she quickly nodded. "How are ya? Pete Melrose. I don't know if you remember..."

Janelle grabbed his hand. "I sure do, Captain. Nice to see you again." She waved to the receptionist, who briefly acknowledged the visitor before continuing with her filing chores.

Pete smiled. "It's Lieutenant, but thanks." Then the door pushed open again and the other nurse he remembered came through. The two men shook hands and then the three moved to the couch and began the task of catching up.

Abby poked her head around the corner briefly from the bathroom. Groaning with a stretch, Abby yawned and then grabbed a coffee before heading out to the waiting room.

"Hi, Pete."

The Lieutenant jumped up and grabbed the woman in a bear hug.

"Hey, Hon. How you doing?"

She smiled and nodded wearily. "It's been a hard row, Pete." Then she turned to greet the others.

"Hey, you two," Abby smiled at the nurses.

The black man bowed and said, "Why, if it ain't Miss Abby Dean. Funny running into you here."

Janelle gave him a light slap to the chest. "Forget him, Sweetie," she said hugging the blonde. "How's Dray?"

"Doing better. Are you guys going into work?"

"No we just came by to see how Dray's doing since you said she'd be in today." After she finished, the nurse took the blonde by the shoulders and gave her the once over.

Abby arched an eyebrow as she was pinned with three sets of very concerned eyes. "Look, it's been rough at times, almost unbearable at others, but really we're fine. And Dray gets stronger every day."

Janelle sighed and let her arms drop. Her practiced eye hadn't detected any bruises or the haunted look a victim of abuse would be sporting...or hiding...which was another good sign.

"So, how is old Iron Sides?" Herman asked.

Pete chuckled easily. "Yeah, that would pretty much describe Dray, alright. Well," he glanced at Abby, "the old Dray, I guess. I mean the new old Dray. You know?"

Abby punched his arm. "Yeah, I know...after the fire but before her rehabilitation from being the anti-social, hard headed, cantankerous, potty mouthed lovable sort you all met at the burn unit."

Janelle found something interesting to look at over in the far corner while Herman smirked.

Herman put his hand on the nurse's arm and gave her a small shake. "Now, who would think such things about the esteemed Andrea Khalkousa?"

A crimson flush appeared on the redhead's cheeks and she glared at the trio petulantly.

"Well, what am I supposed to think after all the wrestling matches I had with the woman for months on end?" Janelle harrumphed and walked over to the magazine rack. "I saw enough to know she's got one helluva temper. And," she put both hands on her hips, "she's not a very good patient, either."

Her eyes flashed dangerously as the others filled the room with good-natured laughter.

Dr. Robert Standling sat behind his desk, his face partially visible behind a mound of files, most of them ranging from 4 to 8 inches in thickness and all of them dealing with a certain firefighter who had just recently undergone extensive plastic surgery.

He was considered one of the top specialists in his field, and at 40, was one of the youngest, too. Although he tried very hard to adapt a serious demeanor befitting his solemn profession, his sandy blonde hair and mustache made him look like a slightly aging Beach Boy.

He slowly flipped through one of the thicker files and held up a few pictures of his patient; pre-op and post-op color photos. He was going through the files, selecting certain pictures to share with another doctor, a certain Dr. Birk, who was presently readying himself for a last psychological session with Andrea Khalkousa.

The lines in his forehead deepened as he thought about the report he'd read at Dr. Matheson's urging. The case had been brought to his attention almost a year previously when Lieutenant Peter Melrose and Dr. Matheson had conferred with him about the possibility of surgery.

It had entailed rather lengthy rounds of visits that would be required before he even went ahead and performed the surgeries. Not having heard from either man for almost three months, Dr. Standling had put the case on the back burner. And then one day, he'd received a fax that asked whether he was still interested in pursuing the case, and if so, would he like to receive documents via fax or post?

After going through Matheson's rather detailed notes, he'd been in a far better position to see how he and the patient could best communicate so that the whole experience of restoring the firefighter's appearance would be a success. It was one thing to look into the mirror and see that your appearance didn't match the image you had firmly in your mind. It was quite another to be faced with the reality that the best the medical profession could do would be a weak facsimile, your past self forever altered and therefore, forever gone.

Standling stretched and then pushed the file away. He'd been very pleased that the patient hadn't suffered any long-term health risks due to the intense thermal injuries, leaving him with a canvass that, while marred, was at least relatively intact. Regardless of the length of time it would take for her to recuperate, Dray had proven to be up for the challenge.

He closed his eyes briefly and could see the last surgery as it played out.

Dray's skin had blistered where the SCBA seal had adhered to her face because of a chemical reaction. Although it hadn't been immediately apparent, there was also a chemical reaction occurring just beneath her skin, deep in the epidermal cells.

The first surgery done to correct this had been one he hoped would never happen again.

His heart rate slowly gathered speed as the images of Dray removing the bandages a good two weeks prematurely hit him. Of course the flesh had been red and raw; you couldn't do skin grafts without a price. But although he'd tried to explain just how temporary that part of the surgery was it became clear that the patient only saw what she wanted, even if the truth was all there was left. The look she'd leveled at him as she saw her reflection in the mirror that first time was enough to freeze anyone's blood rock solid.

There weren't too many nights that weren't filled with the screams of rage and disgust as the patient had all but reduced his examination room to a disaster area. Although some patients had reacted in violent ways, Standling had never seen anyone so completely out of control before. It had been quite the change from the rather stoic woman he'd been dealing with during the pre-op sessions.

Her bandages had lain in tatters, and her hands turned into claws as the puckered and swollen flesh was viewed for the first time.

"What have you done to me? I'll never be able to leave my house again let alone get my job back! You Goddamned charlatan!"

"Ah well." Stretching again, he yawned and checked his watch. It wasn't the first time he wondered exactly how long Matheson was going to take. Rubbing his face briskly, he pulled out an assortment of take-out menus.

Abby had just finished retelling of their adventures at Henderson Point when the receptionist slid open her window. Her eyes clouded over momentarily as a feeling of panic bubbled up and then Abby nodded.

"Say, guys...I've got to go and sit in on something," she winced as a frown passed over Pete's face, "but I'll be back. Gimme about an hour, okay? And then we can all do dinner some place." Pete opened his mouth and then shut it as the blonde hugged him close, whispering. "S'okay, Pete. It's Dray; she's having a bit of trouble with Birk but I think everything will be fine."

Herman pulled the man over towards the magazine rack. "Say, here's a few magazines I bet you haven't read."

Pete cocked an eyebrow his way. "Is that bet large enough to cover dinner, pal? I've already read these plus a few more the receptionist holds behind the counter." He leaned in conspiratorially. "She has a few Bon Appetite mags back there, ya know?"

Janelle blinked at the man. She'd been sure he was going to mention either Playboy or Hustler magazine and was caught totally off guard by his response.

"Bon Appetite?" Janelle asked. "You're kiddin', right?"

Both men turned to look at her.

"What?" they asked in one voice.

The nurse rolled her eyes.

"God, you bachelors. Next thing you'll be telling me you like Martha Stewart!"

Pete's fingers strayed to the crumpled notes in his pocket but he wisely said nothing. By the awkward silence he knew he wasn't alone in his taste in chefs.

Abby followed the receptionist down the corridor and then waited at the door while Dr. Birk's private secretary discretely knocked. At first there was nothing but silence and then, as if telepathy were involved, the woman turned to her and nodded curtly.

"You'll have to wait a few minutes."

Abby nodded slowly and stood outside the door. Only the squeak of the secretary's shoes could be heard as she walked back to an office just off the waiting room.

Abby's hand closed around the brass doorknob, her hair almost standing on end, as a ream of expletives floated under the closed door.

"Dray," she whispered, shaking her head.

# Chapter 19

Psychiatrist Edward Birk tried to remain calm, although his heart was beating like a jackhammer. He should have been used to the sudden and intense outbursts but still they caught the young man off guard. He pulled tapered fingers through his short, brown hair and wondered silently whether Dray was really ready to resume her life as a firefighter.

He peered through the half darkened room and tried to gauge whether the woman was ready to continue. Pricking his ears carefully, he noted the raspy but slowing pattern of breathing and then eased his own respiration. Gone were the days when Dray would just either get up and leave, or worse, rant and rave and then threaten bodily harm to anyone within arm's length. Yes, his patient had made many inroads in their time together.

A miniature grandfather clock ticked on, filling the silence with something that almost sounded like a human heart. Everything in the room was created to give the inhabitants a feeling of security and relaxation.

His attention refocused as Dray began to speak.

"Why do we have to go into this, Birk? I mean, it's not as if we haven't gone over this area before. Just let it be."

Refusing to get into an argument that would lead them nowhere, Birk simply pointed out the obvious.

"I think you still have issues, Dray."

He leaned forward and tried to see past the bandages swaddling the woman's face. He stared intently and then finally, Dray lifted her eyes to look at him. Her venomous gaze did nothing to dissuade his course, however.

"I think there are things you haven't told me, and things you probably haven't told Abby, either. Am I right?"

Dray turned her head and stared at the ceiling. She hated the fact that he could read her so easily, even in the somewhat darkened room. Glancing evilly in his direction, she eyed what she considered to be his preppie clothing. Although probably fairly close to her own age, she was all too aware of his need to project a more mature image, at least in his eyes.

Finally, the psychologist got up and moved to the window and opened the blinds slightly. The comforting semi darkness was shot full of small fingers of sunshine, making her cover both eyes.

"God, Doc. Keep 'em closed."

Loosening his tie just a little, Edward finished jotting down a few notes and then placed his pad on the desk.

"I think we should bring in Abby."

Dray grumbled. "You think a lot, Doc." She propped her upper body up with an elbow. "Tell you what I think..."

The door opened and Abby stepped through.

"I think we should welcome our visitor, Dray, that's what I think. Don't you?"

The firefighter's eyes softened. "Hey."

Abby smiled and approached the divan.

"Hey yourself."

Her hand paused midway to her lover's face, a look of uncertainty crossing her features. Dray's face was still quite swollen beneath the bandages, and although she had acquiesced and was now taking her pain meds, Abby knew just how sensitive she was about the physical state of her appearance. She referred to herself as Claude Raines, the Invisible Man.

Abby knew there was some truth to it. Even though the last few weeks had shown her more of *her* Dray, the truth was that the person she'd fallen in love with almost a year ago was someone who only visited from time to time. But with each day Abby saw an improvement, no matter how slight and she continued to keep her promise of standing by Dray.

Masking a slight exhalation, Abby pushed her dark thoughts away and forced her hand onto the firefighter's shoulder. Her fingers twitched, longing for that moment when the bandages would come off and she could actually run them through a field of dark tresses. And how long it had gotten, the surgery and post medical attention preventing even the smallest of trims to be done.

A smile graced her lips thinking of how Dray had threatened to wear her hair in a topknot. *With my coloring, I'd look more like a pirate than anything else.*

She turned and smiled at the psychologist who was struggling into his sports jacket. "Hey, Doctor Edward. You don't need to put that on just for me." He smiled and nodded, his hand warm and friendly against her palm and she thanked whatever Fate had decreed he would be on their team. He'd been both friend and confidante throughout the whole ordeal, and considered them a couple, sharing information with her about his patient just as he would with any other spouse. In this way, Abby had learned a great many things, things she needed in order to put their relationship into perspective.

"Come and have a seat here, Abby, please." Birk pushed another chair to the foot of the divan and waited until the blonde was settled.

"There, now. Can I get anyone anything before we begin?"

Both women declined refreshments, preferring to get right to the business at hand.

Dray believed she could just gloss over whatever the doctor thought he needed in order to get the much coveted consent form so that she could return to active duty. Abby, on the other hand, knew there were things that needed to be said, and more importantly, needed to be heard. She settled back against the wooden frame of her chair and glanced quickly at the brunette.

Dray steepled her fingers at the top of her chest and willed her breathing to even out. Then counting backwards from ten, she took a slow cleansing breath and began to speak.

"Doc Birk thinks I have things I haven't told him, Abby." She paused. "I suppose that's true." Her gaze swiveled to lock onto the psychologist. "But that part's between Abby and me and not for public consumption." Her eyes flickered once as Abby shifted in her chair. "Fine," she sighed. "Let's just say that the person I thought I was turned out to be a little more than I bargained for. Call it an identity crisis if you like, I don't care. The bottom line is the person I thought was this cruel fuck," her voice cracked, "was actually me," she finished, her voice regaining some of its strength.

Birk frowned and then reached back for his pad and pencil. "So, am I to understand that you won't be going into any detail about this revelation?"

"You sure we have to go into this?" Abby gave her a look and Dray exhaled wearily. "Fine, but I'm only gonna tell what I feel comfortable with and that's it." She shot the psychologist a look. "And I'm not going into any past life experiences, got it?"

The doctor's eyes widened and he leaned forward. "What?"

Dray held a hand up. "Just don't go there, okay?"

His mouth opened and closed a few times and then seeing he wasn't going to get anywhere decided to just be happy with whatever his patient was willing to share. He sighed and then grabbed a newly sharpened pencil. He really couldn't complain: it had taken them almost 25 sessions to get where they were now. If she was willing to really open up, far be it for him to start demanding things she had no intentions of giving up.

"Okay, fine. But this will be conversational instead of strict dialogue on your part, won't it?" He received blank stares. "I mean I can ask questions as we go along?"

The firefighter nodded slowly. "Within reason, yeah. I might not answer but you can ask."

Dray rolled one sleeve up and was in the midst of fiddling with the other when Abby came to the rescue. With a brief nod of thanks, Dray popped another button on her shirt and wiped a bit of moisture from her brow.

Getting rid of some of the secrets she held close to her vest wasn't going to be easy. But she and Abby had come a long way in the past few months and Dray was damned if she was just going to let things slip back down to the point where only one or two word sentences was the norm.

The pleading look on Abby's face tugged at her heart and she knew there wasn't anything she wouldn't do for her. It was time to let go of some of the hate in her life. Cocking an eyebrow at the psychologist, Dray eased a small grin onto her lips and then spoke.

"You got some coffee? If I'm going to tell this I'll need some."

"Okay." He glanced at his watch and then moved around to his desk. "Mrs. Hemplemeyer," he said after pushing a buzzer, "would you have a few sandwiches and coffee brought in from the cafeteria?" He turned and looked at the women. "I know hospital food isn't the best but it's all I can offer right now."

Abby got to her feet. "I know, Dr. Edward. But it's okay, really." She glanced over at Dray. "We're both really pleased that we could take you away from your busy schedule like this. And it was very nice of Dr. Standling to combine visits so that we didn't have to make two trips."

Dr. Birk grinned. "Well, I'm glad I could help." He peered around the blonde and frowned as he caught Dray pulling at the bandages on her forehead. "You'd better leave that alone or

Standling will have your guts for garters. I thought you were getting some of that removed today?"

Dray's hand moved to the back of her neck. "Yeah, this one, in fact. It's annoying me something fierce." Her hand moved back to her hairline but she stopped just short of picking at the tape as a small hand encircled her bicep.

Two sandwiches and twenty minutes later, Dray picked up where she'd left off.

"I guess all the pent up anger I'd suppressed after the death of my son and my marriage, well, it left me feeling like a powder keg. The spark was Debbie's death. And without her," she sighed, "well, I didn't have to worry about controlling my rage. I was a bad ass for a while, you know? There weren't too many people who didn't feel my wrath – some ended up missing body parts."

Abby's dinner did a double roll in her belly that didn't go unnoticed.

"Sorry, Ab," Dray said as she turned to her. "You know, we can just cut things short right now and go home."

The blonde smiled weakly. "No, it's okay. Really. Please go on, Dray."

"Well," Dray said as she turned back to the doctor. "After she was killed...I guess I went kind of crazy. It didn't take me long to find out that it was a guy named Holmes who had done the deed and Percy who had ordered it."

Birk whistled and then sat back. "Not that I'm doubting you, Dray, please. But I'm finding it really hard to wrap my head around the type of life you led."

Dray cleared her throat and stopped any further discussion. "No, it's just been awhile since I talked this long, Doc. I don't wanna cut things short, but I'm not sure how long my throat will hold out before..." she left the sentence dangle.

He nodded easily and patted her shoulder. "Sure, anything you say." He tapped his front teeth with the end of the pencil and then smiled. "We could give it one more hour and make another appointment in a couple of weeks. How about that?"

Dray was busy shaking her head as Abby pushed another tall glass of water into her hand. "Now honey, maybe it would be better."

Dray took a few deep draughts and then settled back against the chair.

"No. No, see I've gotta get it out now. This will be my last session, come Hell or high water."

Seeing the determined set to her features, the doctor nodded and then grabbed up his pad and pencil. "Okay then. Let's just hit the highlights, shall we?"

Dray nodded and then took up where she'd left off. She picked up her lover's hand. "It took me a very long time before I could trust anyone, you know?"

Two sets of concerned eyes watched her carefully, saying nothing but nodding in the right places. They could tell how difficult the story was becoming just by the set to the woman's jaw.

"What got me back on course was a visit from Debbie's husband."

Abby's mouth dropped open in surprise. "She was married? But I thought..."

Dray smiled crookedly. "Yeah, you thought she was just some bull dyke, huh? No way. Debbie was a little more complex than that." She grinned in memory. "She had a loving husband and five kids. He told me that he had something from Debbie he needed to give me." Her eyes became unfocused as the memories bubbled up.

"What was it, Dray? You never said anything about this before."

"It was just a bracelet, Ab, nothing more."

Abby frowned and was just in the midst of asking her lover about the bracelet when the psychologist began mumbling.

"Okay, give me a few seconds here." Birk scratched down a few more notes and then looked up. "So, she was bisexual then?"

"I guess that's an apt description, Doc, but it was my experience that she was with the souls she wanted to be with, regardless of what they had or didn't have between their legs."

Birk nodded but Dray could see by the look on his face that he wasn't convinced. "If she had a husband, wouldn't that be a betrayal to him?"

"My whole life has been about betrayal, in one form or another. Why would my relationship with her be any different?" She swallowed deeply, hoping the man would just stay silent, and then focused on the rapid breathing of the woman beside her. The clock ticked loudly in the background as each person pondered the words.

Abby knew how Dray's mind worked. In her little universe, she betrayed her son by not dying there along with him in her efforts to do her job: protecting him at all costs. She betrayed Debbie Nang by not being there to protect her when it was again, her job. And she hadn't been able to protect Zosia as Ksenka, an officer in a position of power and responsibility. He had let her die. And what's more, she compounded things by not dying in the warehouse fire when by all accounts she should have.

"You mentioned you felt responsible for Debbie's murder," stated Birk as he placed both elbows on his knees, his hands falling loosely between. "Why? Even though you feel you let her down by not doing your duty as her protector, you have to face the fact that she had done just fine before you came along. Why do you feel she needed your protection, Dray? She knew the dangers of being close to you because of your gang connections. As a result of her work, she did it quite often from what you've said."

Dray cringed, each question hitting her like a hardwood baseball bat.

"I owe so much to so many."

Edward Birk leaned back, his hands gripping the armrest.

"Who and why?"

Dray was silent.

"Please explain your thoughts a little more, Dray. I can't help you if-."

"I don't want your help!"

He pursed his lips.

"You say you trust Abby more than anyone alive. All right." He sat forward, his hands palm down on his knees. "Then trust her now. She wants to help you, let her. Let us."

A look of terror passed over eyes of blue and Dray pushed up from her chair. Abby and the doctor remained seated, hoping the woman would accept the space offered and let things flow, opening up to them both.

Dray absently picked at the gauze covering her left temple as she moved over to the window. Although almost a full year had passed since the accident at the warehouse, and in many ways she was still locked in her battle with the flames. Hell's flames could take many shapes, and for Dray, all of them seemed to be pointing an accusing finger her way, biding their time.

Abby's heart wrenched as she began to pick out the almost indiscernible words of her lover. Without a backward glance, she moved up slowly and then just stood by the divan, her leg pressed tightly against the leather as if seeking comfort as well as strength from its bulk.

A ripping sound made Abby turn and both she and the doctor gasped in horror as Dray simply pulled the bandages from her face and upper neck.

"It's all about letting people down, not doing my job, and having people I love simply drop like flies around me. It's about not doing the right thing."

Edward Birk gritted his teeth as the woman's reddened flesh was exposed.

"Whether or not you could have prevented the murder of Debbie is beside the point, Dray. It was out of your hands."

Abby wiped her nose as the tears continued to fall silently like those of her lover.

"Your son died in a fire not because his mother didn't care but because she did," Abby went on. "You were out making a living to support him. And you got these," she fingered the ultra smooth lines just beyond the sleeves of Dray's t-shirt, "by trying to go back inside. In fact, you got these," pointing to the woman's heavily calloused and scarred hands, she ran the same fingers up into the nape of her lover's neck, "because you needed to help your friends."

Blue eyes swiveled down at her and then a fierce gaze replaced the blank look. "And what good did it do?" Dray countered. "Did you know Rodriguez had two kids who are now fatherless? So did Johnson. So did a lot of guys that day...What good did I do?"

Abby gritted her teeth, took her lover's hand and then spoke.

"You've always done good, Dray, always." She paused and glanced at the doctor. "You wear your badges of courage because you need to feel marked, don't you?"

Birk's mouth opened and he whispered, "Dray," before sitting on the edge of the divan beside his patient.

"She never wanted the surgery." He locked eyes with Abby, the wonder clear in his eyes. " Did you Dray? Not really. You wanted to pay for all the times you got to live but the others around you didn't." He ran his hand over his mouth. "You knew it would devastate Abby, and even Pete, if you killed yourself – but if you died in a fire, doing your duty, saving others, then you'd have paid the price and remained a hero in her eyes. That's it, isn't it?"

The firefighter didn't say anything, the words buzzing around her head as she thought of how much control and pressure she had exerted on everything and everyone around her: the life of her son, her ex-lover, the fire department, the hospital – even Abby.

It wasn't her fault Ian had died. If she could finally believe that then she also had to accept that any of the horrible incidents in her past were also beyond her control, too. She would be forced to see that she was only human, after all.

Dray's left eye began to twitch when a small hand clasped her own. Although it was very hard for her to be touched when she was in such a heightened state of awareness, there was a part of her that had already made adjustments regarding the woman that shared her life and her soul. A slow breath of air was released as the other hand moved around her waist.

"I want you to drink something right now, Dray. I think you've been getting dehydrated all day and when you had those painkillers..."

The firefighter nodded slowly, not even registering what her lover was saying, and allowed the woman to sit her on the edge of the divan. It was all so damned clear to her now.

She couldn't control the actions of other people any more than she could control the weather. The doctor was right; her ex-lover's destiny was already pre-ordained. How could she control Debbie's fate when she couldn't even control her own? It was true that everyone made choices but some things were left to chance.

Her eyes remained fixed on Abby's forearm as she brought up the glass the doctor pressed into her hands and drank deeply, emptying the contents in seconds. She stretched her suddenly weightless shoulders and felt the haze she'd been living in begin to lift. It would take time but Dray was finally getting answers to questions she never considered before.

Birk cleared his throat and Dray turned to face him.

"I don't like feeling vulnerable, Doc," she began, "but I guess I have to thank you for forcing my hand and making me face some pretty harsh realities. I might just lose all the sane points I've acquired but I know I let her die in another lifetime," she said pointing to Abby. "I'm not proud of that but we've come to an understanding about it. And as for this life, my son is dead but out of that fire came the person I am today. I might not particularly like how I turned out sometimes, but I'm pretty well stuck with it. And maybe I'm not so bad after all."

Abby gripped her lover's hand and gave her a gentle smile.

"Well," she replied with a look of honesty. "I wouldn't have her any other way."

She moved her hand up to push a strand of dark hair off the sticky mess on her lover's forehead.

"Are you really okay, Dray?" She tried not to stare at any part of her lover's face and just maintain eye contact.

"I'm feeling a lot better now that damned mask is off my face," she said grinning slightly. "So yeah, I guess I'm okay." Dray paused and turned to the doctor. "So what do you think Doc? You're the expert."

He smoothed his tousled hair, tightened his tie, and moved to his desk. "I guess the session is over."

Inferno

Dray rubbed her arms and then squeezed Abby's hand. "You guess?"

"Well, it's up to you. What do you think, did the sessions address everything you wanted it to?" He looked at Abby. "I think she and I had the answers all the time." He shook his head and smiled as she tried to protest. "You had all the pieces too, Abby. But like me, you just needed Dray to put them all together for herself." Both women stood up and came over to the desk. "And Dray? I guess I won't worry too much when you go back to work but if I start getting phone calls from Abby about you chasing fire trucks I'll have you back in my office so quick it'll make your head spin."

A slow smile spread across the brunette's face. "You mean I can go back to work?"

"As long as you pass your physical examinations," Birk nodded and pushed the recommendation he'd just signed across to her. "But I'm going to make sure that Lieutenant of yours makes you debrief after every major fire for the time being – only as a precaution. And if you need to, feel free to come and see me whenever you like, all right?"

Abby hugged him fiercely and he tried not to blush.

"Thanks so much, Doctor Edward. And you know," she pulled away and hugged her partner's arm, "just because our professional relationship is over doesn't mean you can't come and see us every now and then." She looked at Dray. "Say, I'll bet he'd make a good scuba diver, huh?"

"Whoa," he chuckled. "I don't mind going into the deep dark waters of the human psyche but into the dangerous waters of the ocean?" Visions of sharks and a giant octopus pulled at his imagination. "I think not."

"So now what?" Dray asked. "What's next?"

"Go up to see Dr. Standling for your appointment. Just wait here a second and I'll see if he's available since our session ran over." As soon as Dray heard the click of the door close behind the doctor, she turned and hugged her lover.

"I hope he can do something about," she swallowed, "about the mess I've made with my face." Abby looked up, slowly bringing her fingers up to touch her lover's face. Dray felt her heart slow as the woman began peering closely at what she was sure was a hideous sight.

"I'm not a doctor Dray but honestly it's not terrible. And besides, every time I look at you I still see a beautiful woman."

Dray reached up and stroked Abby's face as Dr. Birk came back into the office.

271

"He's free, ladies, so go on up now. They're expecting you."

"Thanks, doc," Dray said sincerely, as she waved her letter. "I mean that."

"Take care of each other," he told them with a smile.

They left the office and proceeded to the elevators, going to Dr. Standling's floor. As they arrived the nurse escorted them into a patient room.

A few moments later Dr. John Standling pushed the door open and just stood shaking his head.

"Damn it, Khalkousa. Can't you do anything you're told?"

Dray bit her lip, preparing for the coming storm and knowing she deserved every word he was going to say.

"You realize you've just jeopardized all my hard work, all the painful hours of time consuming skill at putting Humpty Dumpty together again?"

His eyes narrowed as the patient looked acceptably contrite. Walking purposefully towards her, he stopped a few paces away until the blonde moved to the side, and then firmly took the brunette's face into his hands.

He looked this way and that, nodded a few times, and then sighed deeply.

"Well, I've got good news and I've got bad news."

Dray's heart beat faster at the mere mention of the phrase 'good news.' She'd been so certain all of it would be bad that she hadn't even considered anything else.

Standling almost considered making the woman wait, holding out the information a little longer, but couldn't stand the pleading look both women had on their faces.

"The bad news first." He took out a pen and began to write some notes as he spoke. "First, you're going to have to endure some nasty cortisone shots. I say 'nasty' because they have some rather irritating side effects. They can cause lumping of the tissue, irregular bone spurs and water retention. Next, you'll have to wear a special form fitting mask twenty-four hours a day for at least a week before cutting down that time to only during night time periods."

The doctor paused and looked at Abby. "She gives you the least amount of trouble about this you call me," he said firmly. "If she doesn't want to play by these rules I have other measures I can take." He turned back to Dray with a warning finger. "So do as I say and soon you'll only be wearing the mask immediately after bathing. The pores will be ultra sensitive and we don't want to bruise or irritate them any more than you already have."

He gave the woman a very terse look and Dray looked away guiltily. "It means you'll have to come down to my offices sometime next week for a fitting. It also means you'll be getting quite a bit of gunk all over your sheets until you get the mask. Do yourselves a favor. If you've got expensive sheets go buy cheap ones. By the time the treatment is done you'll have to throw them out." He walked over to the cabinet against the wall, pulled out his key, and then grabbed a few jars. "This stuff is very expensive," he paused as he caught a somewhat crestfallen look on his patient's face, "but I just happen to have a few samples here in my office. Should do you until next week – if you're careful." Dray nodded and went to scratch her cheek but stopped as the doctor began tapping the floor with his foot. "And you'll refrain from picking at the mess you've made instantly, correct?" Both women nodded. "Even if that means she has to tie your hands behind your back 24 hours a day," he said in a firm voice before cracking a smile.

Abby cleared her throat. "You said there was some good news, too?"

"So I did." He plopped both jars into the blonde's hands and then inspected Dray's face again. "I suppose it's somewhat of a miracle, but you should be able to walk away with minimal scarring but only *if* you're careful and do what you're told." He moved his patient's jaw this way and that.

"Oh, thank you doctor," Abby began but got cut off.

"Don't go thanking me just yet. She needs to follow orders," he answered before turning to Dray. "I mean it. You'll have some residual scarring, to be sure, but in time I believe those lines should fade. Not completely, you understand. But look at it this way...scars can be reminders of the lessons we've learned."

Both women locked eyes as the doctor walked out of the office.

# Epilogue

Both women went back to the waiting room to see their friends. Dray held a hand up to shield her eyes from the glare of sunshine coming in the window. She stopped suddenly as an audible gasp reached her ears. *Aw, shit. Well, here we go.*

Pete quickly lumbered to his feet, a painfully tight smile pasted to his face. He wasn't too sure how to react, not having seen Dray since the initial surgery. They'd spoken in phone calls, of course, but Dray had done a fairly good imitation of a hermit and because of it, he'd not really known exactly what to expect.

Nothing could have prepared him for what he was looking at, nothing at all. His knees began to buckle and Janelle grabbed his arm, pulling him back onto a chair. Although the nurse had seen her fair share of burn patients and had seen more than one procedure of skin grafting, plastic surgery and its aftermath were very foreign to her.

"I thought your bandages were set to come off in two or three weeks? Say, it looks too early for those grafts to be exposed to the air. Did Dr. Standling change his mind?"

"Ah, no," Abby answered. "Seems our patient decided that on her own."

"Dray," she drawled.

"I know," the firefighter answered. "I've already been read the riot act once already."

The room fell silent and Herman crossed his arms over his chest and just sighed in resignation. "I find that incredible to believe. Going against medical advice is totally out of character for you," he teased with a warm grin.

Dray smiled at the large man. "How you doin', Herman? Haven't changed either, I see."

Pete got back to his feet, the shock of his friend's condition partially worn off.

"How are you doing, partner?" He looked awkward for a moment and then went on. "I mean other than...well, you know." He pulled at his collar and tried to let the heat of his embarrassment leak out. "Abby's been keeping me in the loop some, but I kinda lost track after the third operation."

Dray knew at that instant exactly how a deer felt in the headlights, she wanted to flee in terror and yet be strong enough to stand her ground. A soothing hand was placed on the skin at the small of her back and she released the tight breath she'd been holding.

"Doc says I'm gonna be okay," she answered. An eyebrow twitched as she watched the man's eyes darting here and there, anywhere but directly at her. "With time the scarring won't be so bad." When no one said anything else she went on. "So," she said, feeling as if she'd swallowed a mouthful of dirt. "How are things back at the precinct?"

The Lieutenant rubbed his face. "Been kinda busy Dray, this year's shaping up to be almost as bad as last year."

Dray pouched her lips out and nodded slowly. She glanced at Abby and then took the woman's hand. "So I guess you're short handed again, huh?"

Pete scratched his chin and sighed deeply, scuffing the tips of his shoes on the rug. "Yeah, you know how it is, always one man short here and there."

Abby reached out and touched his arm. "I've got a tall woman who might fit the bill."

The Lieutenant's head snapped up and he looked from blue eyes to hazel. "You...you mean it?"

"The shrink gave me a clean bill of mental health so it's just a matter of time now to heal up my face."

Pete smiled, moving forward, and carefully pulled the taller woman into a gentle hug. For just a moment, everyone in the room held their breath, and then a deep chuckle from Dray ended the silence.

"Say," purred the brunette as she hugged her partner back full force, "you better stock up on those Wheaties, ya know? I might have a face to heal but that doesn't mean the rest of me will break. C'mere!"

A couple of tears were hastily rubbed off a bristled cheek, as the Lieutenant seemed to melt into the arms of his friend. "Been a long time, Dray. Welcome home."

Abby slipped her arm around Dray and looked up at the smiling firefighter. She knew the truth, they weren't home yet but with each new day the journey was getting easier.